Second Edition

THE
ADVENTURES OF
FLETCHER MACDONALD

Vaud E. Massarsky

Second Edition

Copyright © 2010 Vaud E. Massarsky

To my wife and constant companion,

Felicia S. Massarsky

Without whose inspiration, encouragement, patience,

and counsel, Fletcher MacDonald might never have been.

And to my family and friends who cheered him on.

Special appreciation is given to Sue Fretwell for her

tireless and patient copy-editing.

THE ADVENTURES OF FLETCHER MACDONALD

CONTENTS

THE
ADVENTURES OF
FLETCHER MACDONALD

A SIGN IN INVERNESS

Bone-chilling cold is the only apt way to describe winter weather here in Inverness, Nova Scotia. Arctic winds howl along Cape Breton's Cabot Highway, piling up ten-foot snowdrifts that obscure the life within. That is why I use big, bright yellow banners screaming "TRAVEL" from my second-floor porch to advertise my travel agency to the locals. It's something to look up to, to hope for, beyond the snow.

Scottish heritage is the rule in Cape Breton, a lot of "Mac" this and "Mac" that. I'm an exception—I'm Max Bateman and I'm half English and half German—but I have always felt welcome in this land of the pathologically Celtic. Whether you're a true Scot or not, you become part of the dream if you live here. Along with being steel-willed, strong-backed drinkers, the Scots have a profound mystical side that is manifest in their music. It can evoke a slow and melancholy autumn day one moment and a dizzying tornado the next. Regardless of the tempo, the music summons forth a keen sense of an ancient place and state of mind where skirted men tend flocks in verdant valleys, women bake bread in thatched-roofed cottages, and red-haired children romp with collie dogs, where people are stoic, brave, and above all loyal. The citizenry here is dependable, indomitable, and worthy of inhabiting what we Cape Bretons call our island home, a "rock in the sea."

On this unique day I learned firsthand about the extraordinary abilities of one of these displaced Scots, Fletcher MacDonald, whom I would come to call, with time, my best friend. That's ironic, because we didn't click at all when we were children; he was standoffish and kept mostly to himself. Ditto for my wife, Fiona, who also had known him from childhood.

Fletcher and I were both born and raised in this small fishing and former coal-mining town on the Northumberland Strait. Yet our lives intertwined only after a particular incident set the stage for my lifetime of adventures with Fletcher. I had bought the travel agency a few years before from Stan Hope, who wanted to cash out of the business he had operated for forty years. We made a deal that permitted me to buy the place with little cash but cost me a large percentage of my monthly income, plus I would keep Stan on as an employee until I had paid off the debt. If things failed, I would lose my down payment and Stan would get his business back. It was a fair deal and a fair business, although the competition from internet sites was ferocious. Our edge, for what it was worth, was we could offer the same internet pricing, but we were adept at finding really nice hotels for our clients and scheduling things well. Here, that meant something, and we survive. Loyalty is a big deal here.

My task this morning was to replace those yellow advertising banners I mentioned that hung from the second-floor porch. The signs were my only advertising. Big black block letters on yellow silk, each banner twelve feet long by six feet wide, with wind holes. I had to replace them frequently because the fierce Cape Breton winds ripped them up, but their visibility was worth the expense.

I had two new banners to put up that day. Hoisting them was always problematic because it entailed threading a clothesline through eyehooks at the end of poles that stuck out ten feet horizontally from either side of the porch, thirty feet above the sidewalk. I didn't have a ladder that tall, so I rigged up two ten-foot window poles (borrowed from the old schoolhouse) with bent wire clothes hangers, one on the end of each pole, to thread the eyehooks.

It worked this way: stretching as far as I could from the porch with one pole, I would poke the end of the line, held in the crotch of one of the bent hangers, through the eyehook. Fiona and Stan, reaching out with the other pole, would snag the little end of the line now peeking out from the eyehook and wrap it around the hanger hook like spaghetti. Once they had the line securely attached to their pole, they would pull it through and down—like using chopsticks. I then would tie the line to the banner grommets and hoist it up, one banner on each side of the porch. From the street, this was quite a show. Indeed, a photograph was taken of us hanging the banners, which landed on the front page of the weekly paper with the caption: "Hey, Max, Fiona and Stan: Isn't there a better way?"

It was a ridiculous, royal pain in the neck, and the day Fletcher visited, the problem was worsened because the school had reclaimed the window poles. I tried to jerry-rig some broom handles together with duct tape, but they only sagged in the middle. It had been an hour since Stan and I began to hang the new banners, and we had long passed a boiling level of frustration. The thought crossed my mind that this absurdity had a deeper meaning: why were three adults fumbling like fools on a freezing cold day with these banners? Wasn't there something more productive for us to be doing? The plain answer was no, since we needed to have the advertising, but that didn't make me feel better.

I groused to Stan, "You didn't tell me about this stupid aspect of your business or maybe I wouldn't have bought it."

Stan countered with a snort, "In every business there is toilet bowl cleaning. At least this is out of doors." With that he abruptly left the porch for the warmth of the building.

Fiona, clearly annoyed by Stan's rationalization, snapped, "I think Stan's small and pointed head would be an excellent bowl cleaner." We both laughed at the vision of taking Stan and inserting him into a toilet. As a matter of fact, given the absurdity of our situation, freezing, and no success, we both began to uncontrollably laugh. At that, one of my my ersatz duct-taped window poles collapsed at the tape seam. That did it, Fiona and I threw down the poles and followed Stan inside. We stared at Stan and we both were still laughing at our vision.

"So what are you laughing at?' Stan grumped.

"We think we have a new career for you...one that utilizes your unique qualities, and, you will like this, doesn't involve much physical labor, just the application of your head to a straight forward problem." Fiona's electric blue eyes and fast thin lips, were capturing Stan's attention. She had a clear voice that cut through the denseness of any day or setting. Like church bells, sharp and authoritative.

"So, out with it, smarty pants." Stan was so deliciously interested. I chimed in, "Stan, we will tell you about later.. Need to think it through. There are some mechanical issues."

"Yeah, yeah…probably a hare-brained scheme."

"Well, hair has something to do with it." Fiona was relishing Stan's interest.

From the first floor I heard, "Halloo…Max…Stan…anybody here?"

"Hold your horses, Fletch, I'll be down in a moment."

I closed the door to the porch and gave up on hanging the banners for the day. Stan glared at me in a way that suggested I was a quitter. He tossed the clothesline aside, sat down in an old upholstered chair that was catching the morning sun, and picked up the newspaper.

Fiona said," What's he doing here. I expected he'd be all snuggled up in that stony asylum of his."

"You're too hard on Fletcher. He's a good guy, just a little mal-adjusted."

Fiona snorted, "He's the devil's son, I tell you. Arrogant son of a bitch."

I bounded downstairs to escape the atmosphere of futility and angst. Fiona has always felt that Fletcher is too strange by half.

"Cold enough for you, Fletch?" I asked. He didn't answer the question.

We shook hands. He said "I guess that red nose of yours means either you have been out in the cold or drinking, maybe both, eh?"

"I've been trying to hang those damn banners," I said, annoyed. "The town won't let me put up fixed signs because they say it would be a hazard to pedestrians because of the wind. What pedestrians, I say? Even in the summer, nobody walks anymore. Everybody is in their cars."

Fletcher chuckled. "Max, you have been drinking. Wooden or metal signs the size of your banners, why, in fifty-mile-an-hour winds they would either take flight or lift your shop up and deliver it to Kansas. The town is saving you from yourself. Those cloth banners with wind holes are just the ticket."

"I don't want to be saved. I just don't want to be bothered hanging those banners anymore," I grumbled. I didn't want to talk about it, and I was aware he hadn't come to the agency to discuss my problems. "Tell me, what can I do for you?"

"I want to go to Carriacou, a little island off the coast of Grenada in the Caribbean. Angus McClarren, just before he died, asked me to go there and visit a distant relative and give her some money personally. I guess the warm water and sun are an inducement, too, eh?"

"I thought you found our weather invigorating."

He nodded in agreement. "Extremes reveal values that moderation often leaves hidden. How much more I will treasure our snow kingdom after I have been a place untouched by this virginal purity. There are many people who have never even seen snow and yearn for its splendor as much as we yearn for their snowless warmth."

His philosophizing was lost on me. "Humbug, Fletcher. You're just lusting for dolls in bikinis and long siestas, preferably with a doll without a bikini."

He found this crack amusing. "Ah, Max, there is a delightful coarseness to you, doubtless brought on by your frustrations with the banners. Speaking of which, they represent no small opportunity to understand the mysteries and potentials of life."

"Don't go there," I said, knowing full well his penchant for deeper matters. "Don't tell me that I ought to love this absurd chore. If you think it's so profound, why don't you try it for a few hours, get frost-bitten, risk falling over the balcony, and end up with a goose egg of success?"

"Actually, Max, I welcome the challenge." He pointed skyward. "Shall we go to your roost?"

The last thing I needed was outside interference. "No. Don't worry about it, Fletcher. I need to stop fooling around and get some long poles from the lumber store. I'll do it later."

"I don't need poles. This is simply a problem of mind over matter."

There was that trademark superiority of Fletcher. At school he had earned the moniker of the absentminded professor because, despite his keen intelligence, he would forget his gloves or books or even forget to wear a coat if he was really caught up in his thoughts. He was a very serious student, ending up on the dean's list semester after semester.

Not until I opened up the travel agency and he became a customer did I really get to know him better. In his early twenties he began booking trips to far-flung places. He was working with the Canadian government and private parties to unravel all manner of mysteries, crimes, disappearing people, espionage, and corporate shenanigans. He had become known as the "Scottish problem solver."

In our first encounters, I remember he would enter the shop wearing a heavy tan trench coat with his khaki wide-brimmed and high-crowned hat either on his head or in his hand, looking every bit a seasoned world traveler and a bit mysterious, since the hat's generous brim concealed about half his face. He was of medium height, wiry, glinty red-haired back then, and careful like a crane picking its way along a stream, alert, even wary, at every step and movement. His dark, liquid baritone voice together with this rather elegant demeanor gave him an imperious quality, one I found at first difficult but later discovered was leavened with a whimsical sense of humor. or a practical joke.

He would have a general itinerary worked out in advance for which he would seek my advice concerning the best connections at the best prices. I think he preferred having me do the legwork rather than doing it himself because he was preoccupied with thinking about other matters. That childhood absentminded professor quality hadn't abated with age.

His keenness to have a shot at the banners made me wary. "For God's sake, Fletcher, it's at least twelve feet on the diagonal from the end of the porch to the eyelet at the end of each pole. You think you can free-throw a limp clothesline through a one-inch eyehook at twelve feet? We will be here all week, next month, and next year trying." Oddly enough, his keen expression hadn't changed in the least. "Come on," I said, deciding to show him the futility of the idea. We went upstairs where Stan and Fiona were busied with their independent tasks, Fiona separating brochures and Stan, well, reading the newspaper.

"Ah, the beautiful and charming Fiona. Always a pleasure to set eyes upon you." Fletcher bowed deeply.

"What brings you out of your stony perch. What have I missed that you are about to tell me about?

"Good point. Well, for starters, you skipped a sweater button."

"A true gentleman wouldn't let a lady know of such a gaffe." Fiona was non-plused and busied herself with correcting the error. "*Au contraire*, Mrs. Max, a missed button bears no relationship to he sharpness of your mind. I for one am always missing such things and that doesn't trouble me at all. I rely on my friends to tidy up such trivial matters."

"I need oxygen" Fiona fumed and went outside on the porch.

"And, Halloo, Stan. How goes it? Fletcher was exceptionally warm in his greeting.

"Just waiting until I die. You know nobody gets out of this alive, do they?"

I jumped in. "Here is the clothesline we use. You see, Fletcher, it has no body, it's limp. It can't be thrown with accuracy more than a few inches." He still didn't seem fazed, and I poured it on. "It's not like a spear that you can aim with some certainty. Moreover, the line must pass far enough through the eyehook in order to be pulled through to tie to the banners for hoisting. That's why we use the window pole contraption - to thread the eyehooks with enough line so we can grasp it."

He fingered the white cord with appreciation. "Your approach is ingenious. I'm not denigrating it. But there is more to this than you think. You believe it is impossible to freely throw the line through the eyelet, but I think if you were more precise, you would say that it is virtually impossible, admitting some small chance of success? Am I right?"

I chuckled at his splitting hairs. "Oh, one chance out of a million, no, ten million. Even if I tied the end of the line to a stiff rod and made a type of arrow, the likelihood of getting it through would still be tiny." I became irritated with Fletcher's academic approach to this mundane problem. "At least the old way works. I just have to get the right poles; so drop it, please."

Fletcher wouldn't let it alone, though. "The point is this. Once you admit it can be done, even once in a million tries, then it is removed from the impossible; it becomes a doable feat. The task then becomes identifying what forces and knowledge it takes to succeed as a matter of will and not by chance. To be successful on the first throw, rather than waiting for a million tries to get it right, would prove a mastery of the pertinent physical laws and other forces that are involved. I rank this as very important, so I will try it for you."

Stan came back into the conversation: "Say Fletcher, sorry I bit your head off. A little tension around here this morning. Any way I heard your conversation about the rope and all." He folded his arms across his ample chest. "I would say there is no chance of anybody throwing that line through the hook. It's like saying I could throw a dime a mile. You see, some things are impossible, not virtually, just impossible. Therefore, it's a waste of time to try. Impossible, I say."

Fletcher was delighted with his conviction. "If nothing else, Stan, you are clear, no allowance for ambiguity. So, let me ask you, if I were able to do it, how would you explain it?"

Stan gave him a patient smile. "Well, the word miracle comes to mind, except that I don't believe in them either. I'd have to say athletic prowess, but such a feat is still impossible, so that's out. I'm not holding my breath."

Fletcher was enjoying himself. "I guess that places you in an uncomfortable position. On the one hand, you don't believe in miracles, and on the other, you are sure it can't be done. You need a third way, don't you? Or, maybe we can convert you into a believer in miracles or an extreme rationalist who believes that man can achieve that which can be achieved if he can only find the laws."

Stan said impatiently, "Fletcher, all this yakking is hurting my head. I suggest you get this over with, try a few times, and the subject will be closed." He started toward the door. "You are one peculiar guy, hardheaded like your father. Once he got an idea in his head, there was no stopping him." Fletcher froze, and a look of dawning discomfort came over Stan's face. "I forgot," he said quietly. "You are now about the same age as your father when he died."

Fletcher looked down at the floor. An awkward silence filled the room. Fletcher's sad family history had haunted him, and the community, his whole life. Some say his remoteness, his eccentricities, all stem from that horrible day when his family was destroyed. I now know the tragedy affected his perceptions of the world so that he senses qualities that others miss. He has rarely spoken to me about his lost family, but his study is crowded with pictures and mementos of them, their work as boat builders and fisherfolk, with diaries and accounts going back centuries, chronicling in minute detail the lives of his forebears, who came from Scotland. A jagged, dark rock has a place of honor among all his family history, supposedly taken from the Scottish valley where the MacDonalds lived before they came to Cape Breton.

He had lost his entire immediate family—mother, father, brother, and sister—when their lobster boat, the SeaSwift, went down in a fierce storm. He should have been on that trip, but he was just five and had a bad cold, so he was left with his aged grandparents while the rest of the family went to lobster early on an October morning. A low-pressure cell developed, and by midday the skies had gone dark with giant black thunderheads. Wind-driven hail struck in incessant shotgun blasts with such force that it tore open exposed skin. Twenty-foot waves leapt over the harbor breakwater, tossing the steel-hulled fishing boats around like bathtub rubber ducks. The MacDonalds' wooden boat was probably lifted up and thrown down by the storm gods until it was completely shattered. Days later, remnants of the SeaSwift were spread along miles of our coast, as were parts of Fletcher's family. In the midst of the storm, unbeknownst to his grandparents, Fletcher had left the house and found his way to the very edge of the precipice that overlooked the sea. His grandparents found him yelling, arms outstretched, into the raging storm, "Take me, too! Take me, too!" The funeral drew friends and strangers from all over Cape Breton and even Halifax, two hundred and fifty miles away. The cortege was a mile long. Bagpipes sighed their dirges and stained the memories of all of us with a humbling respect for the things we can't control. From that time on, Fletcher held a special status with us as a living reminder of what can go wrong in our precarious existence.

His grandparents raised him after the tragedy. They had been boat builders and fishermen but were now too old for either.

Fortunately, as a result of years of scrimping, they had more than enough to take care of Fletcher. His grandfather died in his sleep at ninety-six, and his grandmother, not to be left apart from the man she loved for seventy years, passed on weeks later in the same gentle way. At the age of sixteen, Fletcher took over their house at Mabou, where he still lives today. The house is so far out on a high point that it could have been a lighthouse; indeed, the glow from Fletcher's tower study can be seen for miles at sea.

So, in this tragic way, Fletcher is legendary. But he has also built a happier reputation with his exceptional skills at resolving intractable problems of any sort: crimes, business, missing people, and even swords-point political matters. Although he didn't go to college and doesn't have a profession, he can do just about anything, from building a boat, writing music, or designing a circuit board, to comprehending and applying the most sophisticated physics, always coupled with an uncanny sixth sense that trumps book knowledge.

I finally addressed Fletcher, who was clearly lost in thought and had that immobilized look he got when disturbed. "So, do you want to give it a try?"

Fletcher shook himself from his trance, saying, "Yes, yes, it's important. Stan, I think my father wants me to try, too. I feel his presence. Maybe he'll even help." Fletcher started off ahead of us, while Stan and I shared glances confirming our belief that this was a great waste of time, the kind of patronization that one gives to a member of the community who has suffered, even if long ago.

We all stepped out onto the porch where Fiona was having a cigarette. Something she did when she was angered. The wind had greatly increased and blown snow skittered through the air. I kicked the broom handles aside and handed the hank of clothesline to Fletcher. Tilting back his hat, he weighed the line in his hands and then walked over to the left corner of the porch, where one of the long poles extended over the sidewalk and street. He stared at the eyelet at the far end of the pole. It was a little obscured by the flying snow that would occasionally sweep over it. Fletcher then turned back to the porch door, adding another ten feet to the distance that he would have to breech.

"You're not going to throw from there, are you?" I said, intrigued despite myself.

He didn't answer but continued to stare at the eyelet from the back of the porch. His eyes closed, then opened, clearly fixed on the eyelet. He took deep breaths, focusing ever more tightly. He then rubbed his brow, something I have come to know as a sign that he is intensely focusing. I swear there was something happening to the air; it was becoming thick and viscous. A glance at Stanley showed that he felt it, too. Fiona's eyes were tightly focused on Fletcher, and whatever pique she had felt seemed to have dissipated in the moment.

The wind stopped and a hush descended. In one smooth, confident motion, he took the end of the line with his fingertips, opened his eyes very wide, drew his arm back, and with the end of the line just above his ear thrust the line out with a snap like a released spring.

More than the air became still; natural movements all slowed. My eye was able to follow the flight of the line as it passed from Fletcher's hand. It was like a slow-motion film. The end of the line quivered and climbed relentlessly through the air on a direct path to the eyelet. It was as if there were a ramp and the rope was gliding along it to its destiny. I saw the end of the rope pass arrow-like through the eyehook and arc gently down four feet before it stopped, as if it had been pulled through. I remember robotically grabbing the now-threaded line, pulling it down, and tying it to the porch railing. The wind picked up again and the sense of slow motion passed. I was dry-mouthed by the performance. I frankly couldn't believe my eyes. Fletcher detachedly said, "The most beautiful thing we can experience is the mysterious. It is the sense of all true art and science. That is what Einstein said. Do you need me to do the other one, Max?" Fiona wet her lips, and placed her arms around me. He turned to Stan with an ironic grin. "Stan? I think you need to see this again."

I said nothing and watched the procedure all over again. This time there was no sense of slow motion. Everything happened in real time. But the grace, the ease, the certainty were the same. And, yes, the line passed right through the other eyehook and came down the same four feet. Fair to say, I was shaken down to my soul by the feat, repeated twice. How did he do that?

Amid our amazement Fletcher shivered, and I was reminded of the extreme cold. I said distractedly, "Let's talk about Carriacou downstairs, Fletcher." He adjusted his hat a little downward and left the porch.

After he was out of sight and his steps had faded, I whispered to Stan and Fiona, "Am I crazy? Did Fletcher just thread those hooks with one throw each? Did that just happen?"

Stan drew his hand across his mouth and said, "Just lucky, I guess". Despite his nonchalance, I could see the strangeness filling his eyes. I said, "So that's your third way? Lucky...once maybe, not twice. Why not a miracle or an extraordinary ability, Stan?" He shook his head, becoming more positive. "It was just luck, I tell you. Nothing more than that. Maybe he hypnotized us and threaded the ropes while we were under his control". He frowned at this idea even as he said it. "It's not possible that he threw those lines through those hooks at that distance," he muttered. "Just not possible and I refuse to believe otherwise. It's a trick, I say."

"Honey, I saw it, too", Fiona consoled Stan who was clearly agitated. I am a witness so don't think you're mad. You know, I'm feeling sorry I have been so hard on him. I guess he really is something else. Maybe he can't help being difficult with that ability. This is something I'll never forget."

I was stunned to trembling by the miracle I had witnessed, but I got skepticism instead from Stan. Thank God for Fiona. Shaking my head at Stan, I stumbled downstairs after Fletcher. I couldn't make heads or tails out of what I had seen, yet I knew it was a manifestation of a power or ability that was close to being unworldly. It made me very nervous and curious all at the same time.

Fletcher was calmly eyeing the racks of travel brochures. Not looking at me, he said, "Max, Carriacou is a dependency of Grenada, so if you have some brochures on Grenada, then I'm sure there will be something on Carriacou."

I wasn't going for the innocent act. "We have to deal with what happened upstairs," I said firmly.

Fletcher met my gaze with cold calm. "All right. Assume that over a very large number of tries, maybe a million, anyone could eventually throw the line through the eyehook by trial and error. Why? Because the eyehook is well within the range of a human throw, and therefore the potential to thread it is in accord with a natural physical law. Cause and effect. By applying what knowledge I have of physics, coupled with confidence that this could be accomplished, I deduced the right coordinates of altitude and thrust. The core power is the unshakable confidence that it could be done. Everything in the universe abides by law. Einstein, to quote him again, put it neatly: 'God doesn't play dice with the world.' One just has to find the right laws and apply them."

Exactitude to this degree seemed unfathomable. "Everything slowed down for me. I saw the rope move through the air like a slow-motion film." I realized my voice was flecked with awe, and I coughed it away. "Fletcher, why would my perceptions be changed by what you were doing? Did you hypnotize Stan and me? Was this just some sort of trick?"

"I think you know it wasn't a trick," Fletcher said with some asperity. "As to your perceptions, I suspect that you are open to the eddies of time and space more than Stan is. You were able to participate in the forces that were at work. I can tell you that you didn't imagine what you saw. This was the exquisite working of mind over matter, or to put it more objectively, the assertion of dominion over laws both known and unknown with the faith that one can find a way to accomplish the doable, even if one doesn't know exactly how. That's why I told you that this was important. An opportunity arose, unexpectedly, for you and for me, and for Stan, too, to move beyond the shabby perimeters of our daily lives and to harness the powers that are within our grasp to do the seemingly impossible."

He was warming to his subject. "These are the moments when we can soar and capture brief yet telling glimpses of the true scope of the universe. At these times of challenge, if we take the reins of natural law and drive hard to accomplish what we believe ultimately can be done, but rarely is, we can cross through our ignorance to succeed and advance the world's knowledge." As though he knew he was sounding too lofty, he switched gears. "The step-ping-stone to this power, for me, is an abiding certainty that my family is just on the other side of the veil of life. By viewing these challenges as a bridge to them, and the knowledge they now pos-sess, I am able to accomplish things, see things, feel things that would not otherwise be open to me and in the process be nearer to my family. In some way, it was my father's hand that guided the clothesline today, but fully in accord with universal laws that we can still only guess at but know a little better for the effort." Fletcher's voice became weary at the end of his explanation. His strong frame bowed, as if burdened with a heavy load, as he slowly made for the door. The floor creaked and sagged, I thought under the weight of what he knew. He then snapped to ramrod straight-ness. His brow cleared and he pointed to me. "Call Fire Chief Housie" he ordered sharply. "A child, a Cameron child, has been sucked into one of the mine tunnels and is under the sea. We need a boat now to find the Cameron girl. Bring hard-hat divers." He waved at the phone. "I'll be at the wharf. Hurry. She's alive! But the tides, the tides!" He vanished from the shop into the snow.

Stan yelled at me and said something awful had happened on the beach. The radio carried the words of our Mayor McGonigle. "A few minutes ago Sally Cameron, seven years of age, fell in a sink hole above one the coal tunnels underneath Inverness Beach. She was not found in the immediate area where she had fallen in."

The mayor said that rescue workers would be sent into the shafts, but that effort was very risky because opening up a tunnel would mean that all the tunnels would be flooded since they all extended under the sea. There are 13 tunnels and they are all inter-connected. She could have been dragged to any one of them be-cause of intense air pressure. How did Fletcher know? Upon hearing the news Fiona and I ran from the store to be at the pier where the fireboats were. The only entrances that were not truly sealed were escape hatches in the sea, having massive wheels on them for opening. We knew the Camerons very well. They were away and Sally was staying with friends.

When we arrived at the pier it was uncharacteristically alive with the squawking of radios and walkie-talkies as emergency personnel and volunteer firefighters arrived for coordination. The story was now known by all. Sally was on her way to school when she had been sucked into a sinkhole that had opened up on the beach the night before. Owing to air and water pressure changes that create sucking vacuums in the old coal mine tunnels that underlie Inverness and that horizontally stretch a mile or more from the shore out to sea, holes like these occasionally form. The tunnels were sealed decades ago with the failure of the mines, but occasionally their walls broke and the tunnels claimed yet another victim to add to the many miners who drowned literally scratching a living from them. Despite the danger, it was commonplace for everyone, including schoolchildren, to cross the open beach, as part of life here. I feared that in all likelihood, the child met the same fate as unlucky miners, because the police and firefighters failed to find her anywhere near the hole. Soon there would be a typical Scottish funeral for her, too. As I thought of the girl's terrifying path into oblivion, I felt a deep sickness and a sense of responsibility, since I was part of the adult community that had done nothing about those tunnels despite the known dangers.

Every time we have a death from this, the town committee members wring their hands over it, but they pass the problem off to the provincial government because it's too expensive for the town to resolve. Then the government pleads poverty and so on. Seems like five people have died this way over the past decade.

I had made the calls that Fletcher requested and caught up with him at the pier. Fletcher shook his head. "It's awful. I tell you, I keep thinking about that little child being sucked through those tunnels. I know the family well from the Ceilidhs. I can see her dancing joyfully with her brother and swaying to the music when sitting on the steps at Jacob's barn. A very pretty and petite child. Truly an innocent. Just awful." He regarded me more closely.

The gray, wind-whipped seas were breaking violently over the icy wooden planks, throwing bricks of broken pack ice against Fletcher and the men standing with him. Fletcher banged his brow and drew his fists up to the sky. Fletcher had to yell into the ear of the fire chief to be heard. "If she fell in at 8:15 AM this morning, she was dragged about one thousand feet by hydrostatic air pressure. She's in number three tunnel.

The chief screamed back to Fletcher, "Why number three?" Fletcher, his saliva freezing on his face, said, "It's the deepest...strongest pressure. There's a safety hatch five hundred feet out." He pointed toward it and the fire chief nodded in recognition. "It's the only way. Open it and she will be pulled through and shoot up in the air. She won't have been touched by the cold water but for seconds if you are there to catch her. Got to grab her fast before she dies from shock of the water!"

The fire chief screamed "There are 13 tunnels, if you are wrong, all the other tunnels will be flooded and she will die. Give me something more than your belief, damn it!"

"Chief, those are the reasons...that's not a belief...I don't guess...those are the rules. Do it, Chief or she will die!!!" Fiona grabbed Chief's Housie's face, speaking nose to nose, I swear. "Chief, Chief, we have nothing else. He knows things we can't begin to understand. We have to take a chance on him." Though the chief still did not seem completely convinced, he committed fully, and swung into high action, and waved to lower the boat.

Two helmeted divers clambered on board a metal-hulled police boat that had been slung from the pier and dropped into the water. It crashed into the ice, which was not solid yet, but was crowding out the open sea. I and Fiona jumped aboard. The motor exploded in a black cloud of diesel smoke. The divers suited up and the air compressor roared into action. Fletcher and the fire chief clambered aboard, and several men in the prow jabbed at the ice. The vessel shuddered, first slamming against the dock from the violence of the waves and wind. But the powerful motors finally inched the boat out into the rocking sea. The ice blocks hit the hull so hard that it sounded as if each one made a hole in the boat.

Within a few minutes, the boat passed beyond the breakers and stopped about five hundred feet from shore. The divers jumped over the side to find the mine hatch. Everyone peered through the wild mix of wind, snow and seawater as they disappeared. After a moment, the eight rescue swimmers also jumped in. Treading water, they worked to ride the waves while maintaining a circle at some distance from the buoy, bracing themselves and alert for what was to come. For those in the boat the wait seemed interminable. The vessel heaved and fell in the waves as everyone peered into the wild mix of wind, snow and seawater. Fiona and Max took each other's hands. Fletcher again had his hand on his his brow as if willing Sally Cameron to be found.

The Chief said with great worry, "They must have reached the hatch by now. Maybe its stuck."

Five minutes later, a plume of air and water exploded in front of us, like the blow of a whale or an oil gusher, thirty feet high.

Through the rush of water, I had a silhouetted glimpse of what have might been a small body. A flash of a coat sleeve.

Fletcher commanded, "Tighten the circle. She's dead center. Go to the center. She won't last but twelve seconds more!"

Everyone was scanning the sea. Fiona clasped her hands in prayer and I put my arms around her. Then one of the swimmers cried out. "I see her!"

All attention turned to the swimmer and in the direction he powered through the water. He had about 15 yards to go to get a tiny, bobbing head. Some of the other swimmers had started to converge on the goal.

The Chief, placing his arm around Fletcher, said, "If she dies of hypothermia out there, Fletcher, you'll still have done your best.

Fletcher recoiled, "Failure, Chief, is not my best." I cried out, "They've got her!"

The swimmers took hold of Sally and were grabbing life preservers tossed to them from the rapidly closing in police boat. With exquisite teamwork the blue lipped, shivering, soaking wet little girl was soon on board. Her clothes were being stripped off and blankets wrapped around her. But with all the trained personnel ready to help, it was Fiona who was first to take hold of the child and start administering CPR. All the activity ceased and the boat quieted as everyone on board watched Fiona's efforts. She was tireless, rhythmic, persistent. We then heard the gasp, sputter, and cough.

The Chief exploded, "She's alive!"

The word passed quickly around the rescuers. Fiona was hugging Sally, then allowing more trained personnel to take her. I was wearing a huge grin. Fletcher surveyed the scene. Whatever sense of awe and triumph he might have been feeling seemed to transcend the well being of a single child. One might almost call his expression "matter of fact."

****

It was late afternoon by the time Fletcher and I returned to the office. Stan had made a pot of coffee. Fiona was with Sally at the hospital. We put on dry clothes. Fletcher's wet trench coat and hat hung from a pipe in the ceiling.

I said, "Fiona's still at the hospital with the Camerons. Sally's sleeping, but except for broken ribs and a leg, the girl's fine. No brain damage. There'll be pain for a few weeks".

Stan yawned out, "So was it your father helped you find the girl, Fletcher?

Fletcher eyed Stan and calmly stated, "It was my father told me about the tides and the hydrostatic effect they have on the water seeped into those old mine tunnels. That's why I knew we couldn't wait for the tide to return." I asked, "How so?"

Fletcher visibly switched mental gears to explain his thought process. "First, there's a lot of history about these tunnels. Since they were built at the turn of the twentieth century, scores of miners have been sucked through them by changes in air pressure brought about by temperature conditions just above the tunnels because they are near the surface of the ocean bed. When the tides are out, the Gulf Stream warms the air in the tunnels farther out under the sea. When the tides are high, the tunnels cool closer to shore. That temperature difference causes a flow of air back and forth. This morning low tide was at four. Apparently it caused air and water in the tunnels to move out to sea. A vacuum effect opened a sinkhole just as Sally had the bad fortune to be walking above that hidden old shaft. The sucking must have caused her to literally fly through the tunnels. Being small and lithe is what saved her. A heavier grown man, one of those old miners perhaps, would have been dashed against the beams or walls, probably killed. In any case, I knew if we didn't beat the tide, the seeping water would have flowed back and Sally would have drowned."

I asked, "How did you know she was in tunnel three? There are 13 tunnels down there."

"As I have said, the interaction of the outside air temperatures, the Gulf Stream, and the inner air of the tunnels cause a hydrostatic effect. Right now we have much colder ambient air and relatively warmer sea temperatures, so there's a superhydrostatic effect. That creates an air pocket and a vacuum and forces the water that seeps into the tunnels to be driven back out through the same breaks in the wall. When these conditions appeared in the past, the miners would get sucked out to the end of the tunnels, but there was enough oxygen to breathe. Finally, the deepest tunnels had the greatest hydrostatic effect. To suck someone from the ground and beyond the immediate opening therefore made tunnel number three the most obvious candidate.

I was sure that Sally's flexibility would save her, unless she became impaled or had a terrible concussion. At any rate, the only negative consequence that the plan had was right at the end."

"What do you mean?" I asked.

"By opening the hatch, there was a slim chance that the air pressure would not have been forceful enough to keep the water out and she would have drowned. The likelihood was that she would pop right through, though, carried by the air pressure. Thank God, she did. The divers and swimmers did a great job. I was afraid that if they didn't grab her fast, she would die from the shock of the cold water on top of the other traumas."

I sat back, considering all he had said. When it was explained step by step, I could follow it. Another thought came to me. "Why was it so important to rescue her within the hour?"

"I remembered the tides. The reason she was sucked down in the first place was the Gulf Stream current. The low tide, which we had at four a.m., meant that there was a contrasting mix of warm current and cold outside air near the tunnels. At five hundred feet out, they are not too far beneath the seabed, so the Gulf Stream effect, which runs near the surface, would affect them. Temperature change can make a huge difference and set off a violent reaction. It dawned on me while I was here that the incoming tide would surround the tunnels with much colder water temperatures, suspend the hydrostatic effect, and permit the water to flood back into the tunnels again, drowning and freezing Sally. That's why I bolted out of here. The pressure could have dropped at any minute."

Stan, incredulously, "Fletcher, you were five years old when your family's lobster boat when down. I seem to remember you were sick so they left you with your grandparents."

Fletcher and I looked at Stan. I had no idea why Stan would bring this memory up, but Fletcher knew exactly where he was going with it.

Fletcher pounced, "You're right, Stan. My good fortune to have a head cold."

Stan unable to leave this alone, "And yet you remember your father telling his little five year old all about subterranean hydrostatics."

Fletcher, now smiling, said, "I don't believe I mentioned exactly when he told me about it."

Stan, decided not to take the subject any further, and just nodded. From across the street we heard the rhythms of Cape Breton's brand of Celtic music begin to throb from Pete's pub. The Scottish ancestors who populated this area brought with them a form of the music unadulterated by English influences and that tradition is little changed today.

I suggested that we go over to Pete's for a few beers and sandwiches. The music was being played by a local fiddler and his band was entertaining a pubful of people celebrating the successful rescue of Sally. Fiona joined them from the hospital. Surrounded by the happy, the drunk, and the dancing, Fletcher, Fiona and I sat at a table with beer, stout for Fletcher, and we all nibbled on sandwiches. I could see from the shine in Fletcher's eyes that this music was a salve that soothed his soul.

I proposed a toast. "Here's to the day I finally figured out what Fletcher MacDonald does on all those trips he has me book and how he makes the money to support his austere yet lavish lifestyle".

Fiona chimed in, a little drunk, "I wouldn't call him austerely lavish. I think he's more lavishly austere." I said, and nodded to my wife, "I stand corrected."

Fletcher, more relaxed than I had ever seen him, almost dreamily, said, "And just what is it you think you have figured out?

"Well, you, my occasional friend, have been hanging banners for small businessmen all over the globe."

Fletcher aped shock and surprise, "You've got me there, Max. I congratulate you on your perspicacity. I also can't help but note that you and Fiona seem to have something of a feel for the task yourselves. It's possible that in the future, I may ask the two of you to assist me should I find myself facing any particularly formidable banners."

I played out the thought, "I, for one, would decline that invitation unless it involves traveling to one of those exotic destinations you're so fond of making me Google."

Fletcher now being somewhat more reflective, "But what could be more exotic than sitting in a quaint pub on Cape Breton having one's spirits lifted by the most perfect music ever devised by man?"

Fiona snapped, "Dancing to it."

Fletcher, stood up and offered his hand to Fiona, "Ah, Fiona. You've won me over. Accompany me to this greatest of destinations before our travel agent realizes we're gone."

Although I was taken aback a little, I didn't mind too much as Fiona smiled and took Fletcher's hand. He led her to the dance floor where they begin to dance. Fletcher became almost a blur of ecstasy as he lost himself, a long necked crane whirling and stepping to the ancient music which seemed to connect him to all things eternal.

THE OTHER ENIGMA

The dominant male Galapagos tortoise slammed his massive carapace headlong into the tree. Luke Targus, our guide, said that a male tortoise, faced with a tree in his path, would rather keep battering it until it falls over than go around it. Stubborn fellows which, after all, have all the time in the world: their average age at death is two hundred years. Surrounding us were a score of the prehistoric beasts making their way through the rainforest on the uppermost reaches of Santa Cruz Island, the largest in the Galapagos archipelago. These gray boulders were inching forward to better grazing, occasionally extending their accordion-like necks up a few feet to get a better view. Some digressed into copulation, their shells clacking like wooden salad bowls being slapped together. But I kept looking back at the huge beast that methodically slammed into a tree rather than go around it. I eyed the tree's top and saw that its branches were swaying from the siege, undoubtedly the beginning of a very slow but inexorable fall.

Santa Cruz has a peak high enough to contain several microclimates: beach, dry foothills, some arable midlands, and near its top, where we were, a small rainforest held sway. Steam rose from the high forest floor where puddles met the sun. Our path often dissolved into mud from the runoff of the cloudbursts that ambushed us and then disappeared. Paradoxically, up here was plenty of water, but on most of Santa Cruz and the other ten Galapagos Islands grinding drought was the tough iron rule, typified by hot, dry air, eye-burning sunlight, and parched land.

Climate wasn't the only paradox. Because the archipelago is isolated from the South American mainland by six hundred miles of the Pacific Ocean and was never on the main shipping routes, the islands were not inhabited until the early nineteenth century, and then only Santa Cruz. Thus the animal life was spared the depredations of human hunting. As a result, today one can walk among marine iguanas, land iguanas, seals, blue-footed boobies, red-footed boobies and other unique animals, which do not scatter for they have no fear of man.

That very fact was at the heart of the reason Marcia and Joseph Sauer came here for their honeymoon, the return from which was in doubt. Sauer's father, Jacob, met Fletcher and myself by chance on an airplane flight from London to New York. We were all sitting in the same row, Fletcher in the middle seat and I at the window. About midway through the flight Jacob, a man of fifty, neatly dressed in tie and jacket, began to sob openly after making a call from the airliner's telephone at his seat.

Fletcher, his rich baritone voice reduced to almost a whisper but maintaining its soothing authority, offered Jacob his handkerchief. "Excuse me, can I be of any assistance? Shall I call the flight attendant?"

The distraught man wiped his face with his hands. "I'm sorry. I'm very, very sorry." As he spoke the last words, his voice cracked and he began to sob again. His chest heaved with intense sadness.

Fletcher, looking to the floor so as not to embarrass the grieving man, said, "They say a stranger can be the best listener, for he has no vested interest. If it will help, please feel free to talk." Fletcher kept his physical distance and let his voice do the consoling.

Mr. Saurer mimicked Fletcher's low key, quiet style, "Maybe talking will relieve some of my anxiety. You really don't mind?"

With a little more sunshine, Fletcher responded, "Absolutely not. Take your time. This is a six-hour flight, after all."

Jacob took a deep breath. Without doubt he wished to unburden himself. "My son and his new wife have been honeymooning in the Galapagos," he said. "Yesterday, I learned that they haven't returned from a trip to one of the outer islands. Now the police there have reported that, despite a thorough search, they still have not found them. I was to have met my son and daughter-in-law in New York, where we were going to continue the celebration." He became overwhelmed again. "I just can't believe it."

"It will help to stay focused on finding a solution," Fletcher counseled. "Hope springs from thinking well and hard about the facts. And the facts are our friends." The man turned in curiosity at these words, and Fletcher informed him, "Serendipitously, finding missing persons is one of my professional activities as an independent investigator. My name is Fletcher MacDonald, and this is my associate, Max Bateman." Fletcher drew from his jacket pocket his silver business card case. "Here's my card. I wonder if I might ask you some questions to help you sort out the facts, maybe even tease some out of noise.

"Just speaking with you has relieved some of my anxiety. To imagine that something awful may have happened to a young couple just launching their life together is unbearable. Go ahead with your questions. I may not have all the answers."

Fletcher started right in. "Why did they choose the Galapagos for their honeymoon?"

"It was a natural choice. My son is an assistant biology professor who was enthralled early on by Darwin's work on evolution. Marcia is an environmentalist who took a course taught by my son on the interaction of man and mammals, with the Galapagos featuring prominently in the analysis. Animal behavior is an aspect of Darwin's work on species variation that fascinated them both, especially the fact that the Galapagos animals, like those on other remote and uninhabited islands, had never been hunted or molested by man and therefore had no fear of human beings. Indeed, Marcia planned to write a thesis on the interface of man and animals. She had been there once before on a sailing trip. She sought out my son's class because he had built a reputation in this area, particularly his analysis of Darwin's work in the Galapagos. By going there, Joseph planned to study Darwin's observations firsthand. I am very proud of Joseph's commitment to science and to what is clearly the life of close examination. And it seems that Marcia shares his love of science too."

"How did Joseph become so interested in Darwin?"

Mr. Sauer warmed to the subject. "As I think back on it, Darwin was often a central theme of discussions at home. In one way or another, his theory of evolution profoundly affected many aspects of life that we talked about: politics, economics, philosophy, environment, literature. I suppose my wife and I infected our son early with an appreciation of Darwin. When Joseph was young we took him to unusual places in the world so he would have a variety of experiences, natural and cultural." His hand produced a pen with which he easily drew illustrations of birds in different stages of rising into the air.. "Sometimes we might look at how a pigeon flew or why a society had adopted certain traits, and evolution was often a starting point for analysis or conjecture."

"Mr. Sauer, your son has had an enviable life, to be exposed to such rich conversation and experiences with his parents. Now, you say that Marcia sought out Joseph's class. What is her history?"

"Oh, she pretty much had to make her way in the world from a young age," he said in admiration. "She traveled a lot and was an accomplished sailor, having been a crew member on many yachts. Those sailing experiences apparently made her an ardent appreciator of the natural world and she became a dedicated environmentalist. She is very bright, magnetic, and the love of Joseph's life. Until Marcia, he was caught up in his work. But she changed all that, and Joseph's romantic nature was revealed."

Fletcher was getting a good grasp of the situation. "So your Joseph and Marcia were on sort of a busman's honeymoon. Pretty wonderful to have a couple whose professional interests mesh so seamlessly. You speak with such a clear regard for learning and observation and culture in general, I suspect you must be an academic yourself?"

He glanced at Fletcher, impressed. "I see that you are good at your work. Yes, I am a history professor at Cambridge, specializing in eighteenth and nineteenth-century English history."

"Ah, when Darwin's ideas changed everything."

"Oh, yes. I have written a work that demonstrates that evolutionary theory turned the prism through which thinkers and doers of note perceived and acted on their world. I suppose my son couldn't avoid a fascination with Darwin."

"You said your son was planning to retrace some of Darwin's work in the Galapagos?"

"I know they planned to go to Tower Isle, which Darwin visited to record the actual reactions of the animals to humans' presence, both by written record and photographically, and to compare their observations to Darwin's."

Fletcher cocked his head, and aggressively inquired?. "Had they made their visit to Tower Isle before they disappeared?"

"I think they had made a couple of visits. They had hoped to stay overnight there, but the authorities have prohibited anyone, even scientists, from doing that. When we spoke with Joseph and Marcia on the telephone a few days after their arrival, they said that the regulations were unnecessarily hindering important scientific work and they were seeking a way around the rules."

I knew that evading the rules often could lead down ill-advised paths. So I was not surprised by Fletcher's next question.

"What specifically have the police done?"

"They have located and interviewed the local charter boat captain who took them to Tower Isle, a man named Captain Dutch. The Ecuadorian navy sent a team to search Tower Isle on foot, but they didn't find them there. As far as I know, the police are convinced that they aren't on Tower."

"Were there any other places that you knew would have been important to them?"

"Only the rainforest on Santa Cruz Island. They wanted, like any other tourist, to follow the giant tortoises around and to better understand their habitat and ways. They promised to bring me back videos of themselves riding the tortoises." He sighed, becoming morose again. "They were just so excited about this trip."

Fletcher paused before asking his next question. It was cut off by an announcement that the plane was entering its final leg of descent, so we had to buckle up our seatbelts and prepare for landing.

Fletcher continued, "I do hope that you will stay in touch and let me know how things turn out."

Mr. Sauer looked at his watch. "My God, we have been speaking for hours. You have helped me so much by encouraging me to think about things specifically and not to dwell on the worst scenarios. I am deeply appreciative of your time." He extended his hand to Fletcher and myself.

Fletcher said, "Think nothing of it. But do let me know how things turn out."

The plane made a perfect landing, which triggered a few people to applaud. Fletcher thought that act of appreciation rather primitive but sweetly amusing. Mr. Sauer gathered his carry-on luggage from above, nodded to Fletcher, and was on his way.

Catching a cab, Fletcher and I traveled to the University Club, where he had been accorded guest membership despite his never having graduated from a formal academic institution. Always one or another of several members whom he had helped sponsored his stays there when he was in New York. We hadn't been in our rooms but fifteen minutes, when Mr. Sauer telephoned our office cellular line and asked if he could hire Fletcher because the latest reports coming from the Galapagos remained dismal. I said that I would call him back in a few minutes.

"I didn't mention your fees to Mr. Sauer because I wasn't sure if you had discussed them with him on the plane."

Fletcher ruminated a bit and said, "It's Professor Sauer, Max. He lives and loves the life of Herr Professor." Fletcher touched his brow momentarily, "Yet, although he's an academic, judging by his clothes and his well traveled and cultured tastes, I suspect he married very well which accounts for the good life style. Quote him our usual fee, up front, plus expenses, and if he accepts, tell him we will be in the Galapagos in a day or so. Book us at the same hotel where his son and new wife stayed. I believe it was the Academy Bay."

The deal was sealed moments later, and we were off to Ecuador the next day.

****

From the plane I spotted a fast-moving car and a plume of dust behind it traveling in our direction. We circled the little ocher island, which had virtually no vegetation, until the landing gear clanked into position. The plane tipped from side to side like a wavering albatross and bounced down hammer-hard on the tarmac. The terminal had a seedy French Foreign Legion quality. Luke Targus, our assigned guide, found and separated us from the other passengers and ushered us through customs, ahead of short, blackhaired, black-eyed natives and puzzled tourists, and past a painted cinder-block wall announcing: "Fae Bienvenidos Galapagos, Ecuador."

Luke commented on the hellish heat of Baltra. "This is the worst of it. It gets much better when we get to Santa Cruz Island. It's 50 degrees Celsius, 122 degrees Fahrenheit in the sun today. That's the added reason cactus is pretty much the only life here," he said, grinning at the conditions he knew so well. "We'll take a boat over to Academy Bay. If you like, we can stop and swim. There's a spot I know where you can swim face to face with the seals."

We waited for the boat on an outcrop overlooking the Pacific Ocean. Luke was a lean, deeply suntanned, pensive man. His blue eyes rested like jewels in the brown velvet box of his face. We learned that he was of English-German descent; he had no genetic link to the islands or the Ecuadorian nation that owned them. His tie was his unending fascination with the unique natural qualities of the Galapagos and a knack for explaining them well to visitors. He knelt on one knee and scanned his universe from the broken top of a volcano cone on Baltros, the smallest of the islands and home to the only airport serving the entire archipelago. The noon sun fired the waves of the Pacific into white-hot flashes of light amid the cobalt-blue sea that surrounded the island's grainy, dusty brown shores. He watched the waters for our boat as he would have watched the skies for our plane.

He said that before he ever saw the plane, he would hear the grind of the two propellers, then see the plane's shiny aluminum skin piercing the cloudless sky as a small dot, quickly swelling across the canvas until it would seem too heavy to stay aloft. It was a familiar routine, for Luke's entire source of revenue came by plane: tourists, scientists, and environmentalists. People needed his expertise to unveil the mysteries of the islands.

He rose to his full height as he saw our boat approaching. He skated down the side of the eroded volcanic remnant, his brown skin and khaki shorts blending inconspicuously into the baked, crusty earth. Only his white shirt jabbed mercilessly into the dusty tableau as he bounded down to the dock. Once at the bottom, he turned to wave us down.

On the boat to Santa Cruz Island and our hotel, Fletcher said to Luke, "I would like to interview Captain Dutch, the pilot of the boat that took the Sauers to Tower Isle. Were you able to arrange a meeting with him today?"

"Yes, six o'clock. He's expecting you."

I said, "Did you accompany the Sauers on all their field trips?"

"Most, but not all. They did go out on their own, even though guides are required by law here. I now know they went to Tower Isle a second time with Captain Dutch without telling me, which they should not have done. And I am quite sure they spent a day in the highlands without me."

I sensed pique in Luke's voice and pressed on. "What type of trouble does it cause for well-schooled scientists to go out alone?"

Luke grew more exasperated. "For one thing, this is my livelihood. For another, we are assigned visitors and to some extent we are responsible for their safety when they visit the protected areas. I have been under a great deal of pressure by the police because I wasn't more forceful about insisting that tourists take me along on their exploits. I could lose my license because they didn't follow the rules." He had become positively cross by now. "Visitors, including scientists, don't really know how to protect these islands. They walk on sensitive plants, disturb the wildlife, and increase the erosion of the topography. I love the Galapagos Islands. I have devoted my life to them. My role is essential to their preservation. So I'm very unhappy when visitors break the rules."

I hoped to mollify his anger. "I understand fully. Well, we certainly are pleased to have your services."

"Would we have time to go up to the highlands and still make it back to interview the captain?" Fletcher asked.

Luke seemed relieved by the change in subject. "Sure. We'll take a Jeep up to the general area and then walk on the paths that they probably followed. There's a low, grassy place where the tortoises gather. They probably dawdled there for a long time."

Fletcher and Luke continued the conversation concerning the Sauers.

Fletcher took out a reporter's notebook. "What did they want to know about?"

"Of course, they were very informed about the island's flora and fauna and geological history," Luke said, eyeing the notebook uneasily. "The area of interest they probed with me was the interaction of the animals and the people. They wanted to know to what extent the reputed fearlessness of the animals toward man had any flaws in it. You know, whether it was more myth than reality."

Fletcher's curiosity was raised. "And is there some myth to it?"

"A little. Obviously, if an animal took no defensive action against a predator at all, the species would be wiped out at some point."

Fletcher wanted a more definitive answer. "So, what is the reality? Do the seals, iguanas, tortoises, and boobies truly have no fear of man?"

Luke grimaced. "Frankly they should be scared stiff of man, run for their lives, but they don't run fast enough. They trust man. A major mistake. That's why we have guides." He became more discouraged as he broached a related topic. "Some of the islands have lost all their natural wildlife because of the human introduction of cats and dogs, which go wild and feral. It has taken twenty years to get rid of the feral animals from most of the islands and to reestablish some of the original animals, although some species are now totally or almost extinct, like Lonesome George, the last Isabella Island great tortoise. They were hunted to extinction."

That sobering thought quelled further discussion until the boat arrived in Academy Bay. We quickly unloaded, dropped off our things, and had Luke take us up to the highlands to see the giant tortoises. I have already described my fascination with the one fellow whose tenacity was hard to top.

Upon returning from the tortoises, Fletcher and I visited Captain Dutch of the Palistrano, the boat that had taken the Sauers over to Tower Isle twice. He was a rough-hewn Dutchman. His boat was a more handsome affair than himself, with clean lines and two powerful diesel motors. It could sleep twelve passengers in six small cabins and carried a crew of four, including a cook. The Sauers had hired him for a couple of day trips, returning to

Santa Cruz each night despite the captain's suggestion that they should simply anchor off Tower overnight. which would save fuel. The Palisantro weighed twenty tons and drew ten feet, so the three-hour journey one way to Tower Isle was very costly.

Fletcher probed that issue. "Why did the Sauers resist the notion of anchoring overnight?"

The captain ran a hand through his hair, remembering. "There was a disagreement of sorts between them. Mrs. Sauer wanted to stay the night on Tower itself, not on the ship, but Mr. Sauer reminded his wife that staying overnight on Tower was illegal. On the second trip, she was quite insistent about staying. She had asked me earlier if I would object if they went ashore for the night, and I told them that I would look the other way. That also meant we would have to elude Luke, who would obviously object. She even resorted to basically seducing her husband to convince him of the delights of being alone on the island. The whole crew had to avert their eyes and went below. Suffice it to say, Mrs. Sauer prevailed and we overnighted on our second trip out. They took a dinghy ashore with some light provisions and never returned."

Fletcher had a faraway look in his eyes, following some other line of thought. "What species of animals are on Tower?

"Both the land and marine iguanas and many types of boobies, blue-footed and red-footed."

"Is Tower free of feral cats and other predators?"

"Now it is, but for a while we had a problem. Some people squatted a few years back on Tower and introduced dogs and cats. The police had to shoot the animals because they were killing the native wildlife."

This new factor arrested Fletcher's attention. "How long did the squatters remain on Tower? Who were they?"

"They were Europeans, I think from Scandinavia and Germany. They built a hut, and for almost two years they lived there without anybody knowing about it. Finally a group of environmentalists found and reported them. When the police came to take them away, though, the squatters were gone."

"Interesting. Did you ever see them yourself?

The captain's sly manner suggested that he had overlooked a number of infractions. "I saw only the men. Occasionally a small outboard would come into Academy Bay to load up on supplies. They said they were living on Santa Cruz and had an address that they gave the customs authorities that must have checked out. However, I noticed that that boat, fully loaded, crossed a few times in the direction of Tower or Marchena, so I was convinced that they didn't live on Santa Cruz." He spat past the dock and into the swells below. "I didn't care. Live and let live, I say."

"Is there anything left of their encampment?"

"The police found walls and foundations built of stone collected from the island and mortised with ground shells. No roof exists, but one probably did when it all was first built. It is backbreaking work to build out of stone, so they must have hoped to be there for a long time. A year or so after they squatted, a law was passed giving protected status to all the outer islands, including Tower, and making them off limits to settlers of any kind."

"Will you take us to Tower Isle tomorrow?"

The captain checked his log. "I can do it, but I will have to charge you as if we had at least six passengers, to make it worth my while."

I spoke up. "Is that what you charged the Sauers?"

"Yes, exactly."

I was annoyed by the way his eyes never met mine. "It's too much. We will have to find another boat." I was ready to walk away. Fletcher gave silent support by moving slowly back up the dock.

The captain rubbed the two-day beard on his chin. "All right, all right. Pay for five, okay."

"Three and we have a deal," I riposted firmly. Fletcher was already halfway back to the dock.

The captain held up his fingers. "Okay, three." I took the extended hand of the captain and sealed the deal. He continued, "I'd like to leave at six. Will that suit you?"

Fletcher called from the roadway, "We can be ready. Our return must be open, however. We may have to spend the night."

The captain called back, "There's a charge for overnight and extra provisions for you and the crew, and then there's Luke. He'll expect to come along."

I said, "We understand. Just be sure you are prepared for whatever Mr. MacDonald needs. See you tomorrow at six."

Fletcher and I walked back to the hotel. It had a small bar where tourists and locals mingled. We had arranged to meet the local chief of police around eight. Colored Christmas lights hung from the ceiling racks of glasses that hung upside down from slats. The bartender, an attractive middle-aged woman, would just slip the stem of the glass along the slat to the front and remove the glass. Pretty clever. Clusters of nationalities gathered at the tables; it was like the United Nations. There was the German table: blond, loud, and talky. The Japanese group: quieter, less at ease, and observant. Some American teenagers gathered around the only video game, their middle-aged parents, with conspicuous tropical drinks, attempting to soak up the atmosphere with a straw. At an ebullient Italian table, a foursome were giggling and laughing, especially a hyperactive woman who smoked for four and would jump up and then collapse with each joke. A few locals were at the bar. We spied a man in a police uniform sitting alone at a back table. I asked the barkeep if that was Detective Aranah, our police contact, and indeed it was.

We approached and he stood up. "I hope we haven't kept you," Fletcher said and introduced himself and me. He explained that we had been privately engaged by Joseph's father. He then ordered beers for us all. "How is your investigation going?" he asked Aranah.

The police detective looked beleaguered and on the verge of disgust. In a sullen, perfunctory voice he said, "We appreciate any help we can get. The Ecuadorian navy is involved, and they have visited and searched Tower Isle. There is no sign of the Sauers. The Federal authorities are patrolling the waters with an armed coast guard vessel." Perhaps fearing that we thought him incompetent, he gave us some news he had found out. "Did you know that Marcia Sauer had been here before? The bartender, Isabella, remembered her. Isabella has perfect recall. But she says it wasn't hard, since there aren't too many women who have violet eyes and raven black hair. Apparently she made quite an impression here, albeit a wild one. Matilda, the owner of the hotel, will fill you in on what she knows."

Fletcher turned over a circular cardboard coaster and pushed it in the direction of Aranah. "Would you draw Tower Isle, just its coastal make-up, and its special characteristics?"

Aranah, warming to Fletcher, eagerly complied. Within seconds he had sketched added: warming out a circle, with a big dent, like an inverted spike, in the middle of it. He put a peak in the center of the circle and pushed the coaster back to Fletcher, saying, "That's about all there is to

Tower. Not much more than two miles square with that deep inlet and bay and an extinct volcanic cone that goes up a few hundred feet. No water. No shade. No place to hide."

Thinking ahead, Fletcher was tightening his focus. "Outside of this inlet and its beach, what is the topography of the rest of the coastline? Are there any natural places for boats to use as a harbor? And if so, please indicate where on your map."

Aranah took back the coaster and marked a spot on the other side of the inverted spike. "Seal Cove. This isn't a safe harbor because there are too many rocks, but an experienced sailor—with a small boat, no more than thirty feet long, I'd say—could maneuver and anchor. Some boats take tourists there to snorkel and swim with the seals. There's an interesting underwater construction of large holes in the rocks where the seals play a game of hide and seek with humans. From the land, though, it's treacherous to reach. You would have to know the way."

"Tell me, how long do you have the use of the navy, and how much help are they giving you?"

"As long as the pressure from the Ecuadorian president's office remains intense, they'll keep this boat here. They have to give a good show because tourism is so important to the economy. So far the world press hasn't given this much attention, and we want to keep it that way." He paused before he added, "As for my own staff, I have twenty people and three boats to cover an area of one hundred square kilometers within ten thousand square kilometers of surrounding sea. I'm stretched tissue paper thin, but we have many eyes and ears. There are another thirty national park employees who keep us informed. We don't have enough people to do a full-scale manhunt, but we know what's going on most of the time. Unless somebody really wants to hide, which is not impossible. Some of the outer islands are large and have a little water and some arable land. I am sure there are cases where decades have gone by without squatters being discovered."

"What about those squatters on Tower? We understand they were Swedes and Germans. What were they up to?"

"That case was different. We knew they were there, but we tolerated them. They didn't bother anybody. They were ex-yacht rats who fell in love with the islands and wanted to live here permanently. For some people, the isolation and beauty is irresistible. Over the years there have been quite a few people who did the same thing, squat, I mean. But we had to get tough when the Park Law passed, even though I didn't want to evict them. They were gone before we got there."

"Why didn't they put up a fight, even a legal one?"

"If we arrested them, they would have been deported. By scramming, they avoided arrest and deportation."

"I see. Well, thank you, Detective" Fletcher liked this man, I could tell.

The Detective disappeared through the hanging bamboo curtains while Fletcher went over to the bar to talk with Isabella. I tagged along.

Fletcher engaged Isabella immediately. "I understand from the detective that you have a perfect memory. For five dollars, what's my name?" Fletcher put a U.S. five-dollar bill on the bar.

Isabella laughed. "Keep your money, Mr. Fletcher MacDonald." There was a seductive glint in her eyes. She leaned fully against the bar in Fletcher's direction, revealing a disconcerting amount of bosom. Her black eyes, red-lipsticked lips, and smooth, creamy skin created a memorable sight equal to her perfect memory. She opened a beer and placed it before him, got another for me, and made change from his five dollars. "What would you like to know, Mr. Canadian?"

Fletcher was impressed. "You've done your homework."

"I don't have to. It's written all over your face. A little reserved, not noisy, white, English face, and, oh, yes, polite. Canadians are sweet."

He leaned in himself. "I could probably attempt a little character description of you, but I think that might get us both in trouble, and, after all, Canadians are sweet."

Isabella couldn't resist. "Lollypops are sweet, you know." She broke away and busied herself about the bar. I saw the heat between Fletcher and Isabella, but I kept my observations to myself. After mixing a few drinks and making change, she returned to Fletcher and took a sip of beer from his bottle.

"Detective Aranah tells me that you remember Marcia Sauer from a previous visit. Black hair and violet eyes are a rather unforgettable combination. But was there more?"

"Some people sashay in and within a flash the room is a stage and they control and work it. Marcia was such a woman; she understood her sexuality and used it. She played with men like cats play with mice. And, from where I was standing, she never lost sight of what she wanted, be it a beer, a joint, a man, or whatever."

"She must have been here awhile to pick up enough information to determine what she wanted and from whom."

"About three weeks. She blew in here like any other eco-tourist, and ten days later she could write her own ticket. I'll bet that Aranah didn't tell you that he saw her buying pot and somehow or other she never saw the inside of the jug. Aranah just gave her a talking to, privately."

"You're right, Isabella, he didn't say a word. Was she different this time around?"

"Well, she was sporting a big diamond ring and had a handsome husband who clearly enjoyed the thrill of having the most beautiful woman in the room swooning all over him. I guess I would put it this way. The last time, she was fishing. This time she seemed to be feasting on her catch."

Matilda, the hotel owner, came up to the bar to meet us. She and I chatted a little while Fletcher and Isabella finished their conversation. Matilda was a fiftyish, brassy lady from New York City. She and her husband had built the Academy Bay Hotel and Bar. He died a few years ago and she decided to run it year-round. She primarily catered to eco-tourists taking day trips from Santa Cruz to explore the Galapagos. She also had quite a few tourists waiting for charter boats to shape up, or she would handle them after the charter was over. The smallest contingent of guests, mostly bar loungers, were younger people who found their way to the Galapagos by hiring on to be part of a crew on a private yacht. Some of them would quit and stay on the islands for a while and then hire out again to get home.

Pointing to Isabella, she noted, "I see you have met the center of the universe. Isabella is our gossip columnist and has a collective, sometimes selective, memory. Very dangerous."

I moved to focus the conversation better. "Fletcher, Matilda says that the Sauers were in great spirits, had made some acquaintances in the bar, and had plans for several field trips all worked out. She knew that Captain Dutch was going to take them for an overnight to Tower Isle."

Fletcher inquired, "Isabella remembered Marcia from a past trip here. Do you?"

Matilda's face turned stony. "If I had known that Mr. Sauer's wife was Marcia, I would not have booked the room. Her former name was Haupt, Marcia Haupt. One killer woman. In the few days she was here, we had a police investigation for pot, a husband and wife almost killed each other because the husband was caught leaving Marcia's room, and then Marcia left without paying her bill. It was later covered by a total stranger."

Fletcher was puzzled by this portrait. "Did she seem embarrassed to see you?"

"Not one bit. Indeed, she remembered me and even gave me a hug! I guess she recommended our place to her husband." She rolled her eyes. "I should have known there would be trouble."

"Joseph's father told me that you called the police when they failed to return from Tower Isle with Captain Dutch. Do you have any ideas what happened?"

"Nothing solid. Except my sense that, where that lady's involved, something's not kosher, if you know what I mean."

"Thank you, Matilda. I think that's all for now. Max and I are going out to Tower Isle ourselves tomorrow, and we might not be back until the next day. So don't be worried or call the police," he said with a wink.

Matilda left. The bar was still crowded at ten o'clock with drinking and conversation. Isabella was working hard to keep up. I added up all that we learned so far, and I mused to Fletcher,

"Even if Marcia was a firecracker, a femme fatale, it doesn't seem to lead anywhere."

Fletcher pushed away from the bar, pressed his brow, and straightened up. "Ah, and there, my good friend, is where you are wrong. It leads us here! Consider for a moment where we are. This archipelago is one of the most remote places on earth. Its separation from the world created its own variations of animals, not found anywhere else. We are sitting in a bar through which pass very interesting people who have the urge to see the unusual and have made a major commitment in terms of time, energy, and sometimes heaps of money to indulge that urge. Note that Joseph, as intoxicated as he is with Darwin's work, had never visited this place where a substantial part of his core work came together. It took Marcia to bring him here." He bored in on me as he built to his point. "This place, like our home in Inverness, shapes people and thoughts as if they were formless clay. The power of place, call it home, dominates destiny and action, grand and small. It is the cosmic amalgam of time, space, matter, and energy. In the end, even money is only a means to build or return to a place. Place will lead us to the answer, it always does."

I puzzled over his impassioned response as he turned to Isabella.

"Isabella, one last question."

"I am going to hold you to that," she said saucily. "After that, I just want action."

"When Marcia was here before, who did she have her sights on?"

She took a moment to think. At last she brought something sharply into focus.

"A yacht rat. Mid-twenties, curly, dark blond hair. He hung out with a guy and a gal, Selma and Rolf, who I think also shipped in on a yacht and decided to stay. He was a hard catch, though. Independent. He didn't seem to like her splashiness. But toward the end of her stay I saw them together, tight as thieves. Oh, yes, here's a freebie. His name was Olaf. You're out of questions." She reached out and grabbed his hand.

He made no move to withdraw. He merely asked, "Does the clock on the questions start again tomorrow?"

"I think we can arrange that," she said, laughing. "Stick around and find out for sure."

****

We were three hours into the journey when Captain Dutch slowed the engines and pulled us into the bay of Tower Isle. We had seen only one charter boat after leaving Academy Bay, and except for the mechanical marvel of our gleaming white boat, there was no sign of civilization anywhere. No buildings, antennas, cars, even other people. Just what nature had wrought. There weren't even any clouds, just a tableau of the vibrant blue sea, a white crescent beach, some pale-green vegetation, and an ocher thousand-foot high extinct volcano peak in front of us. With plenty of provisions on board, we used a low-horsepower outboard motor to take us to the beach. If we did not return to the dinghy in two hours, it was presumed that we were traveling on foot to the other side of Tower. The dinghy would be picked up by the Palisantro, which would send another dinghy to pick us up at Seal Cove, the place that Detective Aranah had roughly marked out the night before on the coaster map. Fletcher purposely had not informed Luke of the trip and gave Matilda a large sum of money to give him to assuage any hurt feelings. Captain Dutch was also informed to keep quiet about our trip.

After going ashore, we reconnoitered our surroundings. The sun was already blistering hot. Fletcher had on his Tilley and I was wearing a baseball cap, but to little relief. We took shelter from the light and heat behind the only shade on the beach, an Opunto cactus. It stood six feet tall and had ping-pong paddles for leaves. We knew that no one inhabited the island, except that somewhere nearby were the remains of that small abandoned settlement. Fletcher had decided to bypass it and to focus on retracing the Sauers' path. Looming up behind us was the volcano cone, its base covered with thick underbrush and a few trees leading to its top. Animal life was limited but unique. It included, we had learned, many species of birds, especially finches, red-footed boobies, blue-footed boobies, frigates, land and marine iguanas, a variety of lizards, and some seals. Marcia and Joseph would have wanted to find the iguanas and boobies, since those species were unique to the island. Different variations existed on the sister islands, facts that contributed greatly to Darwin's final theory of evolution.

Fletcher had in mind that we should climb up and around the base of the volcano to the spot above Seal Cove that Detective Aranah had identified. He wanted to see if there were any traces of the Sauers' visit, so he felt that we had to do this by land. Many heavy boot tracks littered the beach, undoubtedly made by the navy patrol. We found a sandy, narrow path into the foothills and followed it. It had been made by many expeditions of tourists and scientists seeking to find the boobies. But there had been no visits here since the Sauers.

Fletcher knelt down to examine the foot tracks. The heavy navy-boot prints were gone. He traced the prints over and over again with his fingers and then announced, "Look, we have two distinct types of boot prints. One is much larger than the other, suggesting a male and female. And the smaller one has a definite brand name: Ecco. The larger has a Vibran sole, which we can identify as having many hatch marks. They are not distinct because the sole is well worn. The deterioration of the prints by the wind and sand is exactly the same, so they were made at the same time," he pointed out. "We should see them stop at the site of the boobies."

He bounded ahead, and in a short time we reached a flat place that overlooked the edge of the sea. It was densely crowded with two-foot tall birds with powder blue webbed feet. As we walked along, they didn't move out of our way unless we shooed them. They had absolutely no fear of us, just as advertised. There were even young chicks with fuzzy newborn babies about, but not a single defensive action was taken by the mothers.

The area was largely flat rock with no sand in which footprints would leave a mark. We searched the periphery of the roost for something resembling a trail. I saw a steep decline, then a big drop into the brush. I dropped the six feet or so. The soil was hard packed on the trail. I traveled along it a few hundred feet and saw the outline of tracks that appeared to be similar to those we identified earlier. I called Fletcher to come and examine them.

"Well done, Max. These are the Sauers' tracks." He looked up to gauge where we were. "This is the way to the other side of the island. With a little luck, it will lead to Seal Cove." Sure enough, it did except that the cove was two hundred feet below us and we hadn't found a clear way down.

Our gaze returned to the Sauers' tracks. There were many and they were blurred and basically on top of one another. Fletcher knelt on the ground and examined the tracks as if he were a human magnifying glass. Fletcher really rubbed his brow hard.

"Do you see how the tracks have deep impressions, vastly deeper than the others we have seen? That, plus the chaotic nature of the tracks, indicates a digging in, an attempt at anchoring, telltale signs of a scuffle. We need to find another set of tracks. If they are solo, then we know that one of them either fell off here or was pushed off." I looked up sharply at this suggestion, but he merely went on. "If no tracks, they both fell off the cliff, since the tracks only lead in this direction, not the other way. The grass in the path here is obliterating any tracks forward. There are two ways down, inside the crevice or farther along the edge, beyond the grassy part. I'll navigate the crevice. You take the top. Needless to say, be very careful."

I was anxious for myself but more so for Fletcher. He was angling down a cleft on a sheer face, with only small indentations to secure his feet. He held on to the rock face with his hands, essentially slithering down it. At one point I saw him slip before his legs found a ledge. As for myself, I had yet to find any tracks and wondered if the Sauers had simply turned back, despite the lack of any tracks in the other direction. I lost sight of Fletcher as I turned into the trees. Just a few feet from that turning point, the soil turned soft again and there were boot tracks, clear as day. I was not as good as Fletcher at reading them. I looked hard and finally, coming into focus, was the name Ecco. That would be Marcia's. But there was no sign of Joseph's Vibran sole. Her track continued downward. I moved as quickly as I could, yet I became terribly tangled up in thick underbrush armed with four-inch thorns that ripped at my hands and arms until it looked as if I had been flagellated. Soon, however, I could hear the surf pounding the rocks.

I finally broke through to the edge and found myself still twenty feet above the sea. I looked up to see Fletcher. I could see the crevice, but he wasn't there. I looked down and, lo and behold, he was swimming in the sea in the midst of several seals. I cupped my hands and yelled to him. He looked up, waved, and pointed down and toward him.

Peering cautiously over the edge, I saw that there was a small ledge that I could reach. I nervously stretched my foot to it and let myself down, leaning hard against the cliff wall. Once there, I summed up the nerve and saw several steplike ledges to the sea. Relieved, I made my way down to Fletcher's swimming pool. I called to him saying that I had important news. The water was not cold and was a great relief from the heat and anxiety of the last hour's descent to this place.

Fletcher swam over to me with a seal close in tow. "Meet my friend!" he yelled. He pulled himself up to a ledge right below me. I noticed that he was swimming wearing all his clothes, his backpack, and his shoes! As he dragged himself up and began to take his shoes off, I joined him on the lower ledge. "Why would you swim with your shoes on, for God's sake?"

"Think, Max," he said patiently.

Alarm filled my mind. "No, oh my God, you fell?"

He calmly turned one shoe upside down to let out the water. " Just about the time you disappeared from sight, I lost my footing. I was holding on with my hands, but that wasn't going to last, so I pushed out with my feet, took the leap of faith, and lived to tell the tale. What did you find?"

"Marcia's boot tracks but not Joseph's."

He rapped the shoe lightly on the ledge. "Well, there we have it. Now, cherchez la femme." He rose to his feet and started stripping off his shirt. "We have about an hour's wait until Captain Dutch picks us up. Take off your gear and let's swim with these seals. They nip a bit, but they won't hurt us. Come on."

In short order we were swimming in a natural pool area, separated from the sea by huge boulders. The sea would crash up on those boulders, lowering and raising the pool with the waves. The water was warm and astringently clean. There were about ten brown seals that would slither in and around us. I had my face underwater at one point, and one of them came right up and kissed me on the nose. Now that's a kiss! They did nip at our toes and fingers but clearly never to hurt us. I was quite sad when the Palisantro came by to pick us up because this was great fun. I had to agree with Fletcher: place makes a difference.

Fletcher had Captain Dutch sail toward Point Mejia on Marchena, another island thirty miles away. Also an uninhabited island, it had some dependable water and at one time a small settlement. The plan was to sail to the back side and stay anchored for the night without lights. The next morning we would take a dinghy to shore and approach Point Mejia.

The topography was richer on Marchena Isle than on Tower, a much taller peak, with tall ferns growing along the path we took from the back side of the island to the point in the early morning. Fletcher instructed me that we were to stay close to the ground so we would not be spotted. I asked by whom but he refused to answer. He said that we were looking for the old settlement, which should be visible from up there. I was intrigued by the secretiveness of the mission, but I still wasn't sure what he meant to accomplish.

After an hour of climbing, we found the point. Just below us, we spied a lava stone house and behind the house a clothesline with sheets and clothing flapping in the wind. Fletcher took out his video camera and whispered, "We have to get closer."

We edged back down the spine of the point and circled down to the flat land, keeping a hundred yards away from the clearing. After a while a virtually naked man with tousled dark blond hair stumbled out of the house. He stretched and relieved himself, then walked in the direction of the sea.

In a low voice Fletcher said, "That's Olaf. With any luck, the next person out of that house will be Marcia."

My eyes popped open wide. Now I saw what he had intended in coming to Marchena.

A woman did appear, but she was thin with stringy blond hair, accompanied by another man whom Fletcher identified as Rolf. They moved in our direction but stopped well short of us. We lost sight of them because they were on the other side of the promontory we were standing behind, but we heard their movements.

The woman called out, "Olaf, are we going to Santa Cruz today?"

He yelled back, "No, Selma, tomorrow. We need to do it now."

Just then, who should step out into the morning light but black-haired, violet-eyed Marcia. She hollered, "Olaf, where are you?" He responded and she, covered in a white cotton gown and looking every bit like a goddess, trotted quickly after him, Fletcher recording every second. She reached him while he was standing in the surf up to his calves. She hugged him around the waist, and then they kissed long and hard. Fletcher might as well have been directing the feature *The Long Hot Summer*.

Olaf led Marcia back to the beach and caressed her again. Selma and Rolf slowly approached Marcia with two heavy, short, stout poles. Marcia reclined on the beach and smiled up at Olaf. To my astonishment, he violently kicked Marcia in the side. She yelped and contracted into a small shape. Selma then whacked her with her stick, while Olaf continued kicking her in the middle and then in the face. Rolf took her forearm, laid it on top of his pole, and stomped on it. We could hear the arm break. Marcia's scream pierced our hearts with its awful agony.

Fletcher motioned that we should go, the sounds of the beating still in our ears. We backed up and returned low to the ground.

Upon reaching the Palisantro, Fletcher called Detective Aranah on the ship-to-shore radio. "Detective, we have just witnessed a horrible but consensual beating of Marcia Sauer on Marchena. It appears to be part of a scheme to inherit her husband's money. I believe that she and her cohorts killed Joseph Sauer as part of that plan. I suggest that you wait for them to carry out the rest of it. I am certain they will show up in Santa Cruz with a phony story about how Joseph died. We have a video that corroborates the conspiracy and the beating so you can confront them."

Aranah's voice squawked back. "Okay, but if they don't surface by tomorrow, we will pick them up on Marchena."

The next day, Marcia was brought into Academy Bay by Rolf and Selma. She was a wreck—terribly bruised, scratched around the face, arms, torso and thighs. Her arm was in a sling and her face bluish purple. They said that they had found her yesterday on a ledge at Seal Cove on Tower Isle while they had been boating. Distraught, Marcia told how she and her husband had slipped and fallen from the cliff above Seal Cove. She said that Joseph had slipped first, and in an effort to stop his fall she grabbed his hand and was pulled over.

We sat in Detective's Aranah's office, waiting for the provincial district attorney. One weak air conditioner unsuccessfully battled the ruinously high heat as Aranah and the lawyer walked in.

After the formalities, Fletcher explained his theory: "Four days ago, Marcia and Joseph Sauer did proceed along the top of Tower Isle and reached the cliff overlooking Seal Cove. We have discovered their footprints, and we have taken incontrovertible photographs proving their one-way trek to Seal Cove. I am sure that you will find that they match the shoe wear of both of them, if you can find the shoes. But that makes little difference. We discovered that above Seal Cove only Marcia's shoe tracks continue down to the ledges above Seal Cove. Joseph's do not. His tracks stop at the precipice overhanging Seal Cove. There are many shoe tracks at that point, suggesting a struggle. It is my contention that Marcia Sauer pushed her husband to his death. She did this to receive a life insurance benefit of one million dollars, which his college provides all professors as part of their compensation, plus whatever personal estate he had, and, as a bonus, I think, continuing help from the grieving parents. This money was to be used to pay for a life here with her lover of long duration, Olaf, and their friends, Selma and Rolf."

Everyone present was shaking their heads in disbelief at the sordid and mendacious tale.

"She met Olaf, who was a fellow itinerant yacht hire, three years ago when he was here. Isabella will testify to their being together. He was already close to Selma and Rolf. These are the same four people who became squatters on Tower Island and were to be removed. Except that Marcia had left before the police took action, probably to find a way to support their plans financially. It boiled down to her marrying a rich man whom she could lure to the Galapagos and then kill in such a way as to make it seem an accident with the aid of her friends. They chose the Seal Cove scheme. She would appear frightfully injured and claim that she had survived the fall and was found by Olaf and the gang." Fletcher's lips twisted in disgust. "We have date-stamped video footage of her looking quite well yesterday and having a very warm relationship with Olaf." The emphasis on "warm" left little doubt as to what he meant.

"I suggest that you interview Selma first. Put this theory to her. Let her deny it. And then show her the video. Tell her that if she will confess to being a co-conspirator in the murder of Joseph, the faking of Marcia's injuries, and to the plot in general, a less harsh punishment will be recommended. I have no doubt that she will try and save her skin."

Indeed, Selma cracked exactly as Fletcher predicted, and Marcia, Olaf, and Rolf were on the road to life in prison. Selma was expected to do at least twenty years.

I remained somewhat mystified by how Fletcher had put this all together, and I asked him to explain. "I know it was Isabella who linked Marcia and Olaf for you. But how did you know that there was a plot and that the yacht rats were still here?"

Fletcher was happy to divulge the trail of his sleuthing. "Captain Dutch said that he had seen Olaf subsequent to their leaving Tower. Their modus operandi was to squat on an outer island. The closest one to Tower was Marchena, which had ready-made quarters. And from what I had heard of Marcia's charms, I didn't think Olaf and Marcia would have split so easily after they had to leave Tower unless they had a plan to be back together. Once we found the tracks above Seal Cove and only one set down, well, deduction, my friend, deduction."

"Did you say seduction or deduction?" I couldn't resist ribbing Fletcher. "It seems to me that both played a part in this solution, eh, what?"

Fletcher did blush a bit. "It's all about place. If this weren't the Galapagos, the drive to stay here wouldn't have existed. Its singularity is intoxicating and in this case, lethal. Too bad Joseph wasn't more paranoid."

Fletcher gazed out at the ocean. "In the end, he was too much like the boobies, all too trusting of man, or in this case, woman."

THE EYE OF THE PANTHEON

An ancient grandfather clock solemnly ticked off the seconds in the sumptuous but empty backgammon room at the University Club on Fifth Avenue and 54th Street in Manhattan. Besides the clock's pendulum counting time, the only other sound was the strike of Fletcher's highly polished black banker shoes on the marble floor. The sound of each step ricocheted off the walls and the twenty-foot frescoed ceiling. Fletcher meandered around the tables, straightening a marker here and there. His red hair contrasted brightly with the alabaster white, well-starched collar that topped off his sincerely gray suit.

Fletcher had me scrunched-up in a narrow, virtually airless, hidden chamber in the ceiling. It was invisible from the room itself. A small opening in the wing of a plaster cherub provided just enough room for me to have a clear view of the entire room. I was to record both visually and aurally what transpired between Fletcher and the man he was to meet. Given the power of the man and who he represented, and the possibility of denial that this meeting had ever taken place, these highly unorthodox methods were necessary in Fletcher's mind.

I prayed that the session would be short, since I had to lie flat on my stomach for its duration while I operated both a video camera and directional microphone. I also heard the scratching of mice, or God forbid, rat feet, nearby. I prayed that I wouldn't have to meet them, too.

With one hand behind his back, Fletcher counted the rows, fifteen in all, of the bookshelves that rose from the floor to the ceiling. They were all tightly packed with hoary tomes. He calculated that given the size of the room, about one hundred feet by eighty feet, the walls held about forty thousand books.

The great clock struck one. Along with that strike, a corpulent, banker-type fellow walked through the great doors of the room. He turned around and carefully closed them, pulling the shades down on each of the glass panels for maximum privacy. He fished for something in his pocket and produced a church key with which he locked the doors. The sound of his shoes drummed across the room. Harold Thane, undersecretary to the U.S. State Department, was punctiliously dressed in a dark blue pinstriped suit. As he approached Fletcher, they acknowledged each other's presence by slightly nodding. As they were both wearing suits, although quite different in style, there was a sense that they belonged to the same military, yet from distinct regiments. Fletcher was clearly fit for line action, but Thane's paunch and wizened face had earned him a more distant role.

The older man walked to a picture window overlooking Fifth Avenue and eased himself into a well-padded burgundy leather wing chair. Fletcher followed and took a seat in a matching chair across from him. They said nothing as they peered out the window and waited for the right moment to pick up a conversation that had begun a few days before on the telephone. Although both men had easily socialized in the past, their professional relationship remained stiff owing to the odd reliance of this Goliath upon David.

Clearing his throat, Thane moved first. "You seem well, Fletcher. Your Cape Breton is a tonic, especially in the late fall. I remember well my visit with you there a few years ago about this time. Occasionally I daydream about that night when you, Max, Fiona, and I listened to that old man—what was his name?—play Celtic music on his fiddle. We were in a barn in the country." He became caught up in describing the scene. "Every seat, space, nook, and cranny was filled with awestruck people, of all ages, slapping their thighs and swaying to the music. There were even kids who actually climbed onto the roof rafters to get a better view. Mesmerizing. And how is your friend Max and his delightful wife, Fiona?"

"Max and Fiona are quite well, thank you. Yes, it was a memorable evening. But anytime Angus McLaren played was heaven on earth. With just that fiddle he could make a crowd laugh or cry, dance or reflect. I'm sorry to say that he died last winter, but his daughter carries on the great family tradition of fiddle playing." A more pointed tone entered his voice. "I would be enjoying Indian summer in Inverness right now if it weren't for your rather desperate call. By the way, you seem well fed, Harold."

Thane again cleared his throat. "No need to state the obvious, my friend. Let's get on to business. Your man is Patrice Marshall. He is the CEO of Astra Mineral Corporation, which is the world's largest privately held mining company. Along with diamonds, gold, copper, and silver, they possess deposits of very rare metals." Thane's voice darkened. "One is promethium, thought to have vanished from the planet but which Astra monopolizes in its Namibian mine. Promethium is to future weaponry what uranium was to the nuclear age."

Thane paused and seemed distracted for a moment. "Did you know that it glows in its natural state? A greenish blue and it pulses like a heart."

"I've heard of its strange allure. Just how potent is a promethium weapon?"

"With certain technology, a tiny amount of it can emit a high-intensity electrical field, like a solar storm, that can vaporize all carbon-based molecules. Poof!" Thane burst his hands apart to animate the word. He then became very intense and leaned in Fletcher's direction. "To put a sharp point on it, with thirty milligrams, a tenth of a regular aspirin, it could wipe out all life in a one-mile radius. Imagine, one malcontent, standing below us on Fifth Avenue, becomes an immediate lethal threat to millions of persons." Thane exhaled heavily and leaned back into his chair.

"I have never seen you this troubled. We have faced some dreadful situations in the past, but I detect deeper frustration and apprehension. This awful potential for destruction alone should be enough, but is there more?"

"Economic slavery for us all. Promethium, again with certain technology, can produce unlimited energy without heat or degrading the planet. It's one hundred percent pure electrical energy. No need for converting it into steam to run turbines. All that is needed is a unique coupler. It is the Holy Grail. The barrier to its use has been that it had not been found naturally on earth. Only impractically minute amounts could be obtained from bomb-grade nuclear fuel enrichment. That was until Astra's discovery last year. Astra may have enough promethium for thousands of years."

Fletcher, gazing out the large plate-glass window that gave him a panoramic view of life on New York's grandest street, nodded his head. "That's good news, really. The atomic age redux. But what's the really bad news that has us sitting here?"

"As I said," Thane replied, "we have known about promethium for years, and the technology to harness it has been shared with several countries in a secret consortium, led by the United States and its allies, plus Russia and China. Our greatest concern was that it could empower a small group, an al-Qaeda type, with blackmail power over the world. On the other hand, because there was no known natural source, the threat seemed remote until the Namibian find by Astra."

Thane squirmed in his chair. "The truth of the matter is the technology that both unleashes the energy and creates a weapon, the coupler, has been stolen. Recently someone hacked into a computer transmission that was carrying the critical formulations and technical specifications for the coupler from one engineer to another.

"We had booby-trapped this top-secret data with sensors that were supposed to automatically interrupt the transmission and inform a listening post if there was a leak or a hacking. Unfortunately we were double-whammied. The automatic interruption had been manually shut off by the engineers because of too many false disruptions. And the live human monitor wasn't paying attention when the warning light blinked, so the hacked transmission was completed. It's embarrassing, to say the least. Catastrophic is a better description, like the theft of the atomic bomb secrets. If Marshall has the technology or gets his hands on it, he's unstoppable. We can't allow him to have both the promethium and the means to effectively use it."

Fletcher's demeanor reflected deep concern. "I'd say catastrophic is a mild description. My recollection is that Marshall has a strong interest in politics as well as business. Didn't he engineer a coup in Namibia and put his own man in control? Promethium would give him the tools to build Namibia quickly into the most powerful nation on earth, supplying electrical power throughout Africa, and perhaps globally, as well as creating and controlling the world's cheapest manufacturing center. I can see some good in that, unless he's bent on threatening the world with the lethal aspects of promethium. Would he be content with being the Cecil Rhodes of the twenty-first century, or do you really think he has other aspirations?"

"We think he wants to be the Sun King, and with promethium he can do it. Rule the world! Marshall has aristocratic lineage from both England and France; he's bloody rich, so having such aspirations is, so to speak, in his blood. You are also correct about his political inclinations. Long before the discovery of promethium, he and his firm had bankrolled several politicians to the leadership in countries where Astra's mines are located. To bolster his position in Namibia, he assembled a mercenary force that is very large, well trained, and armed to the teeth.

"We have three choices." Thane raised his hand and counted them out on his fingers. "One, we could physically invade Namibia on some pretext as we did in Grenada, and take over the country and the mine. Two, we could eliminate Marshall. Three, we could persuade him to see our side of the matter and cooperate with us." He proceeded to discuss the consequences of each choice. "The use of overt military power can go very wrong. He's got ten thousand armed men, and the Namibian army consists of another fifty thousand who are well trained and equipped. Furthermore, we don't have much of a fig leaf to explain such an invasion to the world. We could have an entire continent angry with us, causing worldwide repercussions. The second choice, elimination, still leaves the body of Astra intact, and any one of his lieutenants could pick up the same mission. So, option three, persuasion, is by far the best route. We have to try it."

Pointing his finger at Fletcher, Thane said, "We need someone who can make the argument for us forcefully and compellingly, but without being threatening. You have to find something that overcomes Marshall's messianic tendencies. Your friend Martin Hopkins knows Marshall and will drop your name and suggest that you meet to discuss something of mutual interest, but not politics.

We were thinking of art. Marshall is an aficionado of Velásquez, as you are, and there happens to be an upcoming exhibition of Velásquez in Rome, so I thought that you both could meet there."

"Not bad, Harold. Let me see if I have this right. My assignment is to be a connoisseur of Velásquez art, which I am not. I am only an appreciator. Turn the conversation to politics, something that Marshall will find peculiar since I am supposed to be an art connoisseur. And then I am to convince him to give up his promethium to you, and abandon an opportunity to become the next Caesar? How about asking me to levitate while I do all this, just to make it challenging?"

"I don't want to swell your head, Fletcher, but if there is anyone on earth who can find the key to this man, you can. You are uncanny at such things. Everybody at State, and even the president, knows full well that you convinced a terrorist leader to give up atomic bomb suitcases to you. And then he disbanded his group. We'd still like to know how you pulled that off."

"Never give away the magic, Harold. Some things are best left a mystery."

Harold rubbed his large stomach and said, "How about lunch?"

Fletcher rose and chuckled. "Let's see, I recommend the soup de jour, pureed hemlock, and if that doesn't please, try the cyanide sorbet. They're both knockouts."

"You may be a genius in many areas, Fletcher, but your humor is a little flat."

Fletcher shrugged and discretely removed a button mike from under his lapel and left it on a bookshelf near the door. But not before he whispered into it, "Max, I owe you. Were the puns that bad?"

****

Plaza Navona, Rome

"Umm, this tartufo is out of this world. What makes it so sublime?" Fiona swooned.

"Dark-chocolate-covered ice cream, a warm October afternoon, Rome, and staring at Bernini's Fountain of the Four Rivers: that's what makes it sublime!" I was bobbing to the musicians playing accordions and violins in the plaza.

"They call it tartufo because it supposedly resembles truffles," Fletcher remarked clinically. "All that chocolate resembling round, dark balls has made this café, Tre Scalini, famous. Frankly, I don't see the likeness to truffles at all."

"Fletcher, I think you are confusing the mushroom truffle with the confection." Fiona smiled. "These ice cream truffles look like the little chocolate balls we buy at a candy shop."

Looking a bit flummoxed because he rarely got things wrong, Fletcher said, "Mmm, you're right. I was thinking of the mushroom type. Anyway, I think Max has nailed it. It is the magic of Rome that makes this city unlike any other place in the world—carefree, chaotic, and above all monumental. How could it not be captivating: a seventeenth-century plaza with a Bernini fountain, complete with a great church whose bells toll while talented musicians play romantic music; a dozen narrow alleyways, lined with shops and restaurants channeling exuberant people into this magnificent square from all points of the compass; skateboards flying; and sophisticated Roman men and women out for their sacred passeggiata."

Fiona grabbed my arm. and pointed."My God, that woman looks and walks like Sophia Loren in her prime." A woman in a svelte brown suit strutted slowly across the plaza toward three men at the edge of the fountain. Heads turned. To announce her arrival, she gently touched the arm of a lightly bearded fellow. He beamed a neon-bright smile and kissed her hard on both cheeks. They clasped each other tightly around the waist and joined his companions, the eddy of their affection spreading across the plaza, anointing everyone with a romantic gleam intensified by the rich golden sun of the deepening afternoon. I gently kissed Fiona on her temple as we squeezed each other. Fletcher averted his eyes from the tenderness, abruptly leaving the table to more closely inspect the fountain.

I paid the bill to the clinking of silverware by waiters preparing for the next customers, the flapping of pigeons seeking our crumbs, and the shouts of recognition of tourists and lovers finding each other.

We followed Fletcher through the narrow serpentine streets, passing the flag-bedecked Italian parliament and on to our destination of the Piazza di Spagna, the Spanish Steps. Crossing Via del Corso and up Via Condotti, we climbed the famous three tiers of steps to the best view of Rome, where its skyline of history, the Coliseum, the Vatican, and River Tiber wrap together into a living diorama. As we sat atop the steps in the dimming daylight beneath the Church of Trinta del Monti, the scene changed by the minute as the sun melded into the nightlights of the city.

"Tomorrow I meet Signor Marshall at the Museo Rospilli, just a few blocks from here on the Via Del Corso. The museum has brought together the greatest assemblage of Velásquez paintings in history: about one hundred, all sizes, genres, and periods depicting the full scope of the master's works. Tomorrow morning I want you to visit the Pantheon. It's located just a few blocks from here and the Rospilli. From the outside it doesn't have an overwhelming presence, but once you step inside, you will comprehend its significance."

"It was designed by the Emperor Hadrian in AD 120. The oculus, the gigantic hole in the ceiling, is entirely uncovered, so the elements have complete access to the building: sun, rain, snow, anything. On a clear day, the design focuses the sun as if through a magnifying glass, so it appears to be a moving, fiery, molten orb on the walls of the Pantheon. With each second, this circle of light, about twenty feet in diameter, moves clockwise around its perimeter, like a powerful searchlight. To the ancients, it represented the all-seeing, all-knowing eye of God. To my mind, I don't doubt it, for it is one of the few places where the cosmos and earth meet with such dramatic intensity. Some have said that to watch that circle is to come as close as mortals can come to seeing the face of God. I want you to chart exactly where the sun will strike within the Pantheon from four-thirty until five-thirty tomorrow. You will have only tomorrow morning to do these extrapolations."

"Why between four-thirty and five-thirty? What's up?" I hadn't a clue. "I don't see the connection between the Pantheon and convincing Marshall to give up his hold on promethium." I must have looked to be the epitome of befuddlement.

"Suffice it to say, if Marshall is to give up on something as history changing as promethium, the machinery to accomplish this must be equal to the goal. Contact Harold Thane and have him call the appropriate Roman authorities so that the Pantheon is cleared of visitors by four-thirty tomorrow. Marshall and I must have it to ourselves when we arrive. Your charting of the movement of the sun on the walls must be precise. Take photographs so you can be sure to the inch where the sun will be at that time within the building. If my recollection is correct, in the late afternoon the circle of light is just a few feet above the floor. Max, I will wear a wire at the museum. Be sure you record everything and listen for exactly when we leave the museum. You won't have much time to prepare."

"Prepare for what?" I was ignored again. Fiona thought out loud, "You want to show him some cosmic relationship between what he does and the rest of the universe? Is that it, Fletcher?"

"In the abstract, yes, but for it to work, it must seem concrete and tactile. Let's walk and talk. The Trevi Fountain is only a few blocks away, as is Al Moro, one of my favorite trattorias."

Fletcher jauntily trotted down the Spanish Steps. He always became lighter, more animated, when a solution had come to him. As we walked to the Trevi, he said to us, "I have to show Marshall that nothing happens in a vacuum. It's like a ball of yarn. If you pull on one part, it affects another part. The Pantheon is a great example of this principle of harmony and unity. For almost two thousand years it has demonstrated to anyone who looks hard that all forces are intimately and eternally connected: the earth, moon, sun, planets, stars, time, and energy, and everything affects everything else."

Stopping dead in the middle of the sidewalk and speaking in a whisper to us, "Something so big as promethium doesn't go unnoticed in the scheme of things, and I will show him that significance with convincing evidence. I have in mind some theater to make my point, with you and Max as my stars."

I wondered out loud, "Has this something to do with those togas you bought?" I was ignored again and decided to let things roll out as they may.

We continued our walk. "Have you considered a purely business approach to Marshall? Sort of a win-win type of thing?" I asked. "For instance, Fletcher, if he were to cooperate with the Consortium, it would undoubtedly treat this as a symbiotic business relationship, and his Astra company would benefit immensely. If he tries to go alone and threatens force, he stands to lose everything. Working with the Consortium seems much more rational."

Fletcher turned solemn. "Promethium has given Marshall the opportunity to play God's game. That is very appealing and counts for much more than mere dollars. This is not unlike the moment in 1942 when Niels Bohr decided not to work with Eisenberg and advance the Nazis' development of the atom bomb. Bohr had it in his power to secure victory for Nazi Germany, but he sided with the forces fighting for democracy over tyranny. Marshall likewise can use promethium to secure his own imperial dictatorship or release it for the common good."

"Do you really think Marshall sees it in such dramatic terms?" I questioned him.

"How could he not? He holds the key to unimaginable power. Such power makes men think they are God. Of course, they are something less, and therefore vulnerable. And that is what I must demonstrate to Marshall."

I was not entirely convinced. "Sure, Marshall may be drunk on this newfound power. But having hundreds of billions of dollars shifted to him, making him the wealthiest man in the world, cannot escape his thinking. He gets that rich only by absolutely siding with us. Otherwise he takes the risk of being beaten and losing everything."

"Just one other thing," Fiona quietly injected. "If he's on a power trip, the only thing he'll respect is a power greater than himself. I don't think money has a bearing on this. If promethium is so powerful, and he controls it, what could trump it?"

"To use your bridge metaphor, there's always no trump. A hand so strong that even promethium loses. Ah, look, the Fontana di Trevi. Anyone got a penny to make a wish, a really big wish? I certainly have one in mind. Let's have dinner and we'll work out the full plan of action for tomorrow."

****

Fletcher loved the movie *Around the World in Eighty Days* starring David Niven as Phineas Fogg. He never forgot that Fogg always arrived at a destination exactly at the stroke of the appointed hour regardless of the calamities that may have befallen him on the way to the appointment. It was a matter of character. And so, too, did Fletcher regard punctuality as a great virtue. Never hurrying, never revealing any stress associated with arriving exactly on time, Fletcher would stride to a meeting with clockwork accuracy and grace.

The appointed hour for his meeting with Patrice Marshall was three o'clock at the museum in a room reserved for presenting the famous Mars painting by Velásquez. Fletcher was wearing a trench coat and, underneath, his beloved chocolate-brown Harris tweed jacket. His red hair flashed by the guards as he stepped lightly through the exhibition rooms to the Mars painting, walking into the darkened chamber precisely on the dot of three. I was in the guardroom of the museum, listening and recording the conversation via the wire that Fletcher was wearing.

He walked up to a tall giraffe of a man who stood with his hands behind his back, white hair somewhat wildly wavy, and quietly confident. He had a long, narrow face that was tanned a deep brown. One hand leaned on a sturdy black oak walking cane that had a bulbous golden lion's head with what appeared to be sapphires for eyes. A double-breasted blue-blazer over gray flannels and a tie of fine red and gold silk gave Marshall a public school look. In a hushed voice Fletcher said, "Mr. Marshall, I presume? I am Fletcher MacDonald."

Marshall had a surprisingly deep voice that welled up from his stomach and filled the air. "Martin Hopkins says you might have some interesting information about this exhibit. And, yes, I'm Patrice Marshall." Both men shook hands as if in a photo opportunity. No warmth, just a formality.

"Of course, Martin exaggerates. As I recall, his favorite expression is, 'Never let the facts get in the way of a good story.' I'm sure the curator knows a hundred times more than I do. However, I do have one trick up my sleeve. Conveniently, the actual inspiration for the Mars painting is here as well. Come this way." In an adjoining room was a large stone statue of Mars, the god of war.

"This statue, Mr. Marshall, was in the garden of the Spanish Cardinale-Infante, and it was the model for the painting. Velásquez had been sketching it on and off for years. Notice the curious puzzlement on the face of Mars in the painting. He seems unsure and tired, a very curious mental condition for the great mythic warrior. And yet the statue doesn't reveal that worry. It suggests to me that Velásquez understood his mythology quite well. Mars was a warrior who knew war was hell, and he also knew that he could be the tool of the greater gods whose power was superior to his own."

Marshall opined, "Likewise, Velásquez brought almost unbearable torment and meanness to the portrait of Pope Innocent X. The pope's grossly deformed face glowers. At first the pope didn't like it, but he was convinced by his peers that it was a masterpiece of the highest order. I am of the opinion that it was a cruel joke on the sour man by his retainers, for the work was so lifelike it clearly demonstrated what an ugly fellow Innocent X really was. Velásquez pulled no punches and I think, had the pope been honest, he probably would have been happier with the equivalent of major airbrushing."

Fletcher, feeling that he had developed some traction with Marshall, continued to work the art aspect of the conversation.

"Speaking of Pope Innocent, there are three portraits of him in different states of contemplation."

Marshall interrupted. "Mr. MacDonald, why did Martin set up this meeting?"

Fletcher went directly to the heart of darkness. "Promethium. I am here to convince you to sell a U.S.-led consortium of nations all of your promethium."

Nonplussed, Marshall snapped, "Well, that's a waste of time. I'm not selling it to anybody. I certainly will have a word with Martin. Now, I think our tête-a-tête is over." He was marching out of the room when Fletcher called out to him, in that commanding, round, encompassing baritone voice that seems to emanate from the center of the earth, "It is cursed! Promethium is cursed, sir! Give me one minute to explain what I think you already sense."

Marshall stopped in the doorway. "What is this nonsense?"

"That greenish-blue light. The pulse. No one survives it. It's not the radiation. It's a curse. That suspicion, that intuition that promethium carries with it an unknown price is right again...your intuition has never failed you...it is not wrong this time either."

Struck by Fletcher's observation, Marshall walked closer. He cautiously said, "There have in fact been some incidents that are hard to explain. But promethium is a very unusual substance. What do you know about it?"

"It starts and ends with the mythology. As I am sure you know, it is called promethium after Prometheus, who stole fire from the Olympian gods and gave it to the human race out of pity. He was punished for the theft by Zeus, who had him chained to a cliff and daily sent an eagle to tear at his liver. One of the scientists who successfully converted promethium's energy into electricity was Ronald Masters. He was able to manufacture a minute amount from the early atomic bomb experiments. He was killed by an unknown assailant in his lab. Did you know that his death was caused by the tearing out of his liver?"

Marshall violently recoiled. "I had heard of Masters' death, but it was attributed to radiation." He was clearly stunned by the revelation. Sitting down slowly on a bench, he pointed at Fletcher to sit beside him.

"Well...yes...there are some odd things." The words seemed stuck in Marshall's throat. "It could be said that we've had a few peculiar circumstances at the mine and...that they have had a disturbing similarity. Our miners say they feel compelled to see the glow again. When down in the mine, they would seek it out even if it meant leaving their work site and removing massive barricades to gain access to the prohibited area. Promethium seems to have a siren's call about it."

Fletcher asked, "Does it call to you too?"

Marshall nodded his head rapidly. "Yes."

"Have you seen its infamous glow and pulse?" Fletcher's curiosity was authentic.

"Have you ever seen the green flash on the sea just as the sun is about to set?" Marshall questioned Fletcher.

"Yes, I have. In the Caribbean. I'll never forget it."

"Then you know, once you've seen it, you yearn to see again, because it has about it a connection to things that seem outside of this world or outside of the ordinary. It's seductive."

"And this is how promethium has affected you?"

"I've had my men build a lead-protected vision port where I can look at it," he admitted. "I sometimes can't sleep and have to see it again. It burns into your soul; like good blues, it gets under your skin. You can't forget the music, and you want to hear it again. The oddest thing about it is that despite the physical danger, the desire to actually hold it in one's hands is strangely powerful. Sometimes I have to shake myself to not pursue this compulsion."

"As to the mythology, Mr. MacDonald, did you know that there is a star in Andromeda that seems to be largely composed of it? Some astrologists, not astronomers, claim that star is the home of Mt. Olympus."

"No, I didn't."

" So, you do accept that there may be something to what I say?" Fletcher pointed out. "Why risk so much over this? You know promethium's value in the right hands would be a boon to the planet: virtually free energy, ending our use of fossil fuels and all the environmental good that goes with it. Your wealth from it would be secured. On the contrary, if you hoard it and try to exclusively exploit it, you have a double threat, the U.S. and its allies—and the curse. Remember Pascal's choice: better to be a believer in God and pay a ten percent tithe than risk hell."

"If I give it to the U.S., they may use it to force a Pax Americana on the world, ditto for Russia, or China.".

"It isn't the United States and the West alone. It's a consortium of advanced countries: Russia, China, Japan, India, and Brazil. Mr. Marshall, the sides are lining up."

Marshall replied coldly, "The reality is that I have the money and political clout to go my own way with this. I want to be sure that promethium is a positive force for the planet. You can be sure of that. I have been biding my time."

"But, Mr. Marshall," Fletcher argued, "the secret is out about promethium. All the world powers know you have it. One way or another, you will be stopped from hoarding it. You must know that."

"I don't know that. If that were the case, your friends would have already tried. My mine and the surrounding area are virtually impregnable. Namibia and its army and my mercenaries and I are all one. The government of Namibia is not oblivious to the power that will come to all Namibians if they possess the power to fuel the world." His eyes lit with a vision. "Think of the factories we can build, the food plants. In a generation Namibia can be the center of the world rather than barely on the periphery.

Tell your friends that Patrice Marshall and Namibia are not about to capitulate to threats. This fire I own. As to the curse, I won't make the mistake of Prometheus. I'm not giving it to man. I'll sell it to him."

"You're parsing words, Mr. Marshall. You are still in essence giving promethium to the human race. You sense there is something to the curse or you would never have returned to this room. You yourself have been strangely attracted to its power." Fletcher pressed on. "I think it is obvious that you are trying to find a sophistical way of circumventing a curse that you sense may be real. You can't trick the gods with cheap lawyer tricks. You know that there is something to what I say."

"Even if I thought there was something to the curse, don't forget that Hercules finally saves Prometheus from his torture because he recognizes that Prometheus meant no harm. That's me. By my possessing this power, I will be able to impose peace on this world. I will keep order because of my overwhelming power. Basic, isn't it?"

"So, no free will in your world. Only the world according to Patrice Marshall. I am not sure Hercules would rescue you under those terms, because it places you over the gods. But if you are game, I have a test that will prove or disprove the existence of the curse."

Marshall pulled back sharply. "And how will you do that?"

"Do you know that you are only a few blocks from the last

great temple built to the gods who cursed Prometheus? The Pantheon. I propose that you challenge the gods. Go there and swear before them that you are not ruled by them, that you have no intention of giving up promethium, and challenge them on the spot to show themselves or they will be irrelevant and impotent. They were an intemperate lot. If they do not show a sign of anger, then there is no curse. If they do show a sign, you will be well advised to walk away from the promethium to save your hide."

Marshall did not like the idea. "Why should I take this chance?"

"Do you want to end up like Dr. Masters? A liver pecked out. You already know that there is something peculiar about promethium. If you get a sign, then you know the curse is real. You can act accordingly. Distance yourself from promethium. Let it be taken by others who will have to deal with the curse. The gods won't be angry with you because you obeyed them. And if there is no sign, you can proceed with your other plan with more certainty. You can dispense with any nagging concerns that this element has heavy baggage. We can go to the Pantheon now and test the curse."

Marshall's hands were twisted in his lap. "Until promethium, I would never have believed for a moment in such a thing as a curse. My mind still rejects the entire proposition." He noticed what his hands were doing, and he let them fall to his sides. "But I am conflicted, that's true. My rational side not only rejects the myths as fairy tales, but posits that any death associated with promethium is just the result of radioactive poisoning."

Suddenly, Marshall was taken with a new idea. He announced boldly, "The intellect must triumph over the emotions. As I know rationally that curses are for the untutored and foolish, so I will accept your challenge to prove it! And when I leave victorious, my resolve to use promethium my way will be tenfold increased. Tell that to your sponsors. Let's go."

I immediately alerted Fiona at the Pantheon that Fletcher and Marshall were on their way. I ran out the back door of the museum to join her before they got there.

The two lanky men briskly walked out of the museum and reached the Pantheon at exactly five o'clock. As they walked up the steps, Fletcher caught my eye and gave me a slight nod. Once Fletcher and Marshall were inside the building, the noise of the street dropped away as if a giant iron door had fallen down. Their eyes were drawn up the smooth, bare, circular walls. Up, up, fifty, one hundred, one hundred and fifty feet to the top, a gigantic and perfectly round opening: the oculus. At five o'clock the sun threw a spotlight of golden fire twenty feet in diameter through the oculus onto the east wall.

"I am still standing," Marshall said in a sneering voice. "No chains on me. Indeed, I feel quite comfortable in this imperial space. It fits my temperament."

Fletcher knowingly taunted Marshall, "but you have not yet made an oath against the gods if they should try to harm you for giving promethium to man." Fletcher spelled out the rules. "You must be clear. Reject their power over you and let's see if they respond."

Marshall walked to the center of the temple, looked straight up into the oculus, and spoke, "Oh, Zeus and your fellow gods, I now possess your vaunted promethium. It is my ambition to provide its energy for the use of man. Do not interfere with my plans as you did with Prometheus, or I shall resist and damn you! I am more powerful now than you could ever be!" He turned to Fletcher and asked, "Have I made myself clear enough?"

As he spoke, Fiona and I, dressed in white togas, moved from the black shadows created by the contrasts of light in the great room, into the fiery orb of light. We stood against the wall about fifty feet from Marshall and Fletcher, who were in the center of the temple. Our eyes were fixed on Marshall, who strained to see and understand our presence. Due to the intensity of the light of the concentrated sun, our shapes and visages were blurred and hard to sharply decipher, We raised our arms high above our heads, pointing to the oculus. First Fiona and then I repeated in round form, repeatedly, "Thief of fire, blasphemer, usurper. Come, Zeus, and destroy him!" "Thief of fire, blasphemer, usurper. Come, Zeus, and destroy him!" "Thief of fire, blasphemer, usurper. Come, Zeus, and destroy him!" Then we howled as if we were wolves. Our howls filled the giant space with unnatural sounds. Marshall dropped to the floor, cowering. Fletcher knelt by his side. We repeated our chant and howls.

A slow and commanding flapping sound entered the great space. Marshall and Fletcher looked up to see a massive bird with an eight-foot wingspread slowly beating and whooshing through the air of the temple, entering from the mouth of the oculus. Like a black ghost it soared and dived.

Marshall, trembling, uttered, "My God, it's an eagle. It's after my liver! What do I do? What do I do?"

"Recant. Swear to walk away from the promethium," Fletcher prompted him.

Fiona and I slunk away. The bird continued to make slow, wide, methodical circles.

Marshall used Fletcher's torso to steady himself. "Give me my cane." He dropped his jacket, ripped open his shirt, and bellowed, "Here is my liver, Zeus, come and get it. But, I warn you, if you try, I'll smash you if I can with my hands and this cane." He raised his cane and said, "I'm here! Why do you wait?"

Fletcher pulled at Marshall. "Are you mad? Can't you see that you have been given a sign. The gods are watching. Do not anger them more. I know of what I speak."

The eagle continued to circle within the temple, swooping lower, then higher until it was near the top of the oculus. At the zenith of the opening, it dived down like a rocket, swooping so low that the men could hear its feathers ruffle. It came within inches of Marshall's naked torso and flew low to the floor. Marshall covered his stomach with his arms to protect himself from the expected attack. The bird then rose sharply, but this time it soared straight out the oculus and did not return.

The temple was grave-still. Marshall's sweat covered the floor around where he and Fletcher stood. Fletcher was still on one knee but rose to his full height next to Marshall.

Marshall slowly turned to Fletcher. "Looks like I won, Mr. MacDonald. I think you put on a very good show. I just about bought in. Just about. That bird was a plant, wasn't it? And the Greek chorus, your actors. You owe me a suit and a shirt and an apology."

"I've tried to warn you, Mr. Marshall. Perhaps my devices were clumsy, but the truth of the matter is what you already suspect. There is a curse. I advise you to reconsider. I fear you may have gone too far already." Fletcher backed slowly away leaving Marshall standing in the center of the great dome, his grand cane with the sapphire lion eyes firmly in his hand, his chest naked.

Fletcher left by a side door. From the top step of the temple he surveyed the Piazza della Rotunda. He searched the area and saw Fiona and me having coffee in the back of a café. He waved and walked towards us.

Fletcher gave his postmortem. "It almost worked. We had him spooked. He's one tough and brave man. Most would have run out of the building when that eagle appeared. But he stood his ground. He nailed the whole gambit in the end. He's frightened, though, as well he should be. He knows there is something to the curse, but in the end he could not admit that possibility. He is too committed to rationality now to listen to the true whispers of his intuition. I gave him fair notice to heed those whispers." Fletcher was pressing and rubbing his brow and was removed from us.

I sighed. "You know that we almost couldn't pull the sun routine because the forecast called for thunderstorms. There wasn't any way to reach you without tipping off Marshall. But the weather cooperated. By the way, that eagle cost ten thousand dollars to rent for the day, cash. I got him from an animal theatrical service. The bird will naturally fly to his cage that was set up be- hind the temple. He's already back with the troupe. I guess he earned his keep today."

Fiona looked up and said, "Looks as if those thunderstorms are finally coming in. Look at the size of that thunderhead, and behind it a black wall of rain full of lightning. Boy oh boy, it's coming fast. We might as well stay here until it passes."

At that moment, a text message came across my cell phone. It was from Harold Thane. "Tell Fletcher that there has been a volcanic eruption at the Namibian mine. It is completely destroyed. Vaporized. There is now a new, violently active volcano where the mine was." I gave Fletcher the phone so he could read it himself.

The wind started to blow and papers swirled around the piazza. Romans and tourists alike found shelter. The sky went black and the gray-black temple almost disappeared from site, even though it was no more than a few hundred feet away. The black thunderhead that Fiona had spotted was now overhead blocking out all the light. It was like an eclipse of the sun. Its underside billowed and churned. Some lightning cracked along its edges. The day darkened completely to night.

A blinding, end-of-the-world flash of lightning then illuminated the piazza and the Pantheon. It blazed for what seemed like seconds from the oculus itself. A bolt stretched from the cloud through the oculus: the Pantheon itself had been hit.

The strike was accompanied by thunder and a vibration that suggested a volcano was about to erupt under us. From within the Pantheon light licked from under its great two-thousand-year-old doors. We held our breath, thinking that the building would explode or disintegrate. Then the sky opened up, as if a dam holding back all the rivers of the world had burst, and the water came down in waves. I never saw another bolt of lightning, but the thunder rolled on and on, announcing something to someone.

I said, "My God, that bolt was in the temple. Wasn't Marshall still in there?"

Fletcher was already gone and pushing against the wall of rain back to the Pantheon. I was right behind him. We slipped through a side door of the guardhouse, which had been blown open. Upon entering the temple's central chamber, we were assaulted with the sickening stench of singed hair laced with burned wood. There was no light either from the oculus or the electric lights. Fletcher went back to the guardhouse and grabbed a flashlight. He shined it in the huge space and called out for Marshall. The rain was falling hard through the oculus and had created a shallow pool of water covering most of the temple floor. Finally the beam found a black shape in the very center of the floor, directly under the oculus, where Fletcher had left Marshall. We moved to it with reluctance. The light revealed his body, now just a charcoal effigy of Marshall, lying in the pool of water, dissolving rapidly into black sludge. Only the head of the lion cane remained intact, its blue eyes staring up at Fletcher, myself, and the oculus.

MANCHESTER SQUARE

"I love London!" Fiona exclaimed as she pranced ahead of Fletcher and myself and pirouetted on her stiletto-heeled, snaky red shoes. She faced us and waited with her arms akimbo until we reached her. Then she did a half-turn, squeezed between us, hooked her arms into ours, and created a chorus line of three. "Just think of all the scandals and intrigues being cooked up behind these staid Victorian facades. It's so wicked and stately all at the same time—pomp and phony-baloney. And the Brits know it. They don't take themselves too seriously."

I knew the prices of the real estate we were walking by. "These Brits are pretty good at making money, too, Just one of these Manchester Square homes costs what everyone in Inverness makes in a year."

Fletcher opined, "I think they're worth it. Everything that sophisticated life can offer is in London. It's the Koh-I-Noor diamond of cities."

We had just come from the theater in the West End, got off the underground at Bond Street station, and closed a pub after several rounds of beer for me and Fiona and stout for Fletcher. It was about 11 o'clock and the October air was tinged with wood smoke. Decaying autumn leaves skittered over the pavement and gathered in little piles. We turned on to Manchester Square on our way to Durrants, our favorite hotel on George Street. This is where Fiona had leaped with glee just now.

Manchester Square has at its center a small gated park where the privileged with keys can sit on the benches amid the gracious trees and shrubbery and contemplate how lovely life is when one is very rich. Tall brick town houses frame the park, most with high stoops and grand white entrance doors, sporting brass knobs and kickplates shined to mirror quality. Looking up from the street, one can occasionally get a glimpse of the high-ceilinged great rooms inside. As the square is not on a through street, it is serenely quiet, a welcome juxtaposition to the loud and frenzied shopping mecca of Oxford Street only a few blocks back. Black wrought-iron lampposts with weak incandescent bulbs cast a genteel and unobtrusive light on this dignified scene, which, as Fiona rightly pointed out, could mask very foul acts.

Indeed, Fletcher had been engaged by the Manchester Square Association (MSA) to solve what Scotland Yard had failed to do: the sniper murders over the last year and a half of five women, all single and living alone on the square, shot dead with a cyanide dart on their outside door steps. The tabloid press, in its alliterative passion, had dubbed them the "Manchester Maiden Murders." Not only were the inhabitants of the square terribly rattled, but the real estate value was now threatened, and the local Wakefield Museum had seen a catastrophic drop in attendance. The victims were in their early twenties to late forties, and they all had lived on the square for at least three years, some for almost twenty. Some were professional, some not. They all had succumbed to immediate death by a lethal dose of cyanide delivered by a dart gun, literally felling them in their tracks in front of their homes. The police had assigned sharpshooters to the area after the first three deaths, but two more killings occurred. Lady Wakefield, the widowed matriarch and main benefactor of the MSA, and the museum, which was formerly her ancestral home and above which she now lived in a private apartment, recommended that Fletcher be hired. She had been an ardent admirer of Fletcher's for many years.

He had met Lady Wakefield and her husband, Carl, when they visited Cape Breton on a golfing holiday. Fletcher was waiting for a friend at the Ingonish Hotel and was amusing himself with a solo game of chess. Carl asked if he would like a "live" challenger, and that began the relationship. Carl and Lady Wakefield soon learned that Fletcher was known as the "Scottish problem solver" and that he was very much in demand for his services. They had lost their only son, Vachel, on an expedition to the Amazon to identify and preserve rare rainforest mammals from extinction. Near the end of his work, he disappeared with absolutely no sign of his whereabouts. Even though his loss had occurred two years before they met Fletcher, the Wakefields hired Fletcher to see if he could at least provide something more definitive about the disappearance.

Fletcher found him alive in the Villabamba section of Colombia, where he had become a member of a Maoist revolutionary force. Fletcher brought back a video in which Vachel spoke of his rejection of capitalism and democracy. The video also contained a vituperative denunciation of his family. Only a few months after Vachel was found, his head was delivered to the Wakefields with a note from the Maoists accusing him of being a spy for the West.

Despite this ugly turn of events, the Wakefields felt a special admiration for Fletcher because he had at least located their son where others had failed. This admiration prompted them to hire him for several business investigations, and they recommended him to many other people and organizations, which even led to sensitive intelligence work for the governments of several countries. Fletcher's now overflowing client demand as a global problem solver could be largely attributed to the good words and recommendation of the Wakefields.

We had been in London several days carrying out basic investigatory matters that included reviewing what the police would allow us to see, interviews, reading the news accounts, and reconnoitering the area. There were some common threads in the victims' lifestyles: 1. These were uncommonly attractive women. 2. They gave particular attention to how they appeared in public. 3. They all led active social lives and had extensive commitments to charitable organizations; for instance, they were all active in the MSA, holding committee chairmanships from time to time. The police saw nothing of any particular value in these facts, finding that most women in this upscale neighborhood shared those qualities. Fletcher demurred, believing that digging deeper within these commonalities might reveal more finite clues. He asked Fiona and me to re-interview known associates of the victims to do just that.

We arranged meetings at Durrants Hotel, which, as I have said, was close by the square. Durrants was a four-hundred-year old institution, its interior generously paneled with mahogany undoubtedly acquired from a crown colony. Everything was a little askew, the result of a building getting comfortable with its site after four centuries. Shakespeare's plays would have been fresh, as well as the breakthrough ideas of Bacon, Galileo, Hobbes, and Descartes. The hotel was young when Oliver Cromwell brought the wrath of God into London's political affairs. And in grand middle age it celebrated empire with Queen Victoria. It survived the bombings of WWII to tell the tales and now entered the twenty-first century a little wobbly but well marinated.

This was Fletcher's type of place. He preferred establishments that evoked, by their very longevity, respect for the marking of history and as a consequence had a staff who viewed guests as players, great and small, in the scenes of an unfolding epic play. It had a warren of public rooms, most forever permeated with ancient pipe and cigar smoke. The furniture spanned the centuries, so it was eclectic in the extreme, from ancient black yew Edwardian chairs and tables in the taproom to Victorian bric-a-brac stuck here and there. Above the first landing of the interior staircase, ruling the lobby, was an enormous full-length portrait of a beautiful, regal woman wearing a modern formal gown. We all stared at it for a few moments until Fletcher said, "This is our benefactor, Lady Wakefield. She is splendid, isn't she?"

Fletcher chose a very narrow and close room for the investigatory meetings so he could carefully observe the mannerisms and dress of the interviewees. Although Fiona and I would principally interview and report our findings to Fletcher, he would pop in unexpectedly, as he did when we were interviewing Mrs. Evelyn Whitcomb.

She lived on Duke Street, which dead-ended at Manchester Square, and she was a flat neighbor of Ms. Susan Langley, one of the victims, whom she and her husband had known for several years. Mrs. Whitcomb was unusually tall, 5 feet 11 inches, late fifties, of fair complexion, and wore a salt-and-pepper jacket over a demure white blouse and black skirt for her interview in the late afternoon.

Over tea, I began by saying, "It is very good of you to visit with us about Ms. Langley."

With considerable eagerness, Mrs. Whitcomb replied, "I am lucky that because I don't have to work my schedule is quite free. And I do very much want to help find poor Susan's killer, so just ask away."

Fiona pulled up a sheaf of paper. "We have put together from the victims' address books, credit card bills, and other information a list of their friends, acquaintances, frequented stores, restaurants, physicians, and the like. Of course, there are many crossovers, which is no surprise because the victims all lived in the same area. For example, Susan's list had many matches: the mailman, Mr. McPherson; Jim Rice, the owner of Townsends', a local pub; the president of the Manchester Square Association, Lady Wakefield; the local florist, Abigail Hutchinson; and Serge Dahli of Simpson's Drugs, the Arabesque (a Lebanese restaurant), and TopShop, the local supermarket. Is there anything special about these particular matches that would raise your suspicions—something odd?"

Mrs. Whitcomb pushed back some hair from her forehead.

"Odd, you say. Well, we are all a bit odd, including myself, don't you think? Everybody knows and loves Mr. McPherson, and Lady Esther Wakefield is the rock of the neighborhood. Her family has lived at Wakefield House for hundreds of years, and she actively runs the MSA and the Wakefield Museum. Anyone who lives here eventually gets a role to play at the MSA. Susan was the chairwoman of the Park Beautification committee." Mrs. Whitcomb darkened a bit. "That was something I wanted to do, but I was passed over for it. But one has to get over these things, doesn't one? They have given me that post now that poor Susan is gone. Ever since these murders we have lost some very active women at MSA." Mrs. Whitcomb readjusted herself in her chair. She continued, "I don't know Jim Rice well because I and Fred go to a different pub on Marylebone High, but he's got a good reputation. He never lets things get too loud there. The owners of the Lebanese restaurant are young, friendly men. When I pass it, I see lots of pretty women there, so I think it may be a place to be noticed and maybe to be picked up, if you know what I mean. I've known Abigail and Serge for years, nothing unusual there. Have you got other lists for me to look at?" She was quite eager to help.

I said, "There were other matches with the other victims, but not with Susan's list. I wonder if you would look at this one and tell me if you think Susan knew any of these people or had some dealings with the shops." Rita's Beauty Salon, Durrants, La Patisserie, Joanne Falk, Dr. Gupta Singh, Marylebone Ribbon Shop, Sandy's Special Liquors, Speed-O-Printing, Swan's Cleaners, Darrell's Orthopedic Shoes, Mincer's Books, Yesterday's Treasures, Fleet and Jones Photographers, Sally Rulian, Arch Furniture

Mrs. Whitcomb examined the list carefully. "Most of these shops anybody living in this neighborhood would frequent occasionally. I don't recognize the individual names. I know that Susan would put up relatives at Durrants Hotel. Her apartment was small and she had a large family. Now Susan had a thing for ribbons, so I am a little surprised the ribbon shop wasn't on her list. I've bumped into her there many times. It's just around the corner on Marylebone."

Fletcher walked in at that moment. "Liked ribbons, you say, Mrs. Whitcomb? I'm Fletcher MacDonald. How would she wear those ribbons?" He tipped his hat but didn't take it off. His trench coat was still wet with afternoon rain.

"Well, sometimes as a headband in her hair or to hold a ponytail or to add some zip to an outfit. Oh! But she loved to wear wide ones as a choker for going out on a special date or for an event. Wide red or black ribbons, tied off in a bow or cinched with a pin. Looked like a Christmas package for some lucky fellow. She could be very fetching, too fetching at times. I caught my Fred looking at her a time or two."

"Then you think she had lots of ribbons? And how did you know for sure?" Fletcher pressed on.

"Oh, my goodness, yes. She kept them on the inside of her closet door neatly hanging on a bar, like a tie rack. You see, I was in her flat many times over the years to water her plants when she went away. She did the same for us. She kept her ribbons carefully organized. I guess she had a hundred different ribbons. She even special-ordered them."

"How do you know that?"

"Not long before she died, she knocked on my door to show me some exquisite ribbons she had ordered that had just come in.

I remember that the box was from the Marylebone Ribbon Shop. They were satin and had silver threads embroidered in the fabric. Really sumptuous."

Fletcher purred. "Well, that's very interesting. Then you had a key to her flat."

"Oh, yes, so we could water her flowers, as I said."

"Did you know the other victims quite well from the MSA?"

"Pretty well. They were all active, as I said. Other than that, I would just see them on the street. We didn't socialize. They were all so pretty and younger, I didn't want to tempt my Fred too much." She empathetically smiled at Fiona but quickly looked away when nothing was reflected back.

Fletcher took Mrs. Whitcomb's hand and held it tightly between both of his. "You have been of extraordinary help, Mrs. Whitcomb." Turning to us he said, "Do you have any more questions for Mrs. Whitcomb? No? Very good, Max, would you show Mrs. Whitcomb out?"

She seemed reluctant to go, taking her time putting her belongings together, and saying, "If this whole matter weren't so tragic, it might be fun, if you know what I mean."

Fletcher cleared his throat and smiled at the thought.

After Max returned, Fletcher stared at the ceiling and spoke to us. "That makes at least three victims who frequented the ribbon shop. I want you to go over the records of the other two and see if we missed any charges or receipts for that store. And if not, let's speak to the other neighbors and see if they remember any obsession with or frequent use of ribbons. I think it's about time to visit the Marylebone Ribbon Shop."

Fletcher was leaving, his hat in place and trench coat flying, when Fiona pointed to Lady Wakefield's portrait and said, "Whoa! Fletcher, Max, look at her neck. She's wearing a ribbon choker with a diamond clasp. Fletcher, can you remember, does she wear such stuff regularly?"

Fletcher did a double-take, walking up to the painting. "Fiona's right. She does have a fondness for such things. When we see her tonight, we must ask her if she, too, frequents that shop."

****

Fletcher and I were standing amid walls of ribbon spools from alabaster white to black onyx, from one-eighth to three inches wide, and in every imaginable fabric and pattern. The store also sold other notions: lace, buttons, zippers, clasps, thread, and sewing supplies. Fiona found Fletcher, who seemed somewhat overwhelmed by the inventory.

"Sir, how about a black ribbon with a gold stripe to accentuate your red, wavy hair?" Fiona inquired coquettishly, staring quite deeply into Fletcher's eyes.

"All right, quit it. Now what would you do with this three-inch embroidered tapestry affair?" Fletcher's cheeks reddened.

Fiona, here coyly, wrapped it around her hand. "Possibly a hatband," as she pulled it langorously from its spool, "or trim for a lamp shade," holding it aloft, "or maybe, ah, it could even be a choker" Fiona raised and placed it to her neck which she langorously stretched high. Fletcher gasped a bit, "Yes, Amazing. Such versatility! So evocative." He rubbed his brow, looking down to the floor. "I think I'll interview the manager about their customer lists. Where's Max.? Max!" Fletcher looked anxiously for me. I was standing no more than five feet from him observing his awkwardness. Fiona knew how to push his buttons.

Before Fletcher and I found the manager, I said to Fiona sotte voce, "You really got his blood up, dear."

Fiona, squeezing my hand very hard, "Honey, I so wish he had a lady in his life. He's such a wonderful romantic, despite all his strangeness." I smiled and squeezed Fiona's hand right back. I knew the truth of what Fiona had said, and more. If I weren't in the picture, Fletcher would throw himself at Fiona for she was everything he loved in a woman, smart and beautiful. But I am there, and Fiona is completely happy with me as I am with her. I am at peace on that score, albeit odd. But, then again, working with Fletcher, and being his friend, was a case history in things being odd.

Fletcher and I wandered over to the cashier and asked to speak with the manager. A savvy face atop a taut thirtyish body, adorned in a coquettish dress, approached us leisurely.

"I'm Claudette Davis. I own the store. How may I help you?"

Searching her eyes, Fletcher said softly, "May we speak privately? This is a sensitive matter."

"Of course. Follow me." She walked at a slow time-cheating pace to a corner of the store where there were no customers. She started to rearrange some merchandise and said, "Is this better?"

"Yes. Very much. My name is Fletcher MacDonald and this is Max Bateman. We are privately investigating the Manchester murders for the Manchester Square Association."

"Did Lady Wakefield hire you?"

"Yes. Do you know her?"

"Of course, she's an institution in the area."

"Did you know that at least three of the victims purchased ribbons here? Susan Langley was one who placed special orders."

Claudette continued to rearrange the merchandise. "It's just awful. I have the jitters when I walk over there. No. I didn't know her. The only customers I know well are the professional people: tailors, dressmakers, seamstresses who are in here all the time. There isn't sufficient contact with the occasional customer to get to know them well."

"I am a little surprised that someone who might be in here perhaps once a month or more and who special orders would not be familiar to you. Isn't knowing your customers just good business?"

"Maybe for some, but not for me. I'm not a chummy person and I have a lot to do."

"I see." Fletcher showed Claudette a three-by-five index card. "Here are the names of the five victims. Take a look at them. Do any strike a bell?" Susan Langley, Rachell Smith, Anastasia Peabody, Sophie Neidhardt, Emilia Sanderson

"No, none of these names is familiar to me."

A bit incredulous, Fletcher asked, "Do you keep a mailing list that is generated from your sales checks?"

Claudette looked tired of the questions. "Yes."

"If someone places a special order, what is the procedure? Do you keep a record of special orders?"

"We ask for payment in advance. Then we call the customer when the order arrives. Although we don't generate a list of people who place special orders, we do enter them into the computer with a code to distinguish their goods from our regular orders so we don't confuse them with our regular inventory."

"Do you ever deliver?"

"Rarely."

"Would you mind if we checked your computer now to see if any of these names comes up?"

"This is not a good time. How about tomorrow?"

Fletcher became stern, unsatisfied with the woman's reluctance "I'm afraid this is pressing business. If the police come, their presence may be more disturbing than ours."

All right, let's go to my office." Claudette moved more purposefully now. "Give me those names again and I'll enter them."

"Please start with Susan Langley."

Claudette nimbly worked the keyboard. She wet her lips when the screen stopped moving. "Susan Langley is here. She ordered a two-inch-wide satin-velvet ribbon with silver threads on July 15."

"Could such a ribbon be used for choker purposes? Are the addresses and telephone numbers associated with the orders?"

"Yes, to both questions. Chokers are always at least one and a quarter inch wide. But the ribbons could just as well be used for other things."

"Let's search the rest of the names and kindly give me a print-out of the information."

Claudette entered each name, and they all showed up. More important to Fletcher, each woman had special-ordered ribbons that could be used as chokers. Staring with apprehension at Fletcher, Claudette's face lost all its vigor and sureness. "Mr. MacDonald, I don't know what to make of this. We have nothing to do with this. You don't think anybody here does, do you?"

"One more name for the time being. A Mrs. Evelyn Whitcomb?"

"Evelyn Whitcomb of Manchester Square?

"Well, yes."

"She worked here part-time about three years ago during the Christmas season."

"I see. Who has access to these computer records outside of yourself?"

"No one. I am the only person with the password."

"Where do you live, Ms. Davis?"

"In this building, upstairs."

"I will inform the police of these developments, and I suggest that you not make any software changes or delete anything from this computer. The police will need to do a thorough investigation. Thank you for your time."

Claudette's face reddened. As Fletcher and I turned to leave the office, she seized his arm. "How dare you come in here and imply that I or my staff have anything to do with these horrible killings? Get out of my store!"

"Good day, Ms. Davis." Fletcher adjusted his hat downward. Fiona was still in the store as we left for the street.

"Max, call the police straightaway with the information we have about the shop. They need to do a rundown on everybody there, including the owner. Meet me in the taproom at Durrant's as soon as you are finished."

When I arrived at the taproom, Fletcher was sitting on an overstuffed sofa, a pint of stout in front of him, and pressing his brow. "The murderer is getting access to that computer and Ms. Davis seems obviously implicated, yet, I'm uncomfortable with the signs. The crimes have a methodical component that suggests a cool hand, and the crimes have a crazed romantic quality."

I said, "You know me. I always look to the money trail for clues. These murders are negatively impacting the real estate values of the square and the museum. Perhaps someone has a score to settle with the area. Or, someone wants to pick up the real estate at a discount. By the way, the police are at the shop interviewing Claudette. They said they would call us if they found anything definite."

Fiona was sitting with her head in her hands. "Guys, the killer is obviously turned on by women in chokers...ribbon chokers. I don't think this could be a woman's act, so for me that rules out Davis and even Whitcomb. And since all the clerks and the owner of the shop are women, I think it must be a male friend."

"Or a strong woman. I only see the hands of women here."

Fletcher was working up into a lather. "I have the printout of the special orders right here. Susan Langley was called on July 15 by the shop; she was murdered on August 9. Emilia was called on March 15 and was killed on April 3. Sophie was called on November 10 and was killed on January 4. Rachel was called on October 10 and was killed on November 8. Adriana was called on September 21 and was killed on October 6. So we know that the calls didn't immediately set up the killings. The killings always occurred subsequent to those calls. But it looks like those special orders targeted the victims and set these murders in motion. This all leads back to the ribbon shop. But why?"

"Max, who's the detective handling this case?"

"Inspector McGuire. He has no love for us. Says we are meddling and if we cross the line, he'll arrest us for doing detective work without a license."

"Did he thank us for the ribbon shop connection?"

"No. He just reminded me to tell you to keep your distance from the case and him."

Fletcher threw his hands up. "Lovely. We do their work and we are the scoundrels. 'A prophet is not without honor, save in his own country.' Keep your ears open over there to see if Claudette's alibis for each killing hold up."

Moving to the window of the taproom and looking at the back end of the Wakefield mansion fronting Manchester Square, Fletcher, his coat and hat still very much in place on the sofa, said, "Let's go over the facts and inferences we have. All the victims are women, single, attractive, socially active, and live on the square. Each victim places a special order at the Marylebone Ribbon Shop for what could be, but not necessarily is, used as a neck choker. Somehow the killer learns of the order. The victim picks up the ribbon order. Sometime later, a month or two, the victim finds herself in the open on Manchester Square on her doorstep, she is shot with a lethal dart containing cyanide, and dies on the spot. The police have concluded that the dart enters the body from about a forty-five-degree or greater angle and is fired from some distance, as far as a block away. That suggests a sniper shooting from a high window or roof. A search of all the surrounding houses and roofs has turned up no evidence of a sniper. We need to know what lures the victims out and how it is connected, if it is, to the ribbon shop. Tell me again what we know about the incoming telephone records of the victims."

I drew my reporter's notebook from my jacket. "Each of the victims had an answering machine. There are no calls on the machines from the ribbon shop on the day or those just before the shootings, or anything to do with ribbons. The messages all had to do with personal or business matters with people that have been interviewed. There is no crossover between those callers and any other victim. Ditto for incoming local and long-distance calls that the victims answered."

"Were any of the victims' telephones cellular?" Fletcher asked. "If they were, those calls can be traced."

"They all were. In the case of Emilia Sanderson, there is a two-minute call shortly before she was shot made from a disposable cell phone. Scotland Yard traced the phone to a shipment that had been stolen, so it was on the black market. It also wasn't used to make any other calls."

"Ah, I see it now." Fletcher's face became incandescent. He held his brow, "Our murderer leaves no calling cards. She, he, waits until the victim answers calls from a non-traceable phone and draws her out immediately. The ribbon orders themselves are not the trigger, because we know that the orders were all picked up previously. The killer calls later, sometimes as much as a month or more. How were the victims dressed at the time of their shooting. Anyone?"

Fiona replied, "They were all dressed in regular street or business attire, with the exception of Anastasia Peabody, who painted with watercolors at home and had on an artist's smock. As all the shootings took place in the late afternoon or very early evening, between five-thirty and six-thirty, it makes sense that everyone would probably be dressed and be able rapidly to meet someone in a hurry. They were all shot either right on their outside doorsteps or within fifty paces of them."

"But who would they respond to so quickly?" I wondered. "The police? A medical emergency? A friend in dire need?"

Fletcher remembered another matter. "Fiona, you need to visit Evelyn Whitcomb again today. She didn't tell us she had worked at the ribbon shop for a short stint three years ago, at Christmas. A curious omission. Once you interview her, let the police know that they ought to check her alibis for the dates."

The manager of Durrants stuck his head in the parlor and said that Inspector McGuire wanted a word with Fletcher. Before the manager had time to leave, the inspector barged in.

"Now, Fletcher, you don't have a detective's license, you know, and we just can't have you messing about our work, despite her ladyship's fondness for you. You will just have to beg off."

"Won't you have some tea with us, Inspector?" I said.

"No, did you hear me? Butt out!"

I was really annoyed by his sharp tone of voice. "And what about the connection between all the victims and the ribbon shop? You missed that, didn't you? Perhaps if you had been more diligent you would have found this key earlier and there might have been fewer dead bodies to count, sir." I was broiling. "And let me remind you that we are here at the request of Lady Wakefield, who is not too pleased with your performance, and I'm not so sure she's wrong. Mr. MacDonald has probably solved more crimes than you will ever see hatched."

The inspector was surprised at my sharp response. He looked to Fletcher, who sat impassively staring out the window. "All right, I'll have some damn tea. I know you have connections in high places, but that doesn't mean that we have to bow down to you." He sat down in a delicate Sheraton armchair. "I don't like to be gruff with all of you, but there are strict rules, you know, about investigations. This isn't the Wild West or whatever you have in Canada. You can poke around, but don't get in the way of this investigation or get anybody hurt. Or, I swear, I'll lock you up for your own good."

Fletcher interceded smoothly. "Not to worry, Inspector. I wouldn't think of getting in your way. Just consider us your fan club, rooting for your success. If we find something we will tell you. What about the alibis for Ms. Davis?"

"They're not airtight. She has to rely on the other employees remembering that she was in the store. They know that she usually is, but that is all. She can't prove it."

Fletcher harrumphed, "More arrows."

Looking for some sympathy, the inspector explained, "We are getting a lot of heat from Lady Wakefield. The museum has seen a fifty-per-cent falloff in revenue because of the murders. People are afraid to come. She's on my neck daily to resolve this. And she's got the Prime Minister himself calling me about it." He shook his head at such a connection. "Frankly, I'm glad to have your help because this case has the quality of an inside job. These people seem to be sitting ducks. It's really odd." At last he gave Fletcher a compliment. "The break on the ribbon shop was first rate. It's a little hard to admit we missed it."

"Well, I'm relieved that you noticed that we did some good and we're not just causing you grief. As to her ladyship, I'm seeing her this evening and I'll make sure she knows that there is progress on your side as well."

McQuire was obviously pleased by this idea. "That would be very nice and particularly generous of you considering our rather stiff stand against any interference. Bloody nice of you. All right, I'll leave you to your business."

"Inspector", Fletcher intoned, "don't think for a moment that we are unaware of the nastiness of this case and its killing machine qualities. I think we are not dealing with a simple mind bent on destruction, but one which is subtle in its madness."

Fletcher smiled at me after the inspector had departed. "Don't let them get under your skin, Max. But I do appreciate your defense of what we do. You and Fiona are the only people one needs in a foxhole. I have got to run to make dinner with her ladyship. Meet me later in the taproom here and I'll debrief you on what I learn."

****

We rendezvoused in the taproom at ten o'clock. Fletcher was sitting with his chin in one hand and one finger touching his lips as he gathered his thoughts for us.

"For background, the Wakefield Museum is famous for its unrivaled fine private collection of seventeenth- and eighteenth-century paintings, French porcelains and furniture, and its armory.

The vast collection was the fruit of the highly successful Wakefield mercantile family, which traded in luxury goods."

His lips twisted in a wry, puzzled way. "I first saw Lady Wakefield appearing like a queen frozen in a portrait pose at the head of the museum's stairway. She wore a black dress with a bright red sash around the waist. Her thick, wiry, and lustrous silver gray hair shot up from her forehead like a lion's mane and caressed her neck like a fox muff. But as I more closely approached her, I was terrified to see that her face was disfigured. The left side had slipped, creating a freakish, asymmetrical quality, her eyes were at almost a forty-five-degree slant with large blue sacks beneath them, and a great hanging jowl swung freely on the right side. Together we traveled in her private elevator up to her flat on the top floor of the museum. She reeked of acetone, which is often the odor that an excessive gin drinker exudes. Before we alighted, she said, 'The last face-lift went very badly. This is the best they could do to repair me. Let's not talk of it. Pretend I'm the woman you used to know, and delude this old witch.' She burst out of the elevator and its close quarters as fast as she could."

This revelation left both Fiona and me unsettled as he went on. "Her staff had prepared an elegant dinner of steak and kidney pie with a port wine sauce, accompanied with my favorite Côtes de Rhone, Chateau De Pape Vieux Telegraph, all set on a pristine white tablecloth, with full Wakefield silver and Waterford glasses to complement the setting. I'm sorry that you missed that."

I said, "Quite all right. Organ meats are a bit dicey for the cholesterol count anyway. Fiona and I had a divine Dover sole right here, courtesy of her ladyship, according to the terms of our engagement."

"Good. I wouldn't want you to do without. To continue, Lady Wakefield explained that the museum was in danger of closing owing to the loss of revenue, and that the value of the properties in the square had actually fallen but the property taxes had gone up. She said that she could not continue to subsidize the museum much longer and hoped that I could bring this affair to a decisive close very fast.

"She did not have kind words for our Inspector McGuire. She called him a dolt. Apparently he did the inspection of her flat with an assistant when they were searching for evidence of a sniper, and she thought it was slipshod and not very thorough. At any rate, she said that it was impossible for anyone to use her roof because there was no way that a sniper could get through the security of the museum. The elevator can be operated only by recognition of her fingerprint or that of one of her closest staff. She also showed me that hers was the only building on this side of the square and that there was no access to it from another roof."

Fletcher paused to allow us to digest that aspect of what he'd learned.

"I asked her about Claudette Davis, whom she apparently knows very well. She said that Claudette had a married lover, Stephen Laird, who owned a flat on the square where he lived with his wife, until he left her for Claudette. She pointed out to me a six-story brick fellow across the park. When he and his wife broke up, Claudette moved in. Then Stephen tired of Claudette, and she lived there for a time alone. She rents it out for the income and lives over the shop now. Apparently Stephen and Claudette have gotten back together several times, but it never sticks. Thus, we now know that not only does Claudette have a connection to each of the victims through the shop; she also had a perch from which to do the sniping. I'd call the police in, except that I want to talk to her myself first. We are missing a motive and a strategy for getting the victims to respond to her calls to come out."

He looked at us to confirm that these missing elements were essential to the case.

"I then asked about Evelyn Whitcomb. Another bomblet. Evelyn pretends that she and Fred are well off, but Lady Wakefield knows Evelyn has to take odd jobs to keep afloat. Lady Wakefield felt that they ought to sell the place and live where they can afford it. Also, Fred is one serious lech, whom Evelyn keeps on a very short leash. He's so frustrated, her ladyship was certain that he would kill her. It seems to me that we have sufficient dysfunction and prevarication in the Whitcomb family to warrant another visit."

Fiona added to that stew. "When I interviewed Evelyn today, she went on about having forgotten about it because it was such a little assignment, as she called it. Fred was there and kept yelling at her to tell me the truth and to stop pretending that they were rich. Pretty ugly scene. She was very embarrassed. The police also are interviewing her regarding her alibis for the other murders, so she's a wreck. I'll interview her again tomorrow."

Fletcher rejoined, "Lady Wakefield's comments confirm what we have learned about Evelyn. Often pretense presages a fall." He and Fiona nodded, putting Lady Wakefield definitely on their list of suspects.

"As we were talking, Lady Wakefield pulled out a wide red satin ribbon from her skirt pocket that matched her sash. She was using it to tie back her hair. I was intrigued and asked her where she had bought the ribbon.

It was from Marylebone. I then learned that she did place specials orders of ribbons from time to time. I told her that I thought the killer targets women who special-order ribbons at that shop and that if she got a call from someone regarding ribbons, not to follow the caller's requests but instead to call Inspector McGuire or me immediately. She was very upset with that news and asked me to stay awhile longer, until her nerves settled down. It seems to me that, given the agglomeration of her physical problems, the loss of Vachel and Carl, and the possible financial ruin of the museum, she is doing remarkably well. But now we need to focus on Claudette, given that she had access to a flat that gave her perfect aim at the victims., although I am nagged by something I am just missing." Fletcher forcefully pressed and rubbed his brow as if he was trying to force a better answer.

****

We walked out of Durrants at about eleven o'clock. The streets glistened with the night's rain, which had scrubbed the air clean. We visited each spot where a victim had been killed. Indeed, there were unobstructed sight lines from Claudette's Manchester Square flat to each murder location.

Fletcher looked over to the Wakefield Museum and her lady-ship's private flat above it. Her lights were on. Fletcher said he visualized her standing on the museum steps and then being struck by a poison dart. It felt too much like a premonition for him to shake it off. I calmed him by reminding him that the murders happened only in the late afternoon.

We returned to Marylebone High Street and the ribbon shop. Knowing Claudette lived above the store, we went into the vestibule of the building and found her name on the intercom listing. Fletcher's finger hovered over it for a while, and then he pressed it with great force, over and over again. The intercom activated.

"Who is it?" a weary voice asked.

"Fletcher MacDonald. I need to speak with you immediately. It is urgent."

There was a long pause. Finally the buzzer released the lock to the front door. Fletcher bounded up the two flights with us right behind. Claudette appeared in a bathrobe, disheveled and woozy. Upon seeing that there were three of us, she seemed overpowered and meekly held the door open. We walked into her living room, where an open bottle of wine and a glass were set on the coffee table and cigarette smoke twirled up from an ashtray.

Fletcher got right to the point. "Ms. Davis, I now know you have a key to your former lover's flat, which overlooks the square and which would be an ideal perch for a sniper. You have access to the special-order ribbon records that connect the shop to every victim. Your alibis for the times of the shootings are weak, because they rely solely upon your habits, not your actual whereabouts. Your shop employees can only say that you generally were at the shop at those times, not that you actually were. You could have slipped out for fifteen minutes, gone to your Manchester Square flat, shot your target, and returned." His face turned severe. "There's too much to connect you to these crimes. I need a reason not to have Inspector McGuire arrest you on suspicion of murder."

Almost too drunk to be alarmed, she asked, "How did you know about Stephen?" She drained her wineglass in a long swallow. "Stephen and I are still off and on again. Who told you about us?"

"Lady Wakefield."

"No, I can't believe it." As she spoke, she became increasingly agitated. "She wouldn't do that. That's not like her. Get out of here. Get out of my house. I didn't kill anybody!" She started pushing Fletcher, and he forcefully grabbed her arms, and moved her against a wall. With one hand he gently held her chin so she would look into his eyes.

"Claudette, I need something to connect the information in your computer to someone other than yourself, or you are going to jail. What aren't you telling me? I want to believe you."

Claudette pushed Fletchers hands away., and began to sob. "There's nothing else to tell you or the police," she wailed. "Nothing else."

"Think, is there anyone else with a connection to the shop that would give them access to that computer? Think!"

Shocked into responding, she calmed down somewhat. "Of course there's the cleaning people, but they never touch the computer." She searched for other possible avenues. It's never been overhauled. No new software was installed. My vendors don't go near it." A new idea came to her, lighting her features. Yet she hesitated and shook her head, saying, "I can't. I can't!"

Fletcher placed his great hand on her shoulder. "Sometimes you have to go to the heart of darkness, to places you do not want to go, to do things that are against your will. To save yourself, tell me!"

Claudette's face was wet with tears as she slowly said, "I have a silent partner. She never officially comes in the shop. I am under a contractual obligation never to reveal her name, or my loan from her will come due immediately, and I can't pay it. Many years ago she and her husband helped me out when I was broke and in a bad way, on the condition that I would never reveal their association. Her husband died a couple of years ago."

"Why did they help you?"

She hesitated, "I had...I had an abortion. I was sick mentally and physically from it. Everything fell apart: my health, the shop, just everything. You see, I aborted her son's child. He ran away because his parents wouldn't approve of our marriage....He couldn't face the tension over it. I never heard from him again. I became so desperate after the abortion that I called his parents for help, because I had no living family or close friends to turn to. I didn't know how they would react. By that time their son had left, and they blamed themselves for what had happened. I think at first they helped me out of guilt and remorse. But then we became really close. She's like a grandmother to me."

Fletcher's approach became very sympathetic.

"Claudette, your freedom is on the line. Tell me who your silent partner is."

She looked at the floor. "Promise me you will never tell anybody else."

"I can't. You must save yourself."

She whispered, "Lady Wakefield."

"What!" Fletcher was aghast and lost all color. "You and their son, Vachel Wakefield?"

Claudette cried at the mention of his name. "Yes, Vachel."

Fletcher deeply exhaled and lowered his voice. "Claudette, I met Vachel in South America. He told me that he had abandoned someone he truly loved because he feared that his parents would never understand his love for that person. It was clearly you. I can tell you that he was very sorry for his actions, if that is any consolation. Now I must ask you, did you ever show Lady Wakefield how to operate the computer?"

In a low voice she admitted, "There's a slight possibility."

"What do you mean, slight?"

"A year and a half ago, when Stephen and I had a big argument, I became distraught, got drunk, and called Lady Wakefield. I just wanted to talk to somebody, and she had been very kind to me over the years. She came over to the store late on a Sunday night. We talked for hours. Our conversation wandered all over the place." Her voice became more distant as she remembered that night. "We talked about the business, and she seemed fascinated with how the computer kept records of everything. I explained that I could call up inventory information from it even from my cell phone, which was very convenient when I was traveling to buy goods. I showed her how I accessed the information and told her the password to get into the system. It was Vachel's birth date. You see, I still loved him, and this was a simple way to keep him alive in my mind." Claudette began to shake hardly able to continue. "So, she probably would have remembered it."

Ashen, Fletcher rose from the table. "Claudette, the police will have to know everything you have told me. Do not tell Lady Wakefield, though. I will explain to her that you had no choice."

Claudette pleaded, "I don't want to implicate her. There is no way that she's involved. That's madness."

Fletcher said quietly to Fiona, "Stay here with Claudette. Don't let her call Lady Wakefield. Max and I need to go to her place right now."

Fletcher leapt down the stairs with me following him. He ran up the wet streets like an Olympic track star. Breathless, we were outside the Wakefield Museum in just a few minutes. He called her number, but there was no answer. "I know Lady Wakefield is up there. Her lights were on an hour ago, and I saw her silhouette. We need to get in. There must be a night watchman. I'll find out. You look to see if there's a fire escape."

Fletcher pushed a night bell and pounded on the door. After an interminable period, a slow-moving bent-over old man appeared, opened an interior door, and confronted Fletcher through the locked gate.

"I need to see Lady Wakefield. I am a close personal friend. She's not answering the telephone. Please let me in."

"She does not want to be disturbed. Those were her instructions. I just spoke with her. No one is to be let in. I'm sorry."

He went back through the door and locked it.

Fletcher found me at the fire escape, but the last part of it was ten feet off the ground. It only lowered if someone stepped on it.

"I'll climb up your back and pull it down," he said. So Fletcher, who weighed two hundred pounds, stood on my shoulders and pulled himself up onto the lowest rung. It then lowered itself hydraulically so we both could go up. We ran up to the fifth floor, where the fire escape joined the patio. We ran across the patio and opened the door to her quarters. The lights were on. Fletcher went in first.

"Esther, it's Fletcher. We need to talk. Esther!" There was no answer.

We opened several doors—no one.

We came to a double door. A glow of light seeped out from underneath. We swung it open. Lady Wakefield was standing on her bed, against the wall, wrapped in black velvet ribbons like a mummy. One hand, held as a fist, holding a dart pointed at the side of her neck.

"Stop, Fletcher. If you or your friend so much as move an inch, I will plunge this dart into my throat." Her voice was perfectly calm and cultured. "I'm going to do it anyway, but before I do, I'll tell you what happened so that you can tell my story correctly. Vachel, my son, left because of me. I told him that Claudette was a tramp, beneath the dignity of this family, and that he had to let her go." Her disfigured face darkened at the memory. "I drove my only child away. Carl was very angry with me. But after Vachel was executed, Carl did a terrible thing: he swore that he would never touch me again. It was so bad that if he so much as accidentally brushed my skin in passing, he would spit. On the outside it looked as if everything was all right, but on the inside, he hated me and wished me dead." The hand holding the dart dropped slightly as she recalled this terrible period. "Well, I couldn't take it anymore," she continued more firmly. "One night I found one of Vachel's darts, the cyanide-tipped kind he used for self-defense in the jungle, and stabbed Carl while he slept. Because he had a serious heart condition, everyone thought he died from that. Of course, no one would think of doing an autopsy on Lord Wakefield when his wife called their private physician to say that he died peacefully in their bed. No one questioned the cause."

With the softest voice he could muster, Fletcher said, "Esther, why did you kill these women? What were they to you?"

"Look at me! I'm a freak! They were so pretty. I saw them at the Association meetings, perfumed, all trussed up, on their high heels, adored by men and envied by other women, including myself. Slowly I became obsessed with the idea of making them pay for how rotten my life had become, just as I had made Carl pay. The use of the cyanide darts seemed so perfect, because it was immediate and I knew how to shoot because I used to go on safaris."

"I suppose the ribbons marked them in some way that was special to you."

" Yes, that was my key to finding my targets. For me, wearing a ribbon was the most feminine of gestures. Not common, but all women know in their heart that it's a sign of catch me if you can. And the choker ribbon? It is the ultimate tease. The beautiful slave girl with a collar but no leash. That's how I played it when I was young."

Her expression became chilling in its naked cruelty. "Once I learned from Claudette that it was possible to know who was buying ribbons on the square, it became a game for me. I'd watch my targets from my patio, coming and going from their flats. I would put them in the crosshairs of my telescopic sights and toy with the trigger. I would see them at Association meetings, and I would go out of my way to befriend them. They loved to have my attention because I was, after all, Lady Wakefield." Her eyes glazed with the irony. "And they knew I was ugly, so they pitied me. I chose the ones who were still on the prowl, alone, smart, and cunning. And then I carefully planned their destruction. I enjoyed seeing them fall to the ground like wild game shot by a hunter. I would have had them mounted if I could. But that was beyond even my power."

Fletcher seemed in awe of her cunning. "So you telephoned them and somehow got them to come into the street. What would you say?"

She adopted an ugly falsetto. "My dear, Esther Wakefield here. I am having a dreadful problem choosing which color the new museum flags are to be, and I must make this decision tonight. Would you be a dear and come right over and tell me which color looks best?" She scowled at such mummery. "Or some such line, and they would come running out their front doors eager to please, so my aristocracy would rub off on them. And then, poof, down and out. I generally hit them in the bosom, like a viper to Cleopatra." A certain horrible gleam came into her eyes. "Fletcher, aren't you going to try and convince me not to kill myself?"

"Is that what you want, Esther?"

At last her manic expression changed to one of deep sadness. "No, I want my face back, my youth, my son, Carl's love, my life. It's all over, isn't it?"

Fletcher didn't move. "It doesn't have to be. You are very rich. There are some years left. There's a plastic surgeon I know who completely remakes the faces and bodies of wanted men and women. He does it so well that they can become part of the very society that would hang them if they knew who they really were. So, with money and skill there are ways. In my opinion, you are giving up too soon."

"Come on Esther, stop this foolishness. Let me help you start a new life. Don't damage that beautiful body with that dart. It has miles to go before it's finished."

She remained motionless, and Fletcher walked over to her and lifted her down. He took the dart from her hand and tossed it to me. She caressed him and cried.

"We have to get you out of here" he said urgently. "I am going to wrap you up in your blankets and slip you out of town tonight."

"Oh, Fletcher, thank you, thank you."

"Be calm." He placed her down on the bed, rolled her over in the blankets, and, out of her sight, beckoned me over. He took off his belt and cinched it around the cocoon he had made of her. Quietly he mouthed these words to me, "Hold her down."

The next day, Fiona, Fletcher, and I took a long walk in Regency Park to dispel the horrors of the previous night. Lady Wakefield was now safely locked up at Scotland Yard. We learned that Claudette had taken a cell phone with her into the bathroom with which to alert Lady Wakefield.

Fiona said, "It appears that she called up her victims on disposable cell phones so the calls couldn't be traced back to her. She left no voice mail messages but would speak only if the line was answered by the victim."

I asked, "You know what puzzles me? Why would she take the chance of being found out by hiring you? She knew that you were uncanny about solving matters. Why?"

Fletcher gave me a know-all smile. "First, she didn't want to be caught in some humdrum police game and simply nabbed by doltish, in her estimation, Inspector McGuire. Second, I found her son, and in some bizarre way, she probably saw some cosmic balance in her being found, so to speak, by me too." He reflected on the peculiar twists of fate. "There's no folly worse than vanity. If one can't get by it, it will drive you mad. And that's the sum of it."

THE QUEEN OF NIDA

It was late summer on the Inverness beach. Warm zephyrs, born far away in Saskatchewan and Manitoba, lolled down from Prince Edward Island. Beach umbrellas of locals and tourists crowded the sand that in a few months would bear ten-foot snowdrifts abutting a sea jammed with pack ice. But this day kids to grandparents were joyously playing in the Northumberland Strait. The Gulf Stream generously turns a bit west here and runs along the shoreline, raising the summer water temperature to seventy degrees and sometimes more, before turning north to Labrador. This eminently swimmable sea is the open secret with which the natives and the chamber of commerce enjoy surprising a world that assumes only polar bears could love these local waters.

Fletcher MacDonald and I savored, with everyone else, the delicious heat and the golden coloration that the late afternoon sun had given the beach. Fletcher had begun his walk from his home in Mabou, about five miles along the coast to Inverness. Rarely did Fletcher let any day go by without this hike, and in the summer we would often meet up on the beach. I would drive him back home, but not before we had discussed business, talked about high and low events, and had a drink or two to focus the mind.

A sharp gust uprooted a couple of beach umbrellas, sending some of them cartwheeling, followed by sprinting mothers and fathers. I noticed that Fletcher's hat stayed firmly on his head despite the wind, so I asked him how he had it so well anchored.

"Max, it's a Mountie innovation. There is a band, like a shoelace, in the back of the hat, which fits behind my head, just where the neck joins the skull, and holds it in place. It would take a mistral to rip it off."

Just then my cell phone rang, the screen reading: "Unknown caller. Lithuania." Curious, I answered it. "Max Bateman speaking." "Hello, is this the telephone of Mr. MacDonald?"

"Yes, it is. I'm his assistant. May I know your name?"

"Of course. It is Vytalis Sagaritus. I am calling you from Klaipeda, Lithuania. May I speak with Mr. MacDonald?"

"I congratulate you on finding him. It isn't easy to navigate all the international and domestic calling codes. It would be best to explain the nature of your business first to me. I will refer it immediately to Mr. MacDonald."

"We need help in locating my father, Frederick Sagaritus. A couple of months ago he disappeared under ominous circumstances. Our local police have been of only limited help. We fear the worst. We have many thugs and gangs here, so it is possible that he was murdered. If he has been killed, we want to know who did it."

"How did you hear of Mr. MacDonald?"

"The local police chief, Captain Largas, said that Mr. MacDonald had a worldwide reputation for being successful at finding missing persons. Captain Largas remembered that he lived in Canada, so I began a search on the Internet, which led to some news stories that mentioned his home is in Inverness, Nova Scotia. There were several Fletcher MacDonalds listed, but the first one I called knew exactly who I was trying to locate when I mentioned that he was famous for finding missing persons. He gave me this number."

"I admire your persistence. But back to your father: was he involved in activities that would bring him in contact with these thugs, people who might be envious or feel threatened by him?"

"I'm afraid there are many people who might want to harm my father. He owns many businesses here and is well off. In Lithuania, being successful makes you an automatic target for the criminal element. We just want to get to the bottom of it. We are willing to pay whatever Mr. MacDonald's fee is."

"Excuse me for asking, but could there be any other explanations for your father's disappearance?"

"What do you mean, other?"

"Did your father have suicidal tendencies, or were there difficult intimate relationships, family or otherwise, that could explain his disappearance?"

"Absolutely not, yet, to be frank, my father was, I mean, is, a very private man. No one really would know what he was thinking or much of what he was doing at any given time." I stopped myself from reeling off too many questions that always leap to mind at the start of an investigation. Fletcher mouthed to me the question "Who is it?" I put my hand over the telephone and said, " Lithuania...Klaipeda...missing father...businessman...maybe enemies...police clueless...maybe gangs...anxious to know the culprit...will pay any fee."

Fletcher motioned me to hand over the telephone. He rubbed his brow. "Laba diena, this is Fletcher MacDonald. Your Baltic herring is a favorite food of mine. As I recall, Klaipeda is near Nida. Can you find me a place on Nida to stay?"

"Laba diena to you! Your Lithuanian is excellent, Mr. MacDonald. Very good to speak with you. What a stroke of good fortune. We live on Nida in my wife's ancestral home. It is where my father lived as well until he disappeared. Of course, you will stay with us. Thank you."

Fletcher handed the telephone back to me, nodded assent to the deal, and indicated that we were both to go.

"Where is...what is Nida?" I said to Fletcher after arranging matters to get us to Lithuania as fast as possible.

"It's a long and narrow spit of land that juts out from Lithuania into the Baltic. It is thickly blanketed with ancient evergreens and gigantic oak trees that make for magical forests where animist gods and other mythological creatures are thought to live and rule." As usual, his instant recall of obscure facts was nothing short of amazing. "It is the spiritual home of Lithuania," he went on. "The Lithuanians were the last European people to convert to Christianity in the thirteenth century, and they did so reluctantly. Their animist traditions still inform their Christian iconography and dogma, particularly in Nida. Strewn through these dark, nearly impenetrable woods are Lithuania's leprechauns: kneehigh wooden and stone sculptures depicting the gods of the forest and their fierce protectors. They are the embodiment of this ancient religion and are studiously respected because of the various curses and spells that annoying these creatures is thought to trigger. To this day, clandestine forest shrines and pagan rituals having a thousand-year tradition have their anonymous but passionate followers. Lithuania's psyche is radically distinct from all its European, Baltic, and Slav neighbors, and its headwaters are in Nida."

I could only blink at this voluminous detail. "Then I guess we should go there."

****

The rain had been slopping over the windshield of the black Mercedes sedan since it picked us up six hours before in Vilnius, the capital of Lithuania, and it was still pouring while we waited to board the ferry to Nida. The smileless, black-raincoated driver and his equally glum twin wearing the same issue raincoat reeked of the iron-fisted, cookie-cutter clothed, clandestine Soviet era that ruled the Baltic states for nearly fifty years. That numbing sameness was reflected in the countless apartment complexes that were all a sullen gray, built of slab concrete and twenty stories high. Looking like industrial warehouses or cellblocks, they radiated out from Vilnius along the main highway. Only the peasant farmers had it worse: little or no electricity, poor seed, no fuel for tractors, and low market prices. No wonder alcoholism was rampant among all classes and the average age at death was twenty percent lower than in Western Europe.

I had been in Lithuania for six hours, and I hadn't seen a smile yet. People walked head down, hunched over, and seemed to slither along the streets, keeping close to the walls. Partly it was the cold, dank weather. But surely it was also the culture that was still cowed from being defeated so many times over the past ten centuries: subjugated by the Polish, Germans, and Russians. And perhaps there was lingering guilt for making common cause with the Nazis in WWII. As part of that deal the Lithuanians turned over a half million Jews to be murdered by the Germans, which went hand in hand with the destruction of Lithuania's greatest pride: Vilnius University, the Oxford of the East. It was a singular educational center of the world, largely populated and run by Lithuanian Jews, until the Nazis destroyed it and them. Whatever the cause, from the moment we arrived, I felt as if we had entered limbo.

Fletcher had fallen asleep almost immediately after entering the car. I wish I had. It is as if he knew that the drive would be one long, lugubrious dirge. The running lights of the ferry shimmered through the full black, wet darkness as we crossed a bit of the Baltic. We emerged from a slip onto a virtually unlit road and traveled at break-neck speed in silence, except for the distant purr of the giant German motor and the low drum of tire rubber on asphalt. Our headlights seemed no match for the Stygian blackness that enveloped us.

The vehicle came to a halt in a sudden dive into the soft stone of a driveway, with the seething and hissing sound of a stopped steam locomotive. I shoved Fletcher to raise him from his slumber. With the opening of the car door, we were engulfed with the richest evergreen scent I had ever experienced. It was like rubbing one's nose in a Christmas tree wreath. The air was invigoratingly cool, potent, and wet. Lights came on, illuminating the facade of a stone fortress through whose front doors two physically mismatched people emerged. He was stout, round-faced, and pugnacious, while she was tall, slender, and ethereal. Night and day. The hoi-polloi and the elite.

Our driver and his clone conveyed us up to the porch under big, black, official-type umbrellas, upon which the rain hammered and sheeted off and where we met our employers, Vytalis and Christiana Sagaritus, face to face. She was stunningly tall, like the towering pines that we could feel, rather than see, surrounding us, but possessed the grace of a lone egret picking its way through a swamp. He, on the other hand, had the large paws of a bear and carried his great weight with some difficulty. There was no mistaking his brute power. I noticed that Christiana hung back a bit, her hands clasped in front of her as if she were in church.

"Laba diena and sveiki atvyke. Hello and welcome to our country and Nida. Stephan and Klaus will show you to your rooms." Vytalis gave a little bow of the head.

"We have a little dinner prepared, including Baltic herring for Mr. MacDonald. I am sure you must be famished from the long drive," Christiana added.

After being frustratingly taciturn for the whole trip, Fletcher sprang forward towards Christiana and bowed low from the waist. He almost seemed to be preening. "I am Fletcher MacDonald at your service, and this is my good friend and colleague, Max Bateman. We are very pleased to be here, and we will be delighted to have dinner with you. Afterward I will want to get down to work, if you don't mind. I have some questions." Turning to Vytalis he asked, "Is that the Lithuanian cross on the door?"

"You do your research well, Mr. MacDonald. It is indeed. The circle represents the sun, the earth is the inner field, and the intersecting lines, fire."

"And, if I am not mistaken, this cross, now used by Lithuanian Christians, was also a sacred pagan symbol representing conquest and the supremacy of the gods of nature.

The Lithuanian regarded him curiously. "Yes, you are right again. But that is long past."

"It symbolized murder didn't it?" Fletcher's eyes focused hard on Vytalis.

Christiana spoke up. "Yes, again." She spread her arms wide. "You probably know that we were a conquering people, the lions of Europe, until the Poles struck, annexed some of our best lands, and subjugated us for centuries. We really have never recovered. Christianity wasn't particularly good for our nationhood; we were unvanquished before then. But, as my husband said, that is past and we are a free and independent republic, with a future." She bestowed a smile on us. "Now we will let you go to your rooms and we will see you at dinner."

We were escorted by our goon drivers to our rooms on the second floor. Startling me, my room had a life-size crucified Jesus on an even larger heavy oak cross suspended above the bed. On another wall were hung vivid watercolors of a soulful and brooding Jesus. Contrapuntally, the tall and thick dark-oak columnar posts at the foot of my bed were finely carved into giant trolls or dwarfs bearing menacing smiles. They seemed out of place in this very Catholic space. The bathroom towels all bore the Lithuanian cross, which I knew now had a pagan etymology.

After discarding my road clothes and changing into fresh attire for dinner, I walked over to Fletcher's room and knocked. "It's Max. May I come in?" There was no response, but the door opened slowly to a massive space dominated by a life-size stuffed horse in full medieval armor! I craned my neck around the door and saw a virtual army of suits of armor stationed in the room. I jumped when I finally saw Fletcher standing in the lee of the door, against the wall, with his finger to his lips. I walked farther into the room, and Fletcher nudged the door closed.

"Amazing, isn't it? We seem to be in a museum, Max, or maybe something more profound. The past is so very well preserved, as if it is waiting to be reborn." He waggled his finger at the objects behind him. "If you rub your hand over the joints of the armor, you will see that they have been recently oiled. The armor plates have been freshly cleaned. I rather doubt that this is simply a manifestation of good housekeeping. I smell zeal, don't you?"

"Smell? Well, what I see is enough to make me cringe." I gestured towards my room. "I have a full-sized crucifixion over my bed, so lifelike I wouldn't be surprised if it dripped blood on my head tonight. Formidable trolls guard the foot of my bed. It would seem to me that the pagans and Christians are still warring in my room, and I think the Christians are losing. And your room looks like a staging area for a medieval war party."

Fletcher loved all these arcane mysteries. "I've been studying the inscriptions on the armor. The Lithuanians have their own language and alphabet, and it is unlike the surrounding Romance, Slav, or Scandinavian languages. However, I have been able to decipher the word 'Vytautus' on the shields and breastplates. He was their greatest conqueror and most revered king, equivalent in their eyes to Alexander the Great." He cast his gaze on the armor collection. "These are seminal treasures that ought to be in a national museum, yet they are here. Perhaps by right, perhaps not. We must inquire judiciously." Fletcher motioned that we should leave and go downstairs. He was in high gear and clearly exhilarated by his findings and discoveries ahead.

Vytalis gathered us in the elegantly set dining room. We stood behind our chairs waiting for Christiana to arrive, while a maid brought in various offerings and placed them carefully on the table. Entering from a side door, Christiana wore a dark-red velvet dress, her neck adorned with a dazzling necklace of large rubies. Her blonde hair, just hinting of some gray, was pulled back into a tight bun. She rustled a bit as she walked. Her perfume tinged the air with jasmine. I could not have been alone with my silent gasp at her striking beauty and uncommon grace.

I glanced at Fletcher and saw that his eyes were gleaming. He was clearly entranced by Christiana. Vytalis drew back her chair, Christiana took her seat, and we all followed suit. There was no mistaking that we were in the presence of that special quality, that je ne sais quoi, which demands attention and respect.

The dinner was indigenous to Lithuania. Dark-brown bread, sausage, sturgeon, pike, cabbage, kasha, duryanka, a flavored vodka, and an assortment of Baltic herring—creamed, pickled, and with onions. The comprehensive presentation was clearly meant to immerse our palette, too, into Lithuanian culture. As is the custom here, many toasts were raised that evening of welcome, good health, and success in our endeavors, and each was accompanied with a shot of vodka, so the word Sveikatq! ("cheers" in Lithuanian) rang out all too frequently. I remember well one telling exchange between Christiana and Fletcher. Christiana, looking keenly at Fletcher, said, "To our guest who comes from afar, but I suspect will become very near and dear." And Fletcher's response, standing, to his full crane height, " And to the veritas of Dieu and Mon Droit, it's radiance is indisputable, even to this Republican."

I stumbled bleary-eyed from too many toasts into the drawing room. Undaunted by alcohol, Fletcher didn't slip into retirement for the evening, but pressed on with his promised questions.

I could have fallen asleep on the spot and almost did, except the conversation became quite pointed. "I must apologize," Fletcher glanced in my direction, "for my inability to speak your language, whereas you speak English so very well. Where did you obtain such an extraordinary command of it?"

Christiana responded, "We were both given excellent, but very different, educations by our families." She looked momentarily at her husband. "Vytalis was sent to a private school in England, and I was tutored by my father, who was an accomplished linguist," she told us proudly. "He spoke seven languages fluently and even achieved a doctorate in languages. He was one of our nation's great translators of local poetry into other languages. He also operated, at great personal risk and sacrifice, an underground educational system during the Soviet occupation, teaching Lithuanians about their culture because the Soviets were systematically trying to eliminate it, or at least to Russify it."

"Repression of the spirit is a hateful thing," Fletcher responded, concurring. "Eventually it can no longer be tolerated, but before it is confronted successfully, the price paid is unspeakable. Please permit me to turn the subject to a happier note. Mrs. Sagaritus, this was an extraordinary meal, from design to execution. How do you keep such a fine larder in the country?"

"Please call me Christiana. And thank you. One of my husband's businesses is wholesale food, so we are able to have this wide variety. We are very blessed."

Vytalis added, "Mr. MacDonald, the wholesale business was...is...part of my father's overall business, a general wholesaler and importer of a large variety of products, from food to clothing, coal and steel, very integrated and complete. Little importation occurs outside of his operation."

Fletcher's interest surfaced. "But not during the Soviet occupation?"

"It was a state import and distribution authority then, and my father was a first deputy in charge. He acquired the operation when the republic was reestablished in 1991."

Fletcher pressed on at this point. "And so you ate and lived well when others did not, yes?"

Vytalis shot back, "I do not think that you are on the right track. No. My father was not singled out for being pro-Soviet, quite the opposite. In Lithuania under the Soviets, terrible disparities were common. We all had to survive the best we could. Even the patriots of today had to do things they disliked to survive. My father was a partisan, a patriot, and everybody knows that."

"I mean no offense, but somebody deeply hated him, or I wouldn't be here. Please tell me the circumstances of his disappearance."

Vytalis relaxed again, with that point of honor made clear. "Two months ago exactly," he began, "we were with a dozen family members at a nightclub my father owns in Klaipeda. It was eleven. We gathered to celebrate the graduation of a nephew from the local university. We were in a private room down a flight from the bar area. One of the waiters whispered to my father, and he abruptly left the table. I suspected that something was wrong, and after a few minutes I went searching for him.

"I found him having a loud argument with a stranger at the bar. When I tried to break it up, he waved me away, despite my protests, and demanded that I rejoin the family, which I reluctantly did. I didn't mention anything to them and just waited for his return. About fifteen minutes elapsed. I couldn't make any more plausible excuses for my father's absence, so I went back to the bar and learned from the bartender that my father had forcibly taken the stranger outside. My father briefly returned and told the bartender to tell us not to worry, that he would meet us at home. He then left the bar. I explained to the party that my father had some urgent business to take care of. In Lithuania, owing to the black and gray markets, business is conducted at strange times, so this explanation was accepted with knowing shrugs. The family party broke up soon after. I never saw my father again. The ferry operator did see my father cross over to Nida from the mainland before we crossed, so we know he made it here."

He paused to swallow deeply. He was more agitated when he continued. "Early the next morning, I went down to our bathroom here in Nida. I discovered big pools of fresh blood all around and in the toilet. I immediately feared that it was my father's blood, and I called the police."

The tale was very odd, and I asked, "Over the last few weeks, have you discovered anything missing of your father's, such as clothing, special possessions, or perhaps large withdrawals from his bank accounts?"

"No, Mr. Bateman, nothing irregular at all. Indeed, my father kept a large amount of cash and other valuables in a safe, and nothing has been touched."

Fletcher looked at both Vytalis and Christiana and asked, "What have the police discovered?"

Vytalis answered with a scowl, "Not much. No one can or will identify the man in the bar with whom my father had the fight. But that's not so peculiar, because Klaipeda is a major seaport and is frequented by merchant marine transients. However, he was Lithuanian, judging by his speech. The police have interviewed all the people that were at the bar that night and the bartender. The witnesses said the man seemed unknown by my father. The police claim they searched a wide area for people matching the stranger's description, but they couldn't find him. And, on top of that, they can't find any trace of my father." He shook his head at the futility of the police force. "That's why I called you. First, we must find my father, dead or alive, and second, we must punish who did this."

Fletcher responded, "The first requirement is to find out why he disappeared. And, as to punishment, that is the business of the police and the courts. It certainly is not mine. Why are you so frustrated with the police?"

Vytalis exhaled. "The police have long been corrupt in Lithuania. They were the tools of the Soviets and now of the thugs. They are less than useless. They are counterproductive, except for their own purposes. They won't move unless they are paid off, and then it becomes a bidding war between the victims and the perpetrators. So we must take matters into our own hands, even judgment. But, yes, you have only the responsibility to help us find my father and who did him harm."

Fletcher, rubbed his brow a bit, made a steeple of his fingers, thinking deeply. Then he said, "My experience is that people disappear generally as a function of a well-thought-out plan, either that of the missing or of the perpetrator. If the latter, they don't leave calling cards, and if they do, there's a reason. If the former, then there would be an obvious explanation by now: a note, missing cash, coincidental disappearance of a woman he knew, something indicating that your father wanted out of the life he was living. As there is none and there is no ransom demand, I presume that someone wanted him permanently out of the way. Let's start with the bar quarrel. What was the substance of it?"

"Apparently the man with whom my father had the fight was drunk and abusive to a regular customer, a woman of the night that the bar protected. My father wanted him to leave, but he wouldn't, which led to shouting and pushing. Finally my father physically threw him out and, according to the others there, beat him pretty badly outside. Father returned to the bar with blood on his face and hands and told the bartender, as I said, that he was leaving and would go home separately, and not to tell anyone in our party that there was anything to worry about. That was the last anyone saw of my father. The police checked his cell phone records, and there were no calls made."

"How do you know the blood around the toilet was fresh or that it was your father's?"

"It was bright red. The police identified it as my father's blood type, and no one else has access to the house."

"At what exact time did you discover the blood?"

"About five. I went down to relieve myself. The lights in the bathroom were on, so I figured my father had returned and was somewhere else in the house."

"Your father's injuries, if he had any, from the fistfight would have occurred around eleven o'clock. It is unlikely that he would still be bleeding very much at five. Was there any trail of blood to the toilet?"

"No...no blood anywhere else in the bathroom or the house."

"I presume your father, around eighty, like most men of his age, would rise at night to relieve himself once or twice?"

"That is true."

Christiana had been following the conversation closely. She tentatively raised a finger to draw attention and said, "It seems obvious to me that Frederick was followed here by the person he threw out of the bar, who then hid in our house and attacked him in the bathroom and disposed of his body. Many laborers cross on the ferry in the back of trucks, so he could have easily come across and left without being noticed."

Fletcher nodded in assent. "Your conclusions are most logical and probably will prove correct. Do you have any theories about the missing body? If the killer worked alone, given the large size of your father-in-law, it would have been difficult for him to drag the body without help. Indeed, from what I have been told, apparently the blood was confined to the toilet, which suggests that his body was carried away, not dragged."

Christiana continued the narrative. "There was no blood found anywhere else in the house. I think the murderer probably had an accomplice. They could have taken the body off Nida and disposed of it by throwing it in the sea or maybe by burning it. All over Lithuania people burn trash out of doors, a perfect cover for a makeshift crematorium." At our looks of shock, she splayed her hands. "Things like this happen here. We have a lawless and murderous society. Despite your great prowess, Mr. MacDonald, I think this will prove daunting to even you."

Fletcher hardly seemed intimidated by the prospect and chivalrously rose to the occasion, "I promise to give it my all, Christiana, and consider the most implausible as well as the obvious." Christiana responded softly, "I have no real doubts as to your ultimate success, just shall we say, a tenderness for what awaits you in your travails."

Fletcher rose, bowed slightly in Christiana's direction, and inspected a large, horizontal, glass-covered table cabinet of ferocious-looking knives, swords, and other ancient killing devices. I had noticed him gazing at it several times earlier. "Have these been tested for blood stains? Are any items missing?" Surprised by the questions, Vytalis joined Fletcher at the cabinet. "No to both questions. These are all under lock and key. My father, Christiana, and I are the only ones who have keys to the cabinet. The staff has no keys to the case."

"May I have the key?" Fletcher opened up his palm to receive it. "I presume these are from the thirteenth century and earlier. Tools of war."

Christiana walked to the cabinet, slipping herself between it and Fletcher, their clothes now touching, their faces millimeters apart, and dropped the key into his open hand. She eased away from the intimacy she had created. "Yes. They belonged to King Vytautus, our great conqueror. They are mine by inheritance."

"As are the valuable medieval and earlier artifacts in my

room, I presume?"

She was a bit defensive. "I am preserving them so that one day when the Lithuanians have a proper place for them, I will give them to the people as a gift."

"They are exquisitely cared for. Am I to understand that you are a direct descendent of King Vytautus?"

Christiana almost whispered, "With the greatest humility, I must say that the answer is yes." A flicker of pride in her eyes quickly passed. "It is not something that has much importance anymore, of course, except from a historical point of view." Fletcher opened the cabinet and pulled a short broad sword from the case. He took his handkerchief and rubbed the blade fully along its length. I had not seen anything, but a dark residue showed on the cloth. "Max, bring this tomorrow to the police for testing. Odd, but all the other implements have no apparent oxidation or whatever this is."

Vytalis only stared at the sword.

"Gentlemen," said Christiana, "if you will excuse me, I feel I must leave you and retire. Thank you again for coming. I will be fresh to help you in the morning. Good night." All the men nodded a silent acknowledgment as Christiana made her exit.

Fletcher was unusually circumspect. "Vytalis, may I ask you a very delicate question?"

"But of course, anything." Vytalis sat down.

"I notice that your physiognomy and skeleton structure seem not to be classically Lithuanian. Indeed, I would say that there is more Slav in your features. Are you perhaps Polish?"

Our host looked perplexed again, but he answered, "My family came to Lithuania six centuries ago from Poland. Through intermarriage with Lithuanians, I am virtually Lithuanian and," he pointed out firmly, "a partisan. My physique is a throwback, as was my father's. Of what significance can this be?"

"I don't know, Vytalis. But I very much appreciate your answering my question forthrightly. Can you give me a brief overview of your family's economic history in Lithuania? How did it survive World War II?"

"I can take you further back than that. Six hundred years ago, we were titled by the Polish monarch for our military valor in conquering a renegade band of marauding Lithuanian pagans and given a substantial land grant in Lithuania. We led a midlevel noble life here for centuries, making our way with farming. That life was largely ruined with Lithuania's brand of democratic communism that arrived in the 1920s. We were lucky not to be murdered by the proletariat," he growled, showing what he felt about the noble worker. "We barely held on and built up a modest import-export business that operated even through the war. Then the Soviets took it over, giving my family some second-level administrative posts at first because we knew the language and the customs. Later on, my grandfather achieved the top local position in the operation, reporting to a Russian superior in Moscow. My father took over from him when grandfather died." His brow darkened at the memory of their former overlords. "When the Soviets were pushed out, my father put together, at great personal risk to himself, a vast combine of wholesalers, importers and exporters, restaurants, vodka distributer, et cetera. It was, and is, very dangerous to run, because we have no real legal enforcement here. Everyone takes the law into his own hands, like your Wild West. Competition here is truly mortal combat. I am armed at all times." Vytalis opened his jacket and revealed a holstered gun on his shoulder.

As interesting as this family history was, I did not see its bearing on the recent murder. Yet Fletcher seemed fascinated, and he asked, "What of Christiana's family? How were they faring throughout this? What happened to her father, who was apparently leading an active resistance to the Soviets?"

Vytalis became very respectful. "She comes from a scholastic world, and behind that, from an extinguished world where she would have been the legitimate heir to the Lithuanian throne. Her family, who had privately worked to overthrow the Soviets, was totally liquidated, murdered, by them during the occupation. They were professors of language and science, and they used their positions with the students to preach resistance. They doomed themselves," he said sadly. "Christiana had no money, just her heritage and pretensions to the throne."

"Is there any support for a return to the monarchy?"

Vytalis didn't think so. "Probably the peasants and farmers still harbor some warm thoughts for the glory days of Vytautus, but that is all wrapped up with the superstitions, foolishness, and backwardness of the old ways." The prospect, perhaps fueled by all the artifacts populating his house, seemed to annoy him. "We are a burgeoning democracy with a growing capitalistic class that doesn't have time for such nonsense. We are working out our problems. It is all for the best."

Fletcher smiled but pointed out, "There are some healthy constitutional monarchies about, such as—England, Sweden, Norway, Spain, and the Netherlands. Perhaps such a blend would have the power to restore some real order here and end the tyranny of the thugs. It might harmoniously unite the ancient history with the expectations of the present."

Vytalis was irritated by Fletcher's foray into political thinking about Lithuania. He said rather imperiously, "With all due respect, I can't see what this line of thinking has to do with my father's disappearance. He wasn't political, just a businessman."

His annoyance pulled Fletcher up short. He was such a devoted student of history that he could be carried away. He straightened in his comfortable chair. "Quite right, enough of that. Tell me, where have the police looked for your father?"

Vytalis nodded at this return to practicality. "They say everywhere on Nida. They combed the area including the ponds and streams."

"Although Nida is not an immense area, it seems to me that its gnarly forests, groves, and deep dells make it easy to miss places where a body might be hidden or buried. Wouldn't you agree? It is unlikely that they covered it all. Tomorrow I want to search the area. Would you arrange to help us find our way? I would like to go precisely at noon."

"Yes, of course, I will guide you myself."

Fletcher clapped his hands lightly. "Very good. With that plan for tomorrow, I bid you both goodnight." Fletcher left the room to Vytalis and me.

Vytalis eyed the sword intently and then looked at me. "Of

course, I'll inform Stephan. The cook will have some breakfast ready for you as well. You should get some rest. It's midnight already. I'll leave you to retire. Good night, Mr. Bateman."

"Please call me Max. Good night, and thank you for your hospitality. I am sure Mr. MacDonald will get to the heart of the matter—he always does."

****

I arrived at Inspector Vargas's office at the village police station at seven-thirty the next morning. I had planned to leave part of the cloth with an officer for blood testing. I kept another piece just in case the first went astray. To my surprise, Vargas was there and was most amenable to our request, but dismissive of our efforts.

"This killing is gang related. Mr. Sagaritus was operating in business areas, food supplies, bars, and shipping, which are highly coveted by others who will use whatever means to obtain their ways. It's like your Al Capone period here, Chicagoland throughout the whole of Lithuania. Might makes right. We just try and keep it all to the lowest level of mayhem we can". He tapped the sword lightly, as though it were insignificant. "Eventually it will all sort out. I explained to Vytalis there was no need to bring in your Mr. MacDonald, but he says that his father's enemies were too scared of repercussions to strike like this." He gave me a shrewd look. "In my opinion, this is a classic territorial takeover. Frankly his son is probably next for the slaughter, and I have told him so to his face. He has taken precautions at least. Your driver and his twin are his bodyguards, and I can assure you they are pretty tough. They are armed to the teeth and have many scalps on their belts."

The excursion we had taken into Lithuanian history the night before now seemed as remote as a dream. A visit to a police station was always a good way to return to hard ground.

"By the way, do you want this back today, rather than sometime in the unknowable future? This isn't your civil society, you understand. This is the frontier, make no mistake about it." I smiled with understanding, and gave Captain Vargas 400 litas, the equivalent of one hundred dollars to facilitate the process. I returned to find Fletcher and Vytalis just leaving. Both sported walking sticks, the picture of country gentlemen. I trotted after them. "We will have the blood report back today. I had to...oh, well. I had an interesting conversation with your Police Chief Vargas."

Vytalis leaped in. "Yes, he's a very practical man. Just what we need in these days of disorder."

Fletcher, looking skyward and then grasping his brow, started striding at a ferocious pace into the woods, bushwacking where no trails or pathways were evident, leaving Vytalis and me struggling to keep up. The denseness of the forest forced Fletcher to remove his hat, something he resisted doing most of the time. He was following no path that I could see, yet he plunged straight ahead, as if he were homing in on a signal. The land undulated, with deep pits covered with pine needles, moss, and spindly lichen. "Fletcher, slow down!" I called. But he forged ahead, occasionally stopping to raise his head, sniffing the air like a stag.

Fifteen minutes later and a half-mile by my pedometer from the house, I caught up with him, standing on a low ridge. He had found a worn path about two feet wide and well cared for. Even the trees had been pruned back, as was evident by fresh cut marks on the stems and branches. The way ahead seemed clear. Vytalis finally caught up.

"I presume you are familiar with this location. It is where the little people live, isn't it?" Fletcher asked, pointing ahead.

Vytalis showed no such enthusiasm. "Rumor has it so, Mr. MacDonald. But we all know that is poppycock."

"I think we need to explore the dells below."

"You go," he said, waving us off. "This is a fool's errand. There is nothing here. I'll wait for you."

Fletcher was already charging down the cleared path but called up to Vytalis, "Are you sure you don't want to come down here with us?"

"No, too much superstition down there. Just return as fast as you can."

Fletcher bounded ahead and I was following as fast as I could, when Fletcher stopped short and called to me, "Max, we have a friend. I think you know his cousin."

Around a turn, I saw a three-foot column carved into the shape of a troll- nearly identical to the one at the foot of my bed. This time I was sure that by the smile on his face he was muttering, "Go ahead and try getting by me."

"This is another guard troll, isn't it, Fletcher?"

"Yes, I think so. Vytalis is afraid of coming into this sacred area because infidels, a.k.a. Christians, especially Poles, are persona non grata here. The lore is that an infidel will meet his death within an hour of his entering here, and it shall be by the same method as he might kill others. We already suspect that Vytalis and his father were not above brutality to hold on to their empire, so I suppose death from this curse would be particularly painful and gruesome. Voilà, Vytalis's resistance to my entreaty. He knows the rules very well."

This foray into fancy did not seem to be much of a deterrent for a hardheaded man like Vytalis, and I said jokingly, "And for us? I am a Christian after all, aren't you?"

"We will be all right. We are on the right side of the matter. Come on, I have a theory, but there is a big piece missing. That's why we are here."

Fletcher bounded ahead, leaving me with the troll. "So, how spooky are you?" I mockingly said to the statue. To this day, I swear that the thing winked at me.

When I caught up with Fletcher, he was in the middle of a large circular depression. It was ringed with tall trees, creating a little amphitheater in a hidden grove. Although it was nearing noon, only a little light reached the floor of the forest here. Fletcher was sitting on a large log, almost a bench, in the middle of this flat, circular area, staring in the direction of an immense tree. It had a hole about three feet high at its base and four feet wide, making an entrance just large enough to walk through if one bent over. As I stared down at Fletcher, I noticed that the trees surrounding it all had bas-relief carvings in the bark: bears, wolves, vultures, and panther-like creatures. Taken all together, it became clear that the carvings were shaped to face the aperture in the tree, as if they were watching it.

"Fletcher, are we going to look in the hole in the tree or go around? Have you looked on the other side of the tree?"

"The banks are too steep on the other side to see anything. It looks as if the hole leads to a place that is another depression that may have a ceiling of branches and pine needles. Come down here. If you look up like me, you can get a clear view of the carvings."

I jumped down the six feet or so. I was in a bowl surrounded by the carved trees, the log bench in the center and the tree with a gaping black hole or entrance in front of us.

"How do you feel right now, Max?"

"Well, pretty spooked. I actually thought that troll back there winked at me." I stopped to get hold of myself. "I presume we are at a holy spot and these are animist sculptures. This is probably a forest antechamber to a shrine that's on the other side of that tree. Logical, right?"

"Max, sometimes you amaze me. That's spot on. We are here because, as they say, X marks the spot. After studying the armor in my room, I discovered that the breastplates all had, in addition to the Lithuanian cross, the same carved motif. A round circle, guarded by animals, and in the center was an altar. In the study there is an ancient map of Nida. I noticed it was a "sun map," for it traced the movement of the sun over Nida during each month, week, and day in relationship to Christiana's house and to another place nearby. I tracked coordinates to this very place by using the sundial on their grounds and the map this morning."

Fletcher's tone changed from being instructive to questioning. "Max, how do you feel about this place, in your heart?"

I took a deep breath and listened to the silence and then answered. "I feel respect for whatever is here. There is something special, but I can't describe it. It's just a feeling."

Fletcher was very alert. "All religion is like that. It's a feeling that one is in the midst of something more powerful than oneself. It is like being on the edge of understanding, but that full understanding is always a step beyond. Would you agree?"

The spirit was becoming stronger. "Those words feel right. I would add that I sense serenity here as well. Serenity is also part of belief at some level. I feel that here."

"I think we are ready to enter." Fletcher led the charge

through the tree opening.

"Pitch black. Ground is solid, but the tree is wider than I thought. I'm still walking through the trunk. I'm coming out. There is very little light. Just as I suspected."

Fletcher, still with his hat uncharacteristically off, was bending over a small box. My eyes searched the dim light for other information, and then it leapt out at me: a human head on a pike with a Polish flag under the neck, black with blood. After I gathered my thoughts, I asked, "I presume this is Frederick Sagaritus? Should we remove it and bring it back?"

"This is Frederick," he said, agreeing. "This box contains some of his private parts and a finger with a ring with his name inscribed in it. Such ghoulish order bespeaks a ritual offering. It is clear now that Vytalis's father's death was not at the hands of gangs or Mafiosi, but by those who believe that the past represented by this shrine and its supporting culture are viable and most of all potent. I'm very sorry to say, but I am certain that this is work sanctioned by Christiana."

I reacted with surprise, and he continued with inexorable logic. "I think she, or her vassals, cut off her father-in-law's head with the broad sword in retaliation for the subjugation of the Lithuanians by the Poles. I have no doubt that the blood type on the sword will match the one you gave the police. She knew he would go to the bathroom sometime during the night. They waited for him there, whacked his neck, and then decapitated him over the toilet. Those men probably disposed of the body, except for what is here, as she mentioned, by incineration. I also think that the fight in the bar was simply a ploy to throw off suspicion. His head was brought here for some kind of victor's celebration." He stood to his full height. "We will announce this to no one. I think that might unleash more trouble—for Vytautus, for us, for others. This is blood revenge for repression and subjugation we can't even begin to imagine. This is simply something that we must leave be."

"Even if the blood matches," I pointed out, "you have no evidence at all that Christiana did this. It's just a surmise."

He seemed not to have heard me. "Who is the real victim here? Sagaritus? Or the Lithuanian people who have been bled dry by Sagaritus and his breed for centuries? It's obvious that the marriage of Christiana and Vytalis was the quintessential piece in the ascendancy of the Sagaritus family over the centuries. She, and the Vytautus line, were completely subjugated to their will by this marriage. They were the invaders and this was the final triumph. Moreover, what is the law here? Dog eat dog. Look the other way. Should we interfere with the shakeout that is happening? I don't think we should let our morals get in the way of this world righting itself."

"Fletcher, I repeat, you have no evidence."

"I don't need it and I don't want it. To me the fact picture is clear. The moral issue is clear too. Because we have no evidence, as you say, we do not have to reveal what I think is the solution. I don't want to have any more evidence."

"The police chief told me Vytalis is his father's only heir. If he dies, then Christiana gets it all. That places him at risk. Surely we ought to alert him and the police."

"Yes, he is at risk either way. As you said, we have no evidence. Some things must right themselves. This is one of them. We are simply spectators. No one knows we found this place, and that is how things must remain."

We left the grove and found our way back to Vytalis.

"You were right. There was nothing there. It was a waste of time," Fletcher said nonchalantly to Vytalis.

That evening I received a note from the police chief that simply stated: "The blood was that of Sagaritus. No surprise. Yours, Vargas." I gave it to Fletcher while we were waiting for Christiana and Vytalis to call us to dinner. He balled up the note and threw it in the fire.

The great dining table had an alabaster white cloth spread completely over it, with two candelabras lighting each end. The table was wide and long, so we had been placed across from each other at the middle, Fletcher and I on the same side, a good five feet from Christiana and Vytalis.

Observing the delicate features of Christiana, I had a hard time imagining that she would have the strength or the stomach to saw the head off anyone, let alone her father-in-law. I found Fletcher's reasoning fading under the light of her gentle presence.

As she passed me a plate, I carefully observed her hand and fingers. They simply looked unable to carry off such a deed, despite my recognition that Lady Macbeths were not wholly fictional creations. Yet it seemed far-fetched at the moment.

She asked, "Did you find anything today?"

Rather than answer, Fletcher placed his fork down and proposed a toast. "To Queen Nida, may she rule from strength and wisdom forever. Sveikatq!"

Christiana blushed, and Vytalis smiled and said, "Here, here."

"Thank you, Mr. MacDonald, but I am no queen, I have no subjects, I have no rights. Yet I do love my country and my fellow countrymen and our history. I wish to salute the greatest Lithuanian of all : King Vytautus, warrior, protector, and benefactor of all."

We all joined in: "To King Vytautus: warrior, protector, and benefactor of all!" Fletcher asked, "What can you tell us of the history of your great predecessor that makes him so beloved here?"

She was pleased by the question. "I never tire of talking about his reign. He was like so many unique leaders, inspired and modern for his times. He was, of course, born pagan, the last Lithuanian monarch to be so, before converting to Christianity. Despite his pagan roots, he could be quite just. His fairness even extended to the Jews. While no other country would let them live in peace, they were given protection by him, so long as they were loyal to Lithuania. He was a man ahead of his time. His benevolence is what we think of as Christian today. He strove to see that his noblemen treated their subjects with respect and fairness and that the poor were first to be fed and the noblemen last to eat in times of famine." Vytalis added, "He was also a powerful warrior who would not give quarter to his enemies."

Christiana rose from her seat and walked around the table over to Vytalis. She stroked his hair and lovingly kissed his cheek. "Yes, my dear, he gave no quarter to his enemies."

****

The next day we left Lithuania. We were in the waiting lounge in Frankfurt when I noticed a headline below the fold on the front page of the International Herald Tribune, "LITHUANIAN BUSI-NESSMAN EXECUTED." I made a beeline to the newsstand to get a copy. My breath stopped as I read:

"Nida, Lithuania. Vytalis Sagaritus, owner of an influential import-export business headquartered in Vilnius, was found decapitated yesterday by his wife, Christiana, matriarch of the Lithuanian royal line. Police Chief Rigas Vargas told reporters that he attributed the murder to mafia-like warfare between the Sagaritus family and rival forces fighting over controlling the lucrative food and provision business, including the vodka monopoly. Vargas said that the style of killing was clearly that of gangs seeking vengeance. He said that he hoped that the score-settling was over and that peace would return. He noted that Vytalis Sagaritus was the last of his line and that his wife would now control the Sagaritus trade empire. Vytalis's father disappeared under mysterious circumstances two months ago. Vargas also attributed the father's disappearance and probable death to gang violence."

I showed Fletcher the story.

He sniffed. "The world is what it is."

They called our flight to Halifax, and we disappeared into the jetway.

INSIDE THE WEIR

Dark Harbor. If there was ever a name of a place that conjured up bad deeds, that was it. And as things turned out, it lived up to its nasty connotation. Dark Harbor is on Grand Manan Island, in the middle of the Bay of Fundy, about thirty miles by ferry from the Canadian mainland and ten miles as the crow flies from Campobello Island. We were drawn here by Fletcher's receipt of a copy of a letter sent to Louis Moritz, a good friend of his, that read:

Dear Lou: You asked about the last half hour that Fred was alive. As I told the coroner, Fred was in a good mood. He had a few beers as he watched the TV news. I served the salmon I had purchased that day at the Super K. He was about half-finished with his dinner when he began to cough hard. He couldn't clear his throat. Then he began to choke. As I tried the Heimlich maneuver, his face and lips swelled and his eyes bulged. He just stopped breathing, became stiff, and fell to the floor, bright blue. Within minutes, life just left him. One moment normal; three minutes, later, forever gone. God rest his soul. Sue.

A similar death after eating salmon had occurred just a few weeks later on the island. Lou became suspicious that these deaths might be related to the salmon farming that had come to dominate Dark Harbor.

Even the approach to it is eerie, as it shocks the driver or walker with a fast fall from the flat top of the island to the sea floor hundreds of feet below. One winds and switchbacks down to a smallish body of water that is separated from the sea by a high seawall, more of a berm, composed of thousands of sharp-edged rocks—that leads to a small outlet just wide enough for a fishing boat to slip out to sea. Set atop the berm are a dozen driftwood shacks, homes to the local fisherman: one or at the most two-room affairs with a pot-bellied stove for heat, judging by the tin chimneys that stick out like broken arms from each hovel, and clearly no plumbing. On one side the shacks look at the sea, and the other the harbor. What a battering they must take!

Beyond them lies the real reason the little port has a spooky name. Dulse is a dark, almost black-purple seaweed that is both a food and fertilizer. Gathered here for centuries and shipped all over the world, it is rich in B vitamins, minerals, iodine, and salt and is associated with many salubrious health claims. Locals and some gourmets in the great food capitals enthuse about its singular briny taste and crisp texture once it is dried. Floating just outside the breakwater of the harbor and in the nearby coves, the seaweed undulates like a thick, dark burgundy carpet on the waters. Once a year dulse gatherers skim it off the sea, rake it from the shore, and bring it to Dark Harbor for processing. During harvesting, the harbor air is perfumed with the rich nutrient smell of the dulse that locks the mind into the life of the sea.

One reason for the unique seaweed is its unusual habitat, the Bay of Fundy, where the tides are daily miracles. Solid thirty-foot boats lie like dead, swollen seals at low tide that are then brought back to life by the high tide, bobbing and ready for action. Twenty-foot changes in a day are common. All three of us walked in the tidal flat area that led to the harbor and watched how the sea would stealthily creep into it and within an hour flood it with ten feet of water. Many a soul has been caught by these tides and has drowned trying to get back to land. It's like a heart attack: silent, unexpected, and overwhelming.

An unnatural sound now pervades Dark Harbor that didn't exist a few years ago. It methodically and monotonously grinds, whirs, and hums. It is at odds with the cadence of the sea that rises and falls with the waves against the sea wall and that has been soothing hearts for eons. The unholy noise is the sound of feeding machines and aerators that pump life into the salmon-raising pens of GFI Fisheries, Inc. (GFI). Each pen, a thirty-foot-diameter cage rising about ten feet over the water and continuing down to the harbor bottom, holds tens of thousands of fish. In the eight huge pens one can see at the surface salmon leaping and flapping. They are very large fish. Only the thought of crowding into a New York City subway car at rush hour captures what it must be like for them every moment. Being so close to hundreds of thousands of other fish, all penned up, created a voyeuristic quality to the experience; we are free and they are not, in numbers too large to fathom. But then they are only fish, or so I told myself.

We were there to reconnoiter. Louis Moritz had contacted us because of two odd deaths of otherwise healthy men on the island. Louis was a member of the Grand Manan Chamber of Commerce and as such had a heightened awareness of anything that could adversely affect the reputation of the island. The curious aspect of these deaths is that they each occurred within an hour of eating salmon that was raised in these fish farms at Dark Harbor, and the manifestations of death were the same. Since almost a month separated the deaths, this coincidence wasn't popularly known. The autopsies showed that death was due to spontaneous esophageal contractions but the cause of it could not be ascertained. The local doctor who did the autopsies, Lionel Black, was well known to Louis, and they had discussed the matter frankly. Dr. Black felt certain that the deaths had nothing to do with the salmon but rather were just coincidental deaths caused by some reaction to something with which both men had come in contact. Louis remained concerned, because he had read of a few sudden deaths in other places around the world from people who had eaten farm-raised salmon, but he put it out of his mind until a piece of information dropped into his hands.

GFI Fisheries had become the largest single employer and taxpayer on Grand Manan. Outside of tourism, the company represented the only growth industry that Grand Manan had, and the prospects for more growth looked good. At one of the meetings between the Chamber and GFI, members of the Chamber were invited to consider buying stock in GFI and everyone, including Louis, was supplied with material on the subject. One of the obscure pieces of literature referred to people having five percent share positions or greater. Dr. Black was on that list. This coincidence triggered Louis to send Fletcher the note describing the death of one victim and later prompted a call to discuss what Louis feared might be collusion between GFI and Dr. Black. If this suspicion was correct, Dr. Black's judgment regarding the cause of deaths couldn't be trusted. Yet, Louis didn't want to raise the issue with the authorities because Dr. Black was well respected on the Island and such allegations would cause an uproar, especially if they couldn't be substantiated. After all, there wasn't anything inherently wrong in Dr. Black owning stock in GFI for many locals did. Recognizing that Fletcher had a reputation for being an ardent environmentalist and a protector of Canada's wildlife, he had hoped to enlist his help in this matter. Normally Fletcher would not take on a case unless his fees could be paid, but he felt that this was an important public matter and therefore he would pursue it without any hope of compensation.

We met Louis at his home overlooking Whale Cove and across from Hole in the Rock, where the sea and wind had carved an aperture in solid rock the size of a small house. Fiona and I walked out there to take in the view. A very narrow path with a fifty-foot drop on either side to jagged rocks formed a bridge over the Hole, which we nervously walked across to a point where we enjoyed a vista of the open sea, the cove, and two working fishing weirs, the ancient economic mainstay of the island. Roughly the size of baseball diamonds, each weir consisted of slender, long poles driven into the cove floor in the shape of a heart, with each pole supporting a huge fishing net that dropped to the bottom. The sole underwater entrance allowed herring access into the center of the weir, but because of zigzag construction and a one-way flap entrance, leaving the net was next to impossible and the fish were trapped. A boat would maneuver itself directly into the weir, gather up the net and its trapped catch, and then redeploy the net on the poles. The system at one time worked incredibly well because the Bay of Fundy seethed with fish, so the weirs would fill up easily. Now there were fewer fish, so the practice was in decline.

When we returned, Fletcher and Louis had just started to talk. Fletcher introduced us. Fiona and I mentioned that we had taken a walk to Hole in the Rock and the weirs.

Louis said, "Those weirs are family owned, worked by the same families for many generations. There used to be three more weirs in this cove, but since the fisheries crashed only two are being worked now. Around noon the boats will come in and check the nets. I have always found it amazing to see them maneuver their fishing boats right into the center of the weirs, never touching any of the poles that hold the nets together. They are really super at it."

Fletcher asked, "How do the locals feel about the fish farms and GFI?"

Louis sighed "If they could have their way, they would prefer to use the weirs and fish the old-fashioned way. But that's over, owing to the crash in fish stocks. GFI has figured out how to grow vastly more salmon than these guys could ever have fished out of the sea and has given a lot of these fishermen at least some wages, but far less than they would have made in a good year fishing. At one time we had five hundred full-time fishermen. Now we have one hundred, and about a hundred others are employed by GFI to tend the feeding pens and to make repairs. But at least that hundred have full-time jobs. It was the loss of the life of being an independent fisherman that really hurt these people. They loved the adventure and the freedom. They were proud of their jobs."

Fletcher decided to probe more to the heart of the matter. "Do you have the articles about the people who may have died from farm-raised fish?"

"I have copies here in a file." He gave it to Fletcher. "You can see there aren't many, only four, all in Europe, and the connection to farm-raised salmon has not been confirmed." Knowing Fletcher's bent, he added pertinent details. "However, the commonalities are striking. One, they all ate salmon before they died; two, they died within minutes of eating the fish; three, they died from what doctors call anaphylaxis, an allergic reaction, which showed itself in each case by the victims choking, being unable to breathe, swallow, or speak. They rapidly became unconscious and died before emergency help arrived. In none of these cases was there a history of allergies that generally cause anaphylaxis."

Fletcher was pleased that Louis had done his homework. "And what of the victims here? Did they have any allergies?"

"Yes, one victim was allergic to ragweed. As far as I know, that didn't cause his death."

"What work did the victims do?"

Louis splayed his hands. "One was a chef at the Beach Plum Café, and the other worked for the local cable company, handling installation and maintenance. They both were well known, from third- and fourth-generation local families, and had young children. Neither family had any income except what these men made. So they are already on welfare."

Fletcher continued his probing. "Did either one have any medical conditions or abuse problems?"

"No. I had the police department run a check on them for me."

"How do you know that the salmon they ate was farm-raised?"

"We have only one supermarket on the island, the Super K. When Fred, the chef and first victim, died, it was his night off, the only night his wife cooked for him. She told me that she had purchased the salmon that day at the market. And Mack brought home the salmon that night and prepared it himself. When the police got there, they discovered the fish wrapper from the Super K. So there is no question that the fish came from there. I called the store and asked where they got their salmon, and they told me it was from GFI, right here on the island."

Fletcher rubbed his furrowed brow. "Was the fish tested?"

"The police had it tested by a government lab, which reported in both cases that there were no poisons or infectious agents in the meat."

That knocked one possibility off the list. "Could there have been anything unusual in the cooking," Fletcher asked, "such as the oil or spices used? What about side dishes, anything similar there?"

Louis shook his head. "Fred's wife had made a salad, and Mack had french fries. They both had beer but from different breweries."

"You said that Dr. Black did both autopsies. Did he report anaphylactic shock as the cause of death?"

"No, in both cases he cited spontaneous esophageal contractions that brought on choking and asphyxiation. When I asked him why he chose this description of death, he told me that he saw nothing suggesting an allergic reaction to anything, so that to call it an anaphylactic shock was misleading."

What Fletcher thought of this he didn't say. "Have the families pressed for a better answer? Have they gone further than the local police?"

"No. These people are not naturally aggressive. If the police say the case is closed, they accept it. I just can't believe it so easily."

"What about GFI? How did you approach them about this? I presume you didn't accuse them of anything. How did you handle your inquiry so as not to alarm them?

Louis wasn't one for niceties. "I wasn't at all diplomatic. I was pretty frank with them. They have a biologist on staff at all times who monitors the health of the fish and the quality of the food they receive, the water quality, and any other factors that affect the environment. His name is Frank Boynton. I asked him straight out if there could be a connection."

"Did you mention the reports of the other allergic reactions to farm-raised salmon? How did he treat your concerns?"

"He could not have been more cooperative," Louis said, dismissing that angle. "He said that he was aware of these and other concerns and had had discussions with the Canadian health officials responsible for testing fish for contaminants or other problems that might be deleterious to consumers. GFI supplied fish directly taken from the pens for analysis by these authorities. Nothing was found in the fish that could possibly trigger an allergic reaction. He said that the only mild allergen might be the coloring they add to the fish food, carotene, to give a pink color to the fish. Otherwise, their flesh would be almost white, and consumers wouldn't buy it because they expect salmon flesh to be pink."

Fletcher was struck by this point. "Do you know why the farm-raised fish have white flesh?"

"Boynton explained that farm-raised fish feed differently and so that explains the lack of color."

Fiona had been sitting quietly for a long while. "I read somewhere," she chimed in, "that the white color was the result of insufficient exercise and the use of antibiotics to keep the fish healthy."

Louis responded, "That never came up. I guess they probably use antibiotics to ward off infections."

Fletcher walked over to a window that gave a view of the cove, weirs, and in the distance the Hole in the Rock. "Lou, we know that Dr. Black owns some stock in GFI, but just how important is GFI to the economic life of the island?"

Louis opened his arms to include a wide span. "We have a very short tourist season of only two, maybe three months. The rest of the time, it is only GFI and the municipality that provide paychecks here. And those public services, like the police, school, fire department, and water, are largely paid for by GFI property taxes. So we have become more of a company town than we care to admit. All in all, GFI represents about seventy-five percent of the entire economy. I should know, since I have been the head of the Chamber for ten years."

Fletcher seemed satisfied he had learned all he could about the general circumstances. He slapped his knees and rose to his feet. "I think it's time for us to visit some of GFI's installations. Where's the largest one?"

Louis said, "At Dark Harbor. Just take this road to Whistle and then follow the signs to the left." He tapped the table with a finger. "Just be careful of the precipice. It's a long way down if you miss the turn."

Fletcher was soon standing on the edge of the harbor, where the road gave out and the shoreline began. Many boats were perched on their sides, waiting for the tide to lift them. He walked up to a man working on his boat and began to ask him some questions.

"How long have those feed pens been here?"

"About eight years," the old salt replied.

"What do they feed the fish?"

"Fish meal. Mostly ground-up herring and filler."

"Where do they get it?"

The man snorted at the foreign idea. "Beats me. Why don't you ask them yourself?" He pointed a weather-cracked finger. "The supervisor lives in that middle house on the sea wall, just above the pens."

"What's his name?"

"Jared."

"Thanks," he said, tipping his hat.

When we had retreated to the car, Fletcher turned to us. "Fiona, I need you to visit the families of the victims and inquire into what was going on in and around the time of death. I am particularly interested in what else they might have been eating. Tell them that you are a friend of Louis's and that you are seeking information about possible allergies. Also, I want you to go to GFI's main office and ask them about buying wholesale for Cape Breton. Lead them to describe how their salmon is better than other farm-raised and how it compares with the natural variety." He opened the rear hatch. "Do you mind using the bicycle to go back to Louis's and the other places? The island is pretty small and flat. We'll drive you up the hill to the flats."

Fiona relished the idea. "The exercise will be great. Anyway, it all fits the slower lifestyle here anyway." Fletcher glanced at me: that idea had been easy to sell.

After dropping Fiona at the top of the hill, we returned to the harbor. Walking along the periphery of the shoreline was the only way to reach the rock berm that separated the open sea from the little harbor. We scrabbled along the rocks to Jared's shack, which overlooked the feeding pens. A sign hung from the driftwood porch: "Take a seat, you deserve it." We called out, "Anyone home?" and knocked hard on the door, which was held shut with a rope loop.

"Hey, come down here where I can see you." A crusty voice rose from far below the shack, near the water line. Fletcher peered down, shielding his eyes from the sunlight. A shape moved from beneath the catwalk around the pens. We waved and clambered down the loose rocks.

Face to face, it was clear that Mr. McDermott was closer to a hundred than seventy-five. A little man, he was taut and sinewy and brown from being well baked for longer than most men live. He encouraged us to sit down on a tattered front bench car seat removed from a vehicle that must have died long ago.

"Where you're sitting is on the bottom struts of the feeding platform. It's attached to a raft, so it rises and fall with the tides. Neat, huh? So you're a friend of Lou's from Cape Breton?"

"Well, yes, my name is..."

"Fletcher MacDonald, 'the Scottish problem solver.' I know who you are. And you are Max Bateman." I nodded.

Fletcher lit up, "I'm flattered, but how in the world do you know so much about me?"

The old codger shrugged. "This is a small island. Nothing, I mean nothing, happens here that isn't noticed. Once you boarded the ferry to Grand Manan, you became fair game. You showed your license to buy your ticket." A twinkle showed in his eyes. "We know how to Google. You and your partner have become quite famous. And my spies say you're staying at Lou's. It's all straightforward."

"Can you tell me why I am here as well?"

He pushed out his lower lip, nodding. "Lou's been sniffing around GFI since Mack died. He thinks there's something in the fish. I'm a Grand Manan first," he said, making that point clear. "I feed these fish. If there was something going on, my loyalties are first to my friends, not to this corporate machine. I work here because the pay is good and I'm thirty feet from my home, such as it is. Did I get it right?"

"Close enough for me to call you the 'Grand Manan Problem Solver,'" Fletcher said, smiling. "Say, I'd like to see what you feed them."

Jared rose promptly to his feet. "Sure. It's got some carotene so the fish look like salmon when you cook them," he said walking over to a storage bin, "mostly herring, and antibiotics so they don't get sick." He hauled out a huge sack of it, handling the fifty pounds as if it were five pounds. The name on the bag was GFI.

Fletcher ran his hands through the brownish red pellets. It smelled like fertilizer. "Does GFI mix their own feed?"

"They do now. When I first started with them, they bought it from a Canadian company. Then they started mixing themselves. That makes sense, since they harvest herring worldwide. Why buy it from somebody else?"

"Do you mind if I take a handful with me?"

The old man held out his hand. "I don't care. If you find something wrong, let me know and I'll shut them down faster than a hurricane." He stopped, considering the possibility. "The authorities and the company biologist are here regularly testing the fish, though, so I doubt that there is anything upside down."

As Fletcher put two fistfuls in a plastic bag, I said, "Is the company biologist still Dr. Boynton?"

"Right," he said. "Lonely fellow. His family walked out on him a month ago."

Fletcher asked, "May we walk out on the catwalks and look in the pens?"

"Sure, I'll give you a tour. Takes two minutes." We walked up one short flight of steel steps and found ourselves in the midst of the whirring and slapping sounds. Fletcher was right on the edge of one of the pens where the fish were flapping and leaping. At this close range it became clear how tightly packed these fish were; free swimming was impossible. Nor are salmon small fish. They can grow to three feet in length.

Fletcher said to me quietly, "These close quarters remind me of Hitler's railroad cars of people being mechanically brought to their death." He vigorously shook his head as if to erase that picture from his mind.

McDermott had advanced to the end of the catwalk. "Here we have the most mature adults, which we will harvest tomorrow. The ones in the other tank are younger."

Fletcher gazed at them, becoming intrigued. "These older guys are very quiet. What's wrong with them?"

"They're like people. Being always cooped up like this, they lose their zest for life. I think they get depressed, slow down, and don't care anymore."

Frowning, Fletcher inquired along a different line. "Would Super K get their fish from these pens?"

"GFI is a wholesaler. We don't sell locally." Jared explained. "But we have an arrangement with Super K, so they get a little bit for the island's needs, sort of an understanding. They get it for cost so the locals get a break, even after the markup."

"An arrangement?" Fletcher asked, suspicious.

"Yeah. GFI looks the other way when I deliver some fish to the local market myself. An arrangement."

Fletcher accepted that answer. "Well, thank you for your time, Mr. McDermott. If I hear of something, I'll let you know. But somehow I think you will already know it."

Fletcher handed me the small plastic bag of fish feed. "Call Jack O'Brien at his pharmaceutical company, Thurber Drugs, in Moncton," he said as we headed up to the pier. "That is only about a hundred miles from here. Ask him to analyze it for antibiotics. He'll have to send a man down to the ferry slip on the mainland to pick it up. Tell him I need an answer overnight," he said. "Oh, you'd better disguise the feed in a candy or other type box, since everybody knows everybody else's business on this island. While you're making that call, we need to find Dr. Boynton's house, which is supposed to be on this road. Number 108."

"Any further orders, boss?"

Fletcher, deep in his musings, looked up in surprise at the interruption. "No, that'll be fine."

I reached Jack and set up the feed pickup while we searched for Boynton's house. What we found was a wreck. The front yard was strewn with old furniture, rusting appliances, discarded machinery, and trash. We picked our way through the landfill and rang the bell. A fiftyish, grayed, hunched-over man stumbled to the screen door, but he didn't open it.

"Halloo, my name is Fletcher MacDonald. Mr. McDermott said you were GFI's biologist. I've got some questions regarding the salmon feed. Would you mind if I asked you them?"

Through the door he said, "You should go to the company for those questions. If they say I can talk with you, I will." He turned away and receded back into the house.

"Dr. Boynton," Fletcher raised his voice, "if it turns out that there's something wrong with the feed, your cooperation now will help you. I will do my best to see that the authorities know that you placed the public good over your loyalty to the company."

The grizzled man shuffled back and stared at us through the screen. He snorted a little laugh and opened the door. We gingerly walked in. The house reeked of mold and rotting things. With barely any furniture or bric-a-brac, it was empty of life, more like an abandoned place. I noticed furniture marks on the wall, suggesting where a bookcase, a couch, a table had once been. There was a child's crayon picture of a horse drawn on a small part of the wall near the stairway.

We followed Boynton into the kitchen, which was the only room with chairs. "Do you want some cool water? That's pretty much all I have." Opening the refrigerator revealed a space as bare, and dirty, as the house. The pitcher of water was even grimy. Boynton had the presence of mind to be embarrassed.

Fletcher offered, "I'm staying with Louis Moritz. Mr. McDermott told me your family had left. I'm sorry."

"It was a long time coming," he said gloomily. "She took everything and moved to Moncton. Took all the life from the house, as you can see." He snapped out of his bitter reverie and asked sharply, "What do you want to know?"

"What's in the feed besides herring and carotene?"

"Some binder to hold the stuff together and fish medicine."

"What type of binder and fish medicine?"

"I don't see anyone getting sick from a little corn syrup as a binder."

"Sir, and the fish medicine?" Fletcher's interrogating Boynton was tougher than pulling teeth, and Boynton's attitude didn't square with Louis's assessment that Boynton was cooperative. Perhaps his family problems were eating at him.

"A little cephalosporin to kill infections in the fish."

"I have not heard of it."

"It's a chemical formulation related to penicillin."

"Penicillin in high enough concentrations can cause a violent reaction in certain people." Fletcher became very aroused. "Indeed, anaphylactic shock, if I'm not mistaken. How much do you add?"

"One gram per one hundred thousand pounds of fish feed. Not enough to register in a human."

Fletcher continued. "Hypothetically, why would GFI add more?"

"Hypothetically, to keep the fish from dying if they were very sick."

"Hypothetically again. How much would they need to cure them?"

"Probably ten times the normal drug dose, maybe more."

Fletcher pressed Boynton. "Do they often get sick?"

"Sure. They're cooped up and in close quarters, so it's an excellent breeding ground for infections. But if they are sick, the operators are under orders to destroy them. Are we through? I don't know any more. I don't feed the goddamn fish."

"And if the dose were ten times greater, could humans have a reaction?"

"I'm not a medical doctor. I don't know. Your guess is as good as mine."

"Just a few more questions. How long have you worked for GFI?"

"Too long. I gave them my life. I have been working for GFI for thirty years." " I must ask," Fletcher found this line of questioning distasteful, "If you didn't like them, why did you continue to work for them? Surely you could find other employment."

"Let's just say I needed a job and I always had one here."

"One last question. Who checks on the level of cephalosporin in the fish?"

"That's Jared McDermott's job. He's got a test kit. If there's something wrong he notifies me. And he's never called me about a problem with the drug levels. Okay? Finished?"

"Yes, and thank you for your time."

We went straight to the police station. Fletcher explained to the chief that he suspected that the deaths were caused by overdoses of cephalosporin. "You need to know that these fish can be really lethal if drug loaded, and not only to people with allergies. If the concentration is very high, it's a threat to the general population."

"Mr. MacDonald, that is your contention. We have no proof," he said in a flat police manner. "Dr. Black did the autopsies, and he came to a different conclusion." When Fletcher started to protest, he raised a hand to stop him. "We will contact the appropriate health authorities and request that they investigate. But we cannot permit unsubstantiated accusations to be made that may damage a company's reputation and the economy of this island unnecessarily. You are an outsider here who has no idea of our life and needs. Everything you say is pure guesswork, maybe poppycock."

Fletcher sternly stated, "Dr. Black's motives are suspect. He has a lot of stock in GFI."

The captain angrily retorted, "Dr. Black has been the island's doctor for forty years. He has saved countless lives here, and there is not a one of us who doesn't owe him something. He is as good a man as one could ever find." He leaned slightly over his desk. "Are you going to say everybody on Grand Manan can't be trusted because they have an association with GFI?"

"What about Dr. Boynton? He has a record, doesn't he?"

Looking very surprised, the captain said, "That's over twenty-five years ago. How would you know that?"

Fletcher said, "A guess, frankly. What was it for?"

"He borrowed money under false pretenses. Got a year, served three months. He's been clean ever since."

"Captain," Fletcher said, appealing to the man's reason, "with a record like that, he'd have a hard time getting a scientist's job with a regular company. My guess is that GFI found it useful to have a biologist on staff who wouldn't make waves because he was so vulnerable. Someone who might look the other way about antibiotics."

"A lot of people have skeletons. He's been here for a long time, and he has never been in any serious trouble. You're still tilting at windmills."

"The public health requires that that risk of error be taken. Is it not far better to err on the side of caution to protect life? In just a few hours an independent laboratory in Moncton should be able to provide confirmation."

That option didn't appeal to him at all. "I am sorry. I will need more than a private lab report that may have been concocted to damage GFI. I'll need a government lab to substantiate your accusations. Right now," he informed us, "the government has said categorically that the fish are safe."

Fletcher protested, "Just because the fish have been tested before and passed doesn't mean they are safe today." He tried to make the captain see the bigger picture. "We need to be suspicious that, given the size of this operation, there may even be payoffs. This is a big business. The only way to protect the public is to shine a bright light on this so nobody can succeed at hiding anything."

The police officer folded his arms across his chest. "So, everybody is corrupt—GFI, Dr. Black, Dr. Boynton, the Canadian Fish Authority, and maybe me too!"

Off to the side, I said, "Fletcher, come on. Let's think this through. I talked with O'Brien, and he thinks he can have a report on the feed by three tomorrow. We can leave the island, go to the provincial and national authorities, and hold a press conference if the feed proves dangerous."

At that mention, Fletcher stood ramrod straight, holding his forehead "Damn! The clock for destruction of the evidence started ticking when we walked in here. We have to get to Dark Harbor right now."

Fiona had just arrived at the police station. We gathered her up and ran to the car.

Dusk was settling in. We screamed along Whistle Road. When we came to a straightaway down to the water, Fletcher didn't let up on the gas, braking only when we crossed over onto the pebble shore and literally stopped with the hubcaps in the mud.

Fletcher leapt out of the car. "We need a boat to get over to the pens."

I grabbed a flashlight, and we both waded out into the cold waters to the floating boats on the incoming tide, but they all had noisy outboards; none had oars. As we looked for a boat that suited our purposes, we began to see flashes in the water. They were caused by jumping fish.

Fletcher slammed the water with his fists. "Max, what do you hear?"

"Nothing but the sea and the splashing of fish. I looked at Fletcher in horror. "Oh, no!" The motors of the fish farm were silent. We flashed our light on the pens and found the sides were down; the fish had been released. We looked above the pens and saw that the lights were on in McDermott's shack. As we focused on his place, we saw him in silhouette stand up and go inside. Fletcher cupped his hands over his mouth and roared in McDermott's direction, "Right! The islanders come first! Baloney, Mr.

McDermott!" Fletcher's voice, I'm sure, carried across the harbor to its intended target.

We looked back and saw that our car was half underwater owing to the incoming tide. "Well, we are closer to our answer," Fletcher told me. We waded chest deep back to the shore.

Late that afternoon, back at Louis's place, Fletcher's cell phone rang. It was the scientist in Moncton. After he hung up, Fletcher turned to us. "Jack says that the fish feed had ten times the normal level of cephalosporin to fight fish infections. He also said that iodine potentiates the human thyroid and makes the body more sensitive to allergens like penicillin. He wondered if the victims had an exceptionally high sodium intake." Fletcher turned to Louis. "I'm now sure that anyone allergic to penicillin could die from eating the doctored GFI salmon, especially if the victims ingested a lot of iodine, such as in potato chips and other heavily salted food. Now I have to prove GFI did this routinely, but the evidence just swam away and I'm sure the rest of the feed disappeared as well. The company will say that the little feed sampling I got was a one-off."

Louis quietly contributed an important fact. "The chairman and founder of GFI, Arthur McDermott, has a summer place on the island. Do you think confronting him might be of any use?"

"Is he related to the guy in the shack?"

"Yeah, Jared is his half-wit brother."

Fletcher allowed himself a small smile. "This place, like many islands, is really inbred and shows it. Some other time let me educate you about how non-half-witted his brother is. Eccentric maybe, but no idiot. As to meeting King Arthur, does a lion like meat?"

Louis replied, "He's not very approachable, and he hasn't had anything to do with the business for years."

Fletcher harrumphed, "I doubt that. He probably knows everything that's going on. I'm sure he knows that I have his bloody company in my sights, courtesy of your local police chief, who probably tipped off his brother after we left, which explains why the fish were released. My guess is he would like to meet the trouble-makers head-on and bluff his way out one way or the other."

Louis called and to his surprise, but not Fletcher's, invited us all to dinner at nine that evening at the McDermott's. On the way over to the McDermotts', Fletcher asked Fiona again to go over what she had learned about the victims' eating habits.

"Pretty standard diet for a fishing community. Lot's of fish, generally pan fried. Big beer drinkers. For seasoning, they used local dulse. They chew it like jerky; an appetizer before dinner."

Fletcher asked in a low, even voice, "Did both victims eat dulse?"

"Yes. Both of their kitchen tables had glass bottles of the purple stuff. I tried it. It was awful, like eating a salty rubber band."

"Briny, huh?" Fletcher coaxed.

"Yes. Oh! You mean that's the extra sodium Jack was talking about. And they eat it as a snack food!" Fiona hit her head out of a sense of stupidity.

"Okay, now we know the medical connection. How to stop this is another matter."

Arriving at McDermott's mansion, we were greeted by a butler, Sebastian, and were escorted onto a terrace where we were greeted by Mrs. McDermott, a loud, statuesque, peroxide-blonde woman who rattled on with one non sequitur after another. She wore a getup fit for a swimming party, complete with high-heeled shoes with little powder puffs on them. Arthur appeared with a highball glass in his hand and met us heartily, giving Fiona a lascivious kiss on the hand. After the obligatory pouring of a round of drinks, we sat down to dinner.

Mrs. McDermott, or Suzy, got things off to an awkward start by saying sourly, "The only thing good about this island is leaving it. I don't know why my sweetie even comes here when we have such a beautiful home in London."

Louis interrupted, "Mrs. McDermott, it has its charms. Have you gone whale watching?"

Arthur jumped in. "We used to spend more time here when I was active in the business. Now I tend to my philanthropies and let the younger boys play at it. I occasionally offer my advice, but that's all. There are some mighty wonderful things about Grand Manan. Like dulse. I have been away for so long, I've gotten out of the habit of eating it. But, since we've been back, I have been gorging on it again. Sebastian, bring some dulse to the table for everyone." Sebastian brought in a large cut-glass bowl heaped with the shredded dark purple seaweed. The marine aroma overwhelmed the room.

Arthur began to chomp on the dulse while the main course of broiled salmon was delivered. "Suzy, we must always have some dulse on the table in London. I forgot how much I like it. It sharpens the taste." Suzy rolled her eyes.

Fletcher asked, "Is this GFI farm-raised salmon?"

"What else?" Best in the world, don't you think, Mr. MacDonald, or do you believe there is better? Try some dulse with it. It spikes it up like nothing else."

Fletcher moved forward in his seat, touched his brow, and raised his hand to a stop position, "Mr. McDermott, I must warn you that eating dulse and your salmon can be lethal. You've been adding too much antibiotic to the fish food to keep them alive, and when dulse and your salmon are combined it can cause anaphylactic shock. I'm serious. Please don't eat the salmon. I must insist."

"Hogwash, my friend. You and I will have a long talk after dinner, and I'll explain how things really are." Fletcher, lowered his hand, bowed his head, and receded into his chair, holding his chin in his hand. Arthur had a large portion of salmon on his fork and put it down. "Yes, I have heard that you have a bit of a problem with my operation. But before the evening is out, I think I will be able to convince you that your fears are misplaced." He gulped his fish down and followed it with another huge bite. Suzy dug into hers as well, but Fletcher, Fiona, Louis, and myself were far more restrained.

"Well, Mr. MacDonald, tell us a bit about the island you inhabit, Cape Breton, your famous Island in the Sea, as the shanty goes." Suddenly he coughed, and coughed again, and then grabbed for his glass of water and gagged. Fletcher told Louis, "Call the hospital! Tell the paramedics to bring epinephrine!"

Sebastian jumped to Arthur's assistance as he sagged to the floor, pulling the pastel tablecloth with him. Arthur's face turned blue, and his eyes and lips swelled as if he had been bitten by a bee. By the time the ambulance arrived, ten minutes later, Arthur was dead. The injection failed to revive him.

****

We waited, with Louis, for the ferry back to the mainland.

"I don't know how to thank you enough," Louis told us. Our police captain came to his senses with the death of Arthur McDermott. He raided a GFI warehouse that had tons of fish food. Initial testing points to all of it having massive amounts of cephalosporin.

"I'm sure further investigation will prove that GFI was using criminal amounts of antibiotics in the feed so they could raise more fish per pen then they should have." Fletcher commented. "I'm afraid we will never know if there was corruption up and down the system, but I'm sure that GFI will have to be closed for a while. For some like Dr. Black, Boynton, Jared McDermott, or even the police captain, it will be possible to explain away suspect actions or culpability as being prudent decisions that went awry. I suspect that the island is going to be hard hit for the time being. For that I am very sorry."

Louis cheerily said, "A cooperative of GFI employees and local fishermen, backed by the Island's government and the Chamber, has already petitioned the provincial government to allow them immediately to take over the salmon pens and raise the fish themselves while GFI's management is brought to justice. A sinking fund will be created so the cooperative can pay off GFI's creditors and acquire the equipment they have. The authorities have informally told us that the idea will receive a warm reception and forestall adding hundreds to the welfare rolls. So there may not be much of a delay in restarting and the jobs won't be lost, although there will be pay cuts for a while. You should feel pretty good that things might be a lot better for your having come here and shaken things up. Not to mention those who won't die or become terribly sick. You all did a great job."

The ferry arrived and soon Grand Manan began to recede

from us. We could see a weir being worked by a small boat. I turned to Fiona and joked, "Fletcher is probably the only fish who can swim into one of those and swim back out."

FEAST AT THE ALHAMBRA

Alfred Titus looked uncomfortable sitting in Fletcher's study at Mabou Point on Cape Breton. A bald man, he wore a black suit, a white shirt with a dark blue tie, and black shoes—positively funereal. He sat with his hands folded on top of a large, black attaché case. "Mr. MacDonald," he said, opening up the case, "this may be another clue to the disappearances, yet we can't connect it." With some difficulty he wrested a twelve inch long bone from the case and extended it to Fletcher.

"This is the femur of a child, probably ten years of age. It was found on the doorstep to the main police station in Granada a few months ago. You will see that it has the name 'Enrique' carved into it. DNA testing has not revealed a connection to any known missing person. The scientists have determined that the child was alive within the last two years, maybe less. You'll notice that it is, well, fresh for a bone."

Fletcher was holding a glass of Chardonnay. He arched his eyebrows, put down his glass, and rather reluctantly took the bone from Alfred. He turned it in his hands and examined the carved name. He slowly traced each letter with his index finger. Holding it delicately by both ends, he handed it to me. "Max, what do you say about the carved letters?"

I felt squeamish about even holding the specimen, since the crime it suggested was so ghoulish. I could almost feel the life of the child in the bone. Still, I peered at it closely. "Looks like the work of a penknife."

Fletcher smiled indulgently. "Ah, Max, you do not go far enough. The tool is crude, but notice the style. The height and spacing of the letters are nearly identical. A printer would say that the font is consistent. This carving is the work of a perfectionist, albeit using a poor tool. This was the work of someone who values excellence." Fletcher walked over to his window and stood looking out onto the gray sea.

"Max," he said, "do you want another glass of Chardonnay? How about you, Alfred?"

I said, "Don't mind if I do." I returned the bone to Alfred, who had shaken his head to indicate that he didn't want another. Alfred returned the bone to his case and with great ceremony closed the two clasps. He was clearly waiting for an answer from Fletcher. Would he take the assignment?

Alfred was with the Canadian Security and Intelligence Service (CSIS). He had sought out Fletcher to go to Spain to investigate the unexplained disappearance of several adult tourists: four Canadians, two Americans, and an Englishwoman. There were no traces of them and no ransoms demanded. They all had gone to the city of Granada, and several were known to have visited the Alhambra there, the palace and citadel of the Moorish kings. They never returned to their hotel rooms. They just vanished.

The tourists were more dissimilar than not: various socioeconomic strata, disparate ages, both sexes, differing political stripes none of which were extreme, five whites, an Asian, and an African-American. Their families were demanding an explanation, and the press was ridiculing the government in Ottawa about the lack of progress in solving the case. Great pressure was being placed on the police and the CSIS by the prime minister. He was convinced that this was a terrorist action aimed at westerners, although there wasn't a scintilla of evidence of that. No one had claimed any responsibility for the disappearances. There was, until possibly this bone, only one grim commonality. Within a few days of each disappearance, pig blood would be found in the beautiful central fountain and watercourses of the Alhambra and smeared over the doors of the Church of Salvador located in the Albacin, the ancient Moorish quarter that overlooks the Alhambra and its garden, the Generalife. Thus, both the Catholic and the Islamic faiths seemed to be targeted, which added to the inspector's puzzlement.

This wasn't the first time CSIS had enlisted Fletcher's services. The latest was a conspiracy by right-wing Quebec extremeists to blow up Parliament. In that case, Fletcher had infiltrated the malefactors' world and learned of their weaknesses, and with that knowledge the authorities had been able to destroy the fanatics' operations. CSIS was convinced that Fletcher's uncommon chameleon-like abilities were the perfect fit for this operation, for they suspected that these abductions, if that was what they were, were committed by a group, not an individual, whose purpose and goals were unknown.

"Alfred, how is this gruesome evidence connected to the tourists' vanishing?"

"Tangentially at best. I guess the insanity of it all is the correlation. The disappearances, the pig blood, and the carved human bone don't literally connect, but I can't help but think that the extremity of it all does. Do you see?"

Fletcher sat down next to his world globe, spun it about a bit, and said, "I do see, and I sense you may be right. Perhaps the absence of rationality will lead us to the solution." He stopped the globe's spinning with a light tap of his finger. "If we look solely at the disappearances, this is clearly not the work of an organization with a monetary objective, since there have been no demands. We can rule out a gang or criminal enterprise. The abductions, if that is what they are, are too perfect—no traces, no bodies—for them to be the work of hooligans. That leaves zealotry of some sort as a motivator. And that points to religion or politics. If politics, where is the play for power? Religion seems more likely, despite the apparent insult to two central faiths that the blood-smearing incident suggests."

Fletcher manipulated the globe and brought Spain into focus. He rubbed his brow.

"The Alhambra, what do we know of it? It was part of the Islamic Caliphate in the thirteenth century, and therefore the area is suffused in Islamism. Across from the Alhambra and actually overlooking it stands the conquering Catholic Church, epitomized by the Church of Salvador of the Albacin. The ritual pig sacrifices—a taboo animal in Islam—I think rules out the work of Muslims. They wouldn't despoil one of the great edifices of their illustrious past with the blood of an unclean animal. And would devout Catholics desecrate a church? No. But someone who believes that both these faiths are wrongheaded might. Max and I have dealt with all manner of criminals—kooks, psychopaths, and sociopaths—but there is no madness like the type that is driven by the belief that one is acting in the name of God. I have grappled with those who use religion as a cover for some other obsession or scheme, but this subterfuge collapses for lack of discipline.

True religious zealots are in a class by themselves. They are not deterred by the loss of possessions, loved ones, or life itself. This case may be driven by that type of blind faith, because, as I have said, there have been no demands. Instead, we get abstract messages: the pig blood and maybe the bone." He adduced an additional factor. "Abduction is an expensive activity, fraught with tension, especially if they keep their victims alive for a while. There must be a very keenly felt raison d'être driving this, which will make it difficult to root out."

"And if it is religious, does that deter you from taking on the assignment?" Alfred questioned.

Fletcher went on as though he hadn't heard. "Imagine trying to convince the pope to disavow the Catholic Church. That's the measure of the order when dealing with true believers. At least the adherents will be fanatic enough so we can tell by a special madness in their eyes. That can't be hidden long from the careful observer." He was pleased by that notion, and he came over to clasp the inspector on the shoulder. "Sign us up."

****

We could see the Albacin from the archetypical Moorish arches of the Alhambra. Across the ravine rose the terraced ancient quarter of Albacin. The high, blazing white sun made each of the houses into alabaster two-story igloos, all with dusty-pink terra cotta roofs. My eye wandered up the serpentine streets, reaching a high, flat area where the Church of Salvador looked over the Alhambra.

The Alhambra itself was a breathtaking architectural masterpiece. Layer by layer we beheld an increasingly intricate and lacey decorative style. Given the mammoth size of the palace, it was, on close inspection, remarkably delicate. Its many columns were more spindle-like than the heavy-footed variety normally associated with grandeur of this magnitude. Every room had a wooden ceiling carved with the epitome of arabesque designs. Some ceilings were so festooned with carvings that they hung down like stalactites. Other ceilings were brilliant night skies with never ending constellations to marvel at. The overall quality was one of lightness and porosity. The conquering Spanish must have felt that their drab blocky fortresses were quite barbaric in comparison with this exquisite artfulness.

Fletcher was particularly interested in the watercourses, grooves really, that connected the entire palace. These rivulets traversed the palace floor plan like arteries, lazily but inexorably leading from one room to the next and to fountains that acted as pumping hearts. He pointed to one room that, according to our guidebook, was known to be an execution chamber. He remarked that it was designed to allow the poor soul's blood to be mixed with the water in the courses, to be carried along to the outside garden and fountains and then dispersed throughout the palace through many little canals. He imagined that within a few minutes of an execution, all the water courses would turn pale pink to announce the act. And if there were several executions, the announcement would be very red indeed. How interesting a concept to announce the ultimate power of the Caliphate so profoundly, yet with just a rippling sound flowing from point to point, with the color change being the messenger of sealed fate. He conjured up the image of a cluster of household retainers and how they would feel as they went about their daily business in the palace, beholding that the water so benignly playing about them would turn light red from time to time. When would it be their own blood that would color the waters?

At dusk the doors to the Alhambra were locked, so we took the opportunity to visit the Albacin across the ravine. Small cafes amid the dwellings created a warren of activity. We stopped on a wide public terrace that overlooked the ravine, with the Alhambra in the distance, to watch the twilight descend and to have a light supper at a café on the corner. There were a few tourists, but mostly only locals padded along the narrow streets. Small groups, twos and threes, of beggar children—grubby ripped clothes, dirty hair, bare feet, and big black eyes—came up and wheedled for money. The children were persistent, like flies on food. Fletcher seemed remarkably patient and generous with them; perhaps he, like me, reflected on the child's bone that Arnold had presented to us back in Inverness. The waiters gruffly shooed them off, but they would soon return only to be waved off again and again.

Three street musicians set up shop on the other side of the terrace from the café: a bass, a violin, and a cello played by two men and a woman dressed in loose-fitting black clothes. With the last light of day, they played chamber music—pieces as gentle as the breezes that drifted by.

Just as the dark shadow of night gripped the terrace, they changed their tempo and plunged into Ravel. The air became singed with the passion and melancholy of his stirring works. Fletcher vigorously applauded them, even rising to his feet as he did so. He invited them to join us for drinks. They were in their mid-twenties and terribly thin, bordering on being emaciated. They were French but spoke good enough English for us to all communicate easily.

Looking to Fletcher for approval, I asked them, "Will you have dinner with us?" Fletcher nodded his enthusiastic endorsement.

The men exchanged embarrassed looks, but the woman, grabbing the hands of her fellow musicians, said, "We would be most honored and thankful to share a meal with you. We play for money, but sometimes it is not forthcoming, like tonight."

Fletcher was entranced with them. "You play beautifully, with haunting fervor and pathos. I was particularly fascinated by your adaptation of the Ravel A-minor piano trio. I hardly missed the Steinway!" Everyone laughed at Fletcher's informed little joke. He beamed a wide, engaging smile, showing great empathy for these street musicians. Perhaps his feelings sprang from his love of playing the fiddle back in Cape Breton.

The male cellist said, "This restaurant would have been packed at this time last year. But since the disappearances, the number of tourists is down by half."

Seizing the opportunity, I asked, "Do you have any idea what is happening? Are there any local theories?"

The musicians eyed one another. The bassist nodded his head and spoke. "We have a theory, but no one believes us. We have even told the police, but they blew it off." He pointed downward. "There is a very deep ravine between the Albacin and the Alhambra. From here to the Alhambra gardens is almost a mile, although it looks closer. And the ravine drops a thousand feet before it rises up to the Alhambra. You can observe it well from this terrace. The sides and floor of the ravine are, as you can see, full of the thickest trees and brambles. Tourists are often tempted to cross the ravine as a shortcut from here to the Alhambra and vice versa. Most soon find out how impassable it is and give up. Some do press on, but rarely do they emerge on the other side. Instead they follow the streambed at the bottom and come out at the highway in Granada.

The food and drink came. We were all intrigued by this local knowledge and urged him to continue. Digging in, he said, "Granada, like all cities, has its slums and poor. It has street kids who are orphaned and have no homes. They don't go to school. They beg or steal to stay alive. Their clothes are rags and they are completely wild. Some of them are said to live in little more than burrows in the ravine. They lead a miserable life and are despised by the townspeople. The locals stay away from this area for fear of being robbed. We think that these street kids may have become feral and even cannibalistic. That's the reason these tourists disappear."

I dropped my fork. "You can't mean that they ate the tourists."

"That is exactly what we think. Wild as dogs."

Fletcher and I looked at each. We were both thinking of the femur that Alfred showed us. Was there a connection? Did these wild children perhaps prey on one another? Speaking of food, the musicians ate quickly though decorously. In half the time that Fletcher and I consumed our food, they were finished. Fletcher put a hundred euro note into the hand of the violinist. She demurely thanked him with her eyes. "May we play for you a selection of your choosing?" she asked. "You have been so kind." Fletcher said, "Thank you, but how about tomorrow? We would have the anticipation of your exquisite playing to pull us forward through the day. If you can manage it, a chamber music version of

Czech composer Smetana's Moldau would be marvelous. And we would want you to join us for dinner."

"We are fond of the Moldau. It's rhapsodic and very much for the people. We will look for you here around seven. Okay?"

"Yes," Fletcher said, "you can count on it."

They gathered up their instruments and bade us good-bye. We watched them make their way down the steep streets until they disappeared.

"I know you love the Moldau, but it's a symphonic work, hardly fit for chamber music."

Fletcher waved away the objection. "Oh, stripped to its basic melodic line, it is haunting even played on a single instrument. And it's a challenge, isn't it?"

My thoughts returned to the more disturbing part of our dinner conversation. "What do you make of their theory of the cannibalistic street children? If there was anything to it, the police and Interpol would have cleared out that ravine in no time." I dismissed it, but I wasn't sure that Fletcher had.

Fletcher leaned back and mused, "Our young musicians didn't come up with that story on their own. I'm sure that everyone knows that the street kids live in the ravine. What was unusual was the strong hint of empathy for the kids' plight. Notice they said that the urchins live a miserable life and are despised by the locals. Our musicians were sympathizing with them. Maybe they also identified with them." I nodded in agreement. "Street musicians come in contact with tourists more than most, and they know what's really going on in the streets, because that is their territory. I think we need to pay attention to what they said."

Fletcher called to the waiter, who spoke some English, "The musicians say that the street kids killed the tourists. What do you think?"

The waiter shook his head. "Street musicians are a crazy lot. They tell wild stories to make interesting tales for tourists like you. There's nothing to it. The kids might steal but not kill. Anyway, there are too many rats, big rats, in the ravine. Not even the kids live down there. It's too dangerous."

As I suspected and feared, the next day Fletcher proposed that we walk through the blasted ravine, from the Albacin side over to the Alhambra. We donned long pants, hiking boots, and desert jackets for the assault. It was hot even early in the morning, so our garb was already taxing. The downward trip took us on a zigzag route. The sides of the ravine were littered with trash—rusting car engines, cans, tires, plastic bags. The rats were there too. I could see them from the corner of my eye. Sometimes they would walk across our path, not at all inhibited by our presence. They were as large as small dogs. A few dead ones lay bloated from the hot sun. The brush grew over our heads, and the brambles and vines became almost impassable. I could walk on a rat and not even know it until it was too late. A machete would have been useful. Fletcher kept pushing ahead, deeper and deeper, his goal being the dry streambed that drained the ravine. We lost visual contact with the Alhambra, which we knew was somewhere high above us. The underbrush remained thick, and frankly we couldn't see much. We did find many animal tracks in the sand: rats, rabbits, birds, and dogs.

After pushing ahead like this for nearly an hour, the sides gave way to a flat area, where feathery, dusty trees shielded the floor and us from the harsh sun. There was less garbage and trash, but it still seemed to be a wasteland of forgotten things. Fletcher pointed down. I saw the tread of shoes, probably sneakers. Fletcher motioned with his hands that they were large. Indeed, they belonged not to a child but to an adult. We began to follow them. They led up the ravine, rather than down, away from Granada. Grasses began to replace the brush, and the footprints disappeared into a cow path that was quite worn.

Suddenly Fletcher froze, held up his hand, with his finger to his lips for me to remain silent. Then I heard it too. The wistful refrain of the Moldau played on a violin. We must have been only a hundred yards from the source, which we surmised had to be our musicians. We stepped carefully forward. We could now hear the other two instruments as well, but we were too far away to see the musicians. Fletcher sat down on the ravine floor, his back against a willow tree, in full sunlight, to listen to the plaintive music. I remained standing, still being apprehensive about the rats and the unknowns of the ravine. The musicians were playing each movement with great pathos. It was given to the violinist to play the nostalgic refrain, of the great river sweeping by Prague, under the Charles Bridge. It was a piece that Fletcher often played on his fiddle to a recording. He said that it was magical music that would carry him through time to distant places, often entirely new to him. After several minutes, Fletcher rose and we continued to probe.

We kept our distance from the musicians by making a wide circle, hoping to catch a glimpse of them without revealing our presence. At last, through a break in the trees and brush, we saw them. Astonishingly they were completely naked. Their black clothes lay in piles near music stands. After the Moldau, they played Albinoni's adagios. They played with great intensity, despite the heat of the noonday sun. Their nakedness created the sense of a Renaissance painting of mythological beings frolicking in a dell. Their music became ever more alluring and mystical, and now I wanted to stay and listen. I was nodding approval of the scene, but Fletcher put a finger to his lips and pointed ahead. He was clearly on the hunt. Then I heard it, too, a rustling in the brush. In a flash, Fletcher leapt and fell upon something, but I lost sight of him. Coming to the spot where he had disappeared, I saw that he had pinned to the ground a wiggling boy of ten to twelve years of age. A knife with a broad, foot-long blade lay on the ground. I picked it up. Its point was bloody.

"He's been following us." Fletcher was trying to catch his breath and hold the struggling child down. Blood was oozing from a gash on his hand. "Do you live here? Vive usted aqui?" Fletcher asked.

"No, no, esta es casa de Diablo. Diablo vive en caverna," the child sputtered. "I not hurt you. Just need money."

"Toma nostros a caverna de Diablo. Fifty euros." Fletcher let the boy up but held him firmly with one hand. "Max, show this street rat fifty euros." Fletcher's hand was dripping blood. I held the knife in plain view to show that we weren't in any mood to negotiate. I took control of the boy while Fletcher tore off part of his shirt and used it as a bandage. "He says that the devil lives in a cave here. He'll take us there. Just hang on to the knife. He's not above using it on us." Fletcher motioned to the boy to bring us to the cave. "La Caverna, prisa!"

The boy scrambled forward and took us under the back cliffs of the Alhambra, at least a mile and a half from any road. The sound of the music was long gone. It continued to be a wild, over-grown place with thick brush everywhere and no apparent housing of any sort, not even a shack. The cliffs rose perpendicular right to the Alhambra from where we stood. It would not be possible to scale them, for they were too sheer. We walked around the base of the cliffs, looking for a way up. I calculated that to reach the palace on top, we would have to climb a thousand feet almost straight up. The rock was soft sedimentary, and it crumbled at the touch.

The boy took us to a small opening in the cliff wall, largely ob-scured by brush and a large tree. It looked like a cave portal, but only about four feet high. On the ground, in front of the opening, there were many human footprints, some similar to the sneaker prints we had seen before. We ventured into the opening. I turned on my flashlight and saw that the cave had considerable depth. "Caverna de Diablo," the boy announced. "Fifty euros and my knife, por favor." Fletcher gave him the money but not the knife. The boy began to protest, but Fletcher gave him a look that set him running. Fletcher said, "From even a short distance, this opening would vanish from sight because it is so unprepossessing. It could-n't be seen from the Alhambra, and it's just above the brush line, on the back side of the cliff, so one wouldn't see it from the Al-bacin or even if one were walking in the ravine. You would have to be looking for it." He pondered the matter some more and then mused, "It could be the entrance to an escape tunnel from the Al-hambra. Its architects would have certainly introduced many es-cape routes for the kings who lived here. This may have been one. Let's see where it leads." As we went deeper, the cave opening gave way to a large room in which we could stand. It had a foot-wide shaft of daylight in one corner, coming down from a hole ex-iting to the outside. It was cool and dark inside except for our flashlights and the tube of sunlight. The room was about twenty feet square, with an eight-foot-high ceiling. The floor was broom-brushed clean and tidy. Oil lanterns hung from the ceiling, and flashlights were neatly stacked like firewood in one corner. Three mattresses, books in French and English, magazines, some basic tools, a chipped wooden chest, and neatly stacked clothes filled out the room. Under the light shaft was a metal grill set atop a circle of rocks filled with the remnants of burned wood. Various pots, pans, kettles, and scavenged cooking implements were nearby. We went over to the wooden chest.

Opening it, we discovered many human femur bones of different lengths. Carved into each one was a name. Sick with shock, we conducted the loathsome task of looking for what we hoped that we would not find. But unfortunately the third name we saw was "Ernest," one of the Canadians who was missing. There were thirty-five bones, clearly some of children. But most belonged to adults, including "Judith," "Frank," "Roberto," "Cicely," "Geoff," and "Arthur." All the victims who constituted our assignment were here.

Fletcher quickly orchestrated the next steps. "We must take the bones of the people identified by CSIS with us and find the authorities as fast as we can. I don't think it is wise to go out the way we came in, because whoever lives here may return this way. I am sure that there must be a route up to the gardens of Generalife or the Alhambra from this room, perhaps through a tunnel."

As I cast my flashlight around the room to look for another exit, the beam caught a full-length mirror with a wooden frame. To one side of it were black robes hanging from pegs in the rock walls. As I stood in front of the mirror, I saw that the frame was hanging on hinges, like a door. I pulled on it. At first it didn't move. I applied more force, and it grudgingly swung open, revealing another space behind it. Cold, sulfuric air tumbled out. I backed away, fearing that the air was poisonous.

At that moment, Fletcher announced that he had found a passageway up. I told him that I wanted to explore what was behind this door first. I took a deep breath, shined my light into the space, and took a step through the doorjamb, only to stumble and fall into a void. I saved myself from what was below by holding on to the side of the wall. My flashlight fell and exploded into blue and yellow bubbling light as it hit water or something else not too far down. The gas was suffocating. I yelled for Fletcher, who appeared behind me in an instant, grasping my wrists with his iron grip. He screamed at me, "Don't breathe. It's sulfur."

He dragged me from the edge, back into the room, and closed the mirror door. My lungs were burning and aching. Fletcher doused my face with water from a barrel in the room. "Keep wetting your face and nostrils. Blow into this cloth. Try and clear your nose and sinuses of all the sulfur particles you may have breathed in. Don't breathe deeply. Take shallow breaths. Keep expelling what air is in your lungs in short blasts."

By degrees the burning sensation ebbed, and I soon felt that the worst was over. "I think I'm all right."

"That was close, Max. That's a lime and sulfur pit. Any living matter—bone, flesh, hair—would be dissolved in a few hours. Not a trace left." He paused, then repeated himself. "Not a trace left. So that's it."

"What do you mean?"

"The murderers disposed of the bodies in the pit. They kept the femurs as sick souvenirs." I made a face at that, and Fletcher became concerned all over again. "Are you strong enough to walk?" Woozily I stood up and realized that a deep breath still felt like a blowtorch in my lungs. "I'll be all right if I don't inhale too deeply."

Fletcher led me to the passageway he had discovered. We climbed up stairs that had been cut into the rock and ascended almost straight up. The space was more than ample. Every twenty feet or so were flat places to rest. As Fletcher had surmised, this seemed to have the accouterments of a royal escape route.

We started to hear a strange, mechanical heaving from above. Rhythmically it would breathe in and then exhale like a giant bellows. It grew louder as we kept spiraling up. Finally we hit a stone wall that blocked our passage. On the other side was the heart of the mysterious breathing sound. There appeared to be no mortar in the stonework that blocked the way, so we began the process of taking it apart. After an hour, we had dislodged enough stone to feel the rush of fresh air and to see an electric light. The heaving sound became sharp. We redoubled our efforts and made an opening large enough to crawl through. We passed into a chamber that contained a great cylinder that rose and fell, creating the bellows sound. Fletcher yelled to me that this was an electric pump for the watercourses in the Alhambra. He motioned for me to walk around the cylinder. I could see that it was drawing a large bucket of water up from a dark place and then pouring it into a receiving pool that overflowed into a shoot. He yelled over the machinery, "They probably had this powered by slaves or animals before electricity."

We climbed a ladder to a wooden hatchway above the apparatus and pushed through it. To the surprise of gawking tourists in the Alhambra, we emerged in the middle of a pathway near the great central fountain, probably looking like coal miners with a strange and frightening find: several long femur bones.

We hurried to find the Alhambra reception area and had them call the police. We explained who we were, our mission, and what we had found. The police cleared the palace and began to assemble a SWAT team to corner the cave denizens from the ravine as well as from the palace itself. By the time the police were ready to make their assault, about two hours had passed. Several helicopters had been buzzing the ravine, seeking out persons with heat sensors. The place had been entirely cleared of people. Hundreds of police on foot were swarming through the ravine, and specially trained cave fighters who had fought the Basque separatists were ready to go down the way we came. Whoever called the cave home and might have returned there was trapped.

Fletcher and I watched the action from a room in the Alhambra that overlooked the Albacin and the ravine. Suddenly he grabbed my arm and dragged me over to the watercourse that bisected the room. "Look," he cried. "It runs red...it runs red!" We ran out to the great fountain, and indeed the crystal waters were pink. From each side of the fountain the troughs were running light red, and soon the entire palace would be crisscrossed by the ribbons of blood.

Fletcher spoke to the chief of the police and told him that he thought someone had probably committed suicide in the pump room and that the cave searchers should go there without delay. We swiftly opened the trapdoor in the plaza to go down ourselves. Below, we came upon the three musicians. Their bodies were floating in the overflow tank, their wrists and throats clearly slashed in a mutual suicide pact. The world would never be sure of what drove them to this barbarism. Fletcher noted to me as we viewed the grisly sight. "I suspected that the tale they told us last night was more true than false, except that they were starving too, along with the homeless children. Unfortunately, they crossed the moral divide, not the children. A partial confession of sorts to clear their souls. I have no doubt that some tourists wandered into the ravine, where they were easy prey. These ghouls took their money, sold their jewelry and whatever else they could, and then, I think, eliminated what was left of them in the pit. Judging by the smaller bones, I think they preyed on the street kids as well. That's why the boy called it the El Diablo's Caverna."

"But why cannibalism?"

"Terrible things start small. The musicians were certainly hungry, and probably one of the street kids was found dead somehow. Then the musicians did the unthinkable, and it became a way to survive. And maybe they grafted onto it a pseudo-religious-political rationale to justify their actions."

Alfred was waiting for us at the airport in Halifax. "That was a great job, men. You really pulled this together fast. What good luck that you stumbled on to them on your first evening."

"Good luck?" Fletcher exclaimed. "When one is powerfully searching for the solutions to a problem, the very effort attracts the facts. This happens routinely." He was enjoying himself, explicating another of his mystical theories. "You see, when you know what you are looking for, it comes to you, like a heat-sensing rocket. Human beings always want to be noticed for what they do, even the worst. They seek others' admiration, even for horrendous deeds. It is human nature. One just has to be open to being there and to see the signs people leave in their seeking to be noticed. No, Alfred, it was not blind luck at all. Attract the facts, and when those facts present themselves, one must follow them to their ultimate end. If CSIS could ever understand that part of intelligence, then they would have the right to use the name intelligence in the lofty title."

The inspector was quite overwhelmed by this outburst. "No offense, Fletcher. Really good work."

"I cannot be offended by stupidity, only brilliance unnecessarily illuminating my own flaws."

"But there is one thing the office would like to know. Do you think they were part of a wider conspiracy that poses a threat in the West? That type of violence just can't be allowed." Fletcher didn't answer but made his way to the rental car that would take us back to Inverness. Alfred persisted, however. "Fletcher, should we set up a team to look into the possibility that these musicians were part of a larger conspiracy?" Fletcher swung around and grabbed Alfred by the lapels of his black raincoat. "Look, there was no conspiracy. These were people who played beautiful music. They just didn't know how to get along in a less beautiful world and stumbled into a moral abyss. We all live closer to the edge then we care to admit. Let it go."

DOUBLE DOWN

"Fletcher! Fletcher!" I shouted, cupping my hands around my mouth to aim my voice up to his third-floor study. I pounded on his door. He had this maddening habit of getting so caught up in thinking that he would wall out the outside world. He ignored the telephone, so driving the ten miles from Inverness to Mabou and making a five-alarm fire racket was the only way to bring him around when he was in this state. This day, I resorted to throwing rocks at his windows, and I didn't care if I broke one.

Slowly, a side pane opened. A desultory, annoyed voice drifted down to me: "What on earth do you want, Max?" But there was no face to go with it.

"You have an offer of a huge fee, but you have to respond today. We need to talk. Open the door."

Ever since Fletcher's reputation for resolving problems has grown worldwide, I have been handling his calls and business matters from my travel agency. He didn't want to be on the receiving end of requests for his services, nor did he want to negotiate fees. He had even less interest in keeping accounts and the other minutiae of business life. I agreed to handle all of these matters, including filtering out wacky calls and reducing the legitimate inquiries to a short list from which he could choose his next engagement. He works seriatim: never more than one project at a time. The twenty percent commission he insisted that I take for my services was generous and greatly exceeded my income at the agency. Even better, I, and sometimes my wife Fiona, often accompany Fletcher on these trips while Stan Hope, formerly owner of the travel agency until I bought him out, covers for us at the office. These have been some of my most fascinating experiences. We've been working this way for twenty years: not partners, but colleagues and good friends.

As I waited for Fletcher to open the door, I was captivated all over again by the view from this ancient stone house at Mabou. Sited on a bluff overlooking the Northumberland Strait as it opens to the Gulf of St. Lawrence, the sea appears infinite, as if I were on the bridge of a great ship sailing the whole universe. This view, the warm afternoon summer sun, and the lush natural grass made this perch a wonderful place for a picnic.

"I was immersed in a very interesting subject. This had better be worth it," growled Fletcher as he unbolted and threw open the front door. He was disheveled, seemed groggy, and clearly hadn't shaved in a few days. He had his hat pulled low over his face, perhaps thinking it hid his dissolute appearance.

"Is a $250,000 retainer worth it...already wired into the bank?" I snapped.

He was unimpressed. "Not really. How many beds can a man sleep in at one time?" Finally he relented, motioning for me to enter. "But let's hear more, since I won't be able to recapture the interesting spell I was in. Come upstairs. Will you have something to drink? I'm going to have a glass of that delicious Chardonnay from the Okanagan Valley. I have enough left for two glasses. Or are you a teetotaler today?" He knew me better than that. "After the frustration of trying to get you on the phone, that sounds like a just reward. I was just thinking how nice a picnic would be today on your point. Maybe I should call Fiona and have her join us."

Fletcher almost gasped. "No, no, look at me, I can't be seen by your marvelous wife." His eyes pleaded for understanding. The afternoon sun caught Fletcher straight on, warming up that pale, gaunt face. Whatever he had been reading had drained his energy.

Shaking his head, he gave me his backside, left the door open, and plodded his way up the circular narrow stone stairs to his study. It could only be reached by a stone tower that had long, skinny slat windows overlooking the sea. Even during daylight, the staircase was dungeon gloomy, like the bottom of a deep well.

Conversely, Fletcher's study itself was a basket of light, with windows on all sides, illuminating unparalleled chaos. In one corner, a daybed was spread with a blanket of papers, books, and magazines. A brass telescope, set atop a wooden tripod like a small cannon, pointed to the sea. In the center of the chaos was a ping-pong table-size desk with precariously tilting stacks of papers and books laced with bric-a-brac. His gigantic Funk and Wagnall's dictionary, affectionately known as the "Big Dick," rested on its own stand.

He had a three-foot-diameter globe dating to 1932, which could be fully spun and tilted on its axis. New countries and border changes were made with red washable-ink markers, so it had a graffiti-like appearance. He placed pins with colored heads to mark all the places he had been: white pins designated assignments, red pins pleasure visits, and black pins were a mystery to me even after twenty years. Above the large, open fireplace, a broad, wooden mantel held pictures of his forebears. Those of his immediate family, whom he had lost at sea, were all clustered in the middle. I have always been pleased that next to these family shots he added one of me, Fiona, and himself, taken when we were in Arles, France, working on the van Gogh lost painting matter.

I noticed a large, pearly pink conch shell I hadn't seen before sitting on a windowsill. "Fletcher, what significance, if any, does this conch shell have for you?" He rattled around the little kitchenette and produced two crystal wine goblets whose deep facets winked in the intense light. He poured out the contents of the Chardonnay, patiently holding the bottle upside down until the last amber drop fell into the glass.

"I picked that up on my trip to Carriacou. Surely you remember my zombie encounter. It reminds me never to scoff at even the most implausible explanations, for there may be a natural law at work with which even I am unfamiliar. As I recall, you were a little unsure as to my mental status after that eye-opener."

Then he held up the wineglass. "To friendship!" Fletcher seemed brighter as he made his toast.

The wine had an uncommonly rich, buttery texture, coating the mouth, throat, and esophagus with a layer of warmth as it trickled down the gullet. "Ah," I said, "this is a distinctive Chardonnay: hearty, clearly North American, not in the French tradition. Groundbreaking. A great discovery." I raised my glass in appreciation.

Fletcher swirled the sparkling liquid around in his glass, placed his nose deep inside, and took a long sip. "So, what's worth $250,000?"

"Ah, yes, the business at hand. I received a frantic call from a Mr. George Taylor, a lawyer representing the Calvert Brothers, Richard and Stanley, who own the Eldorado Casino in Las Vegas. Apparently a blackjack player beat them out of six million dollars, and they want you to find out how he did it. If he's just been lucky, they don't want to ban him, because if they do, they will never get their money back. And if he's cheating, they'll have him arrested and get back their money via the courts."

"God bless him...win another six million! What do we know about him?" Fletcher seemed now more than a bit interested. I could tell by the energy and crispness that had come into his voice.

"We received a memo from Stanley Calvert that documents the playing history of the winner. I'll read you the key parts:

"The player, Eric Bamba, is an American, about thirty years old, from Los Angeles. Parents are Mexican, from Oaxaca. Until recently he held a low-level kitchen job in a big Las Vegas hotel restaurant. No criminal record. He started playing blackjack at the Eldorado about a year ago, coming in around midnight, after work. Just a $2 dollar-a-hand player with no special ability or any luck. He lost at the rate we expected, about $25 to $50 a night. His only peculiarity was a habit of humming to himself, which occasionally annoyed the players next to him.

One night his luck abruptly changed. He won over $1,000, still betting at most $50 a hand. His big wins were on double downs and splits. This went on for about two weeks, putting him ahead about $6,000, a very big win for a small bettor. Emboldened, he moved over to the $100-minimum table and played a few hands at $100. Then he pulled out an envelope full of cash and made a $5,000 bet, the table maximum, and caught a double down opportunity He increased his wager to $10,000, which he won and left immediately after. He came in the next night and again made a maximum bet that became a double down opportunity. He won it and left after winning the bet. We looked over the videotapes of his play, checked out the dealers, and concluded that he had not been obviously cheating or counting cards but had just been lucky.

He now was ahead roughly $30,000 over three weeks. The next change in his strategy was to continue to play even after he had one big win. Almost like clockwork, he would bounce his bet up to the $5,000 level twice an hour, get the double down opportunity, and win. The rest of the time he played $100 and lost at the expected rate. Obviously we were watching him closely, but we decided to let him play, presuming that he would eventually lose back his winnings. By the end of the graveyard shift, around 10 a.m. the next day, he had amassed $200,000. We had the videotapes of his play scrutinized by pros who earn their living detecting cheats. We even scanned Bamba for RF signals to see if he was wired for computer play or if he was communicating with someone electronically. He was clean. The experts said he was just uncannily beating the probability of winning on the double downs and splits. The pros are sure that he is not counting cards, because he often increases his bet when the deck is not to his advantage."

"Was he still humming while playing?" Fletcher asked, amused. "I would have been laughing. Go, on Max, I rather like our Mr. Bamba."

"At this point, there was another major turn of events. Bamba came in at midnight and asked the shift manager if he could make a $100,000 bet whenever he felt like it. This was over the table maximum and required special permission. We decided that if we didn't let him, he would go someplace else and lose it, so we raised his maximum allowable bet to $100,000. All night long he played and won every $100,000 bet he placed, about $1.5 million in one night. By this time we were in so deep, we didn't dare stop his play.

The next day, he shifted his playing pattern again. He came in at 4 a.m. with $200,000 and played for one hour. He won another $200,000 and left. Since then he has been coming in for one hour, once a week, always at 4 a.m., and picking up between $100,000 and $400,000 every session. We are now out $6 million."

"That's the end of the memo. They found you through Albert Martini, whose daughter you located last year. Apparently Martini and the Calverts are business associates." I lowered their letter until it dangled at my side. "The Calverts want this Bamba fellow nailed. Stanley thinks Bamba has developed a sophisticated cheating method or device, but the other brother, Richard, thinks he is just lucky and his luck will change. I should say that Stanley warned me that Richard has faith only in his gambling buddies to detect cheaters, and he is against the idea of your coming out. Stanley made it clear that he controls the casino, so Stanley's decision is final. Do you want to take this on?" I knew Fletcher disliked employers that did not allow him free rein.

"I'm salivating. Let's go." Fletcher was wild-eyed. "I want to meet Mr. Bamba, shake his hand, and listen to this man hum. Book us on the next flight out of Halifax." Fletcher was gathering up papers as he spoke and throwing them in a big canvas ice bag. He opened an armoire, grabbed some underwear, shirts, and toiletries and announced he was ready to go.

****

Las Vegas at night is one of the singular landmarks on this planet. It can't be confused with any other place. The neon lights turn the otherwise empty black desert into a leaping bonfire of color. A fifty-foot "E" revolves atop the Eldorado hotel tower above a four-sided digital clock announcing the time to a town that would rather forget time. The strip is the unmistakable main aorta that connects downtown with the McCarren Airport, with tens of thousands of platelet cars moving up and down delivering sustenance to the beast. To cap off the uniqueness, where else is one greeted upon leaving a jetway by the sound of clanging, coin-disgorging slot machines. Viva Las Vegas!

On the way in, Fletcher went over some blackjack fine points that he felt I had better know: "You need to know two terms: basic strategy and counting. Basic strategy refers to the way one plays one's cards. This has nothing to do with luck, but just remembering and applying well-known rules for each playing decision. Playing perfect strategy will reduce the house advantage, about 5.5 percent against the player, to almost, but not quite, zero. Counting refers to a system that informs the player if the deck of cards remaining to be played contains an advantage, a disadvantage, or neither for the player. Combining basic strategy and counting can result in a knowledgeable player achieving almost a one percent advantage over the house."

I should have known Fletcher would know all these odds. After all, a man who obsessed about probability theory would know basic facts about casino gambling.

Fletcher continued in professorial mode, "Double downs and splits permit the player to double a bet already made, in the hope that drawing only one card will result in a total hand value higher than the dealer's but without going over This is where Bamba is killing the house. He is winning far more of these hands than even a good counter would. The question is whether he is cheating. Cheating is essentially the use of an external mechanism to win. It can be collusion with a dealer, marking cards, or the use of a computer. So far no one has detected any cheating on the part of Bamba."

A sumptuous limousine bearing the Eldorado logo and chauffeured by a uniformed guard conspicuously wearing a .44 Magnum revolver picked us up and rushed us downtown to the casino. Two other armed guards ushered us into the inner offices of Richard and Stanley Calvert, who were sitting on either side of a long room behind massive desks. You couldn't speak to one without turning your back to the other, sort of a monkey-in-the-middle arrangement. The layout permitted one brother to signal the other without the visitor, the "monkey," knowing it. Richard was short, rotund, sloppy, and bald. Stanley was tall, starched, and bandbox neat, with salt-and-pepper hair, neatly clipped.

Stanley stood up and excitedly walked over to us, pumping Fletcher's hand. "Mr. MacDonald, I have wanted to meet you ever since you found Albert's daughter. He had given up hope and, frankly, nobody can figure out how you found her, not even the police."

Fletcher's eyes sparkled. "I make it a practice of not giving away my magic, but I very much appreciate the compliment. This is Max Bateman, who will be assisting me." He glanced at the other brother, saying decisively, "Now, let's get to it. I want to walk around the casino, especially where Mr. Bamba generally plays, and to talk to the dealers and managers on the floor. I'll need a list of everybody who works in the blackjack pits." As usual, he had thought through everything beforehand. "I'll need it all this evening."

From the other side of the room, Richard roared, "Hey, Mr. Canadian, we give the orders around here." He thumped a fist on his desk for emphasis. "I told my idiot brother, Stanley, that I thought it was absurd to bring out someone who didn't know spit about the game, especially a hoodoo geek from the North Pole and his sleigh dog. We don't need strangers interfering with our business, and we don't take orders from you. You take orders from us!"

Stanley bellowed at Richard, "We've lost six million dollars already. I told you we should have stopped Bamba, but you said his luck had to change and now we really are stuck." It was obviously not the first argument they'd had on the subject. "This man is objective, not one of your gambling buddies, your so-called pros, who will sell us down the river for extra pocket change. Daddy gave me sixty percent of this place because he knew you were just a degenerate gambler at heart."

Richard exploded back. "Daddy was angry with me the day he changed the will, and then he died suddenly. You know that. He would have changed it back. I'm the rightful boss. You're a bean counter...a sissy."

Enraged, Stanley flew across the room like a rocket. "A sissy, huh?" Throwing all his weight into Richard, he knocked him out of his desk chair and onto the floor. With a murderous punch to the side of the head, Stanley knocked Richard unconscious. I couldn't believe Richard Calvert's insults, and I knew that Fletcher would never stand for it. I was about to demand an apology when Fletcher motioned to me not to speak. He slowly walked over to the far corner of the room, where Stanley was still standing over Richard.

Fletcher softly but firmly said, "Mr. Calvert, we will do the job here on one condition: You must keep your brother off the premises as long as I am here. I don't want to see him, hear him, or smell him, or we will leave and keep the fee. Is that acceptable?"

Stanley was clearly torn. "At the moment, I can't stand him either, but he is my family. Banning him from our own casino is asking a lot. Can't you just ignore him?"

"I had no idea that your brother was this violently opposed to your hiring me, or I would not have come in the first place. His belligerence would be counterproductive to my efforts for you."

"I didn't expect him to explode like this. I'm sorry." He waited for Fletcher to respond, but he wouldn't bend an inch. "All right, I'll keep him out of your sight."

Richard came to and crawled towards the door. As he groggily rose to his feet, we saw that his face was fire-engine red. He staggered out the door but not without cursing us all with unspeakable deaths.

Ignoring him, Fletcher became all business. "Who knows Mr. Bamba best here?"

Stanley was clearly glad his brother was gone. "The swing shift boss, May Stalman, was here when he started and has seen a lot of his action. When Bamba's here, I have her stay on through graveyard until he leaves." He gestured toward the floor. "She's downstairs now. Shall I bring her up? Look, I'm sorry about Richard—"

Fletcher cut Stanley off by putting his hands up. "He's your problem, not mine," he said flatly. "Just keep him away from this investigation and me. I want to talk to Ms. Stalman now." He made a face, as though at an odor. "I'd rather do it in the casino though. The air is bad in here."

The Eldorado is one of Las Vegas's oldest casinos, located downtown, the seedier side of Las Vegas. However, the Eldorado has one major draw: it's the only casino in Las Vegas, maybe in the world, that will book any bet, even a million dollars, on one hand of blackjack, one spin of the roulette wheel, or one throw of the dice, so long as you get the OK from Richard or Stanley. High rollers who get stuck on the glitzy strip will come down to the Eldorado and try to get even by making huge bets. Most of the time that strategy loses, but there are true stories about gamblers who made back their uptown losses in a few bets. The legend is well etched in Las Vegas lore that the Eldorado is the only place in town where you can dig yourself out of a gambling hole.

Speaking of holes, the casino itself was just that. Dark, grimy, and probably one of the last places on earth where just about everybody smoked cigarettes. Its gray haze created a pea soup fog that obscured people and their faces, and maybe they liked it that way. The motif was Old Mexico, illustrated by giant oil murals of life and sites south of the border. The slot machines did their clanking, but the blackjack pits were far enough way so that the predominant sounds in the area were the whisking of cards across the felt and the clattering of chips being counted, fanned, tapped, racked, dispensed, cut, and stacked. Highly focused light illuminated each table, especially on the dealer's cards, but it quickly trailed off into dark shadows appropriate for the habitués of this demiworld. A long, heavy, wooden bar had a crew right out of central casting. Dusty, sour-faced, grizzled men—loud cowboys or wannabe cowboys, each with their Stetsons—oozed testosterone, and leggy, busty women were either in close embrace with the men or were scheming to end up that way. Bottles of beer and glasses of whiskey jammed the bar-top.

Fletcher was intrigued by one mural that overlooked the high-limit blackjack tables. He pointed it out to me, rubbing his brow. "This is pre-Spanish. The flattop pyramid depicts Monte Alban, built by the Zapotec Indians, outside of Oaxaca, about two thousand five hundred years ago." The image was vaguely familiar, and I nodded. "It was the home of the aristocracy and priesthood. Their temple was at the top of the grand staircase, which was called the Steps to the Stars." He fanned out his hand to fill out the picture. "These pyramids were built on top of high plateaus and rose five hundred feet beyond the natural land height, presumably to bring the priests and the wealthy, closer to God. As I recall, our Mr. Bamba's family is from Oaxaca. Surely he would recognize this sacred place."

He peered more closely at the mural, entranced by it. "And look at the detail, Max. Each step to the temple in the mural has the exact line etchings that I have seen at the original: tight geometric circles, with arrows pointing precisely to the apex of the temple. That's very—"

"Are you Mr. MacDonald?" a cherubic, black-haired, slightly overweight woman asked.

"Yes, and I presume you are May Stalman? Tell me, where does Mr. Bamba generally sit?"

"He favors those two tables across from the mural you're staring at."

"Stanley said you were on duty the first night he played here. Do you think he sat across from this mural on the first night?" She demurred. "No, Bamba was playing in a lower-limit area several tables over. I remember it well because that night two boozers were yelling at each other. They got in a fight, and one of them threw a bottle of beer at the other. It hit the top of the mural and shattered, and beer ran down the painting. I was near Bamba's blackjack table. We were all watching the dust-up. The porter had to get up on a stepladder to sop up the beer on the wall. I remember that when the play resumed, the dealer had to get Bamba's attention back on the game because he was still fixated on the mural, as if he was in a daze."

"And what about this humming?"

She made an annoyed face. "He sometimes hums so loud that it disturbs the other players. I had to come over a few times and ask him to stop. He would reduce the volume for a while, but he kept on humming."

Fletcher was intrigued by the curious habit. "Can you recall it? Did anyone record it?"

"We have the area miked to detect collusion, but for some reason it doesn't pick up the sound. It seems to blend into the background and so it doesn't come up on the tape."

"Can you imitate it?"

She scratched her head, trying to recall it. "It's sort of singsongy, not so much a tune as a...a...chant. Up and down just a few notes, then a long hum at the same note. Sounds like one of those Hare Krishna fellows."

"Has the mural been reconditioned recently? Cleaned?"

"Cleaned?" she snorted. "Not likely here. As you can see, the charm, if you will, of this place, is that nothing has been changed since when it was built in the late forties."

"What does he wear when he plays?"

She paused a moment. "Jeans, sneakers, a pullover shirt, and generally a light Windbreaker with lots of pockets, including a zippered inside pocket. He's neat, clean, and respectful."

"Does he ever drink?"

"No," she said, finding this bizarre, "and he's a camel. Even when he used to play for long periods, he never ordered anything and rarely went to the john."

"Does he chat with anyone? Is he friendly?"

"No, but he isn't rude. If someone says hello or another player congratulates him on a win, he simply says thank you or smiles. The exception will be when he is asked to stop humming; he only smiles but keeps on with it."

"What about his identification...is it in order?"

"Yes," she said, nodding. "When he first went over the recording limit, ten thousand dollars, I asked for his ID. He has a valid driver's license, Social Security card, and we know where he used to work."

Fletcher pointed at the wall. "Tell me, what's behind the mural?"

She shrugged. "It's the exterior wall on an alley."

"I'd like to look." Fletcher immediately marched out of the casino and I followed. He ran his hands on the outside wall, over the rough stucco surface, looking up to a point about ten feet off the ground.

Fletcher announced, "The mural's about here." He examined the spot more closely. "The wall is solid...all cinder block covered with stucco." He returned inside the casino again and located the swing-shift boss.

"Ms. Stalman, I understand from Stanley Calvert that the professionals say they can't detect anything irregular. How would you characterize his play?"

She waved her hand carelessly. "He's an average player. He plays basic strategy, and frankly he makes a fair number of mistakes. He doesn't count the cards because when he increases his bets, he often does so when the count is very much against him, a big negative count. I have told the Calverts that I think he has some psych going for him."

"What do you mean, 'psych'?"

"I think he has some extrasensory perception that tells him

when to jump his bet. But, of course, I can't prove it. Stanley Calvert is sure he's cheating." She eyed him more closely. "That's why you're here, isn't it, Mr. MacDonald?"

"No, Ms. Stalman. I'm not here to prove he's cheating. I'm here to understand the phenomenon. When do you expect Bamba again?"

"He should be here tonight. He's been on a weekly schedule for six months. Comes in on Tuesday around 4 a.m., plays for an hour, and beats us for two hundred thousand dollars. Just like clockwork."

Fletcher glanced all about the cavernous space. "I notice that you don't have any music, and it's particularly quiet for a casino. Almost a hush. Why is that?"

"The owners like it that way. Their father, Ben, took his gambling seriously, and the brothers have followed that lead, allowing the natural noise of cards and chips to be the backdrop." She showed a slight smile. "During the day shift, between the screaming and yelling of the players whooping it up and the sounds of the slot machines, the gambling noise level is pretty high. Late on swing and especially on graveyard, it's cemetery quiet, except for the occasional hoopla from the bar or a jackpot winner gone wild. We don't have any music, either live or canned."

"So, Tuesday at 4 a.m. is very quiet, right?"

"Yes, deadly quiet."

"Does anything bother him?"

She had to think hard about that. "The only time I saw him become really upset was when the janitor was vacuuming the floor around his table. He cursed that guy up and down. He stopped playing until the guy was finished."

"Do they generally vacuum at 4 a.m.?"

"No. Generally at 6 a.m. This was unusual."

Fletcher was very pleased with all he'd learned. "Ms. Stalman, you are a very observant woman. Thank you. Mr. Bateman and I will be at the bar. Please alert us when Mr. Bamba arrives." Fletcher made for the dark recesses of the bar before Ms. Stalman could respond to his compliment.

Following behind, I said to Fletcher, "Do you think there's an acoustic device involved?"

He was still puzzling through this point. "Something to do with sound, but maybe not a device as such. Go over and stand underneath the mural. I want you to hum softly to yourself in different pitches and look at me as you do it. If I point to you, try to remember the pitch that triggered my pointing."

I tried to divine the reason for this odd request. "Fletcher, how softly should I hum? Do you want me to be heard over the noise of the bar?"

"Very softly. I don't want to hear you. I'm listening for the mural."

"I don't understand."

He said impatiently, "I'm looking for a harmonic response to your humming."

Once again I felt like an idiot carrying out some bizarre idea of Fletcher's, like the time he had me and Fiona dressed up like Greek gods and chanting a curse in the Pantheon in Rome. Yet I headed over to the mural and, trying to be as inconspicuous as possible, started humming. I felt absolutely retarded. But nobody noticed me. I guess it's the nature of a casino: there are lots of eccentrics. I tried a variety of notes, following do-re- mi, until I saw Fletcher point. It was a higher pitch. I kept it in my mind and walked over to Fletcher, as though I was carrying something in my mouth.

"You changed it, Max," he said, disapproving. "While walking over, you shifted pitch."

"I didn't mean to."

"Of course you didn't; it just happened. But I heard it well. It was a high A. That's not uncommon for the paranormal. I ran into it in Carriacou, too, remember? The zombies harmonized on that same note."

"Oh, right, at the graveyard in the sea."

"The mural is resonating to an "A" note. A harmonic is being created. That means that the mural, or something in the wall, is emitting a response to your humming."

"Honestly, Fletcher, I think this is hogwash. Look, if some signal is being generated, the whole process would be unbelievably complicated to communicate and reveal future cards, requiring technology and science the world hasn't even seen. Secondly,

Bamba is a lowly, unsophisticated kitchen helper whose possible access to this type of technology is a ludicrous idea."

Not without some pique in his voice, Fletcher said, "Think back on those vaudeville acts where an opera singer reaches a sustained high note that eventually shatters a crystal goblet. What occurs is that the diva finds just the right note that will destabilize the molecules in the crystal so that it actually is transforming itself into a state other than a solid. Movement from one state to another opens the door to a fluidity of mass, energy, and, importantly, time. And, as to Mr. Bamba's credentials, his sustained win suggests a certain amount of personal control over this phenomenon, and that is all that matters."

At precisely 4 a.m., a dark reddish-skinned Mexican walked along the side of the casino and seated himself at a table with one other player across from the mural. Ms. Stalman started to approach us, but Fletcher waved her away.

"Max, those are pure Indian features. He may not have any Spanish in him at all." This seemed to be an important point for him. "We are going to stand at the column nearest the game and watch . . and listen. I'm now going to hum an A. Try to memorize it."

I listened hard and harmonized with Fletcher. Still, I wasn't sure that I could remember the exact pitch.

Bamba, about ten minutes into playing, began to hum, but it was so soft that Fletcher couldn't hear it. He walked over to the table and sat down a few stools away from Mr. Bamba and beckoned to me to come over. Now I could hear Bamba well. The sound was clearly single note intensive; he would stay on one note for a few seconds and then shift up or down, seemingly arbitrarily. Fletcher played each hand, watching the dealer's up card but declining to raise each time. During a shuffle Fletcher whispered to me, "Hum an A for me".

I tried, but a look of annoyance appeared on Fletcher's face. "That's a G. You are tone deaf. Stay here and play. I'll go to the mural."

Fletcher took up his post and began humming just below the mural. I couldn't hear him, but I knew that was what he was doing. Soon, Bamba's humming became erratic, as if he was searching for a different sound. He seemed frustrated. He then shoved one hundred thousand dollars to the betting circle. He was dealt two cards, totaling twelve, an eight and a four. He looked panicked. He searched up and around, as if for an explanation. He had stopped humming. Normally when he made his big bets he pulled a double down opportunity, but this time it didn't happen. He resumed humming, more rapidly and loudly and changed the pitch more frequently. He drew another card that busted him, because he went over the maximum point count of twenty-one. The hundred thousand dollars was swept away from him. Perspiration appeared on his upper lip. He continued to hum, but it was more fractured. I could tell by Fletcher's tightly held lips that he was steadily humming too.

Bamba immediately pushed out another one hundred thousand dollars, apparently in an effort to catch up. He drew a fifteen. He stopped humming. He drew an ace, then drew a ten and busted. Two hundred thousand dollars lost. He was visibly hyperventilating. He wet his lips and uncharacteristically yelled to a waitress to bring him a beer. Seeing his loss of confidence, the dealer waited for Bamba's next bet. He started to hum again, but it continued to be fractured and disjointed. He bet another $100,000 and lost. He started betting one hundred thousand on every hand, as if he couldn't believe he was losing so badly. With a pinched feeling in my gut, I watched as he lost nine hundred-thousand-dollar hands in a row. Each time he lost, he would look over at the mural in a kind of disbelief.

Over the course of four hours, Bamba proceeded to lose four million dollars.

Finally, flustered to the point of trembling, he asked the dealer to mark his place. He went off to a corner and made a cell phone call. A few minutes later, another Mexican showed up with a bag from which Bamba withdrew piles of hundred dollar bills. His eyes were wide and he looked haunted. While Bamba was stacking his money and buying chips, Fletcher beckoned me to the mural.

Fletcher was very pleased with himself. "Looks as though we are cooking Bamba's goat. I'll explain the details later, but it appears that Bamba was able to know the dealer's hole cards through a curious acoustic phenomenon. I have been able to jam it by humming a similar note." He cocked his head towards Bamba. "The poor bastard could have left when he first realized that his advantage was gone, but he's caught the gambler's disease. He thinks he's invincible and he's chasing his losses. Another hour of this, and the Calvert boys will have back their six million dollars, Bamba will have the same nothing he started with, and then I'll quit. I'll tell Stanley to cover or paint over the mural, and their problems with Bamba will be over."

Just then I saw Fletcher's head go up and turn about like a bald eagle's. He had caught sight of Richard Calvert at the end of the blackjack tables. Instantly infuriated, Fletcher said under his breath, "That cuts it. Come on, we're leaving." He moved away from the mural and walked briskly over to Bamba.

Leaning down he said, "Mr. Eric Bamba, I presume, I'm Fletcher MacDonald. I know you are having a bad day, but don't give up. The gods, I think, are with you again."

Bamba was startled into an open-mouthed stare as Fletcher walked off as quickly as he arrived.

Stanley Calvert saw that we were leaving the casino and ran after us. "Where are you going?" he exclaimed. "We almost have all our money back. Fabulous! What did you say to Bamba?"

Fletcher said coldly, "I wished him luck. Your brother is back in the casino, so we are leaving." He paused long enough to explain the phenomenon. "Bamba is beating you because he is able to enlist the help of the ancient Mexican gods of the Zapotec Indians to transubstantiate himself into the future." Both Stanley and I were stunned by the notion. Fletcher continued, as though speaking to a child. "He's about fifteen seconds ahead of the game in time and thus knows exactly what the dealer's hidden cards are and what's coming." He opened his hands, having cleared up the mystery. "Now you know. I have earned my money. If you want to stop him, you will have to paint over or cover up the mural in front of the hundred-dollar tables or bar him from the casino. If you do none of these, he will break you. I won't help you anymore. You are on your own."

"He has the help of gods?" Stanley could make no sense of this. Instead he offered, "I'll get Richard out of here. Please stay and finish getting our money back."

"I have told you the cause. That is what you hired me to do," Fletcher stated firmly. "Getting your money back wasn't part of the deal. I was doing it out of professional pride. Now, you won't be able to get any more of your money back, but you can stop him if you act fast: cover, paint, or bar. I've said my last to you."

As Fletcher stormed out, Stanley ran over to Richard, saying, "What in the hell did you show up here for? We almost got all the money back, and now Fletcher is leaving."

Richard sneered, "That Canadian hoodoo had nothing to do with it. The wetback's luck changed. That's all. You threw two hundred and fifty grand in the street. Good riddance to him."

****

We returned on an early morning flight from Las Vegas to Halifax. Fletcher was particularly grumpy and didn't want to talk about any aspect of the trip. We took a small plane to Cape Breton and arrived in Inverness in the late afternoon. Emerald, verdant Inverness was a welcome sight. Stan greeted us by saying that Stanley Calvert had left several frantic messages on the telephone. Fletcher and I sat down in the back room, and I poured out some Amontillado sherry. I replayed the messages:

"7:53 a.m. Mr. MacDonald, Mr. Bateman, this is Stanley Calvert. Please call me immediately. We have a serious problem. If you haven't left Las Vegas, come back to the club. Bamba is winning again."

9:45 a.m. "This is Stanley again. He's won back two million dollars. Please call me!"

11:15 a.m. Stanley's voice was somber. "Mr. MacDonald, we have barred Bamba. He won back the six million dollars plus another five hundred thousand. At least call me and tell me what went wrong. You owe us that much."

Fletcher yawned. "I don't owe them anything."

"And by the way, you play blackjack very badly. Why in the world would you hit a twelve against the dealer's five card showing?"

"Back to Bamba," I insisted "Explain this to me again."

Fletcher emitted a long-suffering groan. "Bamba's humming was indeed a chant, an intonation to the gods of the Zapotec. The Zapotec priests created an intricate alignment of sound and planetary movement, which they would activate from atop their religious sites, like Monte Alban outside of Oaxaca, Mexico." He was becoming interested despite himself. "Given the right harmonics, they were able to bend or pull time slightly and thereby change their place relative to the earth, a type of transubstantiation also practiced by early Christians. Today the Eucharist, the conversion of bread and wine into the body and blood of Christ, is a manifestation of this power. The ancient pagan use was to view matter from different vantage points in time, essentially to be in different places at the same time, before and behind where one was physically present at the time of the transubstantiation. This meant one could see what was coming and act on it.

"In this case, Bamba's transubstantiation perspective was at the end of the hand. He could actually see the cards, especially the dealer's hidden cards, as they would be when the dealer revealed his cards to the players at the end of the hand. Bamba was actually looking at the game from a forward position in time, sort of an instant replay in reverse."

"And he would do this how?" I asked.

"To activate this alignment he needed three components. First, the mural's compass orientation had to line up exactly with its real counterpart, Monte Alban, in Oaxaca, which it does. Second, the geometric designs embedded in the steps had to be exact so that they could resonate with certain sound waves. Indeed, the mural was again precisely accurate in this regard," he said admiringly. "Third, the right musical code and harmonics had to be provided." He leaned forward, excited by this part. "Bamba did this by pure accident. His humming was something he picked up from Oaxaca. He did not know that his humming would cause a reaction until he found himself transubstantiated by chance once. Imagine, he suddenly was able to see the dealer's hole cards and the next cards to be dealt. He must have been very surprised! Then he began to try and make it happen, which he succeeded in doing. He eventually chose 4 a.m. to play because it was the quietest period, giving him the best opportunity for the process to work. That's why he was annoyed with the vacuum cleaner, because its high frequency interfered with his connection to the mural."

I remembered that part, and now it made sense.

Fletcher went on, always happy to divulge his own cleverness. "When I was standing at the mural, I hummed essentially a jamming note that cancelled out Bamba's incantation, and his transubstantiation was stopped. I counted on his making the decision that his good fortune would return if he just persisted despite losing. That sense of invincibility is the downfall of most gamblers who have had a big win. And it was working. This was the best way for the casino to recoup, because it didn't alert Bamba that we were on to him and he probably would have tried to win until he ran out of money.

I said with great sternness, "Fletcher, don't you think you let your own arrogance get in the way of your assignment? Richard Calvert may have been crude and discourteous, but you owed him his due. Once they paint over the mural or bar him, Bamba won't continue to play because he knows that the mural was the source of his edge. They can't get all their money back, only what you got back for them."

Fletcher remained unperturbed. "That's right. As long as Bamba thought he might win again, he was liable to lose it all. Eliminating the mural would have convinced even a crazed Bamba that he was finished." He sliced the air with his hand. "But my deal was clear. I was to find, if I could, the cause of Bamba's success, not get back their money. They broke the deal, so I don't feel any remorse for them. My pity is for the few hours during which Bamba must have felt abandoned by his gods."

"And what about cheating? Didn't the help from, as you say, the gods constitute external assistance, and therefore wasn't that cheating?"

Fletcher found that idea humorous. "Since when is getting help from God cheating? God helps those who help themselves, right?" He clearly admired the Oaxacan's pluck. "Bamba was helping himself. I have a clear conscience on this one."

Fletcher departed and I was left to my own thoughts. There was always about my experiences with Fletcher that odd, isolated feeling of never really being on the same plane with him. He says his struggle to reconnect with his destroyed family on the other side of the veil has illuminated the way to these understandings. Finding natural laws and such. Perhaps I haven't experienced sufficient pain to strive for answers the way he does; perhaps life is too easy for me. Yet I wouldn't want to pay the price that Fletcher has paid for his insights, and continues to pay. He's rarely at ease. I'll just have to be content being a spectator.

STEENS MOUNTAIN

Watching over Highway 260, south of Lake Malheur, was a gothic mountain that shot straight up two miles from a flat desert floor that stretched to the horizon in every direction. The mountain resembled a lone shark's dorsal fin in a sea of sand. In an otherwise clear sky with a white-hot sun, a churning inky black cloud the size of Rhode Island was parked over Steens' peak. Lightning bolts wildly snapped within the cloud as if it were Dr. Frankenstein's lab. That's where Fletcher and I were heading.

Like one of those Russian wooden nesting dolls, our trip from Inverness took us on a jumbo jet from Halifax to a smaller jet from Seattle, Washington, to Redman, Oregon, and a single engine plane into Burns, population 2,900, which used the natural desert floor as a runway. Next stop, Frenchglen, population 192, in desolate southeastern Oregon. As promised by our employer, Paul Mitchell, a pickup truck was waiting for us. Next to it, an aged and slightly bent man in worn denim, reminiscent of a well-seasoned Marlboro man, dangled the truck keys from callused yet agile hands. His face, a map of gullies, dry washes, and cracked earth, was shaded by a chocolate-brown felt ten-gallon hat.

"You must be the boys from Canada. I'm Rick. How was the trip?" Fletcher said, "Pretty easy. I see that in Redman there's a pile of new homes being built. How about here?"

"A little. Places a hundred miles away like Redmond and Bend have doubled their population in a few years and probably will again. Not so much here yet. We're just a bit too far from anything...and too little good water. Just some ranchers, miners, tourism folks, and a lot of cows." Rick knocked the dust off his hat with a sidelong swipe at his thigh.

"As I recall," Fletcher said, drawing on his encyclopedic memory, "you get lots of bird-watchers at Lake Malheur. Isn't it famous for having one of North America's largest concentrations of migratory birds?" He was talking in an easy way, not all that different from Rick's cadence.

"Right, they just come and spend a few days. Some bring RVs; others stay at Frenchglen. Some stay here in Burns. I've seen hundreds here when the birds are really moving. But they have no reason to stay. You need something more than bird-watching to make a life, even to live out the rest of your life."

"What feeds Lake Malheur?" Fletcher asked, scanning the desolate scenery.

"The place you are going...the Steens. Two rivers up there, Donner and Blitzen, deliver thousands of acre feet, tons to you, of water."

"Couldn't some of that water be diverted to Burns?"

Rick peered at him more closely. "You sound more like a de-veloper than a cattleman, or whatever you do. Yep, that's possible. And that would change things. Water always changes things in dry places like this." He fished something out of his front pants pocket. "Well, here are the keys. You go down this here road to the inter-section with Route 260 and head south to the Frenchglen Hotel, just a two-story wooden place on the highway. Can't miss it. It's the only building there anyway. Everybody else lives on the ranches. Frenchglen is about an hour. Just keep the Steens to the right of you. By the time you get to Frenchglen they'll seem pretty damn large, and they are. Thirty miles long and two miles high. The Mitchells will meet you at the hotel and take you to the ranch house, where you'll stay." By this point Rick seemed talked out.

"Say, Rick, my name is Max. Is there a rest room around?"

"You've got the whole desert. Nobody's watching, and no-body much cares, Mr. Max."

I wandered off into the flatness a bit and realized that it didn't make too much difference where I was, for you could see twenty miles in every direction. I turned my back and did my business. Even walking a little bit away from what was civilization—Rick, Fletcher, a couple of pickup trucks, and an airplane—a silence rose where the slightest sound had meaning: my urine on the parched earth, the scrape of my shoes, a bit of tumbleweed skipping on the desert floor. Small things made a difference. That was what Fletcher was always teaching me.

****

We had been on the road to Steens Mountain for a half an hour and had seen only one other vehicle, another pickup truck. Dusty red, with rifles hanging behind the driver in the cab. The road stretched ahead of us like a black stripe on an immense tan pavement of desert. The frying-pan heat of the afternoon gave multiple births to imaginary luscious pools of cool water on the road. We would drive within a few feet of them and they would evaporate into the black asphalt.

"Can you see those mirages ahead, or can I only see them because of my angle of view?" I asked Fletcher.

"Yes, I can see them," Fletcher said. "Blue water ahead, right, Max? At least we don't need that water. Imagine if we were truly parched, exhausted, and near death from dehydration. Life or death. Hope or no hope. I guess the loss of hope is even worse than no water."

I wasn't wading into philosophy. "It's the unreality that spooks me. Blacktop, then blue water as sure as the blacktop. What's real? What we see or what we know? Odd."

"And what if one of those mirages was truly water?" Fletcher questioned. "It can happen, but the chances are slim. That is the essence of hope, to strain reality, to squeeze from it a drop of a miracle." Fletcher's voice had lost the easiness of his encounter with Rick. It had returned to that studied, blue tone of his room looking out upon the sea from Mabou point. Not gloomy but not cheery, subdued and heavy.

I changed the subject. "Can you believe the size of the Steens? It's like looking at skyscrapers rising from the desert, like seeing New York City from across the Hudson River. It obviously has a climate of its own, judging by the black clouds, rain curtains, and lightning bolts we can see from this distance. Now that's forbidding."

Fletcher became very interested again in the Steens. "The home of the Wicked Witch, perchance. The moisture from the west must sweep up against the sides of the Steens, and the coolness of the upper atmosphere produces that violent weather we're seeing. The afternoon must be the worst, because the daily heat of the desert rises up and mixes with the cold air and moisture of the peaks to irritate Zeus enough to throw thunderbolts. Mornings, on the other hand, could be lovely. You are right about the rain. Just look at that wall of gray in the far left fold of the mountains. A wall of water. Now that could cause a flash flood. Maybe one of these mirages might just be the real thing. Max, throw on the brakes! Man, that's real water on the road!"

I jammed on the brakes, and the luggage flew from the back of the cab to the front. The motor died, leaving only the sound of Fletcher laughing uncontrollably. He had to get out of the truck, he was so beside himself. He was literally pounding the hood and gasping. "You are so easy. What a straight man. Mr. Impressionable." And a couple of times, "I'm sorry."

I jumped out of the truck. "All right, you son of a bitch, you drive. It looked like water to me." He continued to laugh, making me more exasperated. "You're always setting me up. Well, one day, these pranks are going to kill us. Or I'm going to just shoot you and be done with it."

Fletcher still could hardly contain himself. He had been laughing so hard, he was holding his stomach from the pain. He then began to hiccup, something he did when he laughed uncontrollably.

Fletcher, hiccupping every few seconds, lifted himself into the cab and announced, "Okay, Einstein, next stop, the superdeluxe, Michelin four-star Frenchglen Hotel, where movie stars, politicians, and celebrities from all over the world gather. Hiccup. I am sure that the maitre d', Monsieur Sagebrush, has reserved his finest table for us...out of the two he has." I began smiling, recovering from my outburst. "And I hear that they have the house specialty on the menu: Roast Jackalope, with grilled greasewood for an appetizer, sand sorbet for dessert, and eau de Malheur as a chaser. Hiccup. Oh, how in the hell do we end up in these places?" "You liked the sound of Mitchell's daughter's voice, as I recall."

Hiccup. "Well, there's some truth to that. Her voice had that salty burr of Fiona's." In another life, Fletcher and my wife Fiona would have hit it off, if Fiona didn't kill him first. Frankly, I hoped that Fletcher would find his own Fiona, so he too, could have some real comfort in life. Fletcher continued dyly, "But, aside from that enchanting voice, I was intrigued with the threatened takeover of their land by the government, just like what happened down in Big Bend, Texas. Ranchers on one side; government and environmentalists on the other. I was able to broker a deal down there, and maybe I can do it here too." Fletcher was a tad defensive, realizing that he had tipped his hand about reacting so strongly to the sound of a woman's voice.

"I figure that since they run thirty thousand head at two thousand dollars per head on the hoof, he's worth..." I was calculating when Fletcher stopped me.

"What do you mean, 'on the hoof'?" Fletcher questioned.

"What they get at the market."

"Since when have you become an expert on cattle futures?"

"I researched it as part of the plan to get the ranchers to accept your 'seven plus rights' solution to their argument with the Bureau of Land Management (BLM). Anyway, that means he has sixty million in cattle. His ranch is fifty thousand acres, so that's got to be another, say one thousand dollars per acre, so he's worth at least one hundred and ten million dollars. Might be land rich and cash poor, though."

Hiccup. "You're all numbers."

"I'm just making sure he can pay your bloody fees. Somebody has to be concerned about such things, since you never are."

"Don't nag, Max." Fletcher always became annoyed about money. "Anyway, he paid his retainer up-front, so we don't have to worry." "Fletcher, he didn't pay! You spoke with his daughter, who asked if they could pay here and you said okay."

"Oh, well, they'll pay. I'm not worried. You just said he was rich." Hiccup.

Fletcher started the truck, folded his arms on top of the steering wheel, placed his chin on his forearms, and poked the vehicle back onto the highway. Our speed increased on the perfectly straight road with its little dips and frequent mirages, up to some right balance between our speeding forward and appreciating the massive splendor that enveloped us. Our vehicle was just a speck in this vast desert called the Alvord.

Sagebrush and greasewood were the only plants in the sand and broken-rock landscape. On our right, to the east, like a stalking ghost, the Steens loomed larger. There were dark, greenish patches of extensive vegetation along its east face, lush in comparison to the desert floor. But that green zone ended abruptly at the timberline. From then on up, pure hardscrabble rock was punctuated by a few small white patches where some snow was making a last-ditch fight against the late summer. And it was all capped by that black cloud and the electric show within.

"Like a fist punching up from the center of the earth," I said to Fletcher.

"More technically," he intoned to me, "it's a fault-block mountain formed hundreds of millions of years ago. Pressure from under the desert along a fracture lifted that entire thirty-mile chunk of basalt two miles up." As always he had researched where we were going. "Those steep sides we see are part of giant gorges made by glaciers, some a half-mile deep. It may have been a cataclysmic event, all happening within days."

Just then we passed a dirt road pointing in the direction of the Steens, with a curved sign made of wrought iron over it, announcing in rope lasso typography: "Mitchell Ranch." The road curved and disappeared beneath a depression in the desert. I strained to see where it ended, but it just faded into the dust. There were no houses to be seen.

Up ahead a road sign read: "Frenchglen, pop. 198." In a little bit we came upon a white two-story, typical farm and ranch house, the type built from the late nineteenth century until the 1930s all across the prairies and the West. Ample-sized and inexpensive to build. Simple cubic design, two large areas, one on top of the other, no ornamentation, with a front porch. American Foursquare is the name given to the style. Over the door, a simple sign read: "Frenchglen Hotel." Some aspens flanked the building along a split-rail fence. Besides the dust that we kicked up as Fletcher parked there, nothing was moving in the sweltering heat of mid-afternoon. Fletcher took out his travel diary and plunked himself down on the ground in front of the fence and began to write. He pulled his hat down to shade his eyes.

"Do you want something to drink?" I asked. "I guess we wait here until the Mitchells send someone for us. It would be cooler inside."

"I want to sketch this place and write down my thoughts, so I'll stay here. I could go for an iced tea or a cream soda."

I could see that Fletcher wanted to be left alone. He was surveying the situation and beginning that all too familiar melding of himself with a place. He worked at breathing in its essence so it became part of him. It was his way and I would let him be at it.

I opened the front screen door and found a little general store. No one around. Awaiting me was a lopsided, glass-double-doored refrigerator with soda and assorted other goods to pick through. While searching for iced tea and cream sodas, I found weathered boxes of beef and chicken parts, a plastic-wrapped bowl of pasta, a half-eaten sandwich, and some other remnants of regular life. This was as much a home refrigerator as it was a retail space.

Not finding anything Fletcher wanted, I settled for an Orange Crush for him (I knew he liked the original drink when it had pieces of orange, so maybe he would appreciate at least the sentimental nature of the purchase, if not the drink itself) and a Coke for myself. I never drank much Coke because I always remembered a science teacher of mine who at the beginning of the semester would put some teeth in a glass full of Coke and then at the end show us that the teeth had dissolved owing to the high sugar content of the drink. However, on certain days only a Coke will do, and this was one of them.

I called out, "Anybody here?" Nobody answered, so I put four dollars on the counter and went outside. I could hear a howling in the distance, like a long roll of thunder. A cloud of dust was approaching from the north, between us and the Steens. It got louder and louder until it was on top of us. Swirling in a cyclone of dust was one of those gigantic Hummers, those pseudo-tanks that General Motors built for the macho right-wing crowd. Out stepped a white-mustachioed man, suntanned and lean. A vigorous seventy something.

"I'm Paul Mitchell. Which one of you is Fletcher MacDonald?"

Fletcher jumped to his feet like a twelve-year-old and said, "I guess that would be me. Nice to meet you. That's Max Bateman. You spoke to him on the telephone when you first called. He's going to help me on this project."

Extending his hand in a robust handshake to Fletcher, Mitchell said. "Nice to meet you, and welcome to Steens Mountain, the outback of Oregon. How about riding with me back to the ranch? Max can follow in the truck. Lots to talk about."

Mitchell got back in the Hummer, turned it around, and swung the passenger door open. Fletcher got in, and I scrambled to start the truck and get behind them, throwing the sodas onto the seat. Mitchell blasted off and it was all I could do to keep up. He was going one hundred miles an hour, and then he made a fast left onto the road to the Mitchell Ranch. It was all dust to me from there on out.

We were heading directly towards the mountain. The closer we got, the bigger it loomed, until it consumed the whole windshield. I could see grasses and forests climbing up its sides. And that big cloud was still casting a shadow on the mountain, producing a startling and unreal contrast with the bright daylight everywhere else. A half mile ahead, the Hummer was still ripping along, despite a rutted washboard road. Driving on the desert floor, I wasn't about to fall off a cliff, yet there were deep gullies probably made by flash floods that would have bent an axle and broken my skull if I had slipped into one.

I started to climb up the foothills, and quickly the landscape changed to juniper trees and aspen. The road had deep gashes across it where runoff had dug deep, and they made for some bronco-busting jolts. At last I turned into a flat, wide area and beheld a sprawling log house surrounded by corrals and smaller buildings. The main house was two stories and at least one hundred feet long and fifty feet wide, more of an alpine inn than someone's house.

The Hummer was in front of the corral, and several men were sitting on the fence, watching some spirited action that I couldn't see. I pulled the truck up closer, turned it off, and walked over to the corral. I saw cattle being shoved through a shoot, and those animals were raising hell about it. Something was making them snarl and groan. I looked through the slats and saw ranch hands tackling the cows and dragging the kicking and pawing animals to the center.

A blonde, long-haired woman with an electric-blue cowboy shirt and jeans, an hour-glass figure cinched with a wide leather belt, stood there wielding a smoking branding iron. She pushed it into the side of each cow that her colleagues brought her. She'd then stick the iron into a fire and pull out another one. Each time she brought down the iron, it resulted in a puff of smoke, a loud singe, screaming from the marked cow, and the smell of burned hair and hide. It seemed like awfully dangerous work, given that those cows were angry and hard to control.

Mitchell and Fletcher were standing just a little ahead of me watching the action in the corral from the gate. Mitchell seemed to be enjoying the scene and was animated in his describing it to Fletcher.

Turning to me, Mitchell yelled, "Hey, Max, that's my daughter, Helena, out there! She can brand faster than two men. Come over here." As Helena drew another glowing red-hot branding iron, she saw us watching and gave us a wave. Mitchell cupped his hands and yelled to her, "See you later in the house. The guys from Canada are here."

After we unloaded the truck and put our bags in our rooms, Mitchell offered us drinks in the great room of the house. This room was predominated by a massive fireplace with a twenty-foot opening and fifteen feet high. On either side of it were the trophy heads of bighorn sheep. The walls were covered with photographs of the ranch and its forebears and operations. All the furniture was wooden with red leather seating and backs. The style was alpine through and through, which, given that we were smack in the middle of the desert, was quite an upside-down experience.

Mitchell said energetically, "I was mighty impressed with the work you did in Big Bend, Texas, to get the Federal government and the ranchers to agree to a national wilderness area and to keep the integrity of the ranchers' life style. That piece of work...what do you exactly call it?"

"Seven Plus Rights," I answered for Fletcher.

"In your honor, Mr. MacDonald and Mr. Bateman, I've got some scotch from your Inverness homeland. Will you join me?"

"My pleasure, Mr. Mitchell. That is very thoughtful," said Fletcher. They all clinked glasses with a toast to "Seven Plus Rights" and continued the discussion.

Mitchell kept working to get Fletcher to reveal more of this plan. "I don't blame the environmentalists for wanting to make the Steens a wilderness area. We think it's beautiful too. But to take our grazing rights away will destroy us all. We need lots of land to graze because there's not much grass when you're in country as dry as this. I myself have fifty thousand head, and I can't afford to buy cattle feed for that size of herd. We ranchers don't own most of the land we graze on the Steens, just what grazing rights we have from the BLM." Fletcher nodded, having heard a similar story in Big Bend. If you can get the other ranchers to go along with what you did in Texas, that would be great. Let me see if I have it right: all the ranchers get to keep their home sites on the Steens, a little of the open land surrounding them, and the water rights we have around the homesteads. We trade all the grazing rights on the Steens for ownership of seven times the amount of acreage in valley land."

Fletcher nodded to show that he had grasped the basic plan.

Mitchell continued, "Now, the other ranchers might not like your plan because they'll say there's not enough water on those valley acres for their cattle, but, hell, they will own outright a pile of land instead of having only grazing rights as they do now. As for the water, I've got plenty coming off my property to take care of them, just as I've had in the past. You know, I'm alone at the moment in supporting this approach, but with your help I think we can convince them that this is in their best interests. Anyway, without it we'll just have our rights taken for nothing."

I pointed out, "The ranchers in Texas were about ready to barricade themselves on their land and shoot it out with the Federal marshals. It was very tense. Fletcher had come up with a plan that worked for the native peoples of Canada, who were also ready to make war on Ottawa. He was asked by the bigwigs in the U.S. administration to adapt it for the Texas situation and to sell it to the ranchers. Have you spoken to the Bureau of Land Management about applying the 'seven plus rights' concept here?"

"You bet. Got it covered, but not officially. You didn't know this, but it was the BLM that suggested we contact you in the first place. We're going to bring your plan up tonight when all the ranchers and the BLM are here. I'm told the BLM will go along with your plan. I think that if it looks as though the BLM is compromising, the guys might get past their emotions."

I commented, "For the government this plan works only as a last-resort play. Some conservatives see it as creating a slippery slope of precedent that could lead to major land grabs by ranchers. To avoid the charge of a giveaway, there has to be powerful local resistance. This provides good political cover for the BLM to embrace it. So the situation here is perfect. I'm sure that's why they suggested it."

Mitchell looked perturbed and turned to Fletcher. "It's their emotions I'm really worried about. I hear the ranchers in Texas didn't like the plan at first."

Fletcher finally spoke. "It was, as you say, very emotional. In the end, even this plan means that families who had been walking and riding the same land for one hundred years can no longer use the same land. They are to be given different land, nearby but different. Its characteristics such as good water, trails, shade spots, and cattle paths are all different. That was the problem there, and that will be the problem here. Ranchers become very possessive about the land, even if their connection to it is only by use, not ownership. My experience has been that they come to feel that they have an eternal right to the use of the land.

"Hi, Dad." Helena walked in. "What are you drinking?"

"Scotch. Canadian, Inverness Scotch. Helena, this is Fletcher MacDonald and Max Bateman. Without her this place would dry up and die."

"Don't overstate it, Dad. You're the spirit and powerhouse here. I just do the dirty work. Actually, Mr. MacDonald and I spoke several times on the telephone. I would recognize him anywhere from his fine voice."

Fletcher was preening, I could tell. He arched his back and smoothed his hair. He followed Helena's every move and was searching her eyes for something. I've seen this behavior before, and it has led to complications more often than not. A type of blindness sets in. And apparently there wasn't just one telephone call between the two but several. That was new to me.

Up close, Helena was even more stunning, than the distant view at the corral. That long blonde hair went all the way down to her waist. It was as radiant as gold thread. She had a high forehead. Her walk was spirited, yet she seductively meandered about the room. Her form was statuesque and commanding of male attention. She was a looker; that was for sure.

She sat right down next to Fletcher. Their faces were not more than a foot apart. She gently slapped his thigh and said, "Well, shall I brand you, too?"

A blush came to Fletcher's face, but he didn't drop a beat. "I think you already have."

"Now, Mr. MacDonald, don't let my daughter get under your skin. She's a sweetheart under all that denim and dust."

Helena didn't seem to be slowed down by the work she had just finished. "Say, let me show you around the place. We'll have light for a few more hours. Do you both ride?"

Fletcher seized the chance. "I like riding in the afternoon. My favorite time for the things I like to do best. So, show me the way. Coming Max?"

I hesitated, thinking Fletcher might like to be alone with Helena, but he seemed to be encouraging me, so I nodded an assent. Helena grabbed Fletcher's hand and whisked him out of the room ahead of me. I had to scurry to catch up. We saddled up and turned towards the foothills. The ranch house was soon out of sight.

Fletcher followed right behind Helena along a narrow trail, while I stayed several lengths behind them. I could tell he was admiring those myriad qualities that, in a rush, had altogether attracted him to her, with the seeds having been planted by her captivating voice on the telephone weeks ago. Later that day he admitted that he was entranced. He put it this way: "Her posture is straight, yet loose enough to respond like fluid to each rolling toss of her horse's gait. Her golden hair imparts a heavenly tint to the air. Her lyrical voice is like a violin played by a master, lilting and precise, piercing and healing, all at the same time. Her hips and waist are alluringly, unmistakably feminine. Her words are a potpourri of intellect, understanding, and passion." He was clearly hooked.

We came to a place where white water flowed from the mountain. Helena dismounted and beckoned Fletcher to do the same. We were in a hanging valley overlooking the Great Basin desert and alongside gushing waters that thundered past us, forcing us to raise our voices to be heard. Helena feigned a German accent when announcing the names of the rivers. "These are Donner und Blitzen Rivers, named after the famed reindeer of Santa Claus. They were named by early ranchers. These rivers provide the lifeblood of Lake Malheur and all the millions of birds that exist there. It is the only dependable water source we have, and we own it. Under your plan, this will still be part of our "close homestead," so these waters will be under Mitchell control." She was clearly proud of this ownership.

"I'm impressed that you have studied the plan. Nice to know my work has an appreciative audience."

"A very appreciative and attentive audience." Helena walked over to a precipice where the noise of the rivers receded. "I don't imagine there are many vistas quite as beautiful as this in all the world. Overlooking five hundred square miles of empty desert land, from an alpine setting, with the rushing water of two mighty rivers by your side and the intoxicating fragrance of juniper everywhere." She looked directly at Fletcher. "Do you like the smell of juniper?"

I heard him say, "It is lovely on you."

Upon hearing those words, I said I was going to explore some of the backcountry. I spurred my horse and I crisscrossed the mountain trails to find an even higher vantage point overlooking the desert. My eye caught Fletcher and Helena embracing. I averted my eyes and became concerned that this was going altogether too fast. If Fletcher had an Achilles heel, it was exceptionally smart, aggressive, and attractive women. His normal reserve would sometimes break down and he would leap instead of thinking. It had happened twice before when he was on assignment, and both times things ended badly. Eventually, their respective egos were too strong for harmony and both parties came to the boiling point quickly. Then the resultant personal and professional failures would plunge him into a dark mood for weeks. I hoped against hope this was not going to be a repeat performance.

****

'The great room at the Mitchell house filled with the twenty-five ranchers who owned land on Steens. Ostensibly they had gathered to discuss the BLM proposal. This get-together gave Mitchell the opportunity to have Fletcher present his plan as an alternative and to offer the BLM a chance to be flexible.

"Let's get this meeting going," Mitchell cried from the center of the room. "Find a seat and let's go. John Slosser of the BLM is here to state and discuss their position. I invited Fletcher Mac-Donald from Inverness, Canada, to tell us about the arrangement he brokered between the BLM and ranchers in Big Bend, Texas. It worked out pretty well for everybody there. He's been reviewing our situation and thinks he has a possible solution. After he speaks, there will be time for questions."

The BLM spokesman basically made one excruciating point over and over for the ranchers: the Steens was too beautiful, unique, and significant a place to be grazed into a wasteland. He explained that grazing was not only wiping out unique plant species but also was causing erosion that threatened the very topography of the area. And finally, too many Americans wanted to visit and enjoy this special place, and thus it was unfair to have it tied up by a few ranchers. The ranchers hooted down Slosser several times during the presentation, but Mitchell quieted them and kept the meeting going.

Fletcher then gave an overview of his Seven plus Rights Plan. He asked Slosser in front of everyone if the BLM would be amenable to the plan.

Slosser, as expected, was positive. "Giving you your own land instead of grazing rights is a possibility. The BLM owns most of the valley land surrounding Steens, so it's feasible. And holding back a few acres around your homesteads in the Steens plus the water and mineral rights to them is doable too."

One of the ranchers challenged Fletcher. "There's not much good grazing land in the valley. Who's going to decide who gets what?"

"A committee of ranchers and the BLM will make the allocations," Fletcher said reasonably. "The poor quality will be made up by having a good ratio of exchange, seven acres for each one grazing-right acre surrendered on the mountain. Everyone will get a proportional distribution of land. Each rancher will have seven times more land and value than he now has. This is not meant to be a redistribution of wealth, just a method to help you keep your Steens homesteads and stay in ranching."

"And who's going to control the water?" This question was accompanied by a lot of loud "yeahs" and foot stomping.

"Yes, the core water now comes from the Donner and Blitzen rivers, which are on Mitchell land." Fletcher detected the same undercurrent of resentment of the Mitchells surfacing that I did, something we hadn't expected. "But the control of that water will be in the hands of a joint committee of ranchers, the BLM, and the Mitchell family. You will elect the members of that committee who will protect your interests."

A man who had been quiet spoke from his chair in a deep and commanding voice. "Since the Mitchells already have the lion's share of the Steen grazing rights, that means they get the lion's share of the new land. Since they control the water, that's going to make them the kingpin, and this time we won't have any really good land for grazing, just a lot of land that our forefathers thought wasn't good for anything, and they were right. The little guy is going to be pushed out."

The ranchers roared their agreement.

Fletcher responded, "You will have your vote on the committee and you will have deed covenants giving you rights to the water from Donner and Blitzen."

A thin, middle-aged man stood up on a chair, holding papers in his raised hand, and said, "I have the BLM deal in this hand. Watch what I think of it." He tore it in half and threw it into the crowd. The ranchers gave great howls of support, and many of them started ripping up their BLM copies. Then the same man put his hands up to quiet the crowd and spoke directly to Fletcher.

"You're not from here and you don't know squat about what goes on. So I'll set you straight. Your plan means three votes on the committee, mister, one for the BLM, one for us, and one for the Mitchells. We know that Mitchell owns the BLM, giving the Mitchells control, so your committee idea is bullshit. This is a power play of the Mitchells."

The crowd was really storming now, screaming, "That's right!" and "Somebody had to say it!" They only quieted down when Mitchell bellowed, holding Helena's hand high in the air and saying, "George, nobody cares about this land more than we do, and you all know that. Helena's mother, God rest her soul, cared for many of your children and schooled them. We have all risked our lives in the winter storms to save one another's cattle. We have shared our water with you during droughts. I and my family have been on this land for five generations. I promise you that whatever water comes out of the rivers will be distributed fairly to everyone." Mitchell held up a copy of the Seven plus Rights Plan. "Listen, I have copies of Mr. MacDonald's plan in writing. Give it a chance, study it, and let's keep this conversation going."

"Not so fast, Paul," a rancher replied. "George is right. You would have too much power over us. We can settle this now. We don't have to study any papers." He flipped his plan in the air and let it flutter to the ground. "I know when I'm being railroaded. You're getting the best of this: you keep your water rights to Donner and Blitzen, just below the headwaters. Having first dibs on that water gives you control. You can do what you want to it before it reaches us on the valley floor. We all know that's the law in the West: first use controls. By the time we get you to court because you've screwed us, you could have ruined us."

The ranchers were hooting and saying, "Right!"

"So, Paul, here's the solution. If you give up all control of those water rights, in front of all of us as witnesses, I'll go along, but otherwise I'll fight you and the BLM to the death." With a jerk of his hand he pulled a revolver from his coat, and he shot a round into the roof.

The room went dead still. Slosser said to Mitchell, "Call the police and have that guy arrested. What's his name?"

Hearing that, the other ranchers stood up. One said, "If you try and arrest him, you'll have to arrest us all." Someone else in the crowd pulled out a gun and shot at the ceiling. And then another. It was pandemonium. And the anger was getting out of control.

Fletcher moved deeper into the ranchers and stood up on a folding chair. "Let's take this one step at a time," he called. "The only reason this offer is on the table is that the Federal government doesn't want a public relations nightmare out of this: the government squaring off against ranchers. But if you push them, who will be seen as greedy spoilers and lose big?" The crowd stopped to listen to him. "Putting aside your concerns about enforcement and protection of the water, this plan is obviously better for you than what the BLM has offered. If you reject it, are you going to hold off the U.S. government at gunpoint? If you challenge them in court, it will cost you plenty to fight them and they can outlast you. This compromise is loaded in your favor, and I'm sure we can work out safeguards for everybody."

Just then someone in the crowd reached out and pulled Fletcher off the chair. The crowd backed off their chairs and formed a ring in the center of the room. I ran over to help, but I was throttled by three guys who slammed me down in a chair and held a pistol to my head. The man who assaulted Fletcher was thick-chested and twice his body mass. He smashed Fletcher across the face, lifting him hard against a cabinet. Blood spurted from Fletcher's cheek. I heard Helena's cry to stop, but the roars drowned it out.

Fletcher rose fast, swaying a bit, and then came at the man like a locomotive, hitting him straight on in the face and then in the gut. Again and again in a volcanic explosion of power and anger he pounded the man, who looked utterly surprised by the ferocity. The rancher staggered stiffly backward, and Fletcher struck him with a right cross and then straight on the chin, sending him to the floor, too dazed to stand up.

A commanding voice in the crowd said, "Enough of this. Let's go home." My captors let me up and, grumbling, marched out of the room.

While Fletcher was still trying to catch his breath, a small man called quietly to him. "My name is Stewart Bastide, Mr. MacDonald. May I have a word with you?"

"Sure, go ahead." Fletcher was leaning against a wall to steady himself.

"My family is Basque and we have been working the Steens for about a hundred years. Started as shepherds. Now we run about three thousand head of cattle and have a small place on the western slope." The man turned around to make sure the Mitchells were out of earshot. "We have heard that there's uranium on the Mitchell property, near the rivers. Do you know anything about that?"

Fletcher's fatigue dropped away. "No, first I have heard of it. How do you know? But wait, let's go outside first." Fletcher pushed open the screen door and held it open for the rancher. They walked towards the corral.

"My wife was in Burns a week ago making some photocopies. When she lifted up the copier lid she found a formal-looking piece of paper with a title on it that read something like 'Probability Assessment of Uranium on the Mitchell Ranch, Steens Mountain, Oregon.'"

"Do you have that paper?" Fletcher asked.

"No. A woman my wife didn't recognize, which is unusual because this is a small community, came in right after my wife got there and asked her if there was an original left in the machine. My wife showed her what she had found, and the woman said that it was hers and she took it."

"Was it dated?"

"She doesn't remember. I have asked Paul Mitchell about it, but he says he knows nothing about anything recent. Years ago, in the 1950s when we were building all those nuclear plants, there were rumors that there might be a uranium deposit near the rivers. But then nuclear power went bust and that was the end of it." The rancher lowered his voice. "You know when they mine for uranium they blow everything apart and the land is unsafe for use. And the water is polluted for years. We don't want that."

"Of course you don't." Fletcher said. "I'll look into it. Give me your telephone number and I'll get back to you. By the way, what was the name of that guy who hit me?"

"Jed Baker." The man apologized for his neighbor. "Frankly, I have never seen him so riled up. We all are pretty upset, you know."

"I understand. I promise to call you regardless of what we learn."

The next day, Fletcher asked me to investigate the uranium matter. I spoke to Slosser of the BLM, and he said he knew nothing of it. Indeed, they had a complete analysis of the mining value of the Steens and there wasn't much of anything there. No reference at all to uranium. I asked him about the activity in the 1950s, and he said that it was news to him.

I called the mining claims office in Oregon and discovered that a permit had been granted in 1961 to the Mitchells to explore for uranium, and that it had been assigned to a mining company. The permit expired years ago. As I was being told this information, the clerk noticed that a new document had been filed. She left the telephone and came back and reported that the Mitchells had just renewed the permit. I asked who had filed for the renewal. The form was signed by both Paul and Helena Mitchell, as co-owners of the Mitchell Ranch. I reported this information to Fletcher.

Upon hearing this, Fletcher sought out Mitchell in his study. It was early evening. Fletcher and Helena had planned an evening out. Fletcher spoke. "You were right. Looks like the BLM is going along with all the moving parts of the Seven plus Rights Plan. But I have no idea how we are going to get these ranchers to go along. They don't have much trust in you or the BLM. That's a hard one to crack."

"Don't worry about it," Mitchell said, waving a dismissive hand. "A number of them have called me and apologized for the ruckus the other night. It's over. They see the handwriting on the wall." He looked out the window at the desert below. "The fact of the matter is this new land that they would get is worth about a thousand dollars an acre today and probably will be worth twenty thousand dollars in ten years, because people will eventually move our way once we tap the water from Lake Malheur for de- velopment. There's a population explosion only a hundred miles from us to the west, and it's moving east. One day there will be subdivisions not far from here. It's inevitable. In the meantime, they keep their homesteads and can make a living. They'll go along."

Fletcher looked through the big picture window that revealed the majesty of the Steens. "Paul, you really know how to lasso things up. Say," he added casually, "one of the ranchers at the meeting mentioned a rumor that there was uranium on the mountain. Anything to it?"

Mitchell shrugged at the question. "There might be some, but it would be hard to get at. Some years ago we got excited about it, but it didn't pan out. Not worth the trouble."

"Maybe not fifty years ago, but with the skyrocketing cost of oil, maybe it's worth it now."

"Nobody's mining now," he pointed out, "and under the arrangement, mining has to be grandfathered in before the signing or be approved afterward by the BLM. It's a dead issue to me." "Are you ready to go to the only movie theater in one hundred miles?" said Helena as she swept in. The scene changed instantly from business to the joy of life. She was wearing a bright-yellow dress that lit up the room.

"You two guys going all the way to Burns for a movie?" Mitchell asked.

"Yes, we are, Dad. Time to get away from cattle and the BLM."

Helena strode right over to Fletcher and took his hand in front of her father. She kissed his cheek, which was still swollen and black and blue from the fight. Mitchell looked at Fletcher with surprise and then smiled. "Well, well, I don't remember my daughter being part of the fee."

"Dad, I assure you, we are getting the best of this, as we always do."

Helena and Fletcher left like two high-school kids on a date. Maybe this was the real thing. I turned to Mitchell and said, "By the way, talking of fees, there's a little matter of the retainer and expenses."

"Just tell me how much, and I'll write the check at dinner. Looks as if you and I are eating by our lonesome."

****

"Max," Fletcher whispered to me through the door. "We need to leave by sunrise. Pack up as soon as you can. I'll explain later." I was still drowsy from sleep, but I went to Fletcher's room.

"What's up?" I hissed quietly. "It's four-thirty in the morning. There's still some work to be done with the BLM and the grange, and some of the ranchers need some romancing about the deal. Then there's you and Helena. Why leave now?"

Fletcher's hands covered his face. "We're done here," he said simply. He sat on the bed, put his head down, and ran his hands through his hair. When he looked up at me, it was as if his face were a broken mask. Something terrible had happened, and Fletcher wasn't prepared to talk about it. I left and packed. By five-thirty I had thrown our stuff in the truck. Fletcher left a note addressed to Helena on the table. He asked me if they had paid anything for his work, and I told him that we had settled up last night. He asked for the check, which he tore up and left scattered like petals over his note to Helena.

I had turned the truck to face the driveway and saw Fletcher approaching in the rearview mirror. Helena appeared in a white nightgown and ran up behind him.

In a flat voice she demanded, "What are you doing?" She was still rubbing the sleep from her face.

He stopped but didn't turn around. "Going back to Inverness." He didn't look at her directly but focused on the rising pale dawn.

She moved in front of him and grabbed each arm with her hands. "Look at me. You're ripping me up, Fletcher. Don't you get it? I love you." Her head fell against his chest and she began to sob.

He remained stiff as he said calmly, "There isn't any way you didn't know about the uranium on your land. I know about the permit."

She spoke timorously into his chest, clenching his arms. "My darling Fletcher, I was trying to keep you out of a very complicated situation. This ranch wasn't built on being nice and easy or being honest at every turn. It was built on being tough, hard work, and being smart." Her tone turned practical. "Look around you. This is unforgiving country. It will eat you up if you don't keep an edge. But don't confuse this survival instinct with how I feel about you. I want us to be together. To give us a chance. Dad likes you too."

Fletcher held Helena fiercely by her arms, "I put it all down in a note to you." Fletcher rubbed his brow. "I see now that I was hired to provide a cover so that you and your father could quietly open up the mining claim and at the same time to get all of the other ranchers out of the Steens. They'd be at your mercy, because you would control the water before it went downstream where their new land would be. The water would be tainted from the mining, making it unfit even for grazing animals below, so the other ranchers would eventually have to sell out to you. In time, you would own most of the valley." Helen pulled away from Fletcher, and she was clearly angry at her failure to seduce him. "It also is pretty clear that you and Slosser are in cahoots. I don't buy the story that he knows nothing about the uranium claim. And your father just lied to me about it last night as well."

They just stared at one another. Then, Helena coolly spoke, "This is my Kingdom. I will share it with you because you are the man I want to rule it with. Don't be a Boy Scout."

He abruptly climbed into the truck and signaled me to get on with it. I stepped slowly on the accelerator. From the rearview mirror I saw Helena's white figure fade into the dust. The sun had just popped over the horizon, and its warmth filled the windshield. Fletcher said, "Floor it, Max, floor it! First stop is the house of Jed Baker, the man who hit me. I owe him an apology. Then we have some fast work to do to protect the ranchers from both the BLM and the Mitchells." I pressed the accelerator to the floor and looked straight ahead to avoid seeing my very angry and sad friend.

CARRIACOU REELING

Because I had booked Fletcher for a two-week trip to the Caribbean, I was surprised to see him walk in the office only a few days after he had left. We hadn't, as yet, established a professional investigative relationship like the one we have now. I was simply booking his trips at the Inverness travel agency that I had purchased from Stan Hope, who was now working for me. "Halloo, Max," Fletcher said blithely. "Would you have time for a turkey sandwich and beer while I tell you about my trip to Carriacou. I picked up some lunch for us at Pete's."

"Good memory, Fletcher, I love turkey and beer. Sure, I'll have Stan cover and we can eat and talk in the back office. As you can see, you're the only customer here anyway, and the telephones are so quiet you'd think the lines had been cut." Fletcher grinned. "Now, Max, how could I forget that celebration of Sally Cameron's rescue and that fine dancing with your comely wife."

"Right, the banners, Sally, and you and Fiona. A lot of history was writ in one day. So, why are you back so soon?"

"Let's sit down first. It's a long story, and it starts with Angus McClarren." Fletcher walked ahead, seeming very much at home, slapping his hat against his thigh, as cats do with their tails against a floor when they have something on their minds. His brown, almost black eyes swept over the backroom like tractor beams before settling down in the only comfortable chair.

It was less of an office and more of a catchall for the detritus of my life: file boxes, model ships, wood I intended to turn into a bookcase, even a kayak for those special summer days on the sea. Fletcher settled in on the cat-clawed upholstered sofa, and I carefully slipped into a lopsided swivel chair behind a gigantic teacher's desk that was once the fortress of my tenth-grade algebra teacher. Fletcher took off his hat, placed it and the lunch bag carefully on the desk, and took a thick leather-covered book from the side pocket of his brown herringbone Harris tweed jacket. I could see, as he opened it, that its one-time blank pages were crowded with handwriting. - Fletcher was looking right at me when he said, "You know, of course, that the coroner said that Angus died from a heart attack while he was in bed at home. Unexpected, no hint of trouble. A few weeks or so before his death, while we were playing together at a ceilidh, he told me that he was having a recurring nightmare: black and white zombies were chasing him and trying to drown him in the ocean. He told me that he was so frightened by the dreams, he'd awake shaking and soaking wet from his own sweat. Indeed, as he related the dream, he began to quiver. He said he had a relative, Ruth, living in Carriacou, Grenada, in the Caribbean. Apparently two hundred years ago some Scots from here, including the McClarrens, found their way there as boat builders. She had written him a year ago saying that there had been several unexplained deaths on the island that the locals were sure was the work of zombies, or what the locals down there call, jumbies. She sent him the lyrics of a song reputedly sung by the jumbies when they were on the prowl. And the music was that of an ancient Celtic strathspey. Ruth said she was unnerved by the goings on and feared for her life. Angus by his own admission became obsessed by the music and he began singing the lyrics at ceilidhs and other places he played. Maybe you remember it?" He quietly sang it in his liquid, baritone voice:

Gather your folks from far around,
Understand your life in what they did,
What you don't know, they'll have found:
And set them free when they bid.
And set them free when they bid.

I sat up. "Sure, I remember, Angus would add that to the end of a strathspey instrumental, creating a particularly melancholy and haunting piece."

Leaning back in his chair, and rubbing his hand on his chin, Fletcher said, "Angus told me that the nightmares began when he first started playing the piece. Despite that odd coincidence, he felt compelled to play it. He told me that if anything unusual happened to him, he wanted me to go to Carriacou and do what I could for Ruth to comfort her. When he died, he left me a letter with ten thousand dollars, instructing me to deliver it, less my plane fare, to her in person. So that's why I went."

"Did you tell anybody here about the zombies, er, jumbies and the money?"

"The money, yes, the zombies, no. But I am sure that he died from fright. I kept careful notes on the trip in this diary. Here's what happened:

January 27, 1971. Grenada. Early afternoon, clear, sun showers. Point Salines Airport. Waiting for the flight to Carriacou. When I left home yesterday the weather was bitter cold, so I am happy to be here. Comfortably warm. I came across a newspaper article about Carriacou, its laid-back, unspoiled Caribbean life, and its wooden boat building tradition, rooted in a Scottish heritage. McClarren's verse snapped back to life.

I had to take a small plane from Granada to Carriacou. It was a yellow six-passenger, twin-prop plane sitting like a bedraggled grasshopper on the Port Salinas tarmac in Grenada. It hardly seemed up to the task of carrying people or cargo; more reminiscent of a transportation museum piece. I and my three other companions were led onto the tarmac by a tall, gaunt, somewhat shaky, cappuccino-skinned middle-aged man who was wearing a starched white shirt with gold epaulets, a captain's hat, and black trousers. We had to duck and crawl into the seats. Several times we were moved around to balance the plane, a somewhat disquieting requirement. I was finally positioned in the cockpit, next to the pilot, and I had a clear view of the instrument panel. As I looked about the plane, it was everywhere a bit tattered or shattered, a cracked gauge lens, and everything worn to the point of suggesting possible failure. The little fuselage was stiflingly hot.

The captain climbed into the seat beside me, held down a switch to start the motors, adjusted a few controls, tapped the instrument panel to unfreeze a gauge or two, and began to taxi, all within a fast minute. Weakly, we were aloft, rolling a bit too much from side to side and whining like a lost puppy through the air, while we followed the coastline, which was very near below.

Like a reconnaissance plane, we observed the land close-up: verdant tropical green peaks to the right, the Caribbean to the left with white to brownish beaches beneath. Little brown islets off the coast had white rings of waves around them, upsetting the otherwise tranquil aquamarine seas. A reel came into my mind, and I began to tap my foot to imaginary music and to sing quietly to myself:

I don't know what lies ahead.
I know what lies behind,
But whatever lies ahead,
It will be built on what's behind.

The Captain leaned over and inquired, "You from Windward?"

"No, no, from Canada. Where's Windward?"

"North end of Carriacou, they play music like that." He banked the plane and went on, "That's Carriacou below us, Paradise Beach." Suddenly he stiffened and gasped, crying out, "No! No! Get away from me!"

"What is it? What do you see?"

He simply stared, wide-eyed, and then his chest and head fell sharply against the joystick and the plane began to dive down. As the altimeter showed one thousand feet, the plane began an ear-splitting whine. Some of my fellow passengers screamed as we plummeted.

I didn't have time to move the captain out of the seat, so I took the stick in my hands, pulled up on it, and tried to take the plane out of the dive. The plane shuddered. I feared stalling, but I wanted altitude. I wrestled with the stick to get some stability as the plane swayed from side to side. Finally the aircraft leveled out. I saw clearly the orange windsock of the airport below. I curved upward over the airport. To reach the strip, I had to come in from the water, over some mangroves. I ascended and circled one more time. The strip was pretty long, and I felt confident that we would make it safely if I could bring us in straight and square. The jutting volcano peaks were far enough away, so I had a clear shot at making a circle. We rocked and rolled, but I was able to stabilize and fly back out over the water in a wide turn. One of the passengers was praying. Another put her hand on my shoulder and said, "Thank God you can fly." I didn't tell her that I had never flown before. What I knew was from reading, what I had seen in the movies, and first-order logic.

I made almost a full circle, saw the strip ahead of me, and pointed the nose down. We dropped very fast. I thought we were going to hit the water, so I pulled up hard and leveled out. I took a shot at the airport. I pushed the plane down again and then reached for the switch that I had seen the Captain use to start the motors and turned off the engines in one motion, thinking that I didn't want any more forward momentum. The ground came up faster than anything I had ever seen before. We bounced so hard on the tarmac that I hit my head on the roof but we didn't collapse or roll over, so I hit the floor pedal that I hoped were brakes and prayed that we wouldn't go into the dense mangrove.

A fire engine came up with medics who took the captain away and comforted us as best they could. I learned later that the pilot had died of a heart attack. He, too, had no history of a heart condition, just like McClarren. The rest of the passengers were badly shaken up, but no one was injured. I had to answer a lot of questions from the police, the airline, and immigration. I told them what the pilot had said before he died. Some of the interrogators spoke English quite properly after the Crown, but others talked in a fast patois that was hard to understand. I heard more than once, in hushed tones, the words obeah, the local word for voodoo, and jumbies.

They couldn't believe I hadn't flown before. When they had run out of questions, everyone dispersed, seemingly satisfied that the death of the pilot was from natural causes and that we had all been very lucky. I saw a lot of peculiar grimaces and the downcast, averted eyes of people who wanted to leave the matter quickly behind. I was offered a ride into town, but I declined. I needed to shake out with the short walk to town.

Outside the little two-room airport terminal and the cubicle where I had been questioned, I finally felt that I was on Carriacou itself. A natural slow cadence took over. After all that noise and commotion, quiet descended like a theatre curtain at the end of an act, but to no applause—just the eerie silence of an empty house. The hot, humid air was viscous and moved down my lungs like heavy oil. The sun was intensely bright. It didn't just shine but painfully dazzled, like the white arc of a welder's gun. The trees and flowers were all galactically different from Cape Breton's: palms instead of spruces, hibiscus instead of lupine, voluptuous rather than decorative.

Finally I was completely alone with my thoughts about the airplane experience. The fright that I had seen on the captain's face reminded me of how Angus looked when he talked of the zombies, a fear that drives people to tear at their faces with anguish and disbelief. I found the concept unconvincingly primitive, histrionic and without basis in natural law and so I instinctively rejected it, although I sensed a peculiar legitimacy to it.

As to my landing the plane, I had acted more mechanically than I would have predicted. For some reason I had felt no fear or uncertainty, except for two moments: initially, when I first tried to control the plane and it didn't respond, and finally, when I cut the engines to land. At those times, my perception was one of waiting for a reaction, either good or bad, to my choices. I wonder if my father felt the same way as he fought the storm that finally took the lives of my family members at sea. I wonder if he, like me, did all he could and then had to wait to see if they would live or die. It was then that I wept, not for me but for them. I was shaking with grief for the events of fifteen years ago. It took me quite a while to regain my composure before I could continue my walk to town.

The road came to a seawall with a white sandy beach in either direction and a sharp right turn to the main street of the capital, Hillsborough, a fishing, tourist, and small-cargo entrepôt. It was an utterly magnificent moment: just me and the gorgeous aquamarine sea; a few sailing ships tacking into the wind; blazingly white light; coconut palms; extinct volcanic peaks, carpeted with greenery, reaching up from the sea; and not a whisper of a vehicle. "Wow!" The awful plane ride completely dissolved into the beauty of the present.

Two arms on either side of a long working pier, which they call a jetty, comprised Main Street. Just about every other storefront was a one-room rum shop. A few stools, maybe a table and several chairs, a shelf with a small collection of spirits (mostly Jack Iron Rum, a.k.a. white lightning, one hundred and sixty degrees proof), and the ubiquitous foot-wide, bright-yellow metal bottle cap advertising Carib beer were the standard accoutrement. Silent, knowing proprietors would peer from their retail carapaces and keep order in the generally empty bars.

A bridleless, riderless donkey ambled down the main street amid light car and van traffic and attracted no attention. On the narrow sidewalks walked schoolchildren in neat, well-starched and pressed uniforms. Long-legged young black women wore look-alike beige suits and high heels, supplied as a uniform by the local banks that employed them. There were a few white skins. I saw craggy leather-tan whites with a calm, no-nonsense and focused demeanor as well as lobster-burned-red whites that bounced from one tourist shop to another.

I was approached by a young, lithe, very black man in a Hawaiian shirt who introduced himself as Rafe, the owner of Mango's. He had heard of the plane incident and expressed his admiration of my skills. He already knew my last name and wondered if I was here to visit my relatives, the MacDonalds in Windward. He told me that they escaped from Barbados and became shipbuilders here, that they still build racing boats, and indeed last year one of theirs, the Buddy Mac, won the Regatta. He mentioned that some MacDonalds were light-skinned like me. I inquired about Ruth McClarren, and he said he knew her well for she lived in Windward. Coupled with the late captain's statement about the music in Windward, the existence of MacDonalds here, and the McClarren link, I felt I had just fallen off a cliff into a Celtic story. I rented a car from Rafe and decided to go to Windward the next morning.

I had to get a special visitor's drivers license from the police department, and when I walked in everybody recognized me from the airplane incident. The police clerk, upon filling out the license, asked, too, if I was related to the Windward MacDonalds. I said that I didn't think so but maybe way back I was, since we were all of Scottish descent. The clerk said nonchalantly that many of the Windward people were light-skinned like me, despite the mixing. I was amazed, and a little disconcerted, about the forthright statement of skin complexion as a defining mark. Color seemed to matter. At home, we avoid skin color as a definer, although it is sadly a hypocritical stance. What I couldn't detect was whether the openness was enlightened frankness or patent racism.

I drove off in a four-wheel-drive Jeep, adjusting warily to the English left-side-of-the-road style made more vexing by the narrowness of the roads and some deep four-foot runoff trenches that were perilously close to the edge of the pavement. The solution, not unlike other aspects of the life here, was just to go slow. And if one didn't figure it out by oneself, myriad speed bumps conveyed the message. I counted seventeen in one two-mile stretch.

As I drove up the steep hill to my hotel, a good, dry breeze was hitting the promontory that overlooked Hillsborough and the bay. It carried scents of hot grasses, jasmine, and bougainvillea. In the black backdrop of night, village lights, shore beacons, buoys, and stars sparkled in an easy harmony from inky sea to moonless sky. Upon reaching the hotel, and being quite hungry, I sought out the dining area. A Carib beer and a few airplane peanuts left a huge appetite. There were no customers at the dozen or so tables. Each table sported full dining settings and small vases of tropical flowers. Light evening breezes came in the French doors that overlooked the valley, fluttering the neatly pressed tablecloths. I sensed my presence was almost a disturbance, until a waitress appeared and asked me if I wanted dinner. No quick movements, no fast-paced commercial tone, more of a sloe-gin sort of person. She mentioned that she had heard of the plane episode and thanked me for what I had done. Her voice was more of a whisper and I, too, spoke a quiet assent so as to not to break the mood. I had a fine dinner of callaloo soup (sort of a thick spinach puree), and a sampling of lambi (conch) curry, kingfish Creole, and the obligatory rum punches.

I was woozily finding the way to my room, when I heard sobbing and a tender feminine voice saying, "It's all right, son. You just have a different complexion than they do. You may look different, but you, Marshall McClarren, have Scots blood in you and don't you ever forget it."

"It's not my fault that I'm so black. Mom, they called me a jumbie!" The cracking voice pleaded for answers and comfort.

The tender voice explained quite carefully that there were light-skinned and darker-skinned Windward Scots and that he shouldn't be upset that he was dark complected. She tried to soothe him by saying that whatever had been said was just the taunting of children who would grow out of it. That it was meaningless. He was not comforted. He said, "I'm cursed, Mother, and you know it. Just like Janet and the others. Maybe I should just walk into the sea with the rest."

I didn't want to be seen or intrude, so I reversed direction and found a back stairway to my room. I suddenly felt disheartened by the preoccupation or attention to skin color here. I would have thought that the horrors of past racial subjugation here, as in all of the post-colonial Caribbean, would have made the subject taboo. Instead, it seemed an active force, and probably as hurtful as always, a hurt affecting my own clansmen, MacDonald and McClarren. I was still amazed by the familiar Scottish surnames in this very non-Scottish environment.

January 28, 1971. Carriacou, 10 p.m. 82 degrees F. Back at the hotel. I'd better write now, because I don't want to forget one jot of this day.

Morning came with rooster crows from a thousand places and strong sea scents in the air. I felt reinvigorated and able to get beyond my apprehensions about what might wait for me in Windward. My ablutions quickly discharged, I gathered up my wallet, map, hat, and car keys and hit the road. The day was cloudless and portended to be blindingly bright. I passed only a few vehicles, which would beep a staccato hello on the way. I beeped a return to their good mornings. Motoring down a steep hill, I found the sign demarking my arrival at Windward and then, moving slowly along a narrow coastal road, I came to Windward Pier. Wood and metal shacks lined the road on either side. There were several two-room markets, not as yet open. It was 7 a.m. Ruth McClarren's place in Windward had no street address, but as Rafe put it, "past the grocery store on the sea side of the road, and the fourth blue painted wood house."

I cruised slowly and saw a raw, unpainted, wood boat clearly in its last stages of being built. It was near a blue wooden painted house, and not far from a grocery store, but I wasn't absolutely sure whether it was Ruth's. The boat was on a flat piece of land below the road, about two hundred feet from the sea. I stopped and got out, sidling down the steep hillside to better admire the work in progress. I respectfully approached the upturned hull. I thought of a boat of equal size, the SeaSwift, which had gone down with my family. It had been built by them. It was a fine boat, but no boat could have saved them from the vicious storm that had broken it apart.

"I closely inspected the hull. It was forty or so feet long, with a deep but rounded bottom made of a light-colored wood, maybe cedar, and a keel of a different, darker wood. I ran my hand over the smoothed wood. They probably used a tough hardwood called greenheart from South America for the keel to resist water and termite damage. I admired the clean, subtly curvaceous lines of the hull. It melodically splayed from the stern to a wide bottom and then arched up to a great bow. Recently highly sanded, it smelled of newness. I found a place where dark-brown epoxy had been applied. Undoubtedly a knothole had been filled. The blemish had the effect of a beauty mark, accentuating the overall perfection. Like Mae West, it made them both more glamorous.

I returned slowly in the direction of the car and turned around again to breathe in the site, the majesty of a boat being born. I remember smiling. I felt a strong kinship with this little place, for all the elements I knew so well were here: open sea, building boats, piers, and a very small town. But for the color of the people, a few generations, the tropical climate, and geography, it could be Cape Breton and my family's boat-building compound at Mabou Point. That thought struck me hard. I could almost feel my family here. My exiting footsteps were amplified by the slipping gravel under my shoes as I struggled up the grade to my car.

"Like the boat, do you?" cracked a voice from somewhere on the grounds. I froze, knowing that I was on private property, and I was enveloped with embarrassment at being where I shouldn't be. A grizzled, white-haired man of medium-reddish complexion appeared at the stern of the boat, wearing a blue denim work shirt and jeans. In his hand was a stout knife that he was drawing across the palm of his left hand, as if he were whittling it. He stared at me, waiting for a response. I felt caught. I told him that I was just admiring the boat and was leaving.

Suddenly a young man appeared above me near my car. He was in his late teens, of very fair complexion, red cheeked with huge freckles, and lightning-blue eyes, and yet he had the tightly curled hair and flared nostrils of an African. He said his name was Ali, Alister Kerr, and that the man below was his father, Ian Kerr. Ali was rapidly coming down the hill towards me, and his father was below me with the knife, bookending me between them. When Ali was just about on top of me, he thrust his hand out clearly in friendship. I grabbed it and gave it a relieved hearty shake, but the adrenaline was still galloping through my veins.

We talked about the boat, which was destined to race in the local regatta. And that building boats was a family affair. I had pangs for my lost family again. I went up to Mr. Kerr to offer my hand in friendship and saw that he was scraping the brown epoxy I had seen on the hull from his hands. It came off like hard, dried peanut butter. The knife bit hard into his hand. I introduced myself as a MacDonald from Cape Breton.

Brushing the epoxy scrapings from his hand, Mr. Kerr said, "We've got MacDonalds here." I asked about how these families all got to Carriacou. He said that the MacDonalds were like the Kerrs in that they were all on Barbados at first, where it was hell working the sugar plantations, no different than slaves although they were indentured. Ostensibly they could pay off the travel debt and be free, but there wasn't any way they could pay everything off, with the low wages and new debts always being run up for overpriced food and supplies. He said their ancestors decided to get out around 1820. Most of the Scots were good carpenters and boatmen.

Mr. Kerr closed his eyes and told me that the Scots built crude canoes by night and buried them under the sand. It took them many months. One moonless night they unearthed them and lit out into the sea, crossing to Petite Martinique. The voyage took three days in heavy seas, and they lost many people. But the storm was a blessing, because the plantation owners were sure they all had drowned and didn't bother to search for them. Once making landfall, some went over to Carriacou. They quickly demonstrated their superior boat-building ways to the plantation owners there, who soon were paying them to build boats. The Scots intermarried with the Africans and native Indian population, but he emphasized that many were still light skinned. Not just the MacDonalds and Kerrs, but also several families: the Joneses, Rankins, Skinners, MacLeods, and the McClarrens. I mentioned that I had a letter for Ruth McClarren. He said, "That's my wife!"

At that moment his wife, Ruthy, appeared in the front door of the blue house not far from the boat. Her skin color was more gray than brown, black, or white, but the Caucasian influence was apparent. Her eyes, like Ali's, were bright blue. Janet, the daughter, emerged by her side—curly red hair, violet eyes, and coal-black skin. Now that was one mix of races! She was self-assured and sashayed right over to me. Her name was the same as my lost sister's. She said, "I have never seen a purebred MacDonald before." She pulled and examined my hair. "We have some redheads here, too, same color as your hair and mine, see. It's like boat rust, except it shines." Her voice was soft, and sultry, as if she had come out of a sleep.

I introduced myself to Mrs. Kerr, told her of Angus's death, and presented the package containing his letter and the packet of money. She sat on the ground, sobbing and rocking back and forth for several minutes without speaking. She opened the letter as if it contained loose diamonds and she didn't want to lose any. The banded pack of money fell to the ground. I picked it up and held it for her. She seemed interested only in the letter. She folded it into eighths and tucked it into a pocket in her apron. She took my hand and guided me, in silence, a few hundred feet to a family cemetery which she told me was just for MacDonalds, right on their property. Then Janet erupted and said that not all the MacDonalds were buried there and that there was another place where she would be buried. Mrs. Kerr quieted Janet and confirmed that there was a public cemetery down the road.

Mr. Kerr, strangely ignoring his wife's and Janet's emotions and still stabbing at his hand, got up and walked into the little blue house. He reappeared a few seconds later bearing a violin case. He carefully snapped back the clasps and raised a battered, light-brown fiddle from the case.

He offered it to me. Where jaws had held it for unknown years, the wood was worn to blond. I held it as if it were nitroglycerin or the Guttenberg bible. The bridge was askew and there were countless fissures in the surface. Mr. Kerr said he tuned up this fiddle pretty high, to "A" so it could be heard over the noise and dancing they have at Christmas when the clan gets together and fiddles. About twenty of them still fiddle, although the skill is slowly dying out, like the shipbuilding.

Mr. Kerr lifted the worn bow, tore off some of the loose hair, and began to tune, first by plucking the strings and then by pulling the bow over them. He raised the fiddle to his chin, plunged the bow down upon the strings. An ancient sound let loose—a high, single note that bent the grass towards it—and took its place in the hall of unique and special sounds: the call of the ram's horn, the compelling notes of the soldier's bugle, the tolling of a church bell. At first creaky but then growing smoother as Mr. Kerr's old fingers were lubricated by the energy of the music, an ancient strathspey went forth. It had six turns, each gathering speed. I was near open-mouthed when I heard the melodies of my Cape Breton being played in the tropical sun, and to learn that there were others who played it was almost too much to believe. Tune after tune Mr. Kerr conjured up: jigs, airs, reels, and marches. Each one would be smoother and more intense than the last.

Ali said that his father would go on for hours now and entertain the other family workers who were coming by to play, eat, drink, and dance the whole day through. Mr. Kerr had transported himself to another place with his music, and nothing but exhaustion would stop him.

Janet appeared again and said, "I'm not going to be at the MacDonald place. I'll be at the other place. I'm too black...you'll see." Then she ran towards me, threw her arms around my legs, and began to sob, "Please, please help me." I could feel her tears on my leg. They burned my flesh. My sister would have been her age when the SeaSwift went down. I took her face in my hands. It was awash with tears. She held on to me so tightly that I felt that she knew me. Ali was prying Janet off me. At one point, Janet's watery eyes and face completely leaped into my soul. I felt her agony and fear and knew that there was some awful truth in what she had said. My throat closed and my stomach churned with empathy, but I didn't know how to save her, just as I couldn't have saved my sister. Janet's grasp slowly weakened, and she let Ali take her back to their house. Mr. Kerr kept playing, seemingly oblivious to what had happened, while Mrs. Kerr had turned away from the scene.

I told Mrs. Kerr that Angus wanted me to look after her safety and comfort, and I asked if there was anything I could do. She looked at me and plaintively said, "Take the curse off us before we all die, like Angus." I asked her to explain. In substance, a few years ago people of Windward Scot heritage began dying suspiciously from heart attacks, drowning, car accidents, trees falling, electrocutions, and other strange incidents. There is a belief that bad spirits are on the loose. I asked her if she meant the jumbies, and she said yes. I took her hand to calm her, but I didn't know what to say. I wondered aloud why Janet feared that her dark complexion was a problem, and Mrs. Kerr explained that there were some people on the island who felt that the darker-skinned people were more closely linked to obeah and jumbies. This idea created some cultural schisms on the island. She told me in a hushed voice that I needed to go to Tibeau, the public cemetery, to understand. She pointed me in the direction.

Still trembling a bit from the emotion of the encounter with Janet, I moved the car towards the east, along the coast and a seawall. I passed a large bulldozer that was pushing and lifting sand from the sea and piling it on a dump truck.. This noisy, scarring business was the only unpleasant sight in Windward. It looked and sounded vile. I asked a laborer what they were doing, and he told me that they were excavating for construction sand. I knew from similar activities in Inverness that such sand removal could cause massive erosion and dramatic changes to the shoreline. I asked if that were the case here, and he nonchalantly said that, in some places, the sea had moved almost a quarter of a mile inland from this work. The concrete road stopped abruptly and suddenly gave way to dark, black sand shrouded by the dense foliage of thick-trunked wizened cypress-like trees. The wind was brisk, and the road turned and dived downward, giving me a dramatic view of the Atlantic Ocean, where large waves foamed as they crashed in the distance.

I turned off the motor, and the grove became eerily quiet. The distant waves seemed to crash silently. I studied the gentle slope of the land and the sea beyond. The trees obscured my view some-what, but I made out some small, white stony structures between myself and the sea, a distance of perhaps two hundred yards. I focused very hard on them before I began walking the easy descent. I couldn't quite believe what I saw; they didn't belong there. I moved tentatively on the soft soil, shaded to black by the thick leafage, and focused on one glaringly white structure just within the edge of the sea. As the waves receded, they revealed an upright tombstone.

I noticed other graves, many others, farther down the beach and tombs also awash in the sea. The ocean had engulfed them, washing right through and over them. I walked another ten yards to see splayed out in front of me hundreds of gravesites along a long corridor between the heavy trees and the sea. Some were submerged in the water; with a full tide, all would be soon. This was Tibeau.

Despite the breaking waves, the place was uncommonly quiet. It had that sacred silence that mysteriously pervades ceme-teries, even when they are located in the hearts of cities or along highways. I approached the first gravesite with apprehension, still feeling the residual shock of Janet's pleas and the relationship to burial. To my continued amazement, every marker bore a sur-name of my homeland: Cox, Bethel, Jones, McClarren...and many MacDonalds. The headstones had their inscriptions chis-eled deeply, but not as deeply as what was being driven into my mind. Five thousand miles from my island, I had found clansmen in a place where one would not suspect. Fully, Scotland in the Caribbean. I wandered for hours among the graves, reading each story, dating from 1780 to the present, knowing every name from back home. Some were buried farther back in even darker groves, but all were touched by fingers of the sea. Conch shells and flotsam told the story, that tides and washing water visited every bit of the cemetery. Large crabs poked their heads up from holes near the graves. I stopped myself from wondering what they fed on.

I thought that it was very odd that people would commit their dead here when the likelihood of their tombs being ripped open by the sea was obvious. It was almost as if those buried here had been ostracized or condemned.

Those graves in the front row, facing and standing in the sea, chilled me with the thoughts of human remains being scattered about. I fought the temptation to see if human bones were in the beach debris. I sat on a great fallen tree trunk, part of a tangle of driftwood, which the sea was sliding up to and through. In its arms were two graves whose sides were open to the sea. The inhabitants of those graves were long gone.

I had been alone for a few hours. Yet I felt not alone. So many names and lives, and so familiar. I composed something akin to a sea shanty melody:

I've been traveling the sea,
Didn't have much to do,
but only a lot to see.
Who knew it would be you and you.

Sister, brother, mom, and pop,
Scots of my skin and blood,
Hello, my brood, can I flop,
And let the memories flood?

There's got to be a lot to say,
Across the many years,
Might be nice to stay,
And share the laughs and tears.

Oh, I've been traveling the sea.
Didn't have much to do,
But only a lot to see,
Who knew it would be you and you."

I started to raise myself from my driftwood seat. I took a deep breath and said good-bye silently. As I turned to leave, I found that my foot was caught in something. At first I thought it was a branch, but as I peered into the twisted deadwood, to my horror I found that my foot was wedged between the lid of a grave and its stony box. Somehow I had dangled my foot in the space without noticing, and the lid had shifted. It wasn't so tight that I was in pain, but my foot was securely pinned. I reached underneath my leg to move the lid, but it was too heavy to move. I feared that if it shifted on its own again, the blood supply would be cut off and my foot would become gangrenous.

It was about noon. I was in full sun now, and the tide was clearly rising. It was senseless to yell for help. There was no one about. I hadn't seen anyone on the road since I got there. No boats either. Unfortunately I was positioned far from the road. So my only hope was that someone would come off the road and walk along the sea. As to passing boats, all I could do was wave madly if I saw one. Exacerbating matters was no fresh water and the paradox of being surrounded by water. I was already feeling the sun's fire inside and out.

By 3 p.m. my skin was blistering. The sea was up to my waist. I had drawn blood trying to twist myself out of the coffin's grasp, and indeed I felt that the grip had tightened. I sensed something nibbling at my caught foot. I feared a crab or something else was attracted to the flesh. The waters were reflecting the light onto my face, intensifying the burning and blistering. I saw two boats pass very far from shore, but the reefs kept boating at a distance, so being seen from the sea was unlikely. I heard one vehicle on the road, and I called as loudly as I could, but to no avail.

An hour later my tongue was beginning to swell from thirst and salt. The tide was rising, sweeping up to my collarbone. Another foot of seawater, and I would drown. I was already choking on the waves breaking over me. I heard what sounded like light metal crashing. Just a slam or two from the road. I began to scream and yell as loudly as I could. Two boys appeared on the beach about three hundred yards from me. I waved and yelled, and they ran toward me. They were lanky youths in their early teens or maybe a bit younger. Their faces were eager and inquisitive as they approached, but they slowed down as they drew nearer and their demeanor became somber. I implored, "I'm caught. I need help. Please help me move this slab. I need some water, too, please!"

They approached stonily and examined the situation from about fifty feet. My stream of pleading didn't interfere with their sizing up the situation. Wave after wave crashed over my head as I coughed and sputtered and reached my arms in the air. The boys saw only my head and the flailing arms disembodied from the body below the water.

"Don't go near him. Jumbie! Jumbie!" one yelled and then they backed away.

I stuttered, "I'm not a...a...jumbie! I'm just caught. Help me!" They ran away and were out of sight in a few seconds, clambering into the dark grove. I writhed like Prometheus and yanked at my leg, but the grip was as sure as before. A wave engulfed me and sea-water poured down my windpipe. I gagged and was trying to cough it up when another wave hit me so hard, I swallowed even more water. I convulsed and was hit hard again. These punches were coming faster and faster as the tide rose, and soon I blanked out.

When I came to, the sun was sitting just atop a strangely quiet sea. I was aware of lost body heat. A lower tide left me mostly above water, facing the sunset. I was still atop the dead trunk, my faithful hat on my head. I had a bone chill not dissimilar to that which I might have had in Cape Breton in the minus-twenty-degree winds in midwinter. A sense of futility had seeped into me. In the golden but fading light a figure appeared, then two, then three, and four. They were walking towards me.

I couldn't see any faces yet, just the faint outlines of tallish figures. Behind the first four there seemed to be others, but they were not moving towards me. Indeed, as I looked hard into the otherwise dark brush along the beach, I could see other dark images, like shadows. Out of the corner of my eye, I caught sight of gathering figures on the surf. I was being encircled by a loose necklace of these individuals.

"Halloo," I tentatively called out. The closest ones stopped their forward movement. About one hundred feet separated me from the vanguard. Then one of the forms stepped steadily forward, his or her shape becoming clearer. A loose garment, apparently draped over a body, billowed in the breeze, but the face was not visible.A gust swept up from the sea and the garment was blown wide, revealing only an empty space. No legs, no torso, no face, just the garment standing in the air.

My heart raced, and I thought of poor Angus, and the airplane captain, and the fear which broke their hearts. I guess my last horrible hours prepared me enough for this improbable confrontation so that it didn't kill me too on the spot. Sidling, crablike, off the trunk and up the beach to put some distance between myself and the form, I realizied suddenly that my foot was now free from its trap. I turned to run, only to see hundreds of forms with dim lantern lights, all approaching me from the woods and coming onto the beach. I turned to the sea, and they were there, too, advancing in a corralling motion. I momentarily closed my eyes, turned, and ran in the direction of my car, just to the left of the three closest forms. I picked up speed, but I fell over a grave. I scrambled to my feet only to bump into something invisible pushing me back. It was like a fine web that would flex when I pushed it, but I could not go through it. Everywhere I pressed I could feel the invisible mesh. I stepped back, now standing on the grave I had tripped over, and I became numbingly aware that I was fully encircled by the forms, hundreds of them in many concentric circles from the woods out to sea.

I squatted on the grave, sensing imminent doom, perhaps a suffocation, a devouring, some sort of decapitation, I knew not what. I gathered up my voice and shouted into the arena of shapes, "What do you want? What do you want of me?"

A doleful single A note was played on a fiddle, stretching out the length of a full bow's draw. Then another fiddle and another joined in, all playing the same note, until the atmosphere was saturated. One fiddle struck a full chord, the other fiddles stopped, and a lugubrious air was begun. I was familiar with this piece, which mourned lost loves and lives. As the music rose and occupied the night, names were soberly called out by different voices with Gaelic burrs: Argus McClellan, died 1828; Jonas McQuilkin, died 1828; Sarah McFarlane, died 1829; Rebbeca McLarren, died 1829; Clyde MacLawrence, died 1830. The roll call went in order over the decades and generations. A pause, and the names of my family came: Andrew, my father; Annabelle, my mother; Janet, my sister; and William, my brother, died 1973. A sweet female voice wove through the music and announced the death of Angus McClarren, died, 1997, the fiddler of Cape Breton. A swelling chorus of voices in the hundreds, maybe more, all sang in unison:

I don't know what lies ahead; I know what lies behind. But whatever lies ahead, It will be built on what's behind.

A burred voice then spoke from the garment, "Fletcher, you can set us free, but you must act before the sun sets."

I nervously exhaled. "How? I have no special powers. I'm just one man among many."

"Fletcher." The disembodied voice filled the air. "The children are correct. We are jumbies, or zombies to you. Our graves have been opened to the sea by the excavations. And people believe that we are the walking dead for it. It is a self-fulfilling prophesy: we have become what they believe. We cannot rest. You heard the anguish of the hotel child, Marshall, and the pleas of Janet; they were truthful too. Some of us were relegated here for being less white or too black and not suitable for the family plots, and some were buried here by their families, who cared little that the graves would be tormented by the sea. We here are caught up in a net of disrespect and ignorance. And, yes, we held you for this purpose. Hear us out.

"You heard our plea through Angus McClarren's music back in Cape Breton, and you followed his wishes and came to Carriacou. Over your life, in a thousand ways, you have sensed the interconnectedness of the universe, and acted on that perception. Ideas, just or unjust, course through time and shape the world. Our half dead, tormented status is the result of the energy created by unjust ideas and acts, not unlike the ideas of the inquisition, the holocaust, and slavery. An idea is like mass. It, too, is pure energy, only in a form as unique as a solid, liquid, or gas. When the energy of an idea is unlocked, it affects life just as surely as the energy unleashed from a burning log.

"If you can believe strongly enough in the idea that injustice will be revenged, that you can free us as a pure act of free will, then the force of that idea will set us free. You believed you could fly the plane. Now, with that same certainty, you can free us. You believed you could throw a limp clothesline through a tiny eye-hook, a million-in-one shot, and you did it, twice. The same laws are at work, mind over matter, so long as you believe that you can do this. Will you do this for us before the sun sets? But you must believe you can, and want to do it, for we, in the end, cannot force you. It is the highest law: free will."

"But what of the innocents who have died. Mr. McLarren? The pilot? Perhaps countless others?"

The voice became stern, "Although you have come far, you have much more to learn of natural law. Overarching all is a cosmic fairness, neither good deed nor foul, goes unmarked, yet there is always a matter of scale, and you will come to understand that individual pain, compared to monumental suffering, is accounted for in the balance. You have learned about mind over matter, now you must learn about heart over deeds. Act now or your chance will be lost forever."

"My family was in your roll call. As was Mr. McClarren. Are they here?"

"They are near. They know your struggle, and through your work you come ever closer to them. They want you to do this for all your clansmen."

I wept to see my family, so near but still not here. Yet if I had not come, I would have not known about this closer bridge to them. Through my tears I saw that the sky was darkening fast. The sun was nearly gone, only a sliver of the shimmering orb remained above the horizon. There was so little time, seconds perhaps. I gathered my wits and focused myself on one mental point: that these spirits should, no!, will be set free now. I mentally and physically gave myself to the effort; my extremities, stomach, heart, and mind became one united force with my will. With arms outstretched, eyes shut, I said aloud in a voice coming from my deepest center, "Free them!" My body shuddered, violently shook, and a great fever soared in me.

I opened my eyes to an immense green flash that ripped across the sky, in which the sun disappeared in the burst of that light and the forms were no more. The air was still, and I swear the sea was mirror flat. I was spent; there was absolutely no energy within me. At that moment, the sound of drums, African drums, filled the air. Behind me and along the beach, figures approached – were the jumbies back? No ! I could make out some familiar faces: Rafe of the car rental, the police clerk who had filled out my driver's license application, Janet Kerr, Marshall McClarren, and Ali Kerr, and the youths that I affrighted on the beach. They were all clearly alive.

Ali spoke first, pointing to the sky, "You have driven the jumbies away." As I peered into the night, I could see a line of lights, thousands of them, flowing up from the sea and into the Milky Way, whose brightness and magnitude grew as I watched. I felt sure that my family was part of that light, and that belief brought me comfort. The starlight had the intensity of a baseball night game. The locals each came up to me, and sought out my hand to shake it, and to thank me. Their warmth and appreciation was ironically juxtaposed with the gratitude that I felt sure was in the hearts of that line of ancient Scots, and Arawaks, and Africans, who were now going home above me. I was clearly in two places at the same time, and there was no use in speaking of what I had just experienced. I saw Janet and her mother in the crowd and moved toward them as they moved toward me. We finally clasped one another tightly, with our heads turned skyward, and our tears of awe and release mixed together, forever.

****

"Max, that is the story. I came very close to being with my family again, and I found an even larger family in the process." Fletcher slumped down, exhausted, in his chair. The warm afternoon winter sun was streaming in from a window and was catching Fletcher full force. I saw that he was struggling to stay awake.

I said, "Why don't you rest here for a while? We can go out for another beer after I close up the shop." By the time I had finished the sentence, Fletcher was asleep. And then it occurred to me: Didn't Fletcher say that he was underwater and knocked out? Could Fletcher have died? Could he be a zombie? That's ridiculous.

TENTH MESA

Fletcher was absentmindedly turning over the horseshoe in his hands. We were headed by car to Missoula, Montana, where a longtime mutual friend of ours, Langdon Ochs, owned five acres and an A-frame log cabin along the Bitterroot River. Trout fishing, hiking in the Sawtooth Mountains, story swapping, Scrabble playing, and late night cheap beer drinking on Langdon's porch were the primary goals of this trip. We promised him that we would keep our eyes open for something that had puzzled him for a long time. When he passed through the badlands of North Dakota twenty years ago, he encountered some strange phenomena. As a shortcut to the Montana border, he took a dirt road that had a sign pointing to "Tenth Mesa." After traveling for a good while at night, he pulled over to sleep and awoke to find next to his car an uninhabited, but provisioned, one-room ranch cabin—which he hadn't seen the night before. Inside he found a guest book on a table filled with the names of hundreds of past visitors and the dates of their inscriptions. Some of them were famous people, like General Custer, Frederic Remington, and Theodore Roosevelt. A prominent inscription on its cover said everyone was welcome to use the cabin and requested that visitors sign in. There was no community, no people, just the cabin and this book.

Langdon put his name and the date in the book, as the other visitors had. He was about to leave, when, looking out on the land as the sun was about to rise, he saw a horse and rider on a distant mesa. They vanished from sight the instant the sun popped up over the horizon. He went back to his car and found, on the seat, a horseshoe, still shiny from use. He had no idea where it had come from. When he reached his home in Missoula, he couldn't locate Tenth Mesa on the map. So he asked us to see if we could find it on our trip west. He sent us the horseshoe as a talisman that, he whimsically thought, might help us find the place and maybe the cabin.

We had been traveling across the eastern section of North Dakota for many long hours during a very hot August. The headless wheat stalks offered no hint of relief; just empty straws sucking from a large, waterless bowl. Even the gigantically ugly signs that announced truck stops on Interstate 94 were a welcome interruption from the torturous monotony. These two hundred by sixty foot marquees scarred the pastel blue sky with yellow or red logos and flashed the price of gas as if it were a star headlining a Las Vegas show. But at least they marked time. Just like the destination signs: Bismarck, 200 miles, then 100, miles, then 50 miles; and then Dickinson, 100 miles, then 50, only to start over with another city we weren't going to. At least they reminded us that we were still moving west to our destination. It was 3,349 miles from Inverness to Missoula. Saying it was one thing, driving it quite another.

While Fletcher was fingering the horseshoe, he said, "We're not too far from the Badlands here. Can't be more than fifty miles or so. Hard to believe we will see anything but this flat land forever."

As I drove, I could see the shadow of our car gambol over the wheat. To my blinking surprise, I thought I saw a man on horseback riding along with the shadow and then veer off.

"Fletcher, look out your side window. I think I saw someone riding on a horse alongside the car. Maybe it was an optical illusion, but it lasted for several seconds, and it seemed perfectly real."

Fletcher was so bored that he seemed ready to jump from the car. "I don't see anything but the car's shadow. It's too hot to be riding a horse for pleasure, and nobody uses horses to work the fields anymore." He turned to me and said with a sneer, "I think you are hallucinating. Maybe I should drive for a while." He put the horseshoe in the glove compartment.

I looked again in the direction of the ghost rider—and I saw it again. This time the horse reared and rode off.

"Fletcher, there he is again! He's riding away from us. Do you see him?"

Wearily he said, "No, I don't. But pull over and we'll take a look."

After stopping on the shoulder, we backed up to the point where I thought I had last seen the rider. We walked into the field looking for some evidence like tracks or flattened wheat. Nothing there.

Fletcher called out, "Come here. You're not crazy, after all. Here's a fresh horseshoe."

Upon inspection, we found it was very shiny on the working side, as it would be if it had just been thrown. But there were no tracks nearby.

Fletcher pushed back his Tilley in wonder. "Well, we know they haven't used horses for fifty years to work these fields, and this shoe has absolutely no oxidation on it, so a horse had to have been here within the last few hours. Yet there are no tracks around. It's as though it dropped from the sky." He examined the horseshoe for a few more moments and then shrugged. "Anyway, no sense in standing here like scarecrows. At least we have a souvenir."

Fletcher weighed the horseshoe in his hand and continued to turn it over and over as we walked back.

All of a sudden Fletcher stopped dead and proclaimed, "This horseshoe isn't of modern stamped construction. It has the forging marks of a blacksmith's hammer. It's just like Langdon's." Back at the car, Fletcher compared the two, and indeed they were both from the same period, and even more astonishingly they were the same size. I started the car as Fletcher said, "Interesting. I had Langdon's horseshoe in my hand when you said you saw that image of a rider. The ancients believed that one could conjure up spirits with certain stones or artifacts. I've always thought that there could be a magnetic force operating, which could scientifi-cally explain those claims. After all, this horseshoe is made of pure iron. We'll see." Fletcher rubbed his brow and looked back at the wheat field.

Fletcher and I had met Langdon while he was vacationing in Cape Breton ten years ago. As I recall, he came into the travel agency seeking information on local sites. We started up a conversation. He liked to fish, and we exchanged stories about good spots for trout around our respective homes. I was going to meet Fletcher for lunch and invited Langdon to join us. By the time lunch was over, we had planned a fishing trip on the local Margaree River. We soon learned that we all liked to play Scrabble, so, with my wife, Fiona, we had a Scrabble night, and then another.

Langdon was a great storyteller, especially about the outdoor life in Montana, his birth state. We heard tales about grizzly bears going insane over huckleberries, walking the Lewis and Clark trail, gold mining, Indian powwows, working in the sawmills, Mormon polygamists in the back country—he was a walking radio drama program. He met a lovely local girl on that trip, Stacey Cameron. It was love at first sight, and we thought it might lead to marriage, but he was more wed to Montana and she to Cape Breton for it to happen.

While on the road, Fletcher and I had alternated driving with riding shotgun. Riding shotgun meant you stayed awake just in case the driver fell asleep or was hypnotized by the monotony of the road. Anyway, that was the theory. The reality was, if you weren't driving you were probably sleeping. To relieve the boredom, Fletcher and I would, when we needed gas, food, or a break, pull onto a desolate farm-to-market road and roll into a "population of 158" type of town, looking for the elusive indigenous coffee shop. We would pass up the chain trash places on the interstate exchanges and instead look for the wide main street of a small town. They were pretty much the same across the Great Prairie. Every time we found one of these towns, we would see the relics of dead local restaurants that the national chains had killed. Soap-washed plate-glass windows signaled another mom and pop store eliminated by a Wal-Mart fifty miles away. We would make a beeline to the county courthouse, whose bureaucratic and legal fraternities would support at least one lunch house on Main Street and where the politicos would gather for coffee and schmoozing.

These restaurants or cafés were usually furnished with 1950 Formica tables with steel legs planted on linoleum floors. Bright, energetic waitresses of all ages, sometimes mothers and daughters, would greet you and ask if you wanted "the usual" without ever waiting for the customer to look at the menu. Those menus had their funny spellings of things. Spaghetti came in various permutations: spigetti, spagetti, 'getti', spagett, et cetera. Another favorite butchery would be of veal parmigiana, which produced veal parmeesian, veal parmigana, and the frequent solution, veal parm.

Always, absolutely always, at one big table set with coffee mugs in the early, early morning, the farmers would exchange commodity price news, weather predictions, equipment breakdowns, and maybe some political talk. And later in the day, their wives would arrive and sit at the same table and talk about their type of market prices, the weather, wedding plans, church bazaars, recipes, health matters, and all those things that kept the society intact. For us, it was like looking into the aorta of local civilization and seeing how it all worked. Big cities were too complicated to figure out from one thin slice of their culture, but here just one cup of coffee and a good set of eyes and ears at Hebron's Main Street Café told the whole story. This was our kind of place. Fletcher quipped, "I think I'll take Langdon's horseshoe in for good luck, to protect us from the food." He grabbed it and carried it in his hand into the restaurant, laying it down on the table.

We had coffee with hamburgers and fries. Good and not too greasy. A large man sitting at the big table in the center of Hebron's had his back to us. He wore an old low-slung hat, with longish, wavy brown hair falling beneath it. He tossed some money on the table and strode out of the restaurant, never turning around. I watched him stand in front of the plate-glass window. A riderless horse walked down the street and the man mounted it.

"Fletcher, Fletcher, there he is again...the rider...the horse...in the street." I ran out the door, with Fletcher right behind me. Nothing there. "Did you see him or the horse?"

Fletcher slapped me hard on the back. "No, I didn't see a man with or on a horse. But I think you did. . I am convinced that our little horseshoe is the key to this lock. Let's finish our breakfast and keep pushing along and see if Langdon's Tenth Mesa exists."

We gassed up in Dickinson, North Dakota, around six o'clock. The sun was arching down to thirty degrees over the horizon and moving away from being white hot to a friendly yellow. We planned to leave Interstate 94 and turn north on U.S. Highway 85, which was Badlands country, where we planned to look for Tenth Mesa.

Given the flatness, we could see far to the west as we were traveling. A black line of clouds threatened ahead, but they were pretty far off. Looked like the drought was going to be broken soon. We sailed forward, left the Interstate, and began the northern leg on Interstate 85. By this time, around dusk, the leading edge of the black clouds was overhead and lightning was crawling underneath it. I opened the windows and heard the cracks of thunder ricocheting across the plains. My nostrils filled with the smell of distant water on dry earth.

Some hard splats of rain, like bullets, announced that the storm was on top of us. The raindrops began to bounce on the highway and pelt our vehicle, a Mercedes 240 diesel. The road rapidly became obscured from view by a wall of rain. There had been virtually no traffic anyway, so we weren't worried about hitting an oncoming vehicle, but still we could only crawl along. Thuds began to hit the roof like bricks falling. The windshield was covered in an instant with ice and slush. We were in a major hailstorm. Fletcher slowed down even further, and we both sensed that these ice balls were big and solid enough to shatter the windshield. The car shook with the violence. It felt as if we were in a riot with hundreds of fists pounding on the car and trying to roll it over.

We were still moving forward about ten miles an hour when Fletcher stopped the car, screaming to be heard over the hail. "We can't go forward anymore. There may be a washout or flash flood ahead. It seems as if we haven't dipped down, but it's possible that we are in a wash area. As soon as this pounding lets up, I'll see where we really are."

"I'll go with you."

"No, Max, you should stay with the car. We need to be in different places in case a flash flood hits. I don't know if we're sitting in the middle of a wash or on high ground."

I had to scream too. "How about I go back aways and you go forward? Then we will have a better fix on what to do."

We waited until the hail let up. It was followed by a torrential downpour, a colossal cloudburst. Just as soon as the thunder reached a deafening pitch, it tapered off into a mild, warm rain.

Fletcher commented, "There will be flash floods everywhere. This is an immense amount of water in a short time. When you go out, listen hard for a roar. When flash floods come, they make a howl as they rip down the dry gullies. I'll go ahead and you go back. No more than five hundred paces."

Although the rain was not falling hard, it was being driven by a brisk wind and had picked up fine grains of sand, so it stung when it hit. My flashlight's beam made only a little dent in the black soup as I pushed into the wind. I looked around to see if I could make out Fletcher's light, but all I could see, and just barely, were the lights of the car. I probably had moved a few hundred feet back from the car when I was hit in the face by tumbleweed, knocking my glasses somewhere to the ground. I might as well have been blind. They weren't near my feet, so I felt my way along the wet, gritty mush that covered the pavement and the shoulder.

Despite it being summer, the mixture of hail, rain, and wind created a bone chilling coldness in the air. Between that feeling and my lost glasses, I felt far removed from any sort of normality. I continued to hunt for my glasses. My flashlight didn't help much, because everything was a blur. I was on all fours feeling every inch of the ground. I bumped up against a wooden post and discovered at its base my glasses. Hosanna! Near the top of the post was a battered metal sign with bullet holes in it. On a white background, the name TENTH MESA was printed, with an arrow underneath it pointing right. As the rain had almost stopped, I could see a little farther. I could just discern a dirt road leading from the highway.

As I peered into the darkness, I heard a horse's whinny and the sound of hooves. It was him again. The horse and rider came close to me, so close I could smell the horse's sweat, and the dust swirled up into my nose and eyes. How could there be dry dust in the middle of a rainstorm? I wondered fleetingly. He stopped so close I could hear the breathing of the horse and the thud and scrape of his hooves. He then rode a short way down the road, turned, reared on two legs, pawed the air, and went down the road at a gallop and out of sight.

"Max, where are you? Max? Max?" I heard Fletcher calling, and I could see his light moving toward me.

"I'm over here." I shined my light in his direction. He stopped calling and moved quickly toward me.

"Why are you covered in mud?" Fletcher asked. I told him the story and pointed to the sign. "I swear I saw the rider and his horse again. They were within a few feet of me."

Fletcher examined the ground with his flashlight. The rain was easing up. "Not a sign of a hoof print, Max. I don't know what to make of it." He straightened up, placing his hands on his hips. "Well, Tenth Mesa here we come. We can't go forward anyway on 85 because the road is completely washed out. No more than fifty feet from where we stopped, the pavement has given way into a deep gully that had a wild torrent in it thirty feet across. I saw dead cattle swept by." I made a face, and he nodded soberly. "If we had fallen in, we would have had a dickens of a time surviving. I think it would have caught the car like a bag of candy and carried it pretty far downstream." He glanced at the road sign. "Let's look at the atlas and see what we can learn about the lay of the land around our Tenth Mesa."

We opened the map on the hood and focused a light on the western end of North Dakota. We traced the last part of our route and guessed about where we were on Route 85. Fletcher tilted his head back and forth, making up his mind. "Maybe there's another way north from Tenth Mesa, a ranch road, that will takes us to the Montana border. We have four-wheel drive so we can take most any back road."

"But, Fletcher, what if the road to Tenth Mesa is washed out too? At least on this main road someone eventually will come by. And, to be frank, I'm spooked by that apparition. I'm serious."

Fletcher was having none of it. "Have you noticed there has been no traffic for an hour? I think the weather has been so bad with so many washouts that the road is probably closed on both sides of us. Anyway, there may be some habitation along the way to Tenth Mesa where we can get some directions. It's clearing now, so we will be able to see what's ahead if we take it slow."

"What about the flooding? The same stream that you said washed out the road ahead of us. Won't we encounter it again.? And what about the rider and the horse?"

Fletcher was determined. "That stream is probably down to a trickle now. That's how flash floods work. A wall of water, a huge surge, and then it dries up just as fast as it came. So we'll take our time and see what's what in Tenth Mesa. If it's not passable, we can always turn back." He chuckled as he turned to my other objection. "As to your horseman, why fear what we don't understand? We don't get out of life alive anyway, do we. Maybe he's on our side. Maybe it's all just a mixture of happenstance and serendipity. I say we push along to Tenth Mesa and keep fate guessing rather than sitting here. "But," he said, forcing an exaggerated yawn, "if you want to stay, that's what we'll do."

"Heaven forfend I be the cause of boredom for Fletcher Mac-Donald. All right, let's press on. But I hope you see him next so I don't commit myself to a mental institution."

"Max, you're a sport." He clapped me on the shoulder. "Never fear, Fiona and I won't ever commit you, regardless of how loony you become."

Fletcher turned the car around and made the turn onto the dirt road at the Tenth Mesa sign. It was pretty wide and straight, but we kept our speed down to twenty so as not to outrun our headlights. The earth was muddy, and we plunged into a few very wet places, but nothing daunting in the slightest. But also no sign of Tenth Mesa, despite traveling west for fifteen minutes.

Fletcher noted, "I don't see any telephone or electric wires. There should be wires coming from the City of Medora, 40 miles south of here."

Just then the car dipped forward at a thirty-degree angle. "Whoa," said Fletcher. But it was too late. We went down a slope with our headlights revealing red clay walls on either side as Fletcher, clutching the steering wheel, navigated what turned out still to be a road. It was like a roller-coaster, down fifty feet and up fifty, sharp corners, and another set of hillocks. "By God," said Fletcher, "we are in the Badlands." Our headlights revealed perpendicular walls along this narrow road that now threaded its way through this vertiginous world. Flatness was gone, replaced by its opposite, solid ground undulating like a roiling sea.

I said to Fletcher, "This reminds me of the haunted-house rides at the county fair. Remember how we would travel in a little open car on a track and it would zig and zag in front of hidden monsters that would suddenly leap out of nowhere in a flash of light and then disappear. I'm waiting for the obligatory skeleton to show himself and rattle his bones to the sound of blood-curdling, macabre laughter."

With only headlights to illuminate the way, the world in this up and down place seemed both very close and confined as we traversed the countless gullies from which we occasionally surfaced into the coal-black night. After an hour's bronco-like ride, we encountered a flat place, and Fletcher stopped the car. Flatness was now appealing, whereas it had been so oppressive a few hours ago.

"I can't see a thing, even with the headlights on bright. But we'll stop here and get some sleep. I'll stretch out in the back seat. The sky is clear now, so let's open up the sunroof, get some air, and look at those stars."

Fletcher turned off the engine. The reassuring windbag of the diesel engine fell deadly silent. Turning the key to off disconnected us from modernity, in fact from all external life as we knew it. Fletcher slid open the mechanical sunroof and the silence poured in. All the noise of the last few hours was replaced with an eerie serenity. My ears strained for sound, but there was none to feed them. They searched harder. All my senses accepted this altered state, and they seemed to become alive like a feral animal, aware, vitally aware, of everything and anything.

****

I awoke to the car door opening. Fletcher stood in front of the vehicle. His hat and lanky six-foot frame were silhouetted against a rapidly lightening indigo-blue sky. Only a few stars were barely visible in the last of the night. I could perceive that we were parked on the edge of a wide ravine, across from a flat mesa, that seemed to offer a commanding view of this world. Fletcher's head moved like an eagle's surveying his territory, his sharp eyes missing nothing.

"Max, it will be dawn soon. I must see this place in all its glory from the top edge of that mesa. I want to see the sunrise from that point." With that announcement he disappeared over the precipice. I was still half asleep but I forced myself out of the car. I saw Fletcher running through the ravine, diving through cedars and aspens, down and down to its floor. The light was turning golden quickly. Fletcher was clearly racing against the rise of the sun. I watched him leap and crash through the underbrush more like an antelope than a human. He reached the bottom, dashed along it, zigzagging between the giant boulders, cactus, and shrubs, and then he began his ascent up the mesa. He scrambled along sedimentary rock face. His steps loosened rock as he climbed along the fissures like Spiderman. He would stagger and fall but then pull himself along with his hands and vault forward, like an antelope, from the sheer power of his legs, eventually to reach the top of the mesa. Once there, he ran on its flat surface to the very edge that overlooked what I now saw was a land of infinite little valleys and buttes and mesas all the way to the horizon.

Fletcher raised his arms high and wide, his hands facing outward, turning his face to the sky. In a moment he became lit with an intense yellow, as if consumed with light and heat. The sun literally popped over the horizon and lit up the Badlands like a Broadway sign. To my eternal amazement, within a few moments of this illumination, the tall prairie grasses, standing four feet tall, which had been perfectly still, bowed down, row after row, as the heat of the sun swept over them like a zephyr. It was as if all the grasses were Fletcher's subjects and they were bowing their heads to say, "Good morning, Mr. MacDonald". Then they rebounded back up to begin their day.

Fletcher lowered his arms and put his hands on his knees, apparently to catch his breath from his long sprint. He sat down on the mesa, yoga style, pulled out his diary, lowered the brim of his hat to shield his eyes, and began to write. He wrote until the dawn was complete, the day whole, the sun white, and when the eye could see what the dark of night had hidden. Despite its rough texture, this creased and deeply furrowed place that had so unnerved us on our drive in was now, in full light, a peaceable and colorful land.

The maze of ravines, gullies, and draws created a fantasy of tablelands. Mesas, buttes, and cliffs painted in vibrant to pastel shades from red, to burnt umber, to pale yellows alternating with beach-sand beige and onyx black streaks of lignite. Amid the thick prairie grass were tall cottonwoods and aspens and flowers of delicate hues of purple, blue, green, yellow, and red. The air was alive with the smell of sage. The Badlands seemed a misnomer at the moment. I think Magic Lands would have been my choice. But make no mistake about it, it was much easier to become hopelessly lost and confused here than not. Night skies and bad weather or a winter's storm would bury one here in nothing flat. It just seemed harmless on this bright and clear summer's day, not unlike a sleeping lion on the savannah.

The whole event of Fletcher running to meet the sunrise and my taking in the surroundings must have consumed only an hour, yet it felt like a thousand years of events had occurred. I hadn't taken my eyes off the unfolding scene, and now I was enervated from the experience. Slipping down against a large boulder that supported my back, I fell into a deep sleep. Something woke me and I turned to look back at the car. To my astonishment, I discovered that we were parked within fifty feet of a small cabin I hadn't seen before. I guess I was so focused on watching Fletcher that I hadn't looked around me. This must be Langdon's cabin! Set in a green, grassy area, it was made of split logs with some form of beige mortar placed between the logs to keep out the rain and snow. The dwelling was about fifteen feet square and in good repair. There was no litter around it, no sign of life.

"It was an amazing sight to be able to see the cabin and the car all the way from the mesa. I could feel Langdon's presence," Fletcher called from a few feet away after returning from the mesa. "A modern Mercedes-Benz parked near this nineteenth century stockman's range cabin. Viva extreme juxtapositions! I just made the sunrise. A few seconds later, and I would have missed an extraordinary waking of the world. Max, I felt as if I had witnessed creation."

"With your arms raised, you looked like an Aztec god being adored by his subjects." I salaamed by way of demonstration. Fletcher looked as though he didn't mind such reverence. "I felt humbled by the rise of the sun. Transformed. Connected from the earth all the way up to the sun and into the cosmos. I sensed

again the power and the unity of it all. I find it peculiar, no, fortunate, that things happen that so forcefully remind me of our privileged state of existence and access to all things wonderful. There
is the potential of being one with God in every man, to understand everything, to know all—the power, the glory, and the responsibility. In a very real way, all human beings are God's
surrogates and agents. To treat any person shabbily is to treat
God shabbily; likewise, to be irresponsible besmirches God as if
God himself had acted so. All of this came to me, indelibly fresh,
with the rising sun."

In the bright morning sunlight, we walked around to the front
of the cabin. The road we drove on, just a wide dirt path, had no
tire tracks. There were no signs of vehicles anywhere. Fletcher
knocked on the split-log door. He knocked again and then pulled
on its wooden handle. The door opened easily. He took off his
hat—something he very rarely did—and, as if entering a church,
he reverentially walked through the portal. I was right behind.

The room was impeccably clean and straight. There was a
focal point, but I will come to that later. I was reminded of that
puritan virtue: a place for everything and everything in its place.
Double bunks lined one wall; one pillow and a green woolen
blanket on each bed. Another wall had three shelves with canned
goods, sugar, and flour in glass jars, a few plates, glasses, table-
ware, wooden matches in a box, a coffeepot, and a couple of
cooking pans. A small, iron potbellied stove occupied the wall
across from the door. It had a flat place on top just large enough
for that coffeepot and one small pan. In the middle of the room
was a sturdy rough-hewn table. Two equally sturdy chairs flanked
it. They rose from a wide plank floor. The ceiling was just the
naked underside of the sharply peaked roof. A couple of kerosene
lanterns hung from the rafters. The roof slats were so tight that no
light came in. There were no windows. All in all, the square room
was impeccable, albeit entirely rustic, simple, and matter of fact.
Fletcher said that this was a way station probably used by cowboys during cattle drives or when they were just riding the range.
As for the focal point of the room, it sat on the table. Both
Fletcher and I approached it with awe and great curiosity. A thick,

scrapbook-size leather-bound book was in the dead center of the table. It had the patina of great age. Engraved in gold leaf on its deep chocolate-brown cover were these words:

WELCOME. STAY AS LONG AS YOU LIKE. JUST RE-PLACE WHAT YOU USE WITH WHAT YOU CAN. PLEASE LEAVE YOUR NAME AND DATE WITHIN.

Fletcher opened the great book to the first page. The pages had the feel of parchment rather than paper, rough, rippled, and tough. The first name, clearly made with the scratching quality of a fountain pen or perhaps a quill, was that of Jacques de Mer dated August 11, 1855. A roster followed that covered fifty pages. As we looked down the names, we saw those of George Armstrong Custer, February 10, 1876, Theodore Roosevelt, 1885, and artist and journalist Frederic Remington, 1890. We found Langdon Ochs, dated August 15, 1986, ten years ago to the day. Most wrote in ink but some in pencil. A few placed an X. The entries were also of remarkably modest size. The inscriptions continued all the way to the present time; the last one was only a week ago. One hundred and thirty-three years of continuous use and history.

The book remained here, safe, a testament to the respect of travelers for one another and for history. Given the autographical value of the book, we were both flabbergasted that it had hadn't been purloined long ago. As I think back on that day when we came upon this fantastic book—touching it with our fingers to prove its existence and the signatures proof of the fact that perhaps a thousand souls had rested within those walls over so many years—it felt as if we were holding something of the order of the Declaration of Independence. The signatures in this book were witness to the Cowboy Code: aid to those who need it, respect for others.

I said, "I had always heard that the Badlands were unique. Now I know that was an understatement."

Fletcher pulled out a map from his pocket. It was already folded to a section. "I think we are in the Little Missouri Badlands, about fifty miles north of Medora, North Dakota. This area covers about two hundred square miles. It's not to be confused with the Badlands of South Dakota, about two hundred miles to the south. The Little Missouri Badlands region was Teddy Roosevelt land. This is where he had his ranch in the mid 1880s, just as the signature says. He and his wealthy Easterner friends came here to make a killing on cattle ranching. They had big dreams, though most of these ventures failed or only broke even. The biggest disaster was that of the Marquis de Mores, a Frenchmen who bought huge tracts of land out here and established the town of Medora, named after his wife, Medora von Hoffman, who came with him. They were out to make their fortune and to civilize the area to boot. Madame de Mores would play classical music and do watercolors as part of her effort to tame the roughness. She was regal to a fault. The town of Medora grew to one thousand residents and boasted a packing plant that shipped slaughtered beef to Chicago by refrigerated cars, to avoid the expense of the middlemen. That plan was supposed to be the key to success. Unfortunately the bottom dropped out of the beef markets in the late 1880s and the enterprise and Medora utterly failed. The Marquis and Madame left forever."

Fletcher continued. "Yet Roosevelt was different or became different because of his experience here. He told his sister Corrine, 'My blood seemed to rush warmer and swifter through my veins; and I fancied that my eyes reached to a more distant vision. I could look boldly upon the sun, without quivering in my glance'."

I was always amazed at Fletcher's erudition, but this was particularly unusual. "Fletcher, how is it that you remember his words so well?"

"His love of the land and conservation are rooted right here. His respect for people and hard work and a square deal are also rooted here. In many ways, he took the Code of the Cowboy and made it his. He became a Progressive—we would call him a liberal now—and he never looked back. He often said that he owed his presidency to how his character was refined here in the Badlands of North Dakota."

"I have been here only a few hours, and the difference from any other place is extreme," I said. "The lay of the land makes you think more intricately. Nothing is straight. Everything has a hook and a turn to it. I can easily imagine how this land works against you in bad weather. And yet I can see how, if you survive, it can toughen you as well."

Fletcher was looking back over the ravine. "Between my experience on the mesa this morning and finding this cabin of hospitality and Theodore Roosevelt's signature, I'm reeling, too, from the experience. Maybe I'll try and read a bit. I need some quiet time for it all to seep in. I'll get some apples, bread, cheese, and water from the car and we can have breakfast. Do you mind if we linger here? It's just too special a place to leave. We could spend the night in the cabin and head back to US 85 tomorrow. I don't think heading farther into the outback will bring us to anything but a played-out road."

"Not in the slightest. I've got a book that is feeling unloved, so if I don't fall asleep I might do it some justice."

We fixed ourselves a little feast and, despite all the good intentions to read, we both fell asleep in the warm light of the ascending sun.

****

"I say, my good men, those books are never going to get read that way. Although in my time at the Elk Horn Ranch I was known to fall asleep on the porch with a good book in my hands. But come on now, I don't have all day." A rotund rather short man, mustachioed, and wearing pince-nez spectacles was vigorously tapping our feet.

Fletcher scrambled to his feet and, dusting off his pants and hands, said, "Mr. President. Mr. Roosevelt. To what do we owe this honor? I am Fletcher MacDonald and this is Max Bateman. We are from Inverness, Canada."

"Yes, I know who you are. I've been shadowing your trail since you came within a hundred miles of Tenth Mesa. You watched the sun come up on Tenth Mesa. I was about your age when I first saw this land, in my late twenties.

"Not much difference between Canadians and Americans. Unnatural that we are separate nations, given that we are joined at the hip as it were. Maybe one day that will change. Some of my best riding and hunting partners were Canadian. We are both nations of immigrants, and our strength comes from the working of the great natural lands we both have.

"I gave your friend Mr. Ochs the horseshoe so he could always find his way back. That man has a good heart, and so do you both, or you would never have found us in the first place. You see, Mr. MacDonald, your magnetic theory only goes so far. The last mile is a leap of faith. You are not in a place here as much as a state of mind. Your hearts, as well as the power of your mind, give you access. I hear that you, Mr. MacDonald, have distinguished yourself as 'the Scottish problem solver' and you are making a mark for yourself. I thought I would show you and your good friend around a bit, so you can, how shall I say it, see better. This cabin has been a cowboy station since before my time. What I want to show you is just a little walk beyond it." He strutted off, moving far faster than one would think his weight and huge girth would allow.

Fletcher and I had to run after him to catch up. I said, "This is a great honor for me. You set in motion the conservationist movement that is a model for Canada too."

"I told Congress that to waste and destroy the land would deny our children the very prosperity we ought to hand down to them. Part of that prosperity is knowing the glory of feeling free. You need the wilderness to know freedom." He trudged along the rim of the ravine that the cabin looked over, until we came to a site that divided the land into three separate chasms. He walked out onto a mesa, beckoned us to follow, and made for its point.

He was winded as he spoke. "Maybe the old asthma is showing. It's true that this place made me. Whatever I had known up to this point, this place subjected it to the fire of putting it to practice. Ethics, physical strength, discipline, rigorous thinking were required to survive and understand the Badlands. It could be wicked, especially in winter. Gale force winds would rip the skin off your bones. But then, if you understood her, there was always shelter because of these fantastic formations. More important, you learned never to shirk and to be the best you can be. Everyone relied on each other to survive and succeed. Freedom of the mind and the soul was paid for with hard work. I came to understand that it was the strenuous life, not ignoble ease, that was the elixir of life. That it was better to dare mighty things, even if checkered by failure, than to live in the gray twilight that knows not victory or defeat. Think of the Badlands as nature's purifier. Ah, we are here now."

At the end of the mesa, Roosevelt showed us down a steep cow path that led down to a stream bottom, until we were in the cottonwoods. He guided us along the flat and then stopped and had us look out. We beheld a modern-day saloon, complete with a long bar and stools. A mirrored back wall was lined with an infinite array of liquor bottles. There was a younger man, our age, at a bar. He was talking to someone about the same age. We could hear their conversation, but they were oblivious to us.

YOUNG MAN: A couple came into the showroom today to buy a new car. The sticker price was thirty thousand dollars. I ran a credit check on them. They had average credit. They wanted to finance the car. I gave them the standard pitch of taking ten percent off, rebates, and whatnot, and then I built the cost back up with this and that. So, it was back to thirty thousand dollars, plus interest. In sixty months, that car was going to cost them fifty thousand. And the moment they take possession of it, it won't be worth half of what they will owe.

FRIEND: How do you feel about that?

YOUNG MAN: If I had just pushed the special warranty protection plan, I could have made another two thousand dollars on the transaction. That's how I feel about that. I left money on the table.

FRIEND: I mean how do you feel about the cost to the customer? By any measure, hasn't he been a fool?

YOUNG MAN: That's the way of the world. Take maximum advantage. That's what the customer would do in his relationship with his customers or an employer or whatever. This is laissez-faire capitalism. You make what you can, when you can.

FRIEND: But how do you feel about the customer, personally? Isn't he a fellow human being, a fellow citizen?

YOUNG MAN: He's not my concern. He needs to take care of himself. That's how it works best: if everyone looks after himself first, we all win.

FRIEND: And, if he makes more of the same mistakes and can't feed his family, or educate them, or take care of their health, does that make any difference?

YOUNG MAN: Absolutely not. We live off fools, and the fools eventually die off. If everybody was wise and careful, we would-n't profit, let alone survive. Who in their right mind would pay the profit margins we try for and get? Doesn't make any difference if you're selling cars, legal services, medicines, or oil. You charge what you can get away with. That's the system.

FRIEND: Where do you draw the line? Who isn't a mark for your system? A friend? Your family?

YOUNG MAN: Of course, people close to me I try and help, even if they're weak, although I resent parasites, even if they are my own blood, but what can I do?

Roosevelt spoke. "This is the laissez-faire way. It recognizes no bounds of decency. In its maniacal pursuit of profit and capital, it savages society and any sense of moral order. It is antithetical to a civilized society. That is why I endorsed antitrust legislation, to break the back of robber-baron capitalism with its own medicine, competition. I detest those malefactors of great wealth. And that is why it was necessary to take fifty million acres of wilderness out of the grasp of these robber-barons, who would have stripped and destroyed it forever. Naked capitalism is the natural enemy of morality, because it places greed above all else. Let's move on."

We walked along the path and came to a different ravine. It was the same scene, a bar with the same young men sitting at the bar, discussing the same transaction.

YOUNG MAN: A couple came into the showroom today to buy a new car. The sticker price was thirty thousand dollars. I ran a credit check on them. They had average credit. But they had a high government association rating of ten. So I took off the standard ten percent and gave them the preferential government financing rating, so the car will cost them about thirty thousand dollars.

FRIEND: How do you feel about that?

YOUNG MAN: I don't like it. It's not what you do. It's who you know. Just because they are part of the "party" they get special treatment. I wish I could get into the "party" but they don't want just anyone. No, you have to practice the right religion, be the right race, have the right friends. Well, the world is what it is.

FRIEND: What can you do about it?

YOUNG MAN: Nothing. The government controls everything. Knows what we are doing, saying, thinking. There's nothing we can do.

Roosevelt spoke. "This is the tyranny or dictatorship of elitism. It saps people of the will to be productive. Everyone, except the rulers, becomes slaves to the society. No man should be above the law and no man is above it. Come with me around this point and let's see another story."

YOUNG MAN: A couple came into the showroom today to buy a new car. The sticker price was thirty thousand dollars. I ran a credit check on them. They had average credit. They wanted to finance the car. I gave them the standard pitch of taking ten percent off, rebates, and whatnot, and then built the cost back up with this and that. So, it was back to thirty thousand dollars, plus interest. The law required that I tell them exactly what the car would cost. Over sixty months, that car was going to cost them fifty thousand. And the moment they take possession of it, it won't be worth half of what they will owe. They said that was too much and was there anything I could do about it. I backed out the additions and arranged a better loan, so the car would cost forty thousand dollars overall. They decided that it was worth it and bought the car.

FRIEND: How do you feel about that?

YOUNG MAN: Well, pretty good. The customer wasn't getting a great deal, but buying new cars generally aren't investments anyway. At least they knew what it would really cost. So I feel all right about it. They were informed.

FRIEND: If the law requiring you to disclose the real cost didn't exist, would you have told them?

YOUNG MAN: Probably not. It's very hard to forego our natural instincts to make the most on every sale. But, personally, I feel better about making sales that people can live with. Roosevelt said, "That's what I fought for when I became president. I came to believe that every man holds his property subject to the general right of the community to regulate its use to whatever degree the public welfare may require of it."

Roosevelt continued, "The first requisite of a good citizen in a democratic republic is that he shall be able and willing to pull his own weight. The second requisite is the square deal. Whatever you call it, it is a question always of fairness. And an honest man knows the difference. He can recognize deceit, greed, evil and the rest of it right off. Life here makes things clearer than in easier places to live. I'm glad you have come. Don't forget to put your name in the book. Good-bye and remember, in life as in a football game, the principle to follow is: Hit the line hard." With that he vanished.

We both placed our names in the guest book. Fletcher Mac-Donald, August 15, 1996. Max Bateman, August 15, 1996, and closed the door of the cabin.

"Max, I would rather move on than spend the night here. I think our business is complete and to stay would only detract from the experience. We have news to report to Langdon, although I suspect he knows far more than he let on." I sensed Fletcher's request came from that deep place of respect he had for timing.

"Sure," I said. "Let's be off. Nobody but Langdon, I suspect, is going to believe that we saw and spoke with Teddy Roosevelt. Sort of like the time you put the ropes through those eye hooks. How come these things happen to you?"

"Max, my good friend, as I recall, it was you that Mr. Roosevelt first appeared to, not me! I think your good heart, honesty, and thoughtfulness create an air of acceptance of these special insights so they can occur to both of us. It isn't just happenstance that we are a team. We get along because we share important values. Our friendship is not simply one of what you can do for me and what I can do for you, or for amusement. We help each other be the best we can be."

Fletcher brightened. "And speaking of amusement, we also like trout fishing, Scrabble, and storytelling with Langdon. Missoula, here we come!"

THE TOWN THAT TIME FORGOT

Fletcher, Fiona, and I traveled from Inverness, Cape Breton, to New York City by plane, and then took the train from Pennsylvania Station to Ocean Grove, New Jersey. The seaside town adjoins Asbury Park, a bedraggled, drug-infested beach resort and spiritual home of rock icon Bruce Springsteen. It was a sultry, humid night, not atypical of the summer weather along the Jersey coast. Just before we disembarked, Fletcher pulled from a pocket in his trench coat a crinkled flyer that he had been sent by a client, Jed Bemis. He gravely opened it up and shook his head while reading it. Fiona looked over his shoulder at it and flushed while reading it to the color of her red hair.

> *As long as the vermin*
> *live amongst us,*
> *Christ will not come.*
> *They must be exterminated*
> *To make way for him!*
> *Armageddon Army*

Fiona said, "Every time I see it I want to spit. We'll find them and fix their wagon."

Fletcher, his jaw clenched, jammed the flyer back into his pocket and looked past Fiona.

"Ocean Grove. Next stop, Ocean Grove," the conductor called out.

We gathered our belongings and emerged from the train into the summer night. Parading down the tracks was a busy mix of tourists arriving on vacation and commuters who worked late in the city. Taxis swooped, horns honked, and rock music pumped from the cars of testosterone-spiked males cruising the scene. Most of the people we passed were black and poor as we made our way toward Ocean Grove. The buildings were in a state of disrepair, with gaudy signs advertising cheap products, services, and thrills.

We crossed a noisy highway and walked a short block up a little incline to the gates of Ocean Grove. On the other side of the gates, everything magically changed. Traffic noise was replaced with the hush of old thick-leaved oaks and sycamores that lined streets so narrow that cars were forced to move at horse-and-buggy speeds. Ornate street lamps imparted a gaslight ambiance to the night.

The architectural style was completely Victorian. Fletcher had told us about the buildings on the plane ride. One dollhouse after another, all different in detail and yet all the same in a larger sense. Sometimes called painted ladies, Ocean Grove houses were built in the late nineteenth century. They came in about ten or so basic styles, the plans purchased from Sears and Roebuck. A proper Victorian house had a pointed tower or two, several covered porches, with facades festooned with lacy woodwork and thin carousel columns with infinite turnings and finials. These wooden dollhouses were further enlivened by vivid painting schemes, alternating many colors to produce a kaleidoscopic effect. Twenty-five hundred such Grove houses, pretty much the entire housing stock, thereby defined a subculture having little resemblance to the outside world that had left the Victorian era a long time ago. Ocean Grove had even been designated a National Historic Site, because it is home to one of the largest intact collection of Victorian houses in the United States.

"This reminds me of a theme park or a movie set," Fiona remarked, "except it's real. It's also odd that they are all so very close together. Some of the roofs even touch each other. A fire would burn through this town in no time."

Fletcher instructed, "The reason the houses are so close together is that the lots were purposefully designed to be small to encourage humbleness and equality. It was all part of the master plan put together by Mr. Stokes, who founded Ocean Grove as a Methodist camp for Christian meditation and restoration of the soul. The idea was for this to be a seaside resort for Methodists, and only Methodists.

To this day, the Methodist Church owns all the land. The church leases the land to the homeowners for ninety-nine years, and it is subject to renewal.

"So this is essentially a company town with a twist," he added with a smile.

We reached a green sward called the Pathway, which led to a wide boardwalk that ran along the beach and overlooked the ocean. There we saw, for the first time, the famous yet eerie Ocean Grove beacon of the night. If one were to approach Ocean Grove from the sea, the predominant feature would be this thirty-foot illuminated Christian cross that seemed to be nailed onto the black sky. It actually sits atop a wooden auditorium built in 1859 that seats six thousand worshippers to hear the Good News. A star-blue fluorescent light radiates from the massive cross. It was an unsubtle reminder that we were in the penumbra of a community dedicated to God. For some, this cross is a welcome assurance of safety and for others, a warning.

Fletcher suggested that we sit on a boardwalk bench to get our bearings and rest a bit before we headed on to our final destination, the home of Jed Bemis. Fletcher was surprised by the large sportfishing boat traffic on the sea. There must have been twenty or more boats trolling the ocean waters out just a quarter mile or so from the boardwalk.

By prompting Fletcher, I found out a few more facts pertinent to our visit. "Ocean Grove does not permit the sale of alcoholic beverages, whereas the adjacent towns of Asbury Park and Bradley Beach invite citizens to imbibe with gusto. Until 1981, the Grove had some of the most restrictive blue laws in the United States. It was even illegal to have a car or vehicle of any type on the streets of Ocean Grove from midnight on Saturday until midnight on Sunday. All cars had to be parked outside the Grove. So imagine, when you were here on a Sunday, there were no cars anywhere in this town. Unreal but curiously tolerated almost into the twenty-first century."

Fletcher brought us back to the present. "Those blue laws were exposed and eliminated by a newspaper delivery man who was so angered because he couldn't bring his truck into the Grove to deliver newspapers that he sued the community on the basis of an undue burden on his constitutionally protected rights of inter-state commerce. The New Jersey Supreme Court used this case to strike down most of the blue laws. There are only two remnants: Ocean Grove remains a dry town and no one is permitted to use the beach before noon on Sunday.

"Being shorn of this uniqueness the town experienced a de-cline in its fortunes. These quaint buildings were decaying rapidly, some disintegrating into dust. Coming to the rescue were gays from New York City who were attracted by the below-mar-ket real estate values and the architectural aesthetics of the houses. The Grove residents were so broke that they couldn't re-sist the invasion, and indeed, once they saw their real estate val-ues rise, they cautiously accepted the newcomers. This became a live-and-let-live town, at least on the surface. The gays were probably hoping that the Grove would become another Province-town, Massachusetts, but that didn't happen. A détente with the natives is as far as it went."

"Where does Jed fit in all this?" Fiona asked.

I explained, "He's an old-line Methodist. The family goes all the way back to the settlement's creation in the 1850s. But he's not stuck in the past. My strong impression is that he sincerely feels that the changes have been for the best. He and his friends fear that the recent disappearance and possible murder of two gays who lived in the Grove were masterminded by this Armageddon Army, which is growing more aggressive. First graffiti, then flyers, and now assaults and maybe worse. They seem determined to make Ocean Grove a bastion of prejudice and exclusion again, using Christian fundamentalism as their cover. This Army claims that Ocean Grove has been selected as sacred ground by God and will be one of Christ's estates when he returns to the earth, with the au-ditorium as a temple. Jed says that they have secret meetings to re-store the old blue laws and to eventually create an actual fighting army to force their will on the world. He is sure that the Armaged-don Army printed and distributed this ugly flyer."

Fiona was perplexed. "They seem so conspicuously subver-sive. Why doesn't Jed report them to the authorities?"

Fletcher said, "He has. But he has been faced with reluctance on the part of the authorities to dig into this. They claim that they have no hard evidence. As we all know, the politics of the times look favorably on Christian fundamentalism. Combine that with a history of exclusion and we have a basis for officialdom to look the other way unless they are forced to act. Jed has hired us to develop overwhelming evidence so that the authorities will have good political cover and be forced by overall national public opinion to move against the Army. At a minimum he wants the Army out of Ocean Grove."

The irony of the setting was astonishing to all of us. We all looked out on the most peaceable of night scenes from the boardwalk. The painted ladies were aglow with welcoming candles and joyful twinkling lights festooning their facades. A bronze Lincolnesque statue of the founder of Ocean Grove looked benevolently out on to the boardwalk, where late night promenaders were walking arm in arm under a startlingly huge full moon that hung over the great sea. And yet this tranquility fragilely rested in a thin, filmy layer on a lethal caldron of bigotry that had already claimed innocent lives and could drown the whole town.

Fletcher rose, breaking this moment of collective lucidity, and said it was time to go to Jed's home. A typical Victorian, it was located on a side street a half block from the boardwalk. The rocking chairs on the porch were a welcoming sight. Each window had an electric candle in it. Its tower—they all had towers, generally crooked—looked out on the sea and a little porch which I am sure Fletcher would seek out. It would remind him of his lookout at Mabou Point. The sea breeze solidly slapped the awnings that night.

After being shown to our quarters, we got together in Jed's living room, where his wife and a few other friends were gathered and offered us sandwiches and other snacks they had prepared. They were a quiet and pleasant group, and their underlying soberness seemed at odds with their whimsical house and the lyrical summer night. How very serious they were was soon revealed.

Jed turned on a small window air conditioner and invited everyone into the large living room. He told us that the air conditioner was a necessity—not to cool us off, since there was a good breeze off the sea, but to mask the discussion. I was surprised by this precaution, because it suggested how pervasive the reach of the Army might be. Chairs and sofas had been arranged into a circle for all of us to face one another. Jed asked if we minded if he said a prayer before we began. Of course, we didn't. Everyone bowed their heads. I sneaked a peak at the group to see tightly closed eyes. Jed and his wife held hands so tightly that I could see the whites of their knuckles. In addition, there were four others in the room: a young blonde woman with a busy charm bracelet, a middle-aged black couple, and a fortyish muscular man in shorts and a flamboyant Hawaiian shirt.

After the prayer, Jed laid out the problem.

"Two people have disappeared from our community within the last six months. They were both gays. For the last few years there has been a growing hate campaign against gays primarily, but also against blacks and Jews, which seems to be nurtured by this Armageddon Army. Of course, they never take credit for direct assaults. But the attacks are becoming more frequent and, in our opinion, have turned deadly.

"We are all Methodists here and we care very much about our faith and this community. We have pooled our funds to pay your fees to help us get to the bottom of our difficulties. No one officially admits to the existence of the Armageddon Army, but we are sure that there are as many as one hundred in our area who belong to it. We don't know. Some of them may be politically powerful in this community. We think this because our objections to what they say have been met, in our opinion, with retribution, such as prosecutions for housing code violations that have cost many thousands of dollars, denial of building permits, and most of all ostracism. The Army punishes their enemies by whisper campaigns of slander resulting in neighbors disassociating from those who object to their activities.

"Linda," he said, pointing to the young blonde, "was the target of slander that alleged she had had a late-term abortion, which was untrue. She had no abortion whatsoever. The Clarks," he continued, nodding at the black couple, "were rumored to be selling drugs. Their house was raided a few weeks ago by the police. The charge was ridiculous, but the influence of the Army, as I have said, seems to run to high places."

Fletcher asked, "Who is the ringleader?"

"We think it is John Sample. He came to the community from Illinois about five years ago. That is coincidentally when this Armageddon Army thing started. He holds prayer meetings in his home, and we think that he is the nerve center of the organization. He's not a Methodist, as far as I know."

I asked, "What does he do for a living?"

"I really don't know. He seems to live frugally and doesn't seem to need to work. I see him daily on the fishing pier reading the Scriptures. I think he meets some of his followers there."

Fiona turned to the Clarks. "Forgive me, but the first thing I noticed was that there seemed to be a sharp racial divide between Asbury Park and Ocean Grove. Is that true, even after all the years since the blue laws were struck down?"

The wife shook her head. "Things have changed. We have had a house in the Grove for fifteen years. We have always been Methodists and lived in Neptune. When the barriers to ownership dropped, we began to look in the Grove. Frankly, the people at the church here were warm and welcoming to us. There are more black families here than ever before. This Armageddon Army is another matter. In addition to their being fundamentalists, we know that they are racists from the slurs we have heard from them. We all have seen racist graffiti that is clearly their doing. We know it's their doing because it is always accompanied by a swastika and an extra line on the upper stroke that creates a cross within the symbol."

"It's the gay disappearances that have brought this to a head. I'm sure in my gut that they are dead," said the man with the Hawaiian shirt, whose first name was Mark. "It all began a few years ago with gays being hassled, then the graffiti, then several beatings. But now we have the disappearances. Not a trace. And they all lived in the Grove. Things really got out of control when the Army's so-called Date of Destiny came and went without anything happening. There was a spike in their activity, as if they were desperate for something big to happen even if they instigated it."

"Date of destiny?" I asked, looking at Fletcher. This was the first we had heard of this.

Jed explained, "A few days after we called you, we started seeing flyers and graffiti go up saying that June 6, 2006, was going to be a Date of Destiny and that all "vermin" would die on that day. That was the day when the calendar read 666. Of course nothing happened. But then more beatings occurred, a cross was burned on the beach, and another gay disappeared."

Fletcher asked for a description of John Sample.

Mrs. Bemis answered, "He stands about six feet tall and is grossly overweight. He has a deep voice with the cadence of a preacher at all times. His hair is reddish-blond and is clearly dyed. He wears a black jacket and trousers with a white shirt all year round. He is slovenly, not very attractive. He has very big hands, and I think he is physically powerful."

"Does he go to the fishing pier at regular times?"

"Basically nighttime, about ten to twelve, about now."

Jed said softly, but forcefully, "Whatever you have to do, Mr. MacDonald, to put him out of business, we will back you one hundred percent. He's giving us all a bad name, not to mention the crimes that we are sure he is behind."

Fletcher rose and said, "There is no time to lose." He asked Fiona to interview everybody at the meeting and to get character-istics of the people they believed were members of the Army.

Fletcher turned to Jed and asked, "I noticed a lot of sportfish-ing boat activity. Is Sample a fisherman? Does he have access to a boat?"

"He hangs around fishermen, yet I have never seen a rod in his hands. I am sure he doesn't have a boat. But he has friends in the fishing club and some of them have boats."

"Are the ocean waters regularly patrolled by the police or Coast Guard?"

"Very little. The Coast Guard runs helicopters once a day up and down the coast, but that's all. I think they do it for show."

"I think your wife said that Sample makes an appearance on the fishing pier about now, so Max and I will try to find him. We'll see you later."

The fishing pier was built on pilings and stretched from the boardwalk, over the sand, to extend one hundred feet into the ocean. The waves were breaking on the wooden pilings under the great moon of the night. Fletcher strode along the boardwalk, past couples sitting on the benches staring at the sea, solitary figures strolling along, and the occasional jogger. Some teenagers were huddled on a bench, lighting up cigarettes. The air was much cooler near the sea, maybe by fifteen degrees.

We turned the corner of the boardwalk and started to walk along the pier. It, too, had benches for the public to look at the beach and the sea. Up ahead, sitting on a bench with two other men, was a very large man in a black suit, who fit the description of John Sample. As we drew closer, the conversation abruptly stopped.

Fletcher walked up to the bench where the large man was holding court. The two young men sitting with him rose and walked down the pier. Fletcher sat down on the same bench, and I remained leaning against a railing, a respectable few yards away. Close-up, we were sure this was the man. His girth was such that it took up half of the bench. He was certainly unkempt; he smelled as if he hadn't bathed.

In a flat Midwestern accent Fletcher said, "The Lord has given us a good night. Don't you agree, brother?"

Sample responded in an imperious vein, "The Lord takes care of His flock. Some will die from this heat, but here in the Grove, if you know what you are doing, He takes care of you with the coolness of the sea. Even if, like myself, you can't swim, ocean water cools the air and wraps you with natural air conditioning."

Fletcher rejoined, "Amen, brother. The Lord cools His own. And He smites down the infidels, the apostates, and the blasphemers."

"Amen," responded Sample warmly. "There are many in our midst who fit that description. We must always be on guard to do the Lord's work."

"It's not always easy work either, brother. Abraham was ordered to kill his dearly beloved son, and yet it hurt him to do it. He followed the will of God."

Sample leaned forward a bit, more interested. "Brother, you are right. The Lord's work tries men's souls. But only the truly righteous understand that it must be done to clear the way for Him to return to guide us to better days. And those days are nigh."

"Brother, yes, they are nigh." Fletcher reflected and sighed. "I thought it was so near that I could feel the smell of judgment in the air. And I can still smell it. It is even deeper than ever before."

"Brother, what is that smell you noticed? Was it sulfur mixed with blood?"

Fletcher nodded. "Yes, brother, that was it. Exactly."

"Brother, my name is John Sample. What is your Christian name?"

Fletcher answered respectfully, "George Cumber, from Illinois. I've come here to soak up some old-fashioned religion at the ocean. I come every year to hear the ministers give their morning-by- the-sea sermons. Carries me for the entire year." He pointed at me and explained, "And this is my friend, Bill Starr."

I said heartily, "Wonderful to meet a man who quotes the Good Book as the source of all wisdom."

Sample nodded. "There is no other knowledge, friend."

"Amen to that," Fletcher and I chimed in.

"Brother Cumber, it isn't any accident that we meet on this bench tonight, is it?"

"What do you mean, Brother Sample?"

"You mean you don't know who I am?"

"Brother, I know your heart is Gospel-fearing and white, and that is all I need to know to be your friend."

Sample was very pleased by Fletcher's response. "Things are moving fast towards the final days. Our work is fully operational now. We need more willing hearts and hands because there is so much filth to remove before He returns. I think you and your friend will find more than rejuvenation of your soul this summer in the Grove. You will find meaning and purpose and a way to work for our Lord. A way for you to repay the gift that He has given you. A way to advance the day of the Kingdom of God here on earth."

Fletcher pretended equal delight. "What luck to have met you on the Lord's evening."

"Come, Brother Cumber. Come Brother Starr. Walk with me and I will tell you about things greater than you ever could have believed."

We left the bench behind. Sample walked well despite his girth. Fletcher, with his hands folded behind his back, listened intently. Sample conspiratorially lowered his voice as he disgorged the standard diatribes of the racists against Jews, Negroes, liberals, and gays, all laced together with his belief that Armageddon was near but that it would not come unless the faithful prepared the way for Christ to return and rule. We nodded assent to the slurs.

Fletcher then astounded me by saying, "As I left the train this evening and saw the Negroes raising hell in their lascivious way, I wondered how the Grove protected itself from their proximity. I have even seen on your boardwalk men holding hands. Disgusting and a hideous insult to God. The evil is so near the heart. How fortunate this place has you and your friends working to protect it."

Fletcher had struck the right note. Sample grabbed his arm and said, "Brother Cumber, Brother Starr, I am very impressed with your devotion and understanding of God's way. Perhaps you might like to meet some of us who are working hard to see that the Lord comes to us here in Ocean Grove very soon?"

Fletcher solemnly responded, "Brother Sample, this would be destiny. I am sure the Lord led us to you to be of service to Him. You are clearly His general here, and we will follow you."

"Some do call me His general, but I prefer to think of myself as a foot soldier for Christ." His attempt at modesty made me want to laugh. "You must meet with us at the Embassy Hotel Bar in Asbury Park tomorrow night at midnight. A flicker of doubt crossed his face. "We meet in a bar so as to not bring attention to our work. No one would suspect that the Lord's work would be carried out in such a place. You know that the enemy has many soldiers who would try and slaughter us if they could. Tomorrow we will strike another blow for Him. And perhaps you and Mr. Cumber will want to join your brothers in arms eternally and forever."

"General Sample, we will follow you gladly into hell if that is what it takes to bring Him to earth. Give us the chance to serve!"

"Amen." And we bade each other farewell until tomorrow at midnight.

I was sickened by Fletcher's racist remarks and I let him know it. "Was it necessary to let that slime come out of your mouth?" Fletcher's crisp retort returned in a second. "We needed to seal the deal with him. They need converts more than anything to do their dirty work." As we headed down the boardwalk, he explained further, "Nothing compares to the blind zeal of converts. These people get high on their own propaganda, and having newcomers makes them think that their message is somehow valid because someone else buys it. It makes no difference how low or worthless we are. As long as we are breathing, we swell their confidence."

"Fletcher, I think this is one adventure I'm not going to enjoy." We walked back to Jed's house and Fiona.

"Fiona," Fletcher was rapidly orchestrating a plan. "Tomorrow evening, I want you to scope out the Embassy Hotel Bar in Asbury. Dress to kill for this low-life place. Wheedle anything you can from the owner, bartender, manager, and customers about Sample and his Army. Drop Sample's name and, while you're at it, Jed Bemis's as well, to see if anything registers.

We will be at the bar at eleven-thirty tomorrow evening. Without revealing any connection to us, pass on what information you learned. Rent a fishing boat with a full crew. I want you on that boat from 1 a.m. on, to run dark and slowly near the beach between the fishing pier and in front of the Ocean Grove auditorium until I signal you to pick us up. Be alert to anything resembling a signal, because I'm not sure what we will have at our disposal. Cost is no object. Just be sure you have a boat there."

****

By and large, Asbury Park is where the debris meets the sea. Bruce Springsteen made the town famous singing at the Stone Pony Club, when he was as poor as the people he sang about, belting out his wrenching songs of blue-collar America struggling to find any way to hold its head up. Yet if the Stone Pony defined hard times, the Embassy defined bad times. From a hundred feet outside, the place stank of urine and beer. The hookers, druggies, leather people, and transvestites were the same habitués of Mack the Knife's Berlin bars and cafés. And just as ruthless. Everyone was meat on a hook.

Fletcher and I had carved ourselves out a small spot at the end of the bar. The place was so dark and crowded that it wasn't possible to see more than ten feet. Music blared, and a tiny dance floor had a bizarre collection of enthusiasts. We didn't see Fiona. Although New Jersey had recently passed a no-smoking ban for bars and restaurants, this place hadn't heard of it. The smoke was as thick as being inside the smokestack of a coal power plant. Fletcher had donned a leather jacket, a T-shirt, and jeans. I was wearing a black Motorhead T-shirt, black jeans, and metal-studded wristbands—one of which had a concealed infrared camera to catch what evidence came our way. Fletcher still kept his hat on, which covered that brassy red hair. His pale white skin was turned fire red by the only lights in the joint. He had consumed a couple of bottles of beer because we arrived early. Barflies incessantly came up to ask for handouts, drugs, and worse. It was going to be a hard night for Fiona.

She then appeared from the restroom area. A smarmy gent moved behind her and placed the crook of his arm around her neck, guiding her to a spot at the bar, too far from us to hear her, although she saw us. She gave every appearance that she was interested only in him and that he owned her. She was all tarted up, complete with platform heels, and showing too much skin for my comfort. With some distaste, I aimed my wrist camera and recorded her. Fletcher grabbed his bottle and plowed into the crowd to get closer to Fiona. I followed suit. He emerged one body down the bar from her. He addressed Fiona in a loud and mocking inebriated voice, "Hey, miss, how about a dance?"

Fiona's protector roared, "Get out of her face, you fucking queer!"

Fletcher kept his eyes on Fiona, his thin, lanky body, picking its way ever closer to her, never responding in the slightest to his antagonist.

Fiona gave the man a bear hug and a teasing kiss, and said, "Hey, let me give the guy a thrill. He's probably never been so close to the real thing. Maybe I can turn him on. It will be a challenge. Come on, let me play."

Fiona's manhandler looked confused and then began to laugh loudly saying, "Yeah, let's see if he knows what to do, the fucking queer. Go ahead, sexy, make him hard."

Fiona grabbed Fletcher and dragged him to the dance floor, slinking herself all over him. She whispered in his ear, "Sample meets regularly with a few guys in a basement room that you reach from a stairway in the back of the men's room. Don't ask me how I know. Sample's coming tonight. Most of these people, including my jerk, don't know anything. But the bartender is also the owner, and he's a raving racist. I think he's involved on the periphery. I need a cab to make a fast getaway, or I could get waylaid and not make the boat." She then slapped Fletcher's face conspicuously hard and returned to the bar, saying in a loud voice, "These queers are sick, sick. I need a real man."

In that instant, Fletcher slipped back into the crowd, found me, and wispered Fiona's predicament. I bent low and called a cab on my cell phone, just as Sample walked in, who carefully reconnoitered and spotted Fletcher and then me. Sample raised his head and waved, indicating we were to follow him. Fletcher followed Sample through a door marked "Toilet" and then through one of the stall doors, which had no toilet but an opening large enough for a man to step through. A sheet of plywood covered the opening.

I had caught Fiona's eye and made hand signals that I had made the call, and that the cab would be here in fifteen minutes. I said a prayer that she understood my charade and that she would be able to get out of this okay. Fletcher halted after passing through the opening and called, "General Sample, where are you going?" No response.

A few feet into the opening we discovered a stairway from which we heard a few murmurs of speech and the faint sound of martial music. At the bottom of the stairs, Sample called to us, "Cumber, Starr, put the plywood back." Fletcher saw that part of the wall lying against the stair landing fit the back of the bathroom stall. He replaced it, and we descended into a neon-green lit basement where three men and a woman were wearing white armbands bearing the same emblem as the large flags that draped the walls: a white field with a blue cross over a swastika. I felt a powerful revulsion to the proximity of the two symbols. I moved my wrist camera so that it recorded all of the ugliness.

"Welcome, brothers, to the White Nation of God," said Sample. "These are the other soldiers of Christ." On a table we saw literature that also had the cross-and-swastika image on it, including the flyer in Fletcher's pocket encouraging its readers to exterminate vermin.

Sample advanced to the center of the room. The green light made him look particularly gruesome. He announced, "Let's all pray." The strange martial chant music was silenced. All the people there knew the words of the prayer he spoke and said it along with him: "Hear my words, O Master. We are Your soldiers, waiting for Your orders. We stand ready to use the spear to destroy Your enemies and to throw them from Your house. Our lives are Yours. We fight and we kill in Your name. Amen."

"I want you to meet George Cumber and Bill Starr. They are fellow soldiers. Welcome them to your ranks."

"The small group chanted three times: "Jesus and whites rule! Jesus and whites rule! Jesus and whites rule!"

"We are on the road to glorious Armageddon. And, my friends, here is another tribute to the cause."

Three men lifted a mailbag onto the table with the flyers. The bag was writhing. One of them slammed the bag with his fist. There was a groan from inside. With great difficulty they dumped the contents onto the table. To our horror, it was a bloody body wearing the Hawaiian shirt of the man we met last night at Jed's, Mark. His eyes were blindfolded and his mouth was taped shut. His body was trussed and tied like a turkey. I was nauseated by the scene as I carefully recorded it. Each of the Army louts examined the body like hungry ants.

Sample then addressed us. "Brothers Starr and Cumber, this is your blood initiation rite. You will kill this vermin to prove that you are brave and true, and by doing so you will enter the Armageddon

Army forever and forever. Each man here has sealed his fate with us by digging out the hearts of the vermin while they were alive." Mark's body jerked weakly. "As there are two of you and only one rodent, we have arranged for you to simultaneously kill it with two knives. You, Starr, will cut out his heart and you, Cumber, will cut out his tongue. And, gentlemen, if you should feel not up to it, you will join him. That is the punishment for cowards. But I don't think that applies to you."

Sample was handed a box draped in white, while the others revealed pistols. He ceremoniously withdrew two long knives from the box. I looked at Fletcher, but incredibly he showed no concern. On the contrary, he said to Sample, "Brother, I believe my whole life has been in preparation for this moment. Before we go forward, I want to mention some of the events that led here." He rubbed his brow. "When I was only fifteen I remember this fag..." A loud thumping on the floor interrupted Fletcher. Sample returned the knives to the box and went upstairs.

He quickly came back, out of breath, saying there was trouble in the bar. "We will take care of this on the boat," Sample announced. "Take the vermin up the coal chute. Starr and Cumber, you come with me." We followed Sample up the stairs, escorted by a man with a pistol under his coat. We went through the bar and out into the street. I was very worried that the trouble they were referring to was Fiona. She was nowhere to be seen.

We were ushered to a large van, where the other Army members huddled in the back with Mark. It was towing a boat with an outboard motor. The van ripped away, headlights out, and two minutes later we were on the beach, pulling right to the water's edge. The boat was quickly pulled from the trailer and placed in the sea. Mark's body was hauled into the boat, and then we were, more or less, hustled on. I noticed many sandbags on the bottom of the boat. It was a smallish fishing skiff, with little draft. Eight people were far too much for the little boat.. I was worried we would tip over. We headed into the sea where, ominously, the Ocean Grove cross could be seen... bright and intimidating.

Sample ordered the boat to stop. We were facing the cross, about a quarter of a mile out to sea. From the shore we would have looked like any of the other fishing boats, just smaller. Mark's body was positioned in the center of the boat, and the other men began to tie the sandbags to his appendages and around his waist.

I caught Fletcher's eye, and I could see that it was trained on the pistol of the man nearest to us. Sample was essentially standing guard over the operation that was going so smoothly that it clearly had been done before. Fletcher then turned his hand palm side up to the port side with his thumb out, which meant to me we were to move that way in a hurry. Before I knew what happened, Fletcher had leapt to port, grabbed the pistol, shot it twice in the air, and landed with his weight pressed against the gunwale. The boat listed, and then I repeated the maneuver, forcing the boat to capsize. Fletcher swam to Mark's body as it slid into the water. It was sinking fast because of the sandbags. I dove under it to try and stop its descent. Between us, we were able to drive it to the surface. The other people were flailing in the sea, when we heard the sound of a large boat speeding toward us. Its searchlight caught us in its beam.

Fletcher yelled out, "Throw us a rope, throw us a rope. Pull this man up fast." Fiona was reaching over the side, trying to grab Mark with a long hook. The boat nosed right up to where we were, and ropes and life preservers fell on top of us. Mark had been snagged and was being hoisted onto the boat, when one of the Army members grabbed him and tried to pull him back down. Fletcher, still holding the gun, cracked the guy's skull with it and he fell away. Mark was pulled aboard. We could see the other three men swimming to shore while our boat's captain called the police on a radio-phone. Fletcher sputtered, "Where's Sample?" We looked about and presumed he was one of those trying to reach the shore. We dragged Mark's attacker from the water and onto the boat, and then hauled ourselves up as well. I hugged Fiona as I never had before. We buried our faces into each other's hair.

We were all taken by a rubber dinghy to the beach, where the police and ambulances had converged. The red lights had turned it into a wild-looking bar lounge, all under that never-blinking cross. Armed police boats were picking up the others. Jed and his wife met us with blankets and coffee. They had explained to the police their recruitment of Fletcher. Fletcher in turn laid out that in all likelihood the bodies of the slain Ocean Grovers would be found weighted down with sandbags at the bottom of the sea about a quarter of a mile out or less, directly in front of the Ocean Grove cross.

It wasn't until the next morning that we discovered that Sample had had a heart attack and drowned, according to the coroner. In the late afternoon of the next day, at Jed's house, the events of the previous night were pieced together by Fletcher. In the meantime, divers had found both of the bodies in the location that Fletcher had identified.

"The basic problem we had was that we needed the bodies to prove that a crime had been committed. From the beginning it seemed obvious to me that dropping the bodies to the sea floor was the easiest way to dispose of them. They would decompose and become fish and crab food before they washed up, which wouldn't happen soon since they were weighted down. I thought there was a good chance that Sample had a relationship with someone who owned a boat, since he was always at the fishing pier. When he so rapidly became interested in us as converts, it also became obvious that he had to bond us into his group in such a way that we couldn't reveal what we knew. Making us participate in a ritual killing was a sure-fire way. I must admit that I thought that the attempted killing would occur someplace other than the bar, given the possibility of discovery. I started my story waiting for a diversion that would stop the killing."

Fiona spoke up. "That diversion was me, boys. I was waiting for the taxi and fending off that leach, when I saw a truck unloading a sack at the very rear of the bar, and sliding it down through a trap door. My gut told me there was a body in that bag. I knew you were downstairs and I thought you could use some time, so I went back into the bar, pretended to be drunk, and went up to the bartender. I grabbed him by the lapels and told him I was out to get Sample. I didn't say why. Then I threw a stool into the middle of the floor and bolted. That caused a commotion. The cab was outside, and I pleaded for help from the driver to get me away from the leach. The taxi driver was an enormous black man who got out of the cab and tossed my macho friend across the bar.

Fletcher smiled, "Yes, Fiona, that was the plan. Just like clockwork."

"Whoa, Fletcher, I didn't have a script. What plan?"

"You already knew that we were downstairs and probably in trouble. It was natural for you to cause a disturbance so we could extricate ourselves. Very logical and predictable."

Fiona fumed, "You were just lucky that I made that fuss at the right moment. Anyway, the taxi driver took me to the harbor where the boat was waiting for us, and we chugged out to find you. We heard the pistol shots and then saw the glint of the underside of your boat as it turned over. We were no more than two hundred yards from you when we heard the shots."

There was serious awe in Fletcher's voice as he addressed Fiona, "To be fair, without your diversion at the bar, I would have been forced to use an alternative plan, to buy time and relax their guard by regaling them with stories about their hate targets. In the end, we would have grabbed Sample as a hostage with the knives to create a standoff. Your logical mind led you to make the diversion, I'm not taking anything away from that smart action."

Fiona was still annoyed, "Only that somehow I was doing exactly what you thought I would do."

Fletcher sighed, "Well, yes, but only a smart, quick witted, and resourceful person would have reacted that way. Take some comfort in that."

I hugged Fiona, and whispered, "Let it go, dear, we are alive, and that's what counts."

Fletcher turned to Jed, " You'll soon find out if there were any prominent people in the group last night. But I doubt it. These were losers who found this horrid way to make something of their miserable lives. I also now believe that the entire core group was no more than ten, maybe eight. However, there were sympathizers who gave them some cover, like the bartender at the Embassy.

The political repercussions you experienced were probably the unfortunate result of silent racism. You were complaining about the actions of people whom some secretly applauded. These are the cowards of every culture. Don't forget that Stalin's purges, the Holocaust, Pol Pot's Cambodia, and Rwanda, to name a few atrocities, didn't happen in a vacuum. There were silent masses applauding, or at least tolerating, those murders. Jed, you and your group made the difference. Whether Edmond Burke said this or not, it is eternally true: 'The only thing necessary for the triumph of evil is for good men to do nothing'."

THE WOMAN OF ARLES

Arles is an ancient Roman city snuggled in a bend of the lower Rhône, just before the arable land gives way to marshes and, farther south, the Mediterranean. Despite Arles being the place where Vincent van Gogh produced hundreds of paintings, not one can be found in the city. They have long ago entered the mainstream of the art world and now mostly are owned by museums. It is truly remarkable that in the course of a little more than a hundred years his paintings have gone from being valueless, not even worth enough to pay a pittance of rent, to a single one now worth of over a half-billion dollars. Thus, it is not surprising that his works have migrated to the money centers of the world. Arles, despite its ancient heritage and lovely setting, is not moneyed. Not even the van Gogh museum here has an original van Gogh.

That's the reason Fletcher's curiosity was aroused when he was contacted by the curator of the local museum, Monsieur Lionel Rupert, about a heretofore unheard-of van Gogh painting in Arles. M. Rupert had unsuccessfully tried to track it down. As a result of his inquiry, he heard persistent rumors that there existed in Arles a work of art of substance and style that did not match any of van Gogh's catalogued works. Fletcher at first resisted the assignment, despite his affection for the city of Arles, believing that the extraordinary value of van Gogh's work would surely have flushed out any remaining genuine pieces. As Fletcher had recovered several prized paintings over the past twenty years, his reputation for working within the dark shadows and outsized egos of the art world, especially the niche of very rare art, was well established. M. Rupert persisted and finally won the day with Fletcher by telling him that there was a particularly charming and sophisticated woman, a Claudine Safir, who was well regarded in the community, who thought she might have important and new information, and who was willing to personally discuss the matter with him. Fletcher had a weak spot for interesting woman who might be central to a case. And, truth be told, Fletcher was actually only too happy to return to Arles, a city that he favored. He had previously gone there exclusively to retrace van Gogh's working life through the paintings he had made of the city's landscapes, buildings, and denizens.

****

Not five minutes after we arrived at our hotel, Fletcher, Fiona, and I were having a cognac at the old Lamertine Café, where van Gogh's inimitable night sky illuminates a lazy evening on the cobbled streets. It seemed that some of the same locals as in his Café Terrace on the Place du Forum were ambling toward the unbusy café, which was still known for its conviviality, human warmth, and gentility. The café is now the Van Gogh Café, which seems appropriate enough given that the master had made it legendary. The place bore a stunning resemblance to the scene he made so very famous. As we sat at the round tables, just a few souls meandered by, who might or might not stop for a coffee or something stronger.

The next day we traveled along the Rhône and found Langolais Bridge. As the Golden Gate is unforgettable, unlike any other bridge in the world, so is Langolais Bridge, as immortalized by van Gogh. A side channel of the Rhône is breached here by this lift bridge, which hasn't changed much in hundreds of years. Indeed, just like the painting, Langolais Bridge at Arles with Women Washing, a vehicle was passing over its movable span. Back then it was a horse-drawn covered wagon; now it was a small truck.

I found the mechanics of the bridge remarkably well articulated in the painting, especially given that the master was an avowed Impressionist, which suggested something less than precision in rendition. Both Fiona and I were amazed by his ability to convey the essence of detail with brushstrokes that seemed so wild and extreme. Fletcher was taken by the coloration, unreal but emotionally correct. As he said, "Van Gogh is to the canvas what Shakespeare is to paper. They both go somewhere fantastical to find what is authentic and undeniably real."

M. Rupert arranged for us to meet Mademoiselle Claudine Safir, who he said was a "lubricant of society." By that, Fletcher understood that she was influential, knew how to get things done, and was probably privy to the city's secrets. Although she had an office not far from the famous Place Lamartine, where van Gogh had lived in the now-razed Maison Jaune, she chose to meet us at the gates of the ancient Roman amphitheater L'Arene, which resembles the Coliseum of Rome. Used regularly for events and seating twenty thousand spectators, it lost a top tier of arches and seats while being transformed into a feudal fortification in the Middle Ages. Still, it is very impressive in its imperial Roman grandeur.

We had some free time, so we decided to visit the market outside the ancient walls. Given the agreeable day, so bright, clear, and temperate, the idea was irresistible. The market was chockablock filled with vendors. Some streets are paved with gold, others with ambrosia. Arles is the latter. We all closed our eyes at the same time and inhaled the intoxicating lavender scent that embroidered the morning air of market day. That bright fall October morning revealed a wide redbrick pathway lined on both sides with stalls overflowing with foods and crafts from Provence and its close neighbors. One after the other, herb vendors displayed palettes of reed baskets heaped with spices that ranged from basalt black pepper to golden saffron, from dusty green sage to fire-spewing red paprika, from virginal white peppercorns to earthy shades of mustard.

The nose comes alive in such places, ascending to rule all the other sensory organs. Rich scents transport one away from the commonplace to halcyon plains. A good whiff of oregano, and one is instantly on a warm Mediterranean hillside. Aromas heighten existence by packing each sniff with transporting reveries. Where scent rules, there are no bounds to the imagination.

"Max, Fletcher, come here. Look at these olives. Dark purple, light green, and everything in between. I've never seen so many varieties. I want to sample them all." Fiona had a straw market basket that was already overflowing with flowers. Her nose and flinty red hair were just inches above the olives as she ogled each basket. Her famous heart-melting smile was at its zenith as she romped among gastronomic marvels. She had become a magnificent chef. Even if a day was rotten for me, dinner at her hands always helped me forget my travails. Fletcher was a big fan, too, of her culinary feats and was a rather frequent guest at our home. He'd bring the wine and often some bread and was fond of saying, "Fiona, you are the Chateau Mouton Rothschild of cooking, and I am happily in your irredeemable debt."

I knew that this was not just chivalrous banter on Fletcher's part, for he was for all practical purposes a gourmet and he thought Fiona was a gifted chef. If I weren't in the picture, he would have moved mountains to win Fiona's hand for this and a thousand other reasons.

Fletcher was diverted by all the extraordinary market foods from obsessing over Fiona's cooking, and began eyeing the preserved fruit from Apt, a community in Provence. Pears, apples, pineapples, apricots, tomatoes, melons, nectarines, papaya, mango, and a host of other fruits seem to have their colors intensified and defined by the preserving process. I was standing next to him as he directed the matronly lady presiding over this colorful bounty to fill a clear plastic container with his selections.

"Max," he said, "this lady says that her family has been creating these gems for two hundred years. Van Gogh and his friend Gauguin probably enjoyed them too."

"Hey, boys, what a find! Sugarplum-fairy heaven." Fiona had finally dragged herself away from the olives to see what we were up to. "This is a diabetic's nightmare. But what a splendid way to go. I'm off to the cheeses."

She gave us no time to respond. I watched her purposefully march to the white mountain of Rocheforts, Bries, Camemberts, and other artery-hugging delights. I liked to watch her from a distance, for she always evoked an uncommon intelligence and sharpness mixed with grace and beauty. We have been married thirty years, and my heart still trills at moments like these when I recognize yet again that she has chosen me to bestow these gifts on.

Fletcher slapped me on the back. "You are watching Fiona as if she were a new girl on the block. I guess you are irretrievably hooked on that lady. You are one lucky guy." He smiled in that deeply knowing fashion, with a hint of resignation. We had a special connection between us that didn't need to be explored. "Hard to remember all those good things when she's sure we are fools and lets us know it...and, of course, she's right ten times out of ten."

Before leaving the market to meet Claudine Safir, we found a sunny, grassy spot to rest and have some Brie and wine. Fletcher had a glass of his favorite red, a Côtes du Rhône. He revealed what he thought of van Gogh's work. "Whatever we see, we see with the eye of civilians. We sense something special, and that gives us respectful pause. But what it really is, only an exceptional person can understand and capture. Van Gogh did that. What he shows us is that the clarity that we behold is the product of intensity, which is paradoxical, for intensity is consuming, destructive in its fulsomeness. And what we see, and what he has shown, is eternal. Here at Arles he found a confluence of things natural and man-made—fields and cafés, night skies and bedrooms—that had such an internal intensity that it beckoned him to unlock it and to reveal it so that the world would be able to see the great contrast between what is on the surface and what makes the surface what it is."

Fiona raised herself up from her recumbent position, and addressed us both with a building passion. "It feels so strange, so empty to be in a place so well examined by one person and not to have even one of his works here. It feels like theft to me. Some of those works simply belong here as a matter of right." Fiona expressed this with indignation, which sometimes was a precursor to a Celtic fury, one we hoped would not explode.

****

The entrance to L'Arene, the Roman amphitheater, was cramped and smelled of age. Larger buildings nearby detracted from its size, at least from the perspective of the entrance. The huge stones imparted a pedestrian and officious quality, and lopsided jail-like iron gates blocked the main entrance to the great field within, which was barely visible. By paying a small donation, one could go into the structure through a small doorway.

A cab pulled up and a brown-suited woman with matching shoes and handbag and a floral scarf around her neck alighted. Pert and lively of step, her high heels clacked on the cobblestones as she approached us. She kept her head down, waved knowingly to the ticket agent, and proceeded up the steps to the innards of the structure. The ticket agent motioned that we were to follow the lady, who we presumed was Claudine.

The stairway was cavernous and dark and vaguely smelled of urine. Its width suggested that it had been built to allow hordes of people easy access and egress. We came to the first level, where we could walk out to the seats and see the whole arena. The world opened up as if we were at the center of the universe. A giant oval, football-size with a sandy floor, pulsed under the sun and was flanked with stone steps for seats, rising level after level to the rear walls of giant open arches. All that was missing were the lions and the Christians. Two levels above us and to the center of the oval was Claudine, sitting prettily and waving us up. Fletcher was first to reach her.

"This is a most dramatic place to meet, Mme. Safir. I commend you on the selection, but I can't help but wonder why you felt the need for the drama of it all."

"Monsieur MacDonald, I assure you we of Arles are not without extremes despite our bourgeois ways. Much like our mysterious light, what you see on the surface is one thing; below can be quite another. Vincent van Gogh was no stranger to these matters. The mystery must have appealed to him. May I know who your colleagues are?"

"This is Fiona MacAvoy, wife of Max Bateman, who is my associate. They often assist me on my investigations. But, may I ask, outside of creating a mysterious setting, was there a more prosaic reason for not meeting at your office?"

"But, of course. There are too many there who might whisper. Outside of myself and M. Rupert, I know of no one else who suspects that there is a van Gogh, maybe several, extant in the city. But there are always rumors, and I keep distant from them."

"More than one painting?" Fletcher noted with emphasis.

"Yes. You understand how incredibly valuable they would be. To keep this quiet, M. Rupert had the city council approve your engagement as a marketing consultant to the museum. Except for M. Rupert's knowledge, I am not associated with your work, and I would like to keep it that way."

"Of course. Yet Rupert intimated that you might be very helpful."

"Yes, I know quite a lot. As you know from your history, van Gogh created hundreds of drawings and paintings here. He was always broke and often tried to pay for his needs with his artwork. It's hard to believe that few wanted to buy any, let alone accept them as payment for services or goods. One of his needs was prostitutes, sometimes as models but also for their more regular wares. It appears his affair with Gauguin did not deter him from wanting women as well. There is ample evidence for this conclusion. His paintings, I am sure, must have changed hands for these services occasionally."

Fletcher picked up on that last comment. "Mme. Safir, was Arles a particularly bawdy city in the late nineteenth century?"

"No, probably not any more than any other city."

"Go on. Do you know more of this aspect of van Gogh's life?"

"I think that it was when he and Gauguin started to fall out that he took up with a prostitute—a Madame X, if you will—and that she became a serious love interest.

"Why do you think so?"

"Just conjecture. I am suggesting a hypothesis, you understand. Continuing. We have no paintings of her, but it is very unlikely that he would not have painted her for either payment or out of even affection. He was a very needy person and therefore would easily become very attached to anyone who showed even a passing interest in him. He would try to seal, or worse, buy the relationship with the only thing of value he had, his work."

Fletcher knitted his brow in a tender way. "Are you basing this conjecture on his relationship with the Roulin family? His many paintings of that family support that theory. They befriended him and he became very attached. There is medical opinion that suggests that van Gogh's mental disease carried with it an inordinate desire to have close personal connections."

"Exactement!" Claudine interrupted. "Now suppose that van Gogh and Madame X had a falling out, too. That's not unlikely, because van Gogh was a difficult man, according to Gauguin's letters, which make painfully clear that Gauguin had grown exasperated with van Gogh's temperament. So, too, perhaps, for Madame X. She may have walked out on Vincent and taken the paintings of herself. I imagine that scenario, since the paintings had no monetary value at the time, or perhaps she kept them out of some affection for van Gogh. And it is also possible that she simply liked the renderings and so kept them for herself."

I chimed in, "Yet the puzzle is, how they could have survived here for one hundred years, given two world wars and the well known astronomical rise in the paintings' celebrity and value. If they still exist, what is your theory to explain why they have not surfaced?"

"I agree. I don't think anyone knowing their value would have held them."

Fiona interjected. "Except if there were reasons worth more than all the gold in the world, such as a burning love or hate or mortal fear of some sort. A reason that goes against self-interest and common sense. Something bordering on the insane."

Fletcher leaned far in the direction of Claudine and looked at her in a most supportive and understanding way. "Mme. Safir, do you have something more than conjecture for your Madame X theory?"

A note of reluctance entered her voice. "I...I...know that some people here came from very poor origins, unspeakable pasts. The Industrial Revolution had a huge impact too. People who had earned their livelihood for centuries by farming or herding found themselves impoverished, and they had to adapt to a fast-changing world. Some, it is sad to say, did less than honorable things to survive. My great-grandmother's history is not pretty, and during the wars things did not improve. My parents cobbled enough together to start a restaurant and then a hotel. It became very successful, a place for the powerful to meet and plan. It gave me a strong financial platform from which to rise to the level of the success I have today."

Fiona asked directly, "What is your work?"

"I represent the central government here. I help people get loans from the government and develop trade and business for Arles. I'm sort of the unofficial chamber of commerce."

"You should insist that some of the museums in this country that have van Goghs loan them to your local museum so you have them for local pride and edification," Fiona pointed out.

"I could not agree with you more...so if these paintings appeared, we would try and keep them here."

"Ah, I understand, Mme. Safir. It would be a great boon to the city, wouldn't it? Publicity, tourism, and even the interest-bearing value of loans drawn against the painting or better still, paintings.

And you would not like them to be found and sold to someone else, would you?" Fletcher smiled.

"That's right. If they were found on public property, then they could stay in Arles, or if it could be shown that they were abandoned, the same result would occur."

"You mentioned your grandmother." Fletcher again leaned in close to Claudine, almost like a priest hearing a confessional. "What was her name and how does she figure in this story?"

Claudine looked away from Fletcher and stared down at the seats of the arena. She rubbed her temples as if she had a headache. "I have only confided in M. Rupert what I am about to tell you. My mother and father rarely spoke of my grandmother, Evangeline. It was as if she didn't exist. I was told that my grandfather died in World War I. My father passed away without a word about either. But when my mother was near death, she weakly whispered to me, 'Vincent van Gogh and Evangeline were lovers.' I tried to learn more, but my mother was too far gone to respond to my questions. She died just a day after the revelation. Was she saying that van Gogh was my grandfather? I did a search of city records and found to my dismay that Evangeline had been arrested several times for prostitution. My mother's birth records showed no father. You see, I think my Madame X was my grandmother, Evangeline, and that van Gogh could have been my grandfather. But I cannot prove it. As you can imagine, I have searched to see if there was any evidence of a relationship with van Gogh, or, of course, any paintings. I have found none."

Fiona moved to Claudine's side and put her arm around her shoulder. With that, Claudine began to sob uncontrollably. Her careful composure came completely undone.

Claudine, in a voice hardly audible, said, "I would so like to know if Vincent van Gogh was my grandfather. It would make me feel so special. It would be something that was wholly mine. I would devote the rest of my life to his memory. I think this is true, but I want to know for sure."

In a soothing voice Fletcher said, "No history is more important than one's own. I cannot even imagine the weight of not knowing for certain if I were the grandchild of such a great person. I promise you that I will do everything in my power to find the truth for you."

"Madame Safir, who is the wealthiest family in Arles?" Fletcher asked.

Her voice quavered. "That would be the Fontiers. At one time they owned the entire port area, the grain storage, and great swaths of land in every direction. They have moved away from Arles, except for Martin, who still lives in town. He's one of my closest friends."

"I presume that they were wealthy in van Gogh's time."

"Oh, yes, even more so. Their wealth stems from feudal times. They were at the top of the aristocracy here. They survived the 1789 revolution because they paid off everybody and then befriended Napoleon and helped him bankroll his wars. When the Industrial Revolution arrived, the serfs were thrown off the land and had little choice but to work in the Fontier industries. The Fontiers were a clever and adaptive family. By the way, Martin is a hereditary duke. Here, I'll write down his address and telephone number. As I said, he is my very closest friend and confidant."

"Have you told him the story of Evangeline and van Gogh?"

"Well, yes, I did. So that makes two; I forgot about Martin. But he is close-mouthed. He wouldn't tell anyone else. We have been dear friends since childhood."

"And how did you and the duke become so close? You certainly came from different classes, if you don't mind my saying."

Fletcher stood as he asked that question and looked out onto the arena, pondering, it seemed, a wider picture.

"His mother, Maude Fontier, was a frequent customer of my family's restaurant. She and my parents were friendly, yet they didn't socialize, except at the restaurant. I know that she financially helped my parents add space and a hotel to the restaurant, making it the foremost inn in Arles. They invited me even as a young child to their house and to their seacoast home at St. Maries de la Mer. Martin and I would play together. He became almost like a brother, and the Fontiers, like a second family. I have nothing to worry about in Martin." She paused. "Mr. Mac-Donald, I feel too upset to continue on just now."

Despite the heat of the afternoon, Claudine appeared cold and shaken. I asked her if she would like me to take her home. She declined, turned to us, and waved a little farewell. Just as she was rising to leave, Fletcher, already standing, placed his great hand on her shoulder and said, "I promise to help you in your quest."

After Claudine left, Fletcher asked Fiona to research what life was like in Arles in the 1888-1889 period, at the library and wherever else she could get information, with particular attention to any mention of the Safirs and the Fontiers. In the meantime, I called Martin Fontier and arranged an appointment with him that afternoon.

****

We discovered that the duke, as Fletcher liked to call him, lived on rue Molière, literally across the street from L'Espace van Gogh, which is the serene courtyard garden depicted in van Gogh's Le Jardin de L'Hotel Dieu. This was the garden of the hospital where he went to have his self-mutilated ear bandaged, an act designed to engender pity in Gaugin sufficient to keep him in Arles. It didn't work.

The duke warmly welcomed us. He appeared to be in his seventies and was wearing a burgundy velvet jacket, a cravat, and matching velvet slippers. The Fontier crest was conspicuously embroidered on both the jacket and the slippers. His face was wrinkle-free but tight like a mask—undoubtedly the result of too many face-lifts. He walked with his head tilted upward and his nose quite up in the air as well. His speech was highly mannered and affected. He was the epitome of effete diffidence. An afternoon tea was set for us by his butler, which we took in his garden. The elegance of it all bespoke inexhaustible wealth.

"Is this the family home?" I asked.

The duke spoke in French-tinged English, "Well, not the family home. It is just a property the family owns. I moved here twenty years ago to be close to L'Espace van Gogh. Did you know that I endowed the entire Espace? He paused to emphasize his contribution. "It was the least I could do for poor Vincent. If only I had been alive then, Vincent would never have been so harshly treated." He spoke as if van Gogh were alive. "The room where he was hospitalized after he gave his ear for love, I restored myself."

Fletcher began to say something, but the duke went on.

"I did all the work. Mind you, I mean the sweat work. I restored the wallpaper. I remortared the brick. I plastered the ceiling. And every floorboard I lovingly restored myself: planing, sanding, staining, nailing—all with my little hands. I had to go to the manicurist almost daily!" He chuckled lightly at this revelation. "Just the thought of his feet padding on those boards made me thrill. I wanted literally to put my own body into the restoration as well as my money. That is the reason I let no one do a stitch of the renovation in that precious room of unrequited love. Poor, poor, Vincent."

I found the duke's arch qualities to be stifling, if not ludicrous. The least noxious thing I could think to say was, "It, L'Espace, is a beautiful place, but it must bring many annoying tourists into your otherwise serene world."

"Oh, yes, but they are very respectful and quiet. There is something so peaceful about L'Espace that it drains the 'hoi' out of the 'polloi.'" He laughed at his own limp humor. "Anyway, we are set back behind rather formidable walls, so I can see L'Espace but they can't see me. Indeed, from my bedroom I can see Vincent's hospital room. Sometimes I wave to him. When they close the grounds, I have a key and walk about and do some trimming that the gardeners always forget. Those are blissful periods for me." He sighed dramatically. "I can imagine poor Vincent. If I had been alive, things would have been so different for him. I would have cradled him and made his life much easier."

Fletcher, to my relief, finally involved himself in the conversation.

"I must thank Mme. Safir for directing me to you. I now see that you have a most uncommon appreciation of Mr. van Gogh. She also seems to be most knowledgeable about him as well. And she seems quite savvy."

"Oh, Claudine is savvy, all right. She has had to purr, claw, and God knows what else her way up. But that's in her blood." He laughed, clearly admiring her pluck. "Now she calls the shots with the politicians. She's great fun, and we are as close as two people can be without being one. She and I rather grew up together. Father would send for her to be my playmate at our beach chateau in St. Maries. I learned so much from her. She was more worldly than I was, if you know what I mean. Now, Mr. MacDonald, my spies say you are here trying to find those allegedly missing prostitute van Goghs. I don't know anything about them, except that the idea is preposterous."

"The prostitute van Goghs?" An edge came into Fletcher's voice, and I knew he had picked up on something. "I never heard such a title. How so, your grace, preposterous?" His voice assumed an almost official interrogatory timbre.

"They have no real name because they don't exist. I just like to have a handle for this idiocy. There's a rumor that Vincent was heterosexual or bisexual, a story started and maintained by those who still can't bring themselves to accept that Vincent was just plain gay, no ifs, ands, or buts. But at the time he couldn't openly admit it. He and Gauguin were a duo. It was a terrible cross for poor Vincent and made him crazy, of that I am sure. For many years, once Vincent became somewhat famous, there was a plot to keep his homosexuality secret. The bourgeoisie and his family couldn't tolerate the world knowing that this minister's son was queer. So they cooked up this story that he frequented prostitutes and that there are paintings to prove it. This is an old homophobic line. Vincent was gay through and through, and frankly I resent this cover-up because it is a disservice to his memory and to homosexuals the world over. Here is another example of homosexual glory, and it is undermined by vile deniers."

"It is hardly news, duke." Fletcher seemed to be risking inflaming Fontier. "Almost everybody knows he was homosexual and perhaps bisexual, or at least most informed people tend to believe it."

"Although you are obviously an educated and curious man, you, too, have been duped." The duke waved a hand in disdain. "Vincent used prostitutes only as models. I think his being forced to hide or camouflage his true feelings, especially from his family and his brother, Theo, drove him insane. He was a pure queer genius, and I think it is horrible that his gayness hasn't been made absolutely clear. Don't get me started. So, am I right, are you here to seek these illusions?"

"I am here, so my contract says, to help the van Gogh museum attract more business. If I were to find some heretofore unknown paintings by him and they were exhibited by the museum, I would be earning my keep, wouldn't I?" Quickly changing the subject, he asked, "Did your family keep diaries? I wonder if there was any mention of van Gogh or the life of his contemporaries in them."

The question caught the Duke off guard. "My grandmother Isabella kept a journal. Her possessions were given by her will to the Arles Historical Society. I personally oversaw the gift." He dismissed any value they might have. "I don't know if they would still be legible or just a pile of dust. They were falling apart. I know that later journals were kept occasionally by my father, who remarked on how famous 'this poor painter' had become. My father didn't like Vincent's work at all. He thought it was primitive and garish."

" Do you have any van Goghs?" I asked.

"Ah, not a stroke," he said regretfully. "They are beyond the reach of mere mortal men like me." The duke busied himself with adjusting the position of the tea service on the garden table. "Ah, how wonderful it would be to be able to just look up and see one of Vincent's works whenever I wanted to do so. I would do most anything for that privilege, I assure you."

Fletcher strolled into the portal of the duke's great parlor.

"What a fine place to hang some of van Gogh's work."

Fontier leapt up and followed him. "Oh, no. I would prefer that each painting be near what inspired Vincent. His vistas, his portraits, his perspectives should all look out on the very scenes, just as Vincent did. I would have A Starry Night in its own citadel overlooking the fields of Arles."

Fletcher seemed genuinely impressed. "That is a splendid sentiment. Only a man of your extraordinary gifts could conceive of such a glorious tribute."

"That comes from the heart. I know Vincent's heart. That is what he would have wanted."

****

We returned to M. Rupert's office at the museum right after our visit with Duke Fontier.

"Max, you see how mad the duke is. He denies that van Gogh wanted his paintings to be adored by the world and to fetch high prices, to hang in the finest homes, wherever they might be. He wasn't interested in their staying in Arles. He was painting for the world." Just then, M. Rupert appeared.

"Do you reveal van Gogh's homosexuality, or at least the supposition that he was, at the museum?" Fletcher asked almost sternly.

The curator was offended by the notion. "No, sir, we don't. That is only prurient conjecture. And I don't think the trustees of the museum would want us to raise such unproven speculation. It is irrelevant to his work anyway."

Fletcher didn't seem to think so. "As I recall, every detail of Napoleon's life has been studied to elicit understanding of this great Frenchman. Ditto for Molière, Montaigne, Proust, Zola, and Sartre. We seek every clue to understand what makes someone stand out. Certainly, sexuality is part of that inquiry and therefore hardly irrelevant. Unproven van Gogh's homosexuality may be, but the weight of the evidence is such that it probably deserves some serious mention in your presentations. Has Monsieur Fontier discussed this with you?"

"No. It has never come up in any way. He's a trustee, you

know, and maybe he's the only one who might not object."

"You mean given his persuasion?"

"Yes, of course."

Just then Fiona burst in and asked to speak to Fletcher privately. She was breathless. "I've been at the library. I looked up Claudine Safir. Her birth records indeed show that her grandmother, Evangeline, bore a child 'fatherless' in 1889. More interesting is that the local newspaper ran a story about prostitutes being found dead on the streets from starvation and disease. The article was more a diatribe against them, basically saying that they deserved what they got."

Fiona then opened a sheet that contained a photocopy of handwriting in a book. "Fletcher, this is a copy of an entry in a diary of the grandmother of Duke Fontier, Isabella. I found it at the Arles Historical Society."

Fletcher beamed with admiration. "You beat me to this, Fiona. I just learned from the duke that her diaries were there. Good work."

"This entry is dated August 1, 1898. The translation reads: 'Today J. brought home some rolled-up canvasses and he put them in his closet. They smelled of linseed oil, so I think they were paintings. I asked about them, and he said they were just the filth of the street and that he would soon bring them to the police to prove that some of the artists in town should be expelled for moral depravity.'

"J. refers to Jacques Fontier, the duke's grandfather."

"Look at this entry, August 14, 1898. 'A dirty and emaciated woman came by the house today asking for the return of some paintings that she claimed J. had purchased from her. She said she couldn't live without them and offered to give him back the money. She cried all through her importuning. I told her to go away or I would call the police. She left, cursing J. and making some scandalous accusations.'

"Fletcher, over the next few months several pages of the diary had been ripped out. But a preceding page to one of the missing pages begins: 'J. and I finally talked about the woman. He admitted that...' The next pages are gone."

Fletcher rubbed his brow, and then snapped into action.

"Max, go immediately to L'Espace van Gogh, and if the duke shows up, stay with him. Do not let him alone for a second." He turned his attention to the curator. "Monsieur Rupert, how much would three new van Gogh paintings be worth?"

"Probably over a billion dollars."

Fletcher nodded in agreement with this assessment. "Tell me, if I were to offer you the three paintings in exchange for the museum openly presenting the possibility of van Gogh's homosexuality, would you take the deal?"

All of his distaste vanished instantly. "In a heartbeat." "Do I have your personal assurance of this?"

"Yes, on my honor. But what are you saying?"

"Please call Mme. Safir and the duke. Have them meet all of us at L'Espace van Gogh, in the courtyard at seven. Tell them it is urgent."

It looked as though Fletcher had done it again. I didn't have the foggiest idea of what he knew or where this was going, but I could tell by his conviction that the pieces were coming together very quickly and with a certain amount of theatricality, which was his forte.

****

I had been at L'Espace for only an hour when the duke did indeed show up. It was five-thirty. The garden closed for tourists at five. He was surprised and flustered to see me, saying that he thought we were all meeting here at seven o'clock. He asked me why we were meeting and who would be there, and I claimed that I knew nothing except that it was urgent. He hurriedly left and said he would return at seven. As dusk descended, starlings were flying in all directions and the golden light cast a deep yellow on the courtyard. Fiona, M. Rupert, and Fletcher arrived a few minutes before seven. The clock struck the hour and Claudine was dropped off by a car. The duke, watching for her arrival, rushed from his residence, took her arm, and escorted her into the courtyard.

Everyone gathered around Fletcher, who was standing alone in the middle of the garden. His demeanor was grim. He seemed like a priest at a funeral, and indeed he spoke as if giving a eulogy. "The paths to this holy place come together, and we tonight pay special homage to the greatness of Vincent van Gogh and all that he was."

Fletcher turned to Martin Fontier and spoke to him in a voice of judicial finality. "Duke, you are a man of great passion. This place's manifest beauty is due greatly to your generosity and your hard work. You have enshrined here the qualities of Arles that Vincent loved. But you have also hidden the facts that would reveal to the world that your beloved Vincent did love and have a child with a woman of Arles. Only a man of your great wealth could have indulged this deception of civilization and Claudine."

Martin went crimson and blustered, "This is absurd. I will not be abused like this." He began to leave, but I stood in his way. Fletcher's voice rang out like a tolling bell, "Your grace, I know where the prostitute paintings are. You have made the mistake of hiding them in a public place, so your right to ownership is dubious at best. Now hear me carefully. I also know that you want the world to know about Vincent's homosexuality so that others of similar persuasion can exalt him as a hero. But you must face the fact that it is only a supposition. If you will forgo any interest in the paintings and give them to the museum, M. Rupert has pledged that an entire section of the museum will be devoted to revealing the facts of van Gogh's sexuality. Is that not right, M. Rupert?"

Rupert unexpectedly hesitated. Fletcher glared at the curator and said, "You gave me your word, sir! Don't forget that you don't have possession unless you know where they are. There are only two people who do know, and I am willing to reveal the whereabouts only if you keep your pledge."

M. Rupert turned to the duke. "Yes, Martin, you have my word. If you surrender the possession and all title to the paintings, we will build an entire section devoted to that aspect of Vincent's life and I would want you to design it."

Satisfied with this offer, Fletcher then turned to his next subject. "Claudine, you have suspected since your mother died that these paintings existed. There is oral history from your grandmother, Evangeline, passed to your mother, that van Gogh was the father of your mother, that he loved Evangeline, and that he painted her and she possessed some of those pictures because he could give her nothing else. But you didn't know where they were. You knew in your heart that if these paintings had not been destroyed accidentally, they still were in Arles somewhere, because otherwise they would be famous, and your grandmother would have been revealed as being a prostitute and your mother a bastard."

Fletcher paused before giving her the bad news. "Claudine, the duke has possessed these paintings since his parents died. He kept it from you because of his obsessive need to deny that Vincent had a natural child. Indeed, I think he wanted to forever hide even more than that: that Vincent, in his tortured way, loved Evangeline, your grandmother."

Martin stepped back and grabbed his stomach as if he were going to wretch. He whined to Claudine, whose face showed utter disbelief and horror. "My mother felt sorry for you, Claudine. We were hiding your great heritage to protect our own reputation." Martin choked with tears seeking mercy. "My grandfather was a customer of Evangeline's. He bought Vincent's pictures from her. That is why my mother befriended your family and you at first. It was an act of pity and remorse. But later you became a loved one, really. The lie had gone on so long that it became a truth. Please, please forgive me."

Claudine dropped to the grass. She howled like a wild, wounded animal and tore at the grass, bringing up clods of earth. She yelled at Martin with terrifying hurt in her voice, "How could you lie to me for all these years? I loved you like a brother, but you did not find me worthy of this truth? What was I to you? A toy? An amusement? Your class never stops victimizing, does it? I wish you and your stinking family had been guillotined with the rest of the suffocating scum."

She threw clods of dirt at Martin, fistfuls of them. He stood woodenly, slowly being coated with earth, as if he were being buried while standing. Claudine threw and threw until she exhausted herself and she could throw no more.

Fletcher quietly but resolutely continued. "Yes, Claudine, it is as the duke says. Martin's grandfather, despite his holy tirades against prostitutes, like most men of the time frequented them.

And Evangeline was one of them. She needed money, so she sold Vincent's canvases to him for extra cash. Then, remorseful, she sought their retrieval. Isabella, the duke's grandmother, alludes to this all in her diaries. The duke should have been more thorough in his attempt to erase history, although he came close to doing just that."

Fletcher turned his attention to the duke. He said firmly, "Now, Your Grace, it is time to admit that you have them and to strike a deal here and now in front of these witnesses. The Museum of Vincent van Gogh will forever tell the story you want told. Arles will be blessed with authentic paintings of the master so that the citizens and visitors will be filled with his real light. Claudine's connection to one of the world's most gifted people will be proven. Remember, ownership is a matter of possession, and I know where they are and all that that suggests. Do not force me to question your ownership on technical grounds that will strip you of control, for I then assure you this pledge of the museum will be withdrawn."

Martin's voice was unsteady. "Do I have your word, Lionel, that that special section will be built? And that I can have a say in it?

"Yes. So help me God. This will bring Vincent back home to Arles.

The duke, spattered with dirt, turned his back on us and slowly walked across the lawn and then upstairs to the room where van Gogh had recuperated so many years ago. We all followed behind. He methodically lifted several floorboards, revealing a large space under the floor. Reverentially he drew out a framed picture from the space and then another and another. He leaned them against the wall across from the window that looked out onto the garden. There were three portraits of the same young winsome woman; three van Goghs that had not been seen by the world in over one hundred years. Martin walked over to Claudine and tugged on her hand until she grudgingly went with him over to the paintings. He turned one of the canvases on its back to reveal an inscription:

To my Evangeline, my love for you is as bright as the sun, as wild as the night sky, and as complete and as perfect as a summer afternoon by our bridge on the Rhone. May our child one day know us in better times.

Love, Vincent,
Arles,
16 July, 1889

****

Fletcher was standing again at the preserved fruit stand with its candied delicacies from Apt. I asked him how he knew for sure that Martin had hidden the paintings in the hospital room at L'E-space de van Gogh.

"People of passion, like Martin, are emotionally true but rationally dishonest. He told us that the only fitting place for van Gogh's paintings were near the things he painted. It was no accident that he did the refurbishing of the hospital room himself, leaving him the opportunity of placing the works near the site of van Gogh's passion. Fiona gave us the clues for how the paintings came to be in the possession of the Fontiers. Martin's obsessive actions were a clear road map, once we left rationality as a guide. That's the magic, putting yourself in the mind of the passionate. Once there, what seems like madness becomes perfectly clear. Like why in the world I would buy all this sugar stuff that gives me a headache. Put yourself in the passion, and the answer is clear, albeit crazy. N'est-ce pas?"

MANHATTAN HIGH VOLTAGE

Fletcher had joined Fiona and myself at our home in Inverness for Scrabble and one of her fine dinners. Tonight it was a Bolognese meat sauce on penne and sautéed escarole. She simmers her meat in milk before adding fresh nutmeg and then tomatoes, producing an aroma that is hallucinatory. On Bolognese days my salivary glands are given a lifetime workout. It is usual for Fletcher and myself to think about third helpings on such evenings, and to see the scales the next day in unknown territory. Accompanying Fiona's fine food was one of Fletcher's Côtes du Rhône wines, making for quite an evening, especially in the grip of a deep winter spell, as we were on this night. Despite the soporific quality of the meal and wine, we soldiered through three games of Scrabble, with all of us holding one win apiece, although Fletcher did manage two seven-letter words, and by all rights he should have won hands down. But he got stuck with more than his fair share of vowels for the longest time.

We turned on the TV for inane entertainment and found that The Fritzi Lang Show was just right. Her sharp jabs at U.S. politicians and the occasional Canadian put-down were generally humorous and apt. With brandy for Fletcher and myself and Fiona's sherry, it was a fine way to close the evening.

This evening featured Fritzi working on a new bit they called "Bag the Celeb." She would go out in the audience and have them vote on what males had the best one-liners to lure Fritzi out on a date. Then she went out with the winner on an actual date, and a candid camera filmed her and the guy. They showed one past date where she had been so impossible that the date just walked out, leaving her to pay the bill! It was all very ridiculous and silly fun. Little did we know that we would be asked to put the clamps on "Bag the Celeb."

The next day at the shop I got a call from Ron Steele, an acquaintance of Fletcher's. "Did you see that skit last night on The Fritzi Lang Show?" It turned out Steele had devised the concept and pitched it a few weeks earlier to a different organization, a group called A Fine Offer (AFO). He thought it was stolen by somebody at AFO, but he couldn't prove it. His lawyer told him that there was probably no recourse, since his TV treatment hadn't been registered with the U.S. copyright office. He was desperate and wondered if Fletcher had any ideas, but he also forthrightly said that he didn't have any money to pay Fletcher's fees. He sent a fax of the idea pitch he gave the producers at AFO:

****

CELEBRITY DATE
A CONCEPT FOR A TV SERIES
BY RON STEELE

The host, changing every week, is a flashy, unmarried (divorced OK) female celebrity of TV, movie, music, or news fame, between twenty and whatever, as long as she is hot, powerful, and single. Think Paris Hilton, Scarlet Johannsen, Maureen Dowd, Nora Jones, or even Condoleezza Rice (after she's no longer Secretary of State). Average single guys, chosen by the show for their appeal, are given a chance to have a date with the celeb on the basis of the "line of the week," given in a setup chance meeting at a bar (or other venue changing each week) with the celeb. The guy with the best come-on line and patter is chosen by the audience. The celeb goes out with the guy, and a camera follows them on their first date. Our celebrity host gets to poke fun and withering criticism at the stupid one-liners and the little setup scenes of the average guy (scripted, of course, by us) and to laugh it up on the dates, but she can lace each date with sweetness and interest when and if she wants to.

The audience is a fly on the wall on the celebrity date. They get to see the celebrity close up, in an intimate "real" date, with all the notoriety and stuff surrounding it. The couple goes to fancy restaurants, bars, and clubs. We see the male earnestly squirming to make a good impression and maybe, just maybe, hope against hope, really attract the star for a second date and who knows what else! The audience bears in mind that the celebrity is, after all, unattached and available. The show is a blend of Entertainment Tonight, Cinderella in reverse, and a high-octane "The Dating Game." It can be shaped to appeal to almost all ages, with "hope springs eternal" and "love conquers all" as its power source, with enough cynicism, sarcasm, and irony to keep it hip.

****

Fletcher knew Ron's ethics well enough to be sure that this alleged theft was real. He was also intrigued that Ron's lawyers seemed impotent in the face of the obvious unfairness. He arranged to fly down to New York City and asked me and Fiona to join him. He didn't think this trip would turn into a paying assignment, so he offered to pay for the flight and to put us up at his club. I was worried that we were taking on a few to many nonpaying assignments this year, but Fletcher made the point that overall we had done very well, and a trip to New York always had side benefits, the theater being one. My reluctance was all too easy to overcome.

Fletcher and I met Ron in the Tiger Bar at the club. Fiona was out picking up theater tickets at the discount ticket office. Ron had put on a tie and jacket because of the dress code at the club, but he maintained his artistic style by wearing holey jeans and beat-up sneakers. For a young man, his face was tired and worn. There were deep purple areas under his eyes, and he looked like a hunted, unwell man.

"Mr. MacDonald, I never dreamed you would come all the way to New York to help me," he said gratefully. "As I told you, I am not able to pay you for your time. I was only seeking advice. I hope I made myself clear about the money."

"Stop calling me 'Mr. MacDonald.' Fletcher's just fine," he said mildly. "I may be twenty some years older than you, but I'm not ready for that much respect. This is Max Bateman, my good friend and colleague, who answers to Max. His wife, Fiona, has joined us on this trip as well." He glanced at Ron's attempt at formal attire. "I'm sorry about the stuffy dress code at the club. I know it's a pain, but I must admit I put some stock in dressing up for certain occasions, like the theater. I can't abide people going to a show dressed in jeans." He caught himself as he avoided looking at Ron's denims. "But I digress. Have you discovered if any of the people you pitched the show to worked for Fritzi or the station? Have you been in contact with them since Fritzi began airing the celebrity piece?"

Ron had put some thought to this question. "I called Monica, who is my biggest fan at AFO, and told her about the Fritzi situation. I asked if anyone at AFO had contacts there, and she said that they had no official dealings with the show but they were on friendly terms with the producers and the station." He knew that didn't help much, and he added, "By the way, my lawyer says I don't have any solid copyright or infringement case because I didn't register, even though I did write the idea up on two pages. He says that I would have to clear a lot of hurdles to make a case stick, and the cost would be astronomical."

"Yes, you told me about your lawyer's pessimism. I don't think the solution is legal but a matter of good business. What we know is," Fletcher raised three fingers for emphasis, "One, you invented 'Celebrity Date.' Two, you obviously have the talent to come up with ideas that sell within your business. Three, somebody's profiting falsely on that talent with 'Bag the Celeb.'" Fletcher went on to make a point that really cheered up Ron considerably. "Over the long term, a producer is better off working with you than the idea thief, because you will be a steady idea generator. If we can find out how this happened, maybe we can right the matter for you. Let's go back to your AFO group. How do you know them? Go through each one of them for me, please."

Ron was eager to reply. "I know them all because we have worked together for a few years on different projects. These guys have produced a couple of independent films and one TV show over the last six years. That's a pretty good track record. They have called me in to do film treatments for a few shows that they pitched. None of those worked out, but I got paid for my work. Not royally, but paid.

Lots of other writers work with them on the same basis." His face lit up as he talked, and I could see how much he loved show business. "I also pitch ideas to them, like I did this one, to see if it sticks. If so, they pay for a treatment, and they will pitch it to the stations and cable for TV or film. If they get a deal, I get a union writing contract."

Fletcher patiently repeated, "I want to hear about each one who was in the room when you gave the pitch."

"Oh, that's right. Well, Curtis La Farge is the honcho. He's got a cable TV series running, sort of a chick soap opera. In the end he calls the shots," he observed. "A little gruff and snappish at times. But he's always listening, and he seems to have a perfect memory. He remembers names of characters I've created months, years, after I have mentioned them to him just once in a pitch." He shook his head in wonder at such recall.

"Let's see. Then there's Monica Lash. She works everything in entertainment: film, TV, cable, radio, books, music. She's acted in several films. She's told me that producing is also a route to finding a really good acting role for herself," he said admiringly. "I like her taste in films, and she has a strong casting sense. I might struggle to come up with one or two right star-types for a character, whereas she has ten off the top of her head. She's fantastic. She is also my biggest supporter at AFO. She knows my work and how I think. But she's not pushy. She never says anything at the pitches."

He fell silent for a moment, thinking of the other members. "June Kavner brings some money into the group. Her former husband is an entertainment lawyer. She met him as the producer of industrial films and commercials, but she's given that up for more arty work. The group often looks to her for her thoughts on financing routes."

He spoke more rapidly as the final names came to him. "Joe Masserello owns a film equipment rental operation. One of the biggest in the city. His father started that business, and Joe wants to expand into the creative side. He's got lots of money and contacts within the city to get things done.

"Finally, there's Peter Janwitz. Peter's a new guy with AFO. He's an expert on high-definition transmission and digital. He did some films for cultural organizations on the works of famous painters and places. I think he pitches public TV stations and non-profits."

Fletcher had remained silent, letting Ron talk, but then he asked, "Of all these people, with whom do you have the best and worst relationship?"

"I don't know them outside of the professional setting," Ron said. "My best rapport is with Monica, who is always enthusiastic about my work. It's always nice to have someone rooting for you. I don't have a bad relationship with any of them. Curtis is some-what aloof, but I think that is just his demeanor."

That wasn't the answer Fletcher wanted. "Do you know any-one connected to the Fritzi show?"

"No."

I asked, "If your pitch had been successful with AFO and had they sold it to a TV station, what would you have stood to gain?"

Ron didn't hesitate a moment. "If it went a year on television and had some residuals, maybe a million over five years, certainly five hundred thousand dollars. If it became a hit, perhaps ten mil-lion dollars over ten years."

I whistled. "What's the value to the Fritzi show?"

"If the ratings of the show went up, say ten percent, another million viewers, the show could earn another fifty million dollars a year and the producer would pocket maybe five million of that. Depends on his or her deal. It just might save the show from being cancelled, and that's worth millions to the producer. However you cut it, it's real money. This game is about numbers of people watching."

Fiona walked up to the table and introduced herself. Fletcher and I rose at her arrival, leaving Ron awkwardly still sitting. We took our seats, but the message was transmitted: when a lady comes to the table, gentlemen rise.

Placing her hand on Ron's shoulder, Fiona said, "I think your idea of having men try out their one-liners is wonderful. They generally are so marvelously pathetic." There was more than a hint of sarcasm. "I can see what a natural idea it is to tie it into a real date with a star. Inane, but catchy and should make you a pile.

I hope we catch your idea thief, teach him or her a lesson, and you get your show back."

Ron said, "Thank you. I hope you can."

I persisted with my questioning. "How many others besides us, your lawyer, and AFO knew of your idea?"

Ron made the zero sign with his fingers and thumb. "Although I usually have too big a mouth about my ideas, this one didn't get any play from me at all. I came up with it only a few weeks ago. I immediately called AFO and arranged the meeting where I presented it. That's everyone, so you understand why all the fingers point to AFO."

Fletcher was drawing circular targets on a napkin. He rubbed his brow. "Ron, do you know anybody else who has worked in a creative capacity with AFO or any of the principals? If you do, I need a list with telephone and e-mail addresses ASAP. I also want any addresses and bio material on the principals of AFO that's not on their website."

Ron was happy to comply. "I know of quite a few writers who have made pitches there. I'll scrounge up the addresses." He stopped short, arrested by a disturbing idea. "How am I ever going to pay you for this?"

Fletcher grinned. "I like a man who worries about his debts. You owe us nothing. I told you that. But," he added, "if we should help you to make some serious money on 'Celebrity Date,' how about ten percent?"

I was surprised at Fletcher's dealing. Normally he eschewed such matters or passed them on to me.

"Right now, it's worth nothing. No one will touch it because they will say it's attached to Fritzi's show. So, I'll pay for that magic. Thank you."

Fletcher's expression showed that he expected nothing. "Just give us that list by seven a.m. tomorrow so we can get a jump on matters, all right?"

"You bet."

After Ron left, we snacked on the club's overripe cheese and spongy vegetables. Fletcher looked at his watch. "Did you find us some good theater tickets?"

"Yes," I replied, "a revival of Amadeus. I thought a play about the thief of Mozart's music was right on the mark."

"Say, Fletcher, you went right to the jugular on the fees. I thought you might say five percent. What's up?

"Maybe I'm in a New York state of mind".

At 7:15 a.m. the next day, Fletcher, Fiona and I were having breakfast. Fletcher was reading over the list of authors who Ron thought had pitched ideas to AFO.

"Fiona, I think you ought to call these people and tell them that we are investigating a theft of a TV idea and we want to know if they have experienced a similar problem. Don't reveal Ron's name or AFO's. Tell them that you work for me and that I am in New York doing this investigation. Give them the club's number. I also need for you to snoop around and see if you can get a lead on who at The Fritzi Lang Show is credited with their 'Bag the Celeb.' Find out where the producers and writers for the show hang out before or after the show. There must be a favorite bar. Cherchez le bistro! Max and I are going to pay a call on these AFO principals."

Fletcher telephoned Jeremy Freund, a well known stage and film agent.

"Jeremy, Fletcher MacDonald. I'm in town on an assignment with Max. How are you? I wonder if you could do me a big, big favor. I need to meet en masse with all the principals of AFO, a TV production company in New York. I want to get an angle on how they think and operate. I can't tell you more. Do you know them? Great! That's a good start. That's perfect. Simple and straightforward. I'm at the Princeton-Columbia Club. Let me know if they take the bait. Thanks."

"Jeremy thinks if he tells him that they should meet me because I know a lot of moneyed folks in Canada, they will jump at the chance. Every production company needs access to seed funds. And, in fact, I know lots of people with excess cash, so it's true. He was more than happy to help."

I was trying to refresh my memory about Jeremy. "Was he the agent to Barbara Brownell, who was losing star roles because of a malicious rumor started by her estranged husband that she was an alcoholic? I remember now that the bonding companies refused to do her pictures because they said she was unreliable and too risky. They also refused to reveal their source, saying it was confidential. You found out her husband was behind it and she was reinstated. Her husband did all that because she had dumped him and he was frozen out in a pre-nup. Have I got it right?" "That's the same Jeremy and that's the story. Jeremy is a real mover and shaker. He didn't miss a beat in coming up with a strategy to help us. He's smart, very smart, and he has clout."

Jeremy called about an hour later saying that everything was set. AFO would gather all their partners to meet us today for lunch in a private room at "21." Jeremy himself was going to attend.

Fletcher was grinning. "Just having Jeremy there is a coup for them too. He handles big stars, and this is a way to get closer to him. And it gives us cover to watch how they all interact and to draw them out about how they handle properties." He rubbed his hands together with delight at his cleverness and the prospect of getting to the bottom of things.

We passed through "21's" New Orleans-style, filigreed iron gate facade and its famous procession of dwarf horse jockey statues on every step. We were shown into a private room where all five principals of AFO had already arrived and were sitting at a round table. Jeremy wasn't there, but that was to be expected. Fletcher said he was always late. Jeremy carefully cultivated a mystique that people will wait for an audience with him.

Curtis La Farge, the founder of AFO, introduced everyone at the table, Monica Lash, Joe Masserello, June Kavner, and Peter Janwitz. Fletcher expressed his deep appreciation for the gathering and regaled them with the good things he had heard about the group. He told them that he knew people in Canada and elsewhere who were always interested in the entertainment business as an investment.

Curtis took over and gave a rundown of their past successes and projects in the pipeline. He was controlled and methodical.

Fletcher interrupted him before he was finished. "How do you get good properties? What's your approach?"

Curtis seemed a little shaken at the question. "Well, that's a complicated process. But let me finish about our current projects."

Curtis talked robotically about the rosy prospects of a number of properties, going on and on about the demographics, potential sponsors, and the other business qualities that were pertinent. He didn't, however, address Fletcher's question. One could feel a certain discomfort in the room because of the obvious avoidance. Curtis then turned the conversation over to Monica Lash.

She was very animated and much more at ease than Curtis. "Your question, Fletcher, is really at the heart of the matter. Without good properties, all our good skills and contacts can't turn a loser into a winner. Our job is to attract the best scripts, principally from agents and from certain authors who favor us. We are always on the lookout for good ideas. We have three hooks: a good track record of quality productions, financial successes, and access to capital to finance new projects. I guess the last is the reason we are having lunch with you, despite your good looks. And having a relationship with one of the best film and TV agents like Jeremy is also important."

Right on cue, Jeremy walked in, bright and bubbling and full of kisses for the ladies and handshakes for the men. "Late, late, late, I'm always late for my important dates." he quipped. "Just had a call from Tad Brown. I think he's revving up to sell another million books. Guess the guy likes the atmosphere up there. Good guy and he knows how to pitch. So how's everybody? Has Fletcher written a check yet?"

"Monica was helping me understand how AFO gets good properties, and apparently you are the source."

"These are wise people indeed. Continue, Monica."

"Well, like other production groups, all of us are script scouts. We encourage writers to contact us and bounce off ideas to see if we think they will fly."

Peter Janwitz jumped in, "I'm the newest member of AFO's management. One of the reasons I joined them was that they have a great reputation with authors for listening and intelligently critiquing their scripts and ideas, even in embryonic form. Curtis and Monica have built up a fabulous reputation for encouraging new writers. Most of my previous work was at PBS, and I often heard writers say that the advice they got from AFO, even if they didn't produce their work, was invaluable. Curtis, don't we get about twenty submissions a week?"

"More like fifty, most unsolicited. We do try hard to stay open to new ideas, even if they are not submitted by agents, my apologies to Jeremy. Frankly, if we find a really good script, even if it is not good for us, and if the writer is not represented, we'll recommend an agent."

"Are any of the shows in the past or the pipeline from writers without agents or who just had outlines of ideas?"

Monica said, "Of the twenty or so that represent serious commitments going back five years and forward two years, I'd say maybe five were in scratch form when they came in. Would you all agree?"

June Kavner questioned Monica, "Wasn't Curtis's 'For Every Sparrow' a two-page idea that Ralph Franklin ran by AFO before my time? Were you here then Joe? I know Peter wasn't. Anyway, Fletcher, 'For Every Sparrow' is our biggest moneymaker. It has the highest rating of any cable soap. It has high ratings in Canada too."

Joe Masserello spoke. "Yeah, I was on board then. Ralph gave us a pitch and we all loved it from the start. We gave Ralph a little money and he turned around a full treatment, and the rest is history. Without 'Sparrow,' AFO wouldn't be on the map. But frankly we're no different than anybody else." Addressing Fletcher, he continued, "What type of friends do you have who can make a difference?"

Jeremy jumped in. "Me for one. You know, Joe, your dad built one helluva equipment business. It's great that you are trying to take it to the creative side. You could have sat back and just supplied the industry with lights and cable and made bundles of money, but you wanted to take the bigger risks. I give you credit. There's a lot to learn, my boy, a lot to learn."

Sensing the ice, June Kavner, AFO's key financier, said, "I Understand, Fletcher, how hard it is to get people interested in investing in film or television. The risks are enormous, and the success rate is so-so at best. It's been my experience that entertainment investors always need some other angle; for example, they have a family member involved in the production, they emotionally love the property, they have a financial interest in some sort of allied activity like supplying sets or studio equipment for the production. Indeed that's how Joe's father, and now little Joe, got involved on the producing side. They made deals with the producers for exclusive vendor relationships."

Feeling that he had to redeem himself for being so flatfooted with Fletcher, Joe rejoined, "That's true. That TV dollar gets recycled through the industry, and so people with a way to make money on a TV or film deal as a vendor are obvious investors, since they can get their money back from the deal. That's where I was going, Fletcher. Do you know people, say, on the plumbing end of the business, so to speak?"

"This is a great education. Indeed, I did some work for the owners of Piney Studios in Vancouver. Pretty good sound stage there."

There was palpable awe in the room. Piney Studios was THE busiest sound stage in Vancouver, with at least five projects working at once. Fletcher's bona fides were no longer in question. He could ask them whatever he liked.

I was interested in Peter's connections. "Are you still working the PBS and public interest side of the business at AFO?"

"Well, we have to pay the bills, and there is still a lot less money on that side, so I sort of split my time between it and pure commercial situations. We have two PBS projects working, but the rest are cable, broadcast, and a feature film."

Fletcher used the old 'village idiot' ploy. "Well, I appreciate how you are all educating me. I must sound like the village idiot to you." There were plenty of "ah, no's" and clever make-nice comments. And then Fletcher went for the heart of the matter.. "For me, I'm still trying to understand what distinguishes your production group from others who are equally successful or more so. I thought having access to the best scripts and fresh, new ideas was critical. Would you mind just going around the table and telling me why you would have an edge in that regard? How about you, Joe, going first?" Fletcher put them all on the spot.

"Okay." Joe cooperated but looked very uncomfortable. "Frankly I don't agree with your premise. There are just so many ideas. It's the execution that counts. Curtis is a first-rate producer and we have a great staff. We can take a good idea and make it work. 'Sparrow' I think makes the case. In the end it's a soap opera not so different from a dozen others. Curtis and Monica make sure the scripts and actors and sets work and that the show continues to hold the viewer's interest. AFO executes well. That's not what you want to hear, but that's what I believe. We get enough ideas coming in for ten lifetimes. We just need to choose the ones we can make shine given our skills."

Curtis was next. "Well, I don't disagree with Joe about execution. One of the reasons Joe is important to us is that through him we have immediate access to the best equipment and crews so that we meet our productions on time and on budget. He also has good audience sense. However, I would say that we have an advantage in attracting good ideas. The word is out, largely due to Monica's untiring efforts to encourage authors, that we put our backs into the process, even if there is no payback for us." He nodded, signaling he was finished.

"I love working with artists, especially authors." Monica said enthusiastically. "Curtis was a one-man shop not so long ago. I joined him because he was really open to new ideas and approaches. We expanded that, and now we pull in a lot of opportunities from agents and individuals, many more than shops of comparable size. Indeed, I think if I were a working writer, our shop would come up in the top ten of places to find a producer."

"Well, I think my colleagues have said it all," June smiled. "When I walk in the office and I see hundreds of scripts piled up like stalagmites rising from the floor, I don't feel that we are short on ideas."

From then on we talked about all aspects of the entertainment industry. But the core investigation was over. Now we were picking up subtleties.

****

In line with Fletcher's instructions to Fiona, we found ourselves in the Morgan Tavern, on 49th Street between Ninth and Tenth Avenues. It was 6:00 p.m. The place was packed with people associated with the Fritzi show. The show was taped in the late afternoon, and this is where the staff unwound. We stationed ourselves at the bar and waited for the troops to show up. I had already informed Fletcher that there were no leaks in the press about whose brilliant idea it was to do the "Celeb" bit, but I did know that Variety had said that The Fritzi Lang Show had seen a big rise in its ratings over the last two weeks and that it was attributed to "Celeb."

Three youngish guys walked in and sat at what appeared to be a reserved table. One came over for some beers and greeted the barkeep by name, Sebastian, and said he wanted six Coronas. The barkeep said, "Right, John. You doing the 'Bag the Celeb' tonight?"

The man beamed with a Hollywood smile. "You bet we are, Sammy. It's part of the regular lineup now. It's so hot, we tease them with it in the first half-hour and then run it in the next. No screwing until they get 'Bag the Celeb' first."

I said to Fletcher sotto voce, "Bingo. We must live right. Let's head in their direction."

We moved about twenty feet down the bar so we were within a few feet of their table. But we still couldn't hear their conversation over the clatter in the bar. Fletcher pushed up his hat a bit and said to me, "I'm writing a book on TV writers, did you know that?" I caught on quickly and nodded. "And you're my publisher, Rafe McIntosh of All Canada Publishing. I'm Noah Marvin, your new writer find. Listen and plunge."

Fletcher turned off his stool and stepped over to the Fritzi table. He was effervescence itself.

"Gentlemen, I want to toast you. That 'Bag the Celeb' is fabulous. To brilliance!" As he raised his glass, the others looked askance but then smiled and joined in. "I'm Noah Marvin and that's my publisher at the bar, Rafe McIntosh. He's publishing my book on TV writers, from Your Show of Shows to The Fritzi Lang Show." He spoke in a lower voice. "I'm trying to convince him to hold up printing while I write something on 'Bag the Celeb'. God, it's fabulous. Whose idea was it?"

They pointed their finger at the guy who got the drinks from Sammy.

"And who might you be?" Fletcher was cloyingly exuberant. "Just a nameless, faceless mill hand like these guys. I'm Gideon Wanamaker. Not of the famous Wanamakers of Philadel- phia, but from the poor branch from Weese, Wisconsin, home of Weese Cheddar Cheese."

Fletcher went along and I had to hide a smile. "Weese Cheese. It does spread the cheek muscles. May I and my publisher join you folks?" Charmed by Fletcher, the writers waved us in. "How did you ever come up with that idea?"

Wanamaker tapped his head. "It came to me overnight. I put the pieces together, and then the whole creative team pushed it into the shape that it is. It's evolving with every show."

Fletcher cooed, "It's as original as Ernie Kovac's Nairobi Trio."

Gideon was impressed. "You do know your TV history. You know, those ape costumes are still in the prop department at The Tonight Show."

Fletcher continued with his fawning. "How does Fritzi feel about the extra work? Going out on a real date and all that stuff?"

Several of the writers laughed. "We use local places around the theater, so it's not too much of a hassle for her. And right now it's driving her ratings sky high, so nobody's kicking. We're de- voting almost fifteen minutes to it every show."

Fletcher dashed a look at his watch, and his face fell. "Look, we have theater tickets, but I'd really like to interview you for my book. Is there anyway we could hook up for coffee tomorrow at ten o'clock at, say, the Flame Diner on the corner of 44th and Sixth Avenue? We would like to include something as current as this phenomenon."

Wanamaker loved the idea of being written up in a book. "Yeah, sure thing. What's your telephone number just in case?"

Fletcher gave him Fiona's cell number.

****

We waited for Fiona outside the Music Box Theatre on 44th Street, part of the thousands of eager pilgrims that night to Broadway. Pools of us congregated under venerable marquees whose names alone summoned up reverence for the evanescent, and therefore always unique, experience of the live stage: Imperial, Shubert, Booth, Martin Beck, Longacre, Lyceum, Cort, Broadhurst, Majestic, Lunt-Fontanne, Helen Hayes, and a score of others. Their names reverberated with the two-thousand-year glorious history of theatre from the Greeks, to Shakespeare, to this, the Great White Way. The five-minute bells tolled while we strained to see Fiona's red hair flashing somewhere in the crowd.

Fletcher calmly observed, "How privileged we are to be waiting for your beautiful wife, under this glittering marquee, about to enter this house of sublime delights, in this, the greatest city of the world."

As his last words passed into the air, I saw Fiona dashing toward us, weaving around pedestrians, out into the street, cheeks reddened by the run. I happily waved to her, caught her eye, and she waved back, flashing her great smile at seeing us. In a moment she breathlessly took my arm and Fletcher's, and we all stepped into the soft red plush of the theater, joining an audience restive with anticipation. After taking our seats, Fletcher looked at his watch, leaned over to Fiona, and said, "Precisely eight o'-clock. Well done!"

Fiona pushed a sheet of paper into Fletcher's hand. "Take a look. Ron isn't the only victim." The lights faded.

During intermission, Fletcher studied Fiona's notes. Three of Ron's author friends had also had story ideas show up in some form, or announced as being in production, shortly after pitching to AFO. The lifted ideas all had the same characteristic of not being reduced to a full treatment or script but only presented or discussed as an idea in formation or, at best, an outline. Fletcher addressed Fiona, "I suppose none of these authors sought redress in the courts."

"Same as Ron. Their lawyers said they had no recourse and it was too expensive to pursue. These guys just pitched ideas and hoped something would stick." Act II began, and we grew quiet again. Yet I knew from the look of determination on Fletcher's face, that he would be back on stage tomorrow.

Gideon showed up at the Flame Diner right on time. Fletcher and I waved to him.

Fletcher was ebullient and brimming with energy. "Gideon, how great to see you." His voice took on a note of self-importance. "I see the idea of program generation for the voracious appetite of TV as being one of the great creative stories of our times. In half an hour, an idea that might be a premise for an entire book is consumed. The demand on the imagination to come up with new ideas and approaches to the human condition has never been under such pressure. And yet the product is delivered, and there seems no end to it. Do you ever feel tapped out?"

Gideon was preening like a peacock. "That's an occupational hazard. I'm sure you have heard of writer's block."

"But how does a TV writer handle such a thing when he has been hired to produce week after week? It's very different from a literary writer, where delay only puts off the release of a book. In TV, no ideas means blank air and no job."

Gideon agreed. "You just press ahead. If you can't produce, you have to quit for a while."

"I think if you quit, you are probably through in your business."

Gideon winced at the idea but shrugged. "Okay, I'll go along with that."

Fletcher drilled down deeper. "See if you go along with this too. There's a gal I know who sells ideas to writers for a few thousand and a piece of your hide if the story idea generates steam. This gal gets her ideas from pitches from writers who are unaware that their ideas are going to be sold on the black market to people who run dry of ideas."

Gideon was jolted straight upright. His jaw muscles started twitching beyond his control. Fletcher continued, "This gal heard of an idea by Ron Steele. It went something like this. Unmarried female celebrities go out with average guys selected because they come up with good lines to attract chicks, as judged by an audience. The first date with the celebrity is followed by a candid camera. You know the rest. Sounds familiar doesn't it?

Gideon attempted to bluster. "What are you getting at, Mr. Marvin?"

Fletcher was having none of it. "That you bought stolen goods and passed them off as your own. We have you dead to rights because Monica has admitted it."

Gideon made a move to get up.

Fletcher said firmly, "I wouldn't if I were you. If we release this story, you're through forever. Everything you do will stink and no producer will touch you. So let's just talk quietly."

Gideon, seeing he was trapped, sank back down in his seat. "I'm not the only one in this town who uses her, you know. She runs an idea store. There are dozens of them. She's got a high-priced clientele of people who make their living by feeding the tube with ideas." He tried to explain his own past. "Everybody runs dry. But it isn't theft."

"How, pray, do you rationalize that?"

Gideon licked his lips nervously. "I give the idea words and execution and bring it to life. It's nothing but somebody's dream until I make it into something." He became caught up in this train of thought. "You see, there are lots of ideas, good ideas. But until you have the power to convert them into reality, they stay ideas. So those of us who have access to making things happen, like a writer for a show like mine, can take an idea and make it fly. While the jerk who may have come up with it has no access to the tube and has to go through too many hoops to find a place for it. It won't happen. That's the way it really works. Everybody steals ideas."

Fletcher said, "A nice speech, but you got caught. That's the difference. Monica has set up a neat forum, like AFO, where she attracts writers to discuss their ideas with the hope of having them produced by a legitimate producer. But she siphons off those ideas that are not likely to be produced there and sells them to slime like you for a pound of flesh. You think you're clean because you never had contact with the writer, so there's no way to connect you to the work, except through Monica. Wrong. Follow the money. The cash you deducted from your account. The cash that Monica has.

"We know that Monica is careful to use work that hasn't been copyrighted or is so loosely presented it's too formless for copyright. Or she uses ghostwriters to really cover her tracks.

Those ideas are not yours, and you know it, regardless of the legal niceties. In any event, I have a deal for you. You agree to give twenty percent of your salary from the show to Ron, and if 'Bag the Celeb' turns into its own show, you bring Ron in as a fifty- fifty partner on the basis that you need his help to develop the idea to its potential. Also, you cooperate with the Attorney General to stop Monica and her ilk from this practice, and we can keep your theft out of court. This is essentially a criminal enterprise, so she's liable for racketeering and using false pretenses to convert the legitimate property of others to her gain. What do you say? You want to stay in New York, or go back to Weese, Wisconsin, in disgrace?"

Gideon had long ago slunk back in his chair. There was no breath left in his body and his head was swimming. He said nothing.

Fletcher stood. "Here's Ron Steele's telephone number. Call him, or we will be at your producer's door with the truth in twenty-four hours."

Gideon needed help to stand. He shuffled at first and then left with his head down. Fletcher went into the men's room, washed his hands, and doused his face with water.

The next day Ron came to the club. He was still wearing his holey jeans, but had donned a tie and found a blue blazer. "I was called by Gideon Wanamaker, as I told you. I am to meet his lawyer tomorrow to form a collaboration on 'Celeb.' You know, he didn't sound to be half bad. He said he was sorry, but then we moved on. He asked if we could skip the Attorney General business."

Fletcher exhaled sharply. "That's your call. You are gracious to forgive him."

Ignoring the remark, Ron got to the nub of the matter. "How did you know that Monica was the mastermind?"

"Part of the information that Fiona gathered included that all of the writers that pitched AFO felt that Monica was their best supporter. When you said that she didn't say much at the meetings, that signaled to me that she only told you that you were the greatest, not the group. So she encouraged as many writers as she could to come up with ideas that she would sell on the black market, except those that AFO wanted.

"When we met her and the entire gang at lunch, she was the one who had the clearest picture of how the input at AFO worked, and she was the engine that kept the property input running. Indeed, she was proud of it. Right in your face proud. A smart cookie. Smooth. I have no doubt that she had this in mind from the beginning and used Curtis and AFO as a convenient platform to develop her scheme. As for Curtis, he's a straight arrow and more concerned about doing a good job than scamming. Joe's learning the ropes and frankly is too ham-fisted to be a clever thief. June, well, she's a money person who can make more money in a day that Monica can make in a year with her little scheme. Peter was a possibility. A do-gooder, making very little in a city that costs plenty to live in. But he had not advanced to the stage of being a crook. Of course, there's always hope for him. Once these threads came loose and we had Gideon located, it was logical that Monica was the culprit."

"I'm very grateful to you, Fletcher, and to you, Max and Fiona."

I said, "Don't forget our commission if things work out."

Fletcher put his arm around Ron. "Frankly I think if 'Bag the Celeb' continues to be a big hit, the public gets just what it deserves. Do me a favor and use that mind for something that we will both be proud of."

Ron offered, "'The Adventures of Fletcher MacDonald'?"

Fletcher snorted, "No one would believe it."

ABOUT THE AUTHOR

Vaud E. Massarsky has commercially produced over 70 plays and musicals. He is also the president of a venture capital group, which provides capital for startup businesses and grooms companies for public offerings, as well as being the managing director of a New York City investment bank. He has written over one hundred business monographs as a strategic consultant to presidents and boards of large corporations, public utilities, and academic institutions.

He was born in Hoboken, New Jersey, was an American history major at Columbia University, and studied law at the University of Virginia after which he was a law clerk to the San Francisco Superior Court. He has two children, Tara and Kurtlan.

He and his wife, Felicia, travel extensively. They currently reside in Hoboken, New Jersey. The Adventures of Fletcher MacDonald is Mr. Massarsky's debut work of fiction.